Tell

the Wolves

I'm Home

Tell
the Wolves
I'm Home

A NOVEL

Carol Rifka Brunt

THE DIAL PRESS
NEW YORK

Copyright © 2012 by Carol Silverman

All rights reserved.

Published in the United States by The Dial Press, an imprint of The Random House Publishing Group, a division of Random House, Inc., New York.

DIAL PRESS is a registered trademark of Random House, Inc., and the colophon is a trademark of Random House, Inc.

LIBRARY OF CONGRESS CATALOGING-IN-PUBLICATION DATA
Brunt, Carol Rifka
Tell the wolves I'm home: a novel / Carol Rifka Brunt.
    p.   cm.
ISBN 978-0-679-64419-4
eBook ISBN 978-0-8129-9292-2
1. Teenage girls—Fiction. 2. Loss (Psychology)—Fiction. 3. Friendship—Fiction.
4. AIDS (Disease)—Fiction. 5. Uncles—Fiction. I. Title
  PS3602.R867T45 2012
  813'.6—dc23   2011027932

Printed in the United States of America on acid-free paper

www.dialpress.com

9   8   7   6

Book design by Caroline Cunningham

For Maddy, Oakley, and Julia

Tell

the Wolves

I'm Home

One

My sister, Greta, and I were having our portrait painted by our uncle
Finn that afternoon because he knew he was dying. This was after I
understood that I wasn't going to grow up and move into his apartment and live there with him for the rest of my life. After I stopped
believing that the AIDS thing was all some kind of big mistake. When
he first asked, my mother said no. She said there was something maca-
bre about it. When she thought of the two of us sitting in Finn's apartment with its huge windows and the scent of lavender and orange,
when she thought of him looking at us like it might be the last time
he would see us, she couldn't bear it. And, she said, it was a long drive
from northern Westchester all the way into Manhattan. She crossed
her arms over her chest, looked right into Finn's bird-blue eyes, and
told him it was just hard to find the time these days.

"Tell me about it," he said.

That's what broke her.

I'm fifteen now, but I was still fourteen that afternoon. Greta was sixteen. It was 1986, late December, and we'd been going to Finn's one
Sunday afternoon a month for the last six months. It was always just
my mother, Greta, and me. My father never came, and he was right not
to. He wasn't part of it.

I sat in the back row of seats in the minivan. Greta sat in the row in
front of me. I tried to arrange it like that so I could stare at her without

her knowing it. Watching people is a good hobby, but you have to be careful about it. You can't let people catch you staring at them. If people catch you, they treat you like a first-class criminal. And maybe they're right to do that. Maybe it should be a crime to try to see things about people they don't want you to see. With Greta, I liked to watch the way her dark, sleek hair reflected the sun and the way the ends of her glasses looked like two little lost tears hiding just behind her ears.

My mother had on KICK FM, the country station, and even though I don't really like country music, sometimes, if you let it, the sound of all those people singing their hearts out can bring to mind big old family barbecues in the backyard and snowy hillsides with kids sledding and Thanksgiving dinners. Wholesome stuff. That's why my mother liked to listen to it on the way to Finn's.

Nobody talked much on those trips to the city. It was just the smooth glide of the van and the croony country music and the gray Hudson River with hulking gray New Jersey on the other side of it. I kept my eyes on Greta the whole time, because it stopped me from thinking about Finn too much.

The last time we'd visited was a rainy Sunday in November. Finn had always been slight—like Greta, like my mother, like I wished I was— but on that visit I saw that he'd moved into a whole new category of skinny. His belts were all too big, so instead he'd knotted an emerald-green necktie around his waist. I was staring at that tie, wondering when he might have worn it last, trying to imagine what kind of occasion would have been right for something so bright and iridescent, when suddenly Finn looked up from the painting, brush midair, and said to us, "It won't be long now."

Greta and I nodded, even though neither of us knew whether he meant the painting or him dying. Later, at home, I told my mother he looked like a deflated balloon. Greta said he looked like a small gray moth wrapped in a gray spider's web. That's because everything about Greta is more beautiful, even the way she says things.

It was December now, the week before Christmas, and we were stuck in traffic near the George Washington Bridge. Greta turned around in her seat to look at me. She gave me a twisty little smile and reached into her coat pocket to pull out a scrap of mistletoe. She'd done this for the last two Christmases, carried a piece of mistletoe around to pounce on people with. She took it to school with her and terrorized us at home with it. Her favorite trick was to sneak up behind our parents and then leap up to hold it over their heads. They were not the kind to show affection out in the open, which is why Greta loved to make them do it. In the van, Greta waved the mistletoe around in the air, brushing it right up into my face.

"You wait, June," she said. "I'll hold this over you and Uncle Finn and then what'll you do?" She smiled at me, waiting.

I knew what she was thinking. I'd have to be unkind to Finn or risk catching AIDS, and she wanted to watch me decide. Greta knew the kind of friend Finn was to me. She knew that he took me to art galleries, that he taught me how to soften my drawings of faces just by rubbing a finger along the pencil lines. She knew that she wasn't part of any of that.

I shrugged. "He'll only kiss my cheek."

But even as I said it, I thought of how Finn's lips were always chapped to shreds now. How sometimes there would be little cracks where they'd started to bleed.

Greta leaned in, resting her arms on the back of her seat.

"Yeah, but how do you know that the germs from a kiss can't seep in through the skin of your cheek? How can you be sure they can't somehow swim into your blood right through your open pores?"

I didn't know. And I didn't want to die. I didn't want to turn gray.

I shrugged again. Greta turned around in her seat, but even from behind I could tell she was smiling.

It started to sleet, and the little nuggets of wet ice splatted against the window as we drove through the streets of the city. I tried to think of something good to say back to Greta, something to let her know that Finn would never put me in danger. I thought about all the things Greta didn't know about Finn. Like the way he'd let me know the portrait was just an excuse. How he'd seen the look on my face the very first time we'd gone down for the painting sessions. How he'd waited for my mother and Greta to go ahead into the living room, and in that moment, when it was only the two of us in the narrow hallway inside Finn's apartment door, he'd put his hand on my shoulder, leaned in, and whispered in my ear, "How else could I get all these Sundays with you, Crocodile?"

But that was something I would never tell Greta. Instead, when we were in the dim parking garage, climbing out of the van, I blurted out, "Anyway, skin's waterproof."

Greta pressed her door closed gently, then walked around the van to my side. She stood there for a few seconds, staring at me. At my big, clumsy body. She tugged the straps of her backpack tight against her little sparrow's shoulders and shook her head.

"Believe what you want," she said, turning away and heading for the stairs.

But that was impossible and Greta knew it. You could try to believe what you wanted, but it never worked. Your brain and your heart decided what you were going to believe and that was that. Whether you liked it or not.

My mother spent the hours at Uncle Finn's in his kitchen, making pots of tea for us in a magnificent Russian teapot Finn had that was colored gold and red and blue with little dancing bears etched around the sides. Finn said that pot was reserved for serving tea to his favorite people. It was always waiting for us when we came. From the living room we could hear my mother organizing Finn's cabinets, taking out jars and cans, plates and mugs, and loading them back in again. Every once in a while she'd come out to give us tea, which would usually go cold because Finn was busy painting and Greta and I weren't allowed to move. All those Sundays, my mother hardly looked at Finn. It was obvious that she was being broken up into pieces about her only brother dying. But sometimes I thought there was more. She also never looked at the painting. She'd come out and set the teapot down and walk right past the easel, craning her head away. Sometimes I thought it wasn't Finn at all. Sometimes it felt like it was the canvas and brushes and paint she was trying not to see.

That afternoon we sat for an hour and a half while Finn painted us. He had on Mozart's *Requiem,* which Finn and I both loved. Even though

I don't believe in God, last year I convinced my mother to let me join the Catholic church choir in our town just so I could sing the Mozart *Kyrie* at Easter. I can't even really sing, but the thing is, if you close your eyes when you sing in Latin, and if you stand right at the back so you can keep one hand against the cold stone wall of the church, you can pretend you're in the Middle Ages. That's why I did it. That's what I was in it for.

The *Requiem* was a secret between me and Finn. Just the two of us. We didn't even need to look at each other when he put it on. We both understood. He'd taken me to a concert at a beautiful church on 84th Street once and told me to close my eyes and listen. That's when I first heard it. That's when I first fell in love with that music.

"It creeps up on you, doesn't it," he'd said. "It lulls you into thinking it's pleasant and harmless, it bumbles along, and then all of a sudden, boom, there it is rising up all menacing. All big drums and high screaming strings and deep dark voices. Then just as fast it backs right down again. See, Crocodile? See?"

Crocodile was a name Finn invented for me because he said I was like something from another time that lurked around, watching and waiting, before I made my mind up about things. I loved when he called me that. He sat in that church, trying to make sure I understood the music. "See?" he said again.

And I did see. At least I thought I saw. Or maybe I only pretended I did, because the last thing I ever wanted was for Finn to think I was stupid.

That afternoon the *Requiem* floated over all the beautiful things in Finn's apartment. His soft Turkish carpets. The old silk top hat with the worn side to the wall. That big old Mason jar filled to the top with every possible color and pattern of guitar pick. Guitar pickles, Finn called them, because he kept them in that canning jar. The music floated right down the hallway, past Finn's bedroom door, which was closed, private, like it always was. My mother and Greta didn't seem to notice the way Finn's lips moved along with the music—*voca me cum benedictus . . . gere curam mei finis . . .* They had no idea they were even listening to a death song, which was a good thing, because if my mother had known what that music was, she would have turned it right off. Right. Off.

After a while, Finn turned the canvas around so we could see what he'd done. It was a big deal because it was the first time he'd let us see the actual painting.

"Take a closer look, girls," he said. He never talked while he worked, so when he finally spoke, his voice was a thin, dry whisper. A flicker of embarrassment shot across his face, then he reached for a cup of cold tea, took a sip, and cleared his throat. "Danni, you too—come in, have a look."

My mother didn't answer, so Finn called into the kitchen again. "Come on. Just for a second. I want to see what you think."

"Later," she called back. "I'm in the middle of something."

Finn kept looking toward the kitchen like he was hoping maybe she would change her mind. When it was obvious she wasn't going to, he frowned, then turned to stare at the canvas again.

He pushed himself up from the old blue chair he always painted in, wincing as he held on to it for a second, steadying himself. He took a step away and I could see that, other than the green tie at his waist, the only color Finn had was in the little splotches of paint all over his white smock. The colors of me and Greta. I felt like grabbing the paintbrush right out of his hand so I could color him in, paint him back to his old self.

"Thank God for that," Greta said, stretching her arms way above her head and giving her hair a shake.

I stared at the portrait. I saw that Finn had put me slightly in the foreground even though we weren't sitting that way, and I smiled.

"It's not done . . . is it?" I asked.

Finn came over and stood next to me. He tilted his head and looked at the portrait, at the painted Greta, then at the painted me. He squinted, looking right into the eyes of that other me. He leaned in so his face almost touched the wet canvas, and I felt goose bumps prickle on my arm.

"No," he said, shaking his head, still staring at the portrait. "Not quite. Do you see? There's something missing. Maybe something in the background . . . maybe a little more with the hair. What do you think?"

I breathed out and relaxed my chest, unable to hold back a smile. I nodded hard. "I think so too. I think we should come a few more times."

Finn smiled back and rubbed his pale hand across his pale forehead. "Yes. A few more," he said.

He asked us what we thought of the painting so far. I said it was fantastic and Greta didn't say anything. Her back was turned to us. She wasn't even looking at the painting. Both her hands were in her pockets, and when she twisted slowly around, her face was blank. That's something about Greta. She can hide everything she's thinking. The next thing I knew she'd pulled out her mistletoe and was standing there holding it up in one hand. She waved it in an arc like she was cutting the air above our heads, like she was holding something more than just a scrap of Christmas leaves and berries. Finn and I both looked up and my heart seized. We looked at each other for the amount of time that's maybe one grain of sand in an hourglass or one drop of water from a leaky tap, and Finn, *my* uncle Finn, read me—*snap*—like that. In that tiny slice of a second, he saw I was afraid, and he bent my head down and kissed the top of my hair with such a light touch it could have been a butterfly landing.

On the ride home I asked Greta if she thought you could catch AIDS from hair. She shrugged, then turned and stared out the window for the rest of the drive.

I shampooed my hair three times that night. Then I wrapped myself in towels and crawled under my blankets and tried to sleep. I counted sheep and stars and blades of grass, but nothing worked. All I could think of again and again was Finn. I thought about his soft kiss. I thought about how just for a second, just as he'd leaned in to me, AIDS and Greta and my mother had disappeared from the room. It was only Finn and me in that tiniest of tiny moments, and before I could stop myself I wondered what it might be like if he really did kiss my lips. I know how gross that is, how revolting, but I want to tell the truth, and the truth is that I lay in bed that night imagining Finn's kiss. I lay in bed thinking about everything in my heart that was possible and impossible, right and wrong, sayable and unsayable, and when all those thoughts were gone there was only one thing left: how terribly much I was going to miss my uncle Finn.

Two

Going into the woods by yourself is the best way to pretend you're in another time. It's a thing you can only do alone. If there's somebody else with you, it's too easy to remember where you really are. The woods I go to start behind the middle and high school buildings. They start there, but they stretch up north for miles, toward Mahopac and Carmel, and then farther, to places I don't know the names of.

The first thing I do when I get to the woods is hang my backpack on a tree branch. Then I walk. To make it work you have to walk until you can't hear any cars at all, and that's what I do. I walk and walk until all I can hear are the little cracks and snaps of branches and the swish of the brook. I follow the brook to a place where there's a crumbling dry stone wall and a tall maple tree with a rusted-out sap bucket nailed just above head height. That's my place. That's where I stop. In the book *A Wrinkle in Time,* it says that time is like a big old rumpled blanket. What I'd like is to be caught in one of those wrinkles. Tucked away. Hidden in a small tight fold.

Usually I put myself in the Middle Ages. Usually England. Sometimes I sing snatches of the *Requiem* to myself, even though I know the *Requiem* isn't medieval. And I look at everything—rocks, fallen leaves, dead trees—like I have the power to read those things. Like my life depends on understanding exactly what the forest has to say.

I make sure I bring along an old Gunne Sax dress of Greta's from when she was twelve. It's way too small for me, so I have to wear a shirt underneath and keep the buttons open at the back. It looks more like something out of *Little House on the Prairie* than anything medieval, but it's the best I can do. And then there's my medieval boots. Anyone will tell you that shoes are the hardest part to get right. For the longest time I only had plain black Keds, which I would try hard not to look at, because they ruined the whole thing.

I got the boots, which are black suede with crisscross leather laces right up the front, at the medieval festival at the Cloisters with Finn. It was October, and Finn had already been painting the portrait for four months. This was the third time he'd taken me to the festival. The first time it was his idea, but the other two were mine. As soon as the leaves started to brown and curl, I'd start pestering him about it.

"You're becoming a regular medievalist, Crocodile," he'd say. "What have I done to you?"

He was right. It was his fault. Medieval art was Finn's favorite, and over the years we'd spent hours and hours looking through his books together. This third time at the festival, Finn was already getting thin. It was chilly enough for wool sweaters and Finn was wearing two, one on top of the other. We were drinking hot mulled cider, and it was just the two of us, alone with the greasy smell of a pig roasting on a spit and lute music and the whinny of a horse about to go into a fake joust and the jangling of a falconer's bells. Finn saw the boots that day and bought them for me because he knew I'd love them. He stayed with me at that bootmaker's stall, tying up rough leather laces for me again and again like there was nothing he'd rather be doing. If they weren't right, he'd help pull the boots off my feet. Sometimes his hand would brush my ankle or my bare knee and I'd blush. I didn't tell him this, but I made sure to choose a pair two sizes too big. I didn't care how many pairs of socks I'd have to wear with them. I never wanted to grow out of those boots.

If I had a lot of money, I would buy acres of woods. I would put a wall around them and live there like it was another time. Maybe I would find one other person to live with me there. Someone who was will-ing to promise they'd never speak a word about anything in the present. I doubt I could find anyone like that. I've never met anyone yet who might make that kind of promise.

There's only one person I've ever told about what I do in the woods, and that's Finn, and I didn't even mean to tell him. We were walking back to his apartment from the movie theater after seeing *A Room with a View*. Finn started talking about how all the characters were so enchanting because they were so tightly wrapped and it was so beautiful to watch them try to unwrap one another. So romantic, he said. He said he wished things were like that now. I wanted him to know I understood—that I would do anything to go back in time—so I told him about the woods. He laughed and bumped his shoulder against mine and called me a nerdatroid and I called him a geek for spending all his time thinking about painting, and then we both laughed because we knew we were right. We both knew we were the biggest nerds in the whole world. Now that Finn's gone, nobody knows that I go to the woods after school. Sometimes I think nobody even remembers those woods exist at all.

Three

The portrait was never given to us. Not officially. Not with words.

That's because it was never finished. That's what Finn said. We had to keep going back for just one more sitting and one more sitting after that. Nobody argued about it except Greta, who stopped going to Finn's on Sundays. She said if Finn was only doing the background, he didn't need all of us there. She said she had other things, better things, she could be doing with her Sunday afternoons.

It was a cold cold morning in January, the first day back to school after Christmas vacation, and we were waiting outside our house for the school bus. Our house is on Phelps Street, which is one of the last streets on the bus route. We live on the south end of town, and school is a little way out of town on the north side. By road it's about two miles, but if you cut through backyards and come in through the woods—which I sometimes do—it's much less.

Because our house is one of the last the bus gets to, it's always hard to know exactly when it will show up. Over the years, Greta and I have spent a lot of time out there waiting, staring down the line of front lawns on our street. Phelps has a mix of capes and ranches, except for the Millers' Tudor, which sits up a small hill on the cul-de-sac. It's obviously a fake Tudor, because there was nobody in Westchester except for the Mohegan Indians in Tudor times, so I don't know who the Millers think they're fooling. Probably no one. Probably it never even crossed the Millers' minds. But it crosses mine. Every single time I see it. Ours is the light blue cape with black shutters and a sprawling red maple out front.

That morning I was jogging in place to stay warm. Greta was leaning against the maple, studying a pair of new suede ankle boots she had on. She kept taking her glasses on and off, breathing on them, then cleaning off the steam.

"Greta?"

"What?"

"What better things do you do on Sundays?"

I wasn't sure I really wanted to know. I wrapped my arms around my coat, pulling it in tighter.

Greta turned her head slowly and gave me a big close-lipped smile. She shook her head and widened her eyes.

"Things *you* can't even imagine."

"Yeah, right," I said.

Greta went to stand on the other side of the driveway.

I figured she meant having sex. But, then again, maybe not, because I could imagine that. I didn't want to, but I could.

She took her glasses off again and turned the lenses white with her breath.

"Hey," I called over to her. "We're orphans again. It's orphan season."

Greta knew what I meant. She knew I meant tax-season orphans. Every year it was the same. There'd be the buzz of Christmas and New Year, and then our parents disappeared for all the worst months of winter. They'd leave the house by six-thirty in the morning, and most nights they wouldn't be back until at least seven. That's what it's like to be the offspring of two accountants. That's how it's been for as long as I can remember.

In tax season, when our parents had to leave before the bus came, they used to have Mrs. Schegner across the street watch over us from her living room window. Nine-year-old Greta would stand waiting for the bus with seven-year-old me. Even though we knew Mrs. Schegner was there, it still felt like we were alone. Greta would throw her arm over my shoulder and pull me right into her. Sometimes, if it was taking a really long time for the bus to get there or if it started snowing,

Greta would sing. She'd sing something from *The Muppet Movie* or sometimes that James Taylor song "Carolina in My Mind" from my parents' *Greatest Hits* album. Even then she had a good voice. It was like she was another person when she sang. Like there was some completely different Greta hidden in there somewhere. She'd sing and hold me tight until she saw the bus round the corner. Then she'd say to me, or maybe to herself, "See, that's not so bad. See?"

I didn't know if Greta still remembered that. I did. Even when she was being mean as anything, I could look at her and remember how we used to be.

Greta glanced at me for a second, trying not to be interested. Trying to pretend she didn't care. She put her hands on her hips. "Oh, the drama of it all, June. Your parents work late. Get over it." She spun around and kept her back to me until the bus came trundling up the road.

I went to Finn's with my mother three more times. We'd started going every other week instead of just once a month. And not always on Sundays. I would have loved to go down there by myself, like I used to, at least one of those times. I wanted to have a good long talk with Finn. But every time I brought it up, my mother said, "Maybe next time. Okay, Junie?" which wasn't really a question at all. It was my mother telling me how it was going to be. It started to feel like she was using me and the portrait as an excuse to go down and spend time with Finn. It never seemed to me like they were very close, and I guess maybe she was starting to regret it. Now it was like I was some kind of Trojan horse my mother could ride in on. It wasn't fair, and underneath it all, lying there like quicksand, was the fact that there wouldn't be that many next times. Without ever saying it, it was becoming clear that the two of us were scrapping it out for Finn's final hours.

On the Sunday that ended up being the last Sunday we went to Finn's, Greta was sitting at her desk, painting her fingernails two colors. She alternated—one purple, one black, one purple, one black. I sat on the edge of her unmade bed and watched.

"Greta," I said, "you know, it won't be much longer. With Finn, I mean."

I needed to make sure she understood the way I understood. My mother said it was like a cassette tape you could never rewind. But it was hard to remember you couldn't rewind it while you were listening to it. And so you'd forget and fall into the music and listen and then, without you even knowing it, the tape would suddenly end.

"Of course I know," she said. "I knew about Uncle Finn being sick way before you knew anything."

"Then why don't you come with us?"

Greta put the black and purple nail polishes back on her little wooden makeup shelf. Then she pulled down a bottle of dark red and unscrewed the top. Carefully, she scraped the brush against the bottle's rim. She pulled her knees to her chest and painted her toenails, starting with the pinkie.

"Because he's going to finish that picture one way or another," Greta said, not even bothering to look up at me. "And, anyway, you know as well as I do that if he could have, he wouldn't have even put me in the portrait. It would have been just his darling Junie, all on her own."

"Finn's not like that."

"Whatever, June. It's not like I even care. It doesn't matter. Any day now the phone will ring and you'll find out that Finn's dead, and you'll have a whole life of Sundays to worry about. What'll you do then? Huh? It doesn't matter anymore. One Sunday more or less. Don't you even know that?"

I didn't say anything. Greta always knew how to make me lose my words. She screwed the top back on the polish bottle and flexed her freshly painted toes. Then she turned to me again. "What?" she said. "Stop staring at me."

Four

Tax season always smelled like stew. Most days my mother left her mustard-yellow crockpot sitting on the kitchen counter, slow-cooking something for our dinner. It didn't matter what was in the pot—chicken, vegetables, beans—it all smelled like stew once the pot was through with it.

It was four o'clock and Greta was at play rehearsals at school. She had one of the big supporting parts in *South Pacific,* the role of Bloody Mary, which she got because she can sing like anything and she's pretty dark. Hair and eyes anyway, so all they have to do is put some dark makeup and eyeliner on her to make her look Polynesian. She told us she had to be at the school almost every night " 'til late."

It was a well-known fact that, of all the schools in the area, our school put on the best musicals. Some years there were even people from the city who came to see our shows. Theater people, choreographers, directors, that kind of thing. There was a rumor that once, maybe ten years ago, a choreographer saw the play and thought one of the senior girls was so good that he got her a part in *A Chorus Line* after graduation. Every year that story goes around, and even though everyone says they don't believe it, you can tell really they do. Really they want to believe that a fairy-tale thing like that could happen to them.

The temperature had been in the single digits for a few days, too cold for the woods, so I was home alone, sitting at the kitchen table doing geology homework, when the phone rang.

"Mrs. Elbus?" a man said. The voice was blurry. Watery.

"No."

"Oh . . . right. Sorry. Is Mrs. Elbus there?" Not just watery, but with an accent. English maybe.

"She's not home yet. Can I take a message?"

There was a long pause, then, "June? Actually, is this June?"

This man, who I knew I'd never spoken to before, knew my name, and it felt like he was reaching his fingers right down the phone wires.

"Call back later," I said. Then I quickly hung up.

I thought of that movie where there's a girl babysitting and someone keeps calling, saying he can see her and that she should check on the children, and she gets more and more freaked out. That's what that phone call felt like. Even though the guy hadn't said anything creepy, I walked around the house, locking all the windows and doors. I sat down on the kitchen floor next to the fridge and opened up a can of Yoo-hoo.

Then the phone rang again. It rang and rang until the answering machine got it. And there was that same voice.

"I'm sorry, really sorry, if I frightened you. I'm ringing about your uncle. Uncle Finn in the city. I'll try back later. That's all. Sorry."

Uncle Finn. He knew Uncle Finn. My whole body went cold. I stood up and poured the rest of the Yoo-hoo down the sink. Then I paced back and forth over the brown linoleum tiles of the kitchen. Finn was gone. I knew Finn was gone.

I picked up the phone and dialed his number, which I knew by heart. It rang twice before it was answered, and when I heard the click of someone picking up, a flood of joy spread right through my chest.

"Finn?" It was quiet on the other end and I waited. "Finn?" I said again. I could hear the desperation creeping into my voice.

"I'm . . . I'm afraid not. He's not . . ."

I hung up the phone quick. The voice was the same. It was the same man who'd left the message on our machine.

I ran up to my room. It had never seemed so small. So shrunk down. I looked around at my stupid fake candles and my big dumb collection of *Choose Your Own Adventure* books, my gaudy red comforter with the fake tapestry print on it. The city seemed like it was a thousand miles away. Like without Finn it didn't have the weight to stay put. Like it might just float away.

I crawled under my bed and closed my eyes tight. I stayed under there for two hours, breathing in stale stew, pretending to be something ancient and entombed, listening for the back door to open so I could press my hands tight over my ears before I had to hear someone playing that stupid answering machine message again.

Five

What Greta said—that she knew about Finn being sick before I did—
was probably true. She wasn't there when I found out. The day I found
out, I was supposed to be going to the dentist with my mother, but
then, without saying a word, she turned left on Main instead of right
and the next thing I knew we were at the Mount Kisco Diner. I
should have known something was weird about the whole thing from
the start, because Greta and I always went to the dentist together and
that time it was just my mother and me. Maybe she was hoping I'd be
so relieved not to be going to the dentist that the news about Finn
wouldn't seem so bad. She was wrong about that. I like going to the
dentist. I like the way the fluoride gel tastes, and I like that for
the twenty minutes I'm sitting in Dr. Shippee's chair, my teeth are the
most important thing in the world to him.

We sat in a booth, which meant we had a jukebox. Before I even
asked, my mother passed me a quarter and told me to pick some songs.

"Something good, okay?" she said. "Something happy."

I nodded. I didn't know what we were about to talk about, so I
chose "Ghostbusters," "Girls Just Want to Have Fun," and "99 Luftballons." The jukebox had both the English and the German versions of
that song. I chose the German because I thought it was cooler.

My mother ordered a cup of coffee, no food. I ordered lemon meringue pie and chocolate milk.

"Ghostbusters" started to play as I flipped through the jukebox songs. I turned the pages, reading the titles one by one, wondering if I'd made the best choices. Then my mother's hand was suddenly on top of mine.

"June," she said, looking like she was almost going to cry.

"Yeah?"

She said something so softly I couldn't hear any of it.

"What?" I asked, leaning across the table.

She said it again, but I could only see her lips moving, like she wasn't even trying to make herself heard.

I shook my head. The jukebox blared out Ray Parker Jr. singing about how he wasn't afraid of ghosts.

My mother pointed to the space next to her, and I walked around to her side of the table. She took my head in her hands and pulled me in so her mouth was almost touching my ear.

"Finn's dying, June."

She could have said that Finn was sick—even really sick—but she didn't. She told me straight out that Finn was dying. My mother wasn't always like that. She wasn't usually one for harsh truths, but this time she must have figured it would mean less talking, less explaining. Because how could she possibly explain something like this? How could anyone? She pulled me closer and we stayed like that for a few seconds, neither of us wanting to look the other in the eye. It felt like there was a traffic jam in my brain. A hundred different things I was supposed to say.

"Lemon meringue?"

The waitress was suddenly standing there holding out my pie, and I had to pull away and nod. I looked at that ridiculous fluffy cheerful meringue and couldn't believe that only a few minutes ago I was a girl who would have wanted something like that.

"What kind of dying?" was what I finally said.

I watched as my mother traced her index finger against the table. *AIDS,* she wrote. Then, as though the table was a blackboard, as though it could remember what she'd written, she rubbed it out with the flat of her hand.

"Oh." I got up and went back to my side of the table. The pie sat there taunting me. I stabbed my fork into that stupid hopeful meringue and pulled it apart. Then I slid closer to the jukebox and pressed my ear against the speaker. I closed my eyes and tried to make the whole diner disappear. As "99 Luftballons" started up, I sat there waiting for Nena to say "Captain Kirk," the two words in that whole song I understood.

Six

The coffin wasn't open at Finn's funeral, and everyone was grateful for that. Especially me. I'd been imagining his closed eyes. His thin-skinned eyelids. I'd been wondering how I would stop myself from laying gentle fingers against them and sliding them open. Just to see Finn's blue eyes one more time.

The funeral was exactly a week after the phone call. It was a Thursday, and we were missing the afternoon of school for it. I was pretty sure that was the only reason Greta agreed to come. This was also one of the few days in my life that I'd ever seen both my parents off on the same day during a tax season.

My mother brought along the portrait Finn had painted of the two of us, because she thought it might be a nice thing to put up somewhere to show the kind of man Finn had been, but when we got to the parking lot of the funeral home she changed her mind.

"He's here," she said. Her voice was a strange combination of anger and panic.

My father parked the car and looked out the window. "Where?"

"Right there, can't you see him? On his own, on the side there."

My father nodded, and I looked too. There was a man sitting hunched on a low brick wall. A tall skinny guy who reminded me of Ichabod Crane from "The Legend of Sleepy Hollow."

"Who is it?" I asked, pointing out the window.

My mother and father both turned to look at me in the backseat. Greta elbowed me in the ribs and said, "Shut up," in her meanest voice.

"You shut up," I said.

"I'm not the one asking stupid questions." She straightened her glasses, then looked away.

"Quiet. Both of you," my father said. "This is hard enough for your mother."

It's hard for me too, I thought, but I didn't say it. I kept quiet, knowing that the sadness I was feeling was the wrong kind of sadness for a niece. Knowing that Finn wasn't really mine to be that kind of sad over. Now that he was dead, he belonged to my mother and my grandmother. They were the ones people felt bad for even though it seemed like neither of them were even that close to him. To everyone at Finn's funeral, I was just the niece. I stared out the car window and understood that I was in a place where nobody knew my heart even a little bit. Nobody had any idea how many minutes of each day I spent thinking about Finn, and, thankfully, nobody had any idea exactly what kind of thoughts they were.

My mother had arranged for the funeral to be held at a funeral home in our town instead of in the city, where all of Finn's friends lived. There was no argument about it. It felt like she was trying to gather him up. Like she was trying to keep Finn all to herself.

My father looked over at my mother. "So, should I leave it in the trunk?"

She nodded, her lips pressed together tight. "Just leave it."

In the end it had been my dad who drove down to the city to pick up the portrait the day after Finn died. He went at night, and none of us offered to go with him. My mother had a key to the apartment, which Finn had threaded onto a piece of red silk ribbon. We'd had that key for years, but I'm not sure anybody had ever used it. My mother always said it was a "just in case" kind of thing. Something Finn wanted us to have.

My dad didn't get home until late that night. He banged the door coming in, and even I overheard him and my mother talking.

"Was he there?" she said.

"Danni—"

"Was he?"

"Of course he was there."

I thought I could hear my mother crying then.

"God. Just thinking about him . . . You'd think things would turn out a little bit fair. Just a little bit."

"Shhhh. Danni, you have to let it go."

"I won't. I can't." There was quiet, then, "Well, where is it anyway? You did get it, right?"

He must have nodded, because the painting was on the table in a black garbage bag the next morning. I was the first one up and I found it there looking like nothing special. I circled the table once, then reached out to touch the bag. I pressed my nose against the outside, searching for a scent of Finn's, but there was nothing. I opened the bag and stuck my head inside, breathing in deep, but the chemical plastic smell smothered anything that might have been wound up in the canvas. I closed my eyes and breathed harder, slower, tightening the bag around my neck.

"Hey, dorkus." I felt a slap land hard across my back. Greta. I pulled free from the bag.

"I won't stop you if you want to end it all, just let us keep the painting, okay? It's gross enough without another dead-body story all over it."

Dead body. Finn was a dead body.

"Girls?" My mother stood halfway down the stairs, pulling her pink quilted robe around herself. She squinted at us through sleepy eyes. "You're not messing around with that painting, are you?"

We both shook our heads. Then Greta smiled.

"One of us has been trying to commit suicide with the garbage bag, that's all."

"What?"

"Shut up, Greta," I said, but she couldn't. She could never shut up.

"Found her down here with her head halfway in that bag."

My mother came over and hugged me so tight I thought she might suffocate me. Then she held me away from her.

"I know how you felt about Finn, and I want you to know, Junie, anytime, anytime you need to talk—"

"I was not trying to kill myself."

"It's okay," she said. "You don't have to say anything. We're all here. Me, your father, Greta. We all love you." Behind my mother, Greta goggled her eyes at me and mimed hanging herself with a noose.

There was no point arguing, so I just nodded and sat down at the table.

My mother picked up the plastic bag and took it upstairs. She said we needed a break from the portrait for a while and that she was putting it someplace safe. That was the last I saw of it until the day of the funeral.

Now we walked up the path toward the front door, Greta and I falling behind our parents. My father stopped and put a hand on my mother's arm.

"Go on ahead," he said, pointing up toward the front steps. "Go find your mother. See how she is."

My mother nodded. She was wearing her nice black wool coat over a narrow black skirt with a dark gray blouse, and she had on a little black hat with a veil. She looked good, like she always did. It was snowing lightly, and the snowflakes kept landing and sitting on the top of her hat for a few seconds before they melted into the black felt.

My grandmother was in the entrance hall, talking to someone I didn't know. She was nothing like my mother, but that was the story of the Weiss side of the family. It seemed like Finn and my mother had looked at their parents and decided that, no matter what, they did not want to turn out like them. So there's Grandpa Weiss, who was a big army guy, and then there's Finn, who went off to become an artist. And there's Grandma Weiss, who spent her whole life cooking meals and ironing clothes and getting her hair done for Grandpa Weiss, and then along comes my mother, who would pay anything not to have to iron or cook real food, who cropped her hair short so she wouldn't have to worry about doing anything with it. If the trend continues with Greta and me, that would mean neither of us would ever want to work in an office, which so far was true for me. If things went my way, I would be working at a renaissance fair as a falconer. I wouldn't have to worry about climbing career ladders or getting promotions, because falconry's not like that. Either you're a falconer or you're not. Either the birds come back to you or they fly away.

My father waited until my mother walked into the funeral parlor. Then he turned to the two of us. I noticed a thin strip of bristle along his jawline, where he'd missed shaving, and I noticed that his brow was constantly furrowed that day. Like a juggler who had to concentrate too hard to keep all the balls in the air. He didn't seem sad about Finn dying. If anything, I thought, he acted like it was a relief.

"I want you two to tell me if you see that man come in, okay?"
We both nodded.
"For your mother's and your grandmother's sake, got it?"
We nodded again.
"Good girls. I know this is rough, and you're both doing a great job." He squeezed my shoulder, then Greta's. "Things will settle down after this, okay?" We nodded once more. He looked at us for another second, then turned to jog up to the open front door.

Greta and I stood there on the ice-crusted front path. Sometimes it felt really obvious that I was taller than Greta even though she was older than me. I leaned in to her and nodded my head toward the man.

"Who is he anyway?" I whispered. I was almost certain she wasn't going to tell me, and I was right. She said nothing, just gestured for me to walk down the path toward where he stood. I glanced up and saw that he was staring right at me. Not at Greta. Only me. He leaned forward like he was about to stand up, like he thought I was coming over to greet him. I was about to turn and walk back the other way, but Greta laid a hand on my arm and pulled me on. We walked until we were maybe a room's length away from the man. Then Greta stopped, waited a second, and cleared her throat.

"He's one of those people who weren't invited to this funeral," she said, loud enough for him to hear.

I looked over at the man who a second ago had seemed to be trying to catch my eye, but now he'd looked away. He'd plunged his hands into his pockets and was staring down at the sidewalk.

"What'd you say that for?"

"I'm not telling you a thing," she said.

The reason Greta knows things that I don't is because she spies. There are places in our house where you can hear everything. I hate those places, but Greta loves them. Her favorite is the downstairs bathroom because hardly anybody uses it, so nobody remembers someone is in there. Even if you are noticed, you can shout out, "Just a minute," before unlocking the door to let someone in. By that time you've heard everything.

I don't like to overhear things, because, in my experience, things your parents are keeping quiet about are things you don't want to know. It doesn't feel good to know that your grandparents are getting separated because your grandfather lost his temper and gave your grandmother a slap across the face after fifty-two years of being married with no problems at all. It doesn't feel good to know ahead of time what you'll be getting for Christmas or birthdays so that you have to act surprised even though you're a terrible liar. It doesn't feel good to know that your teacher told your mother at a conference that you're an average student in math and English and that you should be happy with that.

Greta raced ahead to the door of the funeral home. When she got there, she stopped and turned around.

"On second thought," she said in a loud clear voice. "On second thought, I will tell you." She wiped melted snow off her cheek with the back of her hand.

I felt cold and sick. It was always the same with Greta's information. I wanted to know, but I was scared to know. I gave her the very slightest tip of my head.

She pointed to the man and said, "He's the guy who killed Uncle Finn."

I twisted my head back to look at him, but he'd already turned to go. All I saw was a tall skinny man crouching to get into his small blue car.

I sat in the front row during the funeral service, trying to listen to all the nice things people had to say about Finn. It was stuffy in that room, and dim, and the chairs were the kind that forced you to sit up straighter than you wanted to. Greta didn't sit up front with us. She said she wanted to sit in the back row, and when I turned to glance at her I saw that her head was down, her hands were over her ears, and her eyes were closed. Not just closed but squeezed tight, like she was trying to shut the whole thing out. For a second I thought she might have even been crying, but that didn't seem likely.

My mother gave a short speech about Finn and her as kids. About what a good brother he'd been. Everything she said was vague, like the details might stab her if they got too sharp. After my mother, a cousin from Pennsylvania said a few words. Then the funeral director babbled on for a little while. I tried to listen, but I couldn't stop thinking about the man outside.

I didn't want to think about how Finn got AIDS. It wasn't my job to think about that. If that guy was really the one who killed Finn, then he must have been Finn's boyfriend, and if he was Finn's boyfriend, then why didn't I know anything about him? And how did Greta know? If she'd known Finn had a secret boyfriend, she would have taunted me about it. She never missed an opportunity to let me know I knew less than she did. So there were two possibilities. Either she just found out about this guy or none of it was true.

I decided to believe the second one. It's hard to do that, to *decide* to believe one thing over another. Usually a mind makes itself up on its own. But I forced myself, because the idea that Finn would keep such a big secret from me made me want to throw up.

The service ended and everyone filed out of the building. A few people stopped to talk in the entry hall, but I went straight out the door and tried to find the little blue car. There was no sign of it. Or the man. The snow had started to come down harder, turning the streets and lawns white and perfect. I zipped my coat up as high as it would go, then I looked down the road in both directions, but there was nothing to see. He was gone.

Seven

After a snowstorm is one of the best times to be in the woods, because all the empty beer and soda cans and candy wrappers disappear, and you don't have to try as hard to be in another time. Plus there's just something beautiful about walking on snow that nobody else has walked on. It makes you believe you're special, even though you know you're not.

I was wearing this pair of orange mittens that Greta had knitted for me when she was in the knitting club in fifth grade. They were huge and sloppy and the thumbs were in the middle instead of on the edges. I didn't bother with the Gunne Sax dress, but I did change into my medieval boots. It wasn't actually all that cold, and I walked in farther than I usually did, across the little brook that ran along the bottom of the hill and then up the hill on the other side of it. I tried not to think about Finn and all the secrets he might have kept from me. I tried to keep my mind on the story I was telling myself, where I was the only one strong enough to hunt for my village and I had to trek across the snow to track deer. Girls weren't supposed to hunt, so I had to tie my hair up and pretend to be a boy. That's the kind of story it was.

There was a layer of old frozen snow under the fresh stuff, and for every step I took up the hill I slipped down a bit. By the time I finally got to the top, I sat down, exhausted. It was all quiet and I let my eyes fall closed. For a second I saw Finn's face and I smiled, pressing my eyes closed harder, hoping to keep him there. But the picture disappeared. I let myself tip backward so I was lying flat out in the snow, looking up at the twisted patterns the bare tree branches made against the gray sky. After the land settled around my body, everything was still, and even though I tried to keep my brain in the Middle Ages, Finn kept sneaking into my head. I wished he'd been buried instead of cremated, because then I could take off my gloves and press my palms to the ground and know that he was there somewhere. That through all those molecules of frozen dirt there was still a connection. Then the guy from outside the funeral home came into my thoughts, and I felt a blush of stupidity. Of course someone as amazing as Finn would have a boyfriend. Why wouldn't he? This must have been the guy who'd called that day. The English guy who knew my name. The guy who was calling from Finn's apartment. He was actually *in* Finn's apartment. With *my* uncle Finn. A hot tear ran down my cheek.

Then, into the silence, over the top of everything, came a long, sad howl. For a second it felt like the sound had come from inside me. Like the world had taken everything I was feeling and turned it into sound.

By the time I sat up, there were two howls. Dogs maybe. Coyotes or wolves. The howls weren't steady. Both of them had a kind of cracked-voice sound to them, and they were staggered. One would start, then a few seconds later the second one would come in. Then more. Three or four. I listened hard, trying to hear how far away they were, but it was like the sound was everywhere. Near and far. Wrapped around the trees and the clouds. The howls grew louder, and a picture of a big lunging gray wolf with tons of matted fur popped into my mind. For a single dumb moment it really did feel like I was in the woods in the Middle Ages, when wolves could take away babies or eat a person whole.

"I'm not afraid," I called out across the hills. Then I ran, stumbling and tripping. I misjudged the jump and plunged one boot into the brook, then scrambled up the other side, grabbing on to thin saplings, steadying myself. A few minutes later I came out of the woods, into the school parking lot. Almost all the cars were gone and I stood there for a minute, doubled over, catching my breath.

"Shoot," I said, looking down at my right hand. I kicked at the big pile of dirty plowed snow at the edge of the parking lot. One of the mittens Greta had made me was gone.

Eight

"Do you want to go to a party?"

Greta wasn't smiling when she asked me. She wasn't even looking at me. She was bent over her dresser as I walked past the door to her room on my way down for breakfast.

I was sure I'd heard her wrong, so I stopped and waited for her to say something else. I must have looked like an idiot standing there in the hallway with my mouth hanging open.

Greta turned and eyed me up and down.

"Par-ty," she said, enunciating every syllable and exaggerating her lip movements. "Do. You. Want. To. Go."

I stepped into her room, which still had the same white furniture it had when she was seven and the same pink walls with that thin strip of Holly Hobby wallpaper across the top. From the way the room was decorated, someone who didn't know anything about Greta would think a nice little girl lived there. I sat on the edge of her bed.

"What kind of party?"

"The good kind."

"Yeah, right."

Greta knows that for me there are no good parties. I'm okay with one or two people, but more than that and I turn into a naked mole rat. That's what being shy feels like. Like my skin is too thin, the light too bright. Like the best place I could possibly be is in a tunnel far under the cool, dark earth. Someone asks me a question and I stare at them, empty-faced, my brain jammed up with how hard I'm trying to find something interesting to say. And in the end, all I can do is nod or shrug, because the light of their eyes looking at me, waiting for me, is just too much to take. And then it's over and there's one more person in the world who thinks I'm a complete and total waste of space.

The worst thing is the stupid hopefulness. Every new party, every new bunch of people, and I start thinking that maybe this is my chance. That I'm going to be normal this time. A new leaf. A fresh start. But then I find myself at the party, thinking, *Oh, yeah. This again.*

So I stand on the edge of things, crossing my fingers, praying nobody will try to look me in the eye. And the good thing is, they usually don't.

"I don't think so," I said.

"Oh, come on, June. I promise it won't be awful."

I raised my eyebrows at her. The whole thing sounded too sincere. Not like Greta at all.

"Really. Cross my heart." She put both hands over the middle of her chest. I tried hard not to smile, but I could feel my face betraying me.

"Well, where is it?" I said after a while.

"Don't know yet, but Jillian Lampton's organizing it. You know Jillian Lampton, right?"

I did know Jillian. She was one of the lighting people for *South Pacific*. She had dyed black hair that she wore in a sharp bob. I always thought she looked kind of how I'd like to look someday. Jillian was a junior, a class below Greta, but she was probably older than Greta.

This is something that only a few people know. Greta's a senior, but she's only sixteen. None of her friends know her real age. Not a single one. We moved from Queens to our town when I was five and Greta was seven. Greta was supposed to go into second grade, but instead she got put in third. Her last teacher had recommended it. She said Greta wasn't being challenged and told my parents she could easily hold her own if she skipped a grade. Apparently my father wasn't sure, but my mother thought it was a fantastic idea. "Opportunities don't come swimming back to you if you throw them away." That was her big motto. Mostly for Greta. As if opportunities were slippery little fish.

Greta didn't care either way. So they did it. Even though she was already one of the youngest kids in her class, she skipped a grade. Now she's at least a year younger than everybody else in her class, almost two years younger than most. But she keeps it quiet. At her birthday parties, my mother would put an extra candle on her cake, just for show. The tradition was that every year Greta would decide which one was the "liar candle" and, if she could, she'd leave that one burning. She was scared that blowing that one out would reverse all her wishes. The age thing is on her school records, but other than that it seems like it's mostly forgotten. Sometimes I can tell though. I would never say anything to Greta, but sometimes I can see that she's a lot closer to being a kid than her friends are.

"I don't know, Greta. I don't think Mom—"

"Don't worry about Mom. I'll deal with Mom. It's a month and a half into tax season. Mom won't care." Greta put both hands on her hips and cocked her head to the side. "So you're coming?"

"I . . . Why do you want me to?"

There was a flicker of something in Greta's look. I couldn't tell whether it was a flicker of love or regret or meanness, and then she said, "Why *wouldn't* I want you to?"

Because you hate me, I thought, but I didn't say it.

Three years ago we stopped having Keri Westerveldt babysit us during tax season. Greta was put in charge. My parents trusted her. "You're both sensible girls," my mother said. That first year without Keri Westerveldt, Greta kept track of everything I did. She helped me with my homework and sat next to me on the bus on the way home. She made us little American cheese and mayonnaise sandwiches for snacks and we'd sit up in her bedroom eating them, pretending to be the kind of orphans who had only each other in the world. The house would be so still sometimes, so quiet and empty, that it was easy to believe it was true. If she'd asked me to a party back then, I wouldn't have hesitated for a second. Even though I hate parties, I would have said yes. I wouldn't have doubted her at all.

It's hard to say exactly when we stopped being best friends, when we stopped even resembling two girls who were sisters. Greta went to high school and I was still in middle school. Greta had new friends and

I started having Finn. Greta got prettier and I got . . . weirder. I don't know. None of those things should have mattered, but I guess they did. I guess they were like water. Soft and harmless until enough time went by. Then all of a sudden you found yourself with the Grand Canyon on your hands.

"Come on. Please, June?"

"I don't know, maybe," I mumbled. I wanted to believe her intentions were good. I stared right down deep into her eyes, squinting to find the place where all this had come from. But I couldn't see anything. Then the idea came to me that maybe somehow it was Finn. Maybe when you're dead you can crawl inside other people and make them nicer than they were before. I don't really believe in that kind of thing, but I smiled at her anyway. Just in case. Just on the off chance that it was Finn looking out through Greta's eyes.

"So you'll go?" she said.

I looked around her room. In every corner, clothes lay crumpled and piled. Lipsticks and eyeliners that had rolled to the edge of Greta's uneven desk rested against a photocopy of the *South Pacific* script. A crushed 7Up can sat on top of an unsolved Rubik's Cube. In the upper right-hand corner of her mirror, she'd wedged photo booth pictures of herself and her friends, and I saw my feet sticking out. An old picture of me, of us, my dirty white sandals and the edge of my yellow polka dot sundress peeking out from under all the rest.

Maybe it was the fact that Greta still kept that picture close at hand, or maybe it was how surprisingly good it felt to have Greta asking me to do something with her, or maybe it was that I knew this was my last real year with her. She'd already gotten early acceptance to Dartmouth. It didn't seem possible, but in six months she'd be out and gone. It could have been any of those things, or it could have been that the party just felt far away. I knew there'd be time enough to bow out later. Why spoil the moment now? Maybe that's why I found myself nodding my head.

"Okay," I said, half-smiling. "I guess I'll go."

Greta clapped her hands together and did a little hop off the ground. Then she reached over and lifted my braids up onto the top of my head.

"I'll fix you all up," she said. "I still have some Sun-In, and Megan said that it can work even if it's not summer if you stand really close to a lightbulb. And we can do makeup." She stopped for a second and let my hair fall back down onto my shoulders. She picked her glasses up off the top of her dresser and put them on. Then she looked at me hard.

"We're back, right? Like we used to be? I'll help you forget all about Uncle Finn. Now that Finn's gone, you and me . . ." Greta was smiling. Giddy almost.

I pulled away from her and stared.

"I don't want to forget about Finn."

That's what I said. It came straight from my heart and out my mouth, and although it's as true as anything, I've spent a lot of time wishing I hadn't said it. Wishing I'd told Greta that, yes, we were back. That we were best friends again. That everything could be like it used to be.

She tried to turn away fast, but before she could, I saw the look of disappointment that flooded across her whole face. She fidgeted with something on her desk, keeping her back to me. When she faced me again, the look was gone, replaced by her usual condescending repulsion.

"God, June. Do you always have to be such a moron?"

"I—"

"Just go. You can go."

I got to the door, then turned around.

"Greta?"

She let out an annoyed sigh. "What?"

"I didn't mean—"

She waved the back of her hand at me.

"I don't want to hear it. Just go. Get out."

Nine

Uncle Finn wasn't just my uncle, he was also my godfather. Greta's godparents were the Ingrams: Fred Ingram, who was a quality control manager at Pillsbury, and Becca Ingram, his wife. They have one son, named Mikey, who's younger than me by a couple of years. Greta and I have known Mikey since the day he was born with that weird port-wine-stain birthmark across his shoulder. In the summer, the Ingrams came around a lot for barbecues, and Mr. Ingram always brought his own meat. If we went up to the town pool to swim or had the sprinklers on, Mikey would always wear his T-shirt because of that birthmark. Even in front of Greta and me, who had seen it all before.

The Ingrams were okay, but you'd never know they were Greta's godparents. Finn took the job of being my godfather seriously. I asked my mother once why Finn wasn't Greta's godfather too, and she said that when Greta was born, Finn hadn't settled down yet. He was still "out and about," traveling here and there on a whim. That sounded okay to me, but according to my mother it wouldn't have been suitable.

She said that even if Greta had been born after me, she still wouldn't have asked Finn to be a godfather again because he ended up taking the whole thing to heart too much. She didn't expect him to take so much interest, and now that I was older she thought it was becoming a distraction. Once, before he died, she said it might be a good thing for me not to be able to rely on him so much.

I hated that. And I hated when she said any sentence that started with the words "A girl your age . . ."

I knew Greta hated that I got Uncle Finn and she got stuck with the Ingrams. It wasn't like Finn ever said Greta couldn't come along to anything. He never excluded her. She excluded herself. Sometimes she would say, "I don't want to intrude on your special godfather time with Finn," in her snotty tone. And I never argued with her because I did want Finn to myself.

Last summer, Mikey tried to kiss Greta. She told him it was gross because he was her godbrother and that was like incest.

"But you can kiss June," she said. Mikey went red, not knowing where to look. Nobody wanted to kiss me, not even Mikey, and Greta wanted to make sure I knew it one more time. But what I could see was that Greta always remembered the godfather thing. It was always right on the edge of her mind. I'd lucked out with Finn, and she knew it.

Ten

The portrait finally came out of that ugly black garbage bag on the Tuesday morning after Uncle Finn's funeral. There was supposed to be only a two-hour delay that morning, but it kept snowing hard and fast, and we ended up getting the whole day off from school. I like snow days. Especially when there was already piles of snow on the ground and you can go out and walk two or three feet above the grass and pretend you're in a cloud heaven.

When we were little, before Greta turned mean, the two of us would disappear together into the backyard in our fat snowsuits. We'd lie on our backs, both trying not to blink when the snowflakes hit our faces. Greta said that once a snowflake landed right on her eyeball so that she could see every little delicate detail of it. Every single crystal. Just for a second. Like it was carved right into her eye. She said it was the most beautiful snowflake she could ever imagine. More beautiful even than angels. Then she ran into the house. She clutched at my mother's skirt, crying and crying because she knew I'd never be able to see that snowflake. She knew she'd never be able to show that perfect thing to me. That's a story my mother tells sometimes to show what Greta and I used to be like. Sometimes I believe it. Sometimes I don't.

"We have to get it framed," my mother said. My dad had made his way in to the office, but my mother stayed home with us that day. She was pacing the kitchen, holding the bagged painting to her chest. The

kitchen smelled of scrambled eggs and coffee, and the snow was coming down so thick I couldn't even see the car outside in the driveway.

"We don't have to," Greta said. "Who says we have to?"

"That's just what you do with a painting," my mother said. "One of
you take it out. Let's have a look."

There was nothing to be afraid of. That's what I told myself. I
reached for the bag. My mother handed it to me, then took a step
back. Greta leaned in close as I laid the whole thing down on the table
and tugged the bag off.

There we were, me and Greta, staring up at ourselves from the
kitchen table. My hair was the way I always had it—two thin braids,
one on each side, tied together at the back—and Greta had her glasses
on, because Finn told her he thought we should look the way we always did. That the portrait should be true. The way Finn painted me
made it look like I knew some kind of massive secret but I was never
going to tell anyone. He should have painted Greta like that, because
that's more what she's like, but instead he made her look like she'd just
finished telling a secret to someone and now she was sitting there,
waiting for a reaction. If you look at that portrait you can see what a
fantastic painter Finn was. I can't even begin to understand how he got
the thoughts out of someone's head and onto the surface of a canvas.
How can thoughts that are invisible be turned into smudges of red and
yellow and white?

None of us could take our eyes off the portrait. My mother put her
arms around our waists and eased in between us. I soaked in every
brushstroke, every shading of color, every angle and line in that painting. I could feel my mother and even Greta doing the same. I could
feel them wanting to dive into that canvas. My mother's grip grew
tighter and tighter around me until I felt her hand forming a solid fist
around my shirt. She twisted her head away and wiped her cheek
against the sleeve of her sweater.

"You okay?" I asked.

My mother nodded quickly, eyes fixed on the painting. "It's such a
waste. Look at this. Look at what he could do. He had all the opportunities in the world. . . ."

I thought she was going to cry, but instead she broke the moment with a quick hard clap. Then, in an overly cheerful tone, she said, "Okay. Frames? Ideas?"

I cocked my head to the side. "Does anyone think it looks . . . I don't know . . . different?"

"I don't know," Greta said, rubbing her chin, pretending to consider it, "you still look like a doofus."

"Not now, Greta," my mother said, letting out a long slow breath.

But the painting did look different. The last time I'd seen it was the last time I went to Finn's. The paint had still been wet, and Finn was there looking smaller than I'd ever seen him before. His vision was going, and he said he'd never be able to get it right. He put a hand on my shoulder and said, "Sorry, June. Sorry it's not so great." He said we'd keep working on it.

We. That's what he said. As if I had something to do with it.

"Everybody finished looking?" my mother asked, reaching for the portrait.

"Just a sec." I searched the painting for the thing that had changed. I looked right into my eyes, then Greta's. No. Nothing was different there. Then I noticed the buttons. There were five buttons right down the front of my T-shirt. Once I saw them, I couldn't understand how I hadn't seen them right away, because they didn't even look like something Finn would paint. They looked like something a kid might paint. Each one was solid black with a little splotch of white to make it look like light was reflecting off it. Why would Finn put buttons on a T-shirt? I touched my fingertip to the top button. The paint was thicker than it was anywhere else, and somehow that made me sad.

I looked at my mother and Greta and decided not to mention the buttons.

"Okay," I said. "I'm done. You can put it away."

On Friday after school we went to the frame store downtown. Chubby little Mr. Trusky told us he understood how important it was that we were all happy with the choice, and he let us stay a half hour after he flipped the CLOSED sign on the door. Over and over my mother had Mr. Trusky frame up the portrait, and over and over one of us decided it wasn't quite right. At the end of that day the painting was still un-framed. It went back in the trunk of the car, back in the same black plastic bag we brought it in.

"We'll try again tomorrow," my mother said in the parking lot. "He says he's got more."

"Why don't you just go by yourself?" Greta asked.

"Absolutely not. This is something Finn made for the two of you. This is your responsibility."

"Well, then, I say we go for the plain black wooden one."

I hated the plain black wooden one. It made us look sarcastic.

Each frame Mr. Trusky put around the portrait seemed to change everything about it. The one my mother liked was called Valencia and was made of dark wood with some small carvings around the edge that looked like coffee beans. I thought it made the whole portrait look boring.

"I like the gold one. The old-fashioned one."

"Surprise, surprise," Greta said.

It was called Tuscan Gold, and I thought it looked classy. Like the painting could go right into a museum with that frame around it.

"Finn would like that one," I said.

"How do you know what Finn would like?" Greta asked, her voice sharp. "Have you managed to jump rope your way to the land of the dead now?"

Sometimes it amazed me the way Greta remembered things. When I was nine I had an idea about time travel. I thought that maybe if I jumped rope backward fast enough, I would go back in time. If I could just churn the air hard enough around me, I could make a little bubble that went backward. I didn't believe that anymore. I didn't believe anyone could have that kind of power.

My mother looked like she might break down any second, so I nudged Greta.

"Tomorrow. Maybe tomorrow we'll see things clearer," my mother said.

And somehow we did. We chose the first one Mr. Trusky showed us the next morning. Maybe we chose fast because Greta had found a good excuse not to come with us, so it was only me and my mom. Or maybe it was because we were worn down or maybe because it really was the best frame. It was medium brown with beveled edges, and it almost seemed to disappear around the canvas, letting the painting be itself.

"Leave it with me for a couple days. I'll have it all framed up by, say, Tuesday morning." Mr. Trusky scribbled on a pad.

"Leave it?" I said.

My mother put a hand on my shoulder. "He can't do it right now, honey. It takes some time."

"But I don't like the idea of leaving it here. Away from us."

"Come on, now, don't be rude. Mr. Trusky's doing his very best." My mother smiled at Mr. Trusky, but he was still writing on his pad.

"I'll tell you what. I'll come in special tomorrow afternoon, just for you, and I'll bring it over to your house when I'm done with it. Okay?"

I nodded. It would still be away overnight, but it seemed like the best deal I was going to get.

"Say thank you to Mr. Trusky, please, June. This is awfully nice of him."

I thanked him and we left. Mr. Trusky kept his promise, and the painting came back to us the next day. He propped it up on the kitchen counter so we could have a good look.

"Now, that's one handsome piece of art," my father said, hands on his hips.

"And the frame is perfect. We do appreciate everything you've done," my mother said.

"It makes all the difference, you know," Mr. Trusky said.

Both my parents nodded, though I'm not sure they were even listening.

"And what about you, June? Are you happy?" Mr. Trusky asked.

It was the kind of question you had to say yes to. But really I wasn't. All I could see was me and Greta shoved into that frame together. No matter what happened, the two of us would always be trapped inside those four pieces of wood.

Eleven

"Can you sign for it . . ." The mailman pointed at a line halfway down a paper on his clipboard. His cap was tipped down with the peak covering his eyes. He scanned the list of names. ". . . June. June Elbus."

This was on an afternoon a couple of weeks after Finn's funeral, when I was the only one home. I nodded and took the pen from his hand, which was shaking a little. As I signed my name, I could see out of the corner of my eye that the mailman was peeking into the house. After I signed, he handed me a box.

"Thanks," I said, glancing up at him.

He stared back at me, and for a moment it seemed like he wanted to say something to me. Then he smiled and said, "Yeah. Right. It's fine . . . June."

He turned to go, but then he stopped and stood there for another moment, his back to me.

I started easing the door closed, but the mailman still stood there, not moving. For a second it looked like he was about to turn around. He put a finger up in the air like he was about to say something, but then he didn't. He just let his hand drop and walked away.

I went straight up to my room and scooted onto my bed. I sat cross-legged with the package on my lap. The box was entirely covered in tape. It was like someone had taken a roll of brown packing tape and wrapped it around and around in every direction until the box completely disappeared. I tried to find an end to pull, but I couldn't, so I used scissors to cut through the top. It wasn't my birthday and it was two months past Christmas. There was no return address on that box. Nothing at all except my name and address written in black permanent marker on top of the tape.

Inside were two big overpacked blobs, one smaller than the other. I opened the smaller one first. As I got down to the last few layers of bubble wrap and newspaper, I started to feel what it was. Then I saw a flash of brilliant blue with gold and red, and I realized that it was the lid of Finn's Russian teapot. I almost dropped it right onto the floor. After all that careful packaging, I almost let it slip right out of my fingers. I quickly moved on to the bigger piece. Ripping at it. Desperate to see the whole pot again.

The last time I'd seen that teapot was that last Sunday we went to Finn's. That Sunday when Greta didn't want to come along. That day, my mother and Finn were arguing about the pot. He wanted her to take it but she wouldn't. He held it out to her with two hands, and she batted him away.

"Stop being like that. We'll see you again," she said.

Finn gave me a look like he was checking to see if it was okay to tell the truth. I looked away. I wanted to go into another room, but Finn had a one-bedroom apartment and there was nowhere else to go except the tiny kitchen, which was behind two swinging doors like they had in the Old West.

"Danni, just take it. For June. Just let me have my way for once."

"Ha. For once. That's a good one." My mother's voice was shrill. "We don't need your teapot and that's that."

He walked across the room toward me, with the pot cradled in his hands.

My mother gave me a look. "Don't you even think about it, Junie."

I sat there frozen. My mother headed Finn off, grabbing at the pot. Finn held it up over his head, trying to hand it to me.

Right then I thought I could see into the future of that teapot. I could see it smashing against the wood floor of Finn's living room. I could see all those shiny colored pieces catching the light of the sunset through Finn's big windows. I saw half a dancing bear, a bear with no head, just legs, kicking up toward the ceiling.

"You silly old woman," Finn said. He always called my mother "old woman." Since they were kids, she told me once. And they had other jokes between them. Finn would call her "mutton dressed as lamb," which wasn't really true, and then she'd call him "lamb dressed as mutton," which was true. Finn did dress like an old man, with brown-buttoned cardigan sweaters and big, clunky old man shoes and handkerchiefs in his pockets. But it looked good on him. It looked right.

"You silly, silly old woman."

My mother stopped reaching for the pot. She smiled the tiniest little smile.

"Maybe," she said, her whole body drooping. "Maybe that's what I am."

Finn lowered the pot and took it back to the kitchen. He was so pale that the colors of the pot looked garish next to him. I would have liked to have taken it from him. It didn't have to mean anything. It didn't have to mean we wouldn't see him again.

"June," Finn called from the kitchen in his hoarse, worn-down voice. "Can you come here a sec?"

When I got in there, he hugged me. Then he whispered in my ear. "You know that pot's for you. No matter what, right?"

"Okay."

"And promise me you'll only serve the best people from it." His voice was cracking, splintering up. "Only the very best, okay?" His cheek was wet against mine, and I nodded without looking at him.

I promised. Then he squeezed my hand and pulled away from me and smiled.

"That's what I want for you," he said. "I want you to know only the very best people."

That's when I broke down and cried, because I already knew the very best people. Finn was the very best person I knew.

That was the last time I saw that teapot at Finn's house. The last time I ever thought I would see it. Until the day it showed up on my doorstep.

I ripped open the rest of the packaging, then stood the teapot on my dresser. It was exactly the same. I picked the lid up from my bed and went to put it on the pot. That's when I saw there was something inside. At first it looked like just a scrap of the packing paper, but it was folded too neatly. Then I saw my name on it. *For June.* A note? Maybe from Finn? A rush of joy and fear rose up in my chest.

I rewrapped the pot with all the bubble wrap, but I kept the note out. I settled the teapot into the box and looked at it again. No return address and no stamps. How could there be no stamps? For a second I had the stupid thought that maybe the ghost of Finn had brought me the teapot. But then the mailman came back into my head. When I thought about it, it hit me that there was nothing official at all about what he was wearing. A navy blue baseball cap and a navy jacket? My parents would have killed me for opening the door. But there was something more than that. Something about the way he'd looked at me. What was it? Why was there something familiar? And then it clicked. It was the guy from the funeral. The guy who Greta said was a murderer. A chill shimmied through my body. He'd come right up to my front door.

I grabbed the note off my bed and slid the box to the very back of my closet. I vaulted down the stairs and grabbed my coat. I stuck the note in my coat pocket and then, even though it was getting dark, I left for the woods.

Twelve

26th February, 1987

Dear June,

    My name is Toby. I was a very close friend of your uncle Finn, and I was wondering if it might be at all possible for us to meet up. I think you might know who I am because we spoke once on the telephone. I sincerely apologize if I distressed you on that occasion. Also, I know you saw me at the funeral. I was the man nobody wanted to see.

    Please don't take this the wrong way or be afraid, but I would advise you not to tell your parents about this letter, or even your sister, as I think you know how they might react. I think you are perhaps the only person who misses Finn as much as I do, and I think just one meeting might be beneficial to us both.

    This is what I suggest: I will be at your train station at 3:30 P.M. on Friday 6th of March. If you meet me there, we can ride the train somewhere. Talk in peace. Would that be all right?

    I don't know what you've been told about me, but it's probably not true.

    With much hope of seeing you soon,

                      Toby

That's what the letter said. I had to read it sitting on the curb under a streetlamp in the school parking lot, because it was too dark in the woods by the time I got there. A few kids from the play were out there waiting for their mothers to drop off dinner. I stayed in the far corner of the lot with my hood up over my head, hoping nobody would see me.

Once I'd read the letter, I shoved it back into my pocket and walked right into those dusky woods. It was wet and icy, but I didn't care. I walked and walked until I got to the brook. All along the edge of the water there were paper-thin sheets of ice pressed with brown leaves. But the middle still ran, quick and snaky, like it was worried it might get caught. I jumped across the brook and walked a bit farther before I sat down on a big wet boulder. I must have gone farther than I thought, because I could hear the same sad howling I'd heard the last time I was in the woods. Or maybe it wasn't that I'd gone farther; maybe those wolves, or whatever they were, were coming closer. I unfolded the note and tried to read it again. I sat there squinting my eyes to see the words one more time, but I couldn't. Even with no leaves, the trees shaded out any light that was left.

But it didn't matter. I didn't need light. The words of that note were already burned into my mind. *You are perhaps the only person who misses Finn as much as I do.* What was that supposed to mean? What was it supposed to mean that some man who thought it was a good idea to pretend to be a mailman and show up on the doorstep of his boy-friend's niece's house thought he missed Finn, *my* uncle Finn, as much as I did? This man who'd killed Finn. I could have shouted out right along with those wolves. I could have let a warm howl turn my breath into a ghost in those cold winter woods. But I didn't. I sat there, quiet.

I thought about tearing that note up into a thousand little pieces. I thought about dropping the pieces into the fast, cold brook and watching them float away. But I didn't. I folded it up into a thick small square, tucked it back into my pocket, and turned for home.

Thirteen

"Mom?"

"Yes?"

"What's gonna happen to Finn's apartment?"

It was later that same night. I'd waited until Greta was in bed. My dad was watching the late news, and my mother was washing out the crockpot in the kitchen. She had on her yellow rubber gloves, and her shoulders shook with the effort of scrubbing. You could tell how far into tax season it was by what my mother did at night. Now she was still doing dishes before going to bed. By mid-March, the crockpot would sit soaking overnight in the sink and she'd be on the couch with my father, both of them with eyes barely open, folders of paperwork on their laps.

When she heard my question, she stopped scrubbing and stood staring out the dark kitchen window for a few seconds. Then she pulled off the gloves one at a time and tossed them into the sink. When she turned around she was frowning a little, but I could see she was trying not to.

"Let's sit down." She pointed down the hall, toward the living room. "Go on. I'll be there in a minute."

The folded note was still in my pocket and I slid my hand in there, letting my fingers riffle the edges. I looked at my mother, thinking she had no idea what I was holding on to, thinking I would tell her when the right moment came along.

In the living room, the portrait's eyes were on me. We'd hung it just a few hours after Mr. Trusky dropped it off. At first my mother said it should go in our rooms. Greta's for a month, then mine for a month, switching back and forth like that. Finn meant it for us, she said. Greta said right away that she didn't want it in her room. It creeped her out and she didn't like the way Finn had painted her. She said he'd purposely made her look like an idiot. And, she said, she didn't like the way he'd painted me either.

"Why not?" I said. "I think it looks okay."

"Of course you think it looks okay. He made you look better than you've ever looked in your whole life. You *would* like it."

She was right. I did like myself in that portrait. There was a kind of intelligence in my eyes that I was pretty sure wasn't there in real life, and I seemed smaller. Greta and Finn and my mother all had the same slim bones. My father and I were the lumbering ones, the misshapen bears. But in the portrait, Greta and I were almost the same size.

Still, if you looked at Greta and looked at the portrait, you could see that Greta was prettier in real life and prettier in the picture, and I told her that.

"I'm not prettier, you dweeb. I'm just older. Can't you even tell the difference?"

It was a nice thing for her to say. In her way. With Greta you have to look out for the nice things buried in the rest of her mean stuff. Greta's talk is like a geode. Ugly as anything on the outside and for the most part the same on the inside, but every once in a while there's something that shines through.

"Well, then, I'm going to be selfish," my mother said. "I don't think it's fair that the painting stays locked up in one person's room forever, so I'm going to suggest that we hang it over the mantel. Any problems with that?"

Greta groaned. "That's even worse. It'll creep out the whole living room. Plus, absolutely everyone who comes here will see the thing."

"I'm afraid that's the way it's going to be, Greta. June, any problem with that?"

"No. That's okay."

"That's done, then. We'll have your father hang it."

Since it's been up, I've caught my mother staring at it. Not just once, but a bunch of times. All that time at Finn's it was like she was completely uninterested, almost repulsed, by the portrait, but since it's been in our house she's seemed almost obsessed with it. I've seen her eyeing it the same way Finn did. Tilting her head. Muttering things to it under her breath. Walking close, then backing up. This was usually at night, after I was supposed to be in bed, and if she caught me standing there she'd give me an embarrassed smile. Then she'd walk out of the room, acting like nothing had been going on.

I'd made sure that Greta wasn't around when I asked about the apartment. I thought she probably knew all the horrible details of what was going to happen to it. She probably knew that it'd be scrubbed with bleach until there wasn't even a hint of lavender or orange left. She probably knew exactly who the new owners would be and that they were horrible people who'd turn that apartment into some kind of dumpy place with TVs and stereos and wires all over the place. Finn hated wires. He hated having stuff plugged in everywhere.

At first, when my mother came into the living room, she didn't say anything. She looked up at the portrait, then she looked at me. She sat next to me on the couch, close, with her arm around my shoulders. She smelled of lemony dish soap.

"Junie," she said. "You need to understand some things about Finn." She turned her face away from me, then turned back. "I know how much you loved your uncle. And I did too. He was my baby brother. I loved him to pieces."

"Love."

"What?"

"Love, not loved. We can still love him."

My mother raised her head.

"Of course we can. You're right. But the thing about Finn is that he didn't always make the best choices. He did whatever he wanted, whenever he wanted. He didn't always . . ."

"Care what other people wanted him to do?"

"Yes."

"He didn't care what you wanted him to do."

"That's not the important thing. The important thing to understand is that Finn was a free spirit and a good man, but maybe sometimes he was a bit too trusting."

My mother said this kind of thing about Finn a lot. How he never grew up. She said it like it was a bad thing, but to me it was one of the very best things about him.

"So what does this have to do with his apartment?"

"Nothing. Just, well, Finn had a different . . . lifestyle. Do you see what I mean?"

"I know Finn was gay, Mom. Everybody knows that."

"Of course you do. Of course. So let's just leave it there. Okay? We don't need to worry about the apartment anymore." My mother rubbed my back and smiled. She started to stand, but I wasn't done.

"Well, what if I wanted to go there?"

My mother shook her head, then stared up at the portrait for a long time. When she finally looked at me again, her face was serious.

"Look, June, there's a man living there. Okay? He was Finn's . . . special friend. Do you see what I mean?" My mother grimaced slightly, though I could tell she was trying to hold it back. "I didn't want to get into this. . . ."

Special friend? I stifled a laugh. *Special friend* reminded me of kindergarten field trips. It made me think of holding hands with Donna Folger and looking both ways before crossing streets.

"What's that supposed to mean?" I said.

"I think you know what it means. Now can we drop it?"

I was still laughing a little, but as the whole thing started to sink in, my smile faded. Finn had never told me that someone would be moving into his apartment when he died. Why wouldn't he tell me something huge like that?

I felt for the note again. *The only person who misses Finn as much as I do.* That's what it said. Toby. I knew the special friend's name. And I knew he'd called me from the apartment, but I guess I figured he'd find a new place to live.

I would have asked my mother then and there why nobody had ever mentioned this special friend, this Toby, to me, but I couldn't bear to do it. To embarrass myself like that. To make it seem like this was a big deal to me. For the last few years I'd considered Finn to be my best friend. The very best. Maybe I was wrong about that.

I nodded at my mother without looking her in the eye. Suddenly the thought of telling her that Finn's *special friend* had come right to our front door, that Finn's *special friend* knew that I was the only one who missed Finn as much as he did, that Finn's *special friend* had asked me to meet him, seemed impossible.

"Yeah, okay. I'll drop it," I said, and although I held it back with every muscle in my body, what I really wanted to do was cry. Not only because Finn had never told me about this guy, but because there was no way to ask him about it. And until then I don't think I really understood the meaning of gone.

Fourteen

"Remember that party?" Greta grabbed me and whispered in my ear as I came out of the upstairs bathroom. My hands were still wet and I rubbed them on my sweater.

"Ummm?"

Greta let out an exasperated sigh. "Yeah, you do. Remember I asked if you wanted to go to a party? Jillian Lampton? Remember?"

I hadn't exactly forgotten. I think I just filed it away somewhere. Or maybe I thought it was all a joke in the first place. Some cruel thing Greta had said just to see what I'd say. I nodded anyway.

"Yeah, well, it kept getting put off, but now it's tonight."

"Tonight? But—"

"I told Mom they need help with the play."

"I'm not in the play."

Greta rolled her eyes and took a deep steady breath. "Yes. I know. You'll be at the party."

"Oh." I'd never lied to my parents about where I was going. I'd never had anywhere to go before.

"You can bring Beans too. If you want."

I hadn't been friends with Beans for years. Not really. When Beans first moved here from Ohio in third grade, with her Dorothy Hamill haircut and her 4-H badges sewn on the outside of her backpack, she had no one. Back then we were best friends. For a long time, all the way through to the end of elementary school, Beans was my only friend. Because that's how I've always been. I only need one good friend to see me through. Most people aren't like that. Most people are always looking out for more people to know. In the end, Beans was like most people. After a while she had dozens of friends, and by fifth grade it was pretty obvious that even though she was *my* best friend, I wasn't hers.

Somehow my whole family seemed to have missed the thing where Beans and I weren't good friends anymore. I could call her up and she would be nice and everything, but it would be weird. No matter how many times I told my mother that Beans had tons of other friends, my mother couldn't stop seeing it the way it used to be between us. Maybe I didn't want her to, because then she would start nagging me to find some new friends. I didn't want to explain to her who I was. That I was the weird girl who carried a worn-out copy of *The Portable Medieval Reader* in her backpack, the girl who only wore skirts, usually with medieval boots, the girl who got caught staring at people. I didn't want to have to tell her that people weren't exactly lining up to hang out with me.

Plus, once you had a friend like Finn, it was almost impossible to find someone in high school who came anywhere close. Sometimes I wondered if I might go through my whole life looking for someone who came even a little bit close.

Greta unzipped her purse. "Mom was so happy we were doing something together. You know what she did?"

I shook my head.

"She gave me ten bucks." Greta grinned and pulled out the ten-dollar bill from her purse, flashing it in front of me. "She said I should take you out for ice cream after. So we're set. Are you still up for it?"

"I guess."

"Good. Bring boots. And dress really warm. It's in the woods."

"Greta?"

"Yeah."

"You know that guy at the funeral?"

"Yeah."

"He was Finn's boyfriend, right?" I was trying my best to act like I didn't care one way or the other.

Since that day with the teapot, I thought I saw Toby all over the place. I couldn't remember exactly what he looked like, just the shape of him, which made it worse. There were tall lanky men everywhere, and on first glance any one of them could have been Toby.

For the past few days I'd been waiting to catch Greta off guard. I thought if I asked her something when she wasn't expecting it, she might tell me more than she meant to. What I'd learned over the years was that playing dumb was the best way to do it. As soon as she thought I didn't know something, she'd jump in with everything she had.

"Congratulations, Sherlock. That only took you a few centuries to figure out."

"That's not all I'm trying to say."

"All right, then, what?"

"So he's living in Finn's apartment now?"

"That's right. Life ain't fair. You kill a man and end up with a great apartment on the Upper West Side."

"So you think he definitely gave Finn AIDS. You're sure."

"Not just sure, I know he did it on purpose. That guy knew he had AIDS when he met Finn. He knew it."

"How can you know that?"

"I just do. I've heard things."

"So he really is like a murderer?"

"Exactly." Her tone had changed. She seemed suddenly pleased that I was interested in what she knew. I thought that maybe I could tell her about the teapot and the letter and about the train station on March 6. Maybe she'd listen and be impressed that I had my own news for once. But I couldn't get the words out. The letter said not to tell anyone, and maybe Toby was right. Maybe even a murderer can be right sometimes.

"Okay."

"Okay what?"

"That's all. I just wanted to make sure."

"Whatever, June. Grow up. It's all over now."

"Yeah. I know it is."

I called Beans. I guess I thought I should make the effort, but she said she couldn't get out. So it would just be me. Me and a bunch of Greta's friends.

Later, on our way down the stairs for dinner, Greta poked me on the shoulder, then slipped a note into the back pocket of my jeans. *Party canceled.* It turned out a lot of people couldn't get out. But Greta had already lied to our parents, so I had to go to the play rehearsal with her anyway. I would have to sit there in the back of the auditorium on those red velvet seats, watching her turn into Bloody Mary over and over again.

Of course, I was relieved that the party was canceled. It wasn't only the shy thing, the total social retardation. It was more than that. I wasn't interested in drinking beer or vodka or smoking cigarettes or doing all the other things Greta thinks I can't even imagine. I don't want to imagine those things. Anyone can imagine things like that. I want to imagine wrinkled time, and forests thick with wolves, and bleak midnight moors. I dream about people who don't need to have sex to know they love each other. I dream about people who would only ever kiss you on the cheek.

That night I sat in the school auditorium and watched Ryan Cooke, with all his golden charisma, singing about enchanted evenings. Mr. Nebowitz, the director, kept stopping Ryan, making him sing certain parts of the song over and over again, telling him to let the words show on his face.

"We should be able to read your face like a poem. Even if you don't say a word, every person in that audience should know exactly how you feel." Mr. Nebowitz was young, with lots of dark curly hair. It was the end that he wanted Ryan to get right. The part about holding on and never letting go.

Ryan tried again and again. I couldn't see much difference, but Mr. Nebowitz said, "Better. Getting better." He let Ryan go off and then called Greta to the stage.

"'Happy Talk,' okay?"

Greta nodded and walked onto the stage without any makeup or costume. Just her, in jeans and T-shirt. She didn't even take her glasses off. She pulled her hair back with one hand and closed her eyes for a second. Mr. Nebowitz started on the piano.

"Straight through," he said, nodding at Greta.

She sang it the whole way through, and I couldn't see or hear a single mistake. When she finished, Mr. Nebowitz clapped and turned to the rest of the cast, who were sitting out in the audience, and said, "This is the standard I'm looking for, people." Then he looked back at Greta on the stage and thanked her for all the effort she was putting in. Something like that would have embarrassed me beyond belief, but Greta just took an exaggerated clownish bow, the top of her head nearly grazing the stage, and got a big laugh from the other kids. I laughed too, because that was the first time in so long that I'd seen her loose and jokey like that. It made me glad I'd been forced to go to the rehearsal.

Greta left the stage and I thought about Toby again. I thought that *special friend* could mean anything. It didn't have to be a big deal. Maybe Finn never mentioned him because he was nobody. It was my mother who used the word *special*. Finn would never call someone that. Not with a straight face anyway. Maybe it was just luck that the guy had ended up with Finn's apartment. Maybe Finn felt sorry for him.

The rehearsal ended at around eight-thirty. I stayed put in my seat and watched Greta and Ryan and a bunch of other kids from the play sitting on the edge of the stage, legs dangling, laughing. These were the kids Greta hung out with now. The smart kids. The ones who weren't only smart but popular too. The ones who could do anything. Ryan Cooke and Megan Donegan and Julie Contolli. Greta looked happy up there. Relaxed. Like this really was some island in the South Pacific. But she also looked younger than the rest of them. Lined up like that I didn't know how everyone couldn't see how obvious it was. Ryan had a little mustache. Megan's and Julie's legs were women's legs. Full and shapely. Greta's thin legs hung from the stage and made her look like a kid on a swing.

Mr. Nebowitz said good night to everyone and asked Greta if she had a minute. One by one the kids jumped off the stage and grabbed their coats and bags. Greta followed Mr. Nebowitz out of the auditorium. I stayed in the back row, waiting, thinking I shouldn't leave without Greta.

"Hey, you there. I'm shutting the lights." I could see it was Ben Dellahunt, who was a junior and the assistant stage manager for the play.

I nodded in the shadows.

"I'm just waiting for my sister," I said. "I'll go in a minute."

Ben was one of those kids that you thought might be rich when he grew up. Not because there was anything that great about him, but more because he was the kind of guy who always seemed to have a plan. He always had his hair in a ponytail, and there was a rumor that he'd actually invented a new computer language, but that probably wasn't true. He wasn't the best in his class, but he was pretty smart. Smart enough. He put a hand above his eyes and squinted at the back row, like he was looking way out to sea. Then he started walking up the central aisle. When he got closer he looked me over, zeroing in on my feet.

"Hey, you're the girl with the boots." He smiled and nodded like he'd solved some kind of puzzle. He was about to sit down next to me, but before he did, Greta came back through stage left. She stood on-stage, looking out over the rows of seats.

"Are you coming or not?" she called, already turning to leave.

"Yeah. Coming," I called back. I said goodbye to Ben, then jogged to catch up with Greta. She stormed ahead, leaving me paces behind for the whole walk home. When we finally got there, she didn't say a word. She just ran up the stairs, straight into her bedroom, and slammed the door behind her.

Fifteen

Since Finn died, I'd been spending a lot of my weekend time in the woods. My parents would go to the office to get in a few extra hours of work, Greta would go to extra rehearsals, and I would head to the woods. Sometimes I'd take my coat off and tuck it behind the stone wall so I could feel the pain of the cold right through my body. Sometimes it was good to feel like a wretch of a girl who didn't have the right clothes to keep her warm.

It wasn't like I used to do something with Finn every weekend, but there was always the possibility. The phone could ring early in the morning—usually on a Sunday—and Finn would be on the other end, asking if anyone wanted to go out someplace. He always did that, asked if *anyone* wanted to go, but I knew he really meant me.

"You're in love with Uncle Finn," Greta said one Sunday after he called.

She'd been watching me from the other side of the kitchen. Watching my face light up as I listened to Finn saying it was a good day to go to the Cloisters. After I hung up, Greta stood there for a second and smiled. Then she said that thing to me, about being in love with Finn, and I could have punched her. I clenched my fists and shoved them deep into my pockets and walked out of the kitchen, but she followed.

"Everybody knows it."

I stopped and closed my eyes, my back still to Greta.

"You know what I heard Mrs. Alphonse say?" she said.

Mrs. Alphonse was a friend of my mother's from the garden club. My mother didn't even like gardening, but she still went to garden-club meetings one Thursday night a month, to drink coffee and talk to other moms who probably also didn't do much gardening.

My back was still to Greta, my fists pulling tighter and tighter.

"I heard her asking Mom about you and Finn. *'It's a bit strange for a girl to spend so much time alone with her uncle, isn't it? Not that I'm saying there's anything funny going on. I don't mean that at all.'* That's what she said, but I could tell she meant that she thought something was very wrong with it. And I could tell she'd been talking about it with other moms. And poor Mom, she didn't know what to say. . . ."

My fists had started to loosen because I was listening so hard to Greta. But then I thought about Mrs. Alphonse with her stupid tightly permed hair. Why did Mrs. Alphonse even need to think about me and Finn at all?

"Just letting you know, that's all. What you're putting Mom through and that everybody knows."

"Which everybody?" I asked, though I hadn't meant to say a word.

"Well, if you think that Mrs. Alphonse wouldn't talk about it with Kimmy, you'd be wrong. And if you think Kimmy wouldn't tell, like, everybody she knew, then, well, whatever."

Kimmy Alphonse was a girl in my class who seemed pretty average. I'd never even thought about her until now.

"So go on and meet up with your precious uncle Finn. Enjoy yourself."

I couldn't let Greta get away with all that. Let her yank every bit of joy from my Sunday without saying anything.

"There's nothing gross, because Finn is gay and everyone knows that." I turned to see if I'd gotten Greta, if her smile would fade. But it didn't. It got wider.

She waited a second and then said, "I said *you* were in love with Finn. I didn't say Finn was in love with you, did I?"

And what could I say to that? Nothing. As usual.

That day I did go out with Finn. I took the train down and met him in Grand Central, and then we went to the Cloisters, which was our favorite place. Ever. Usually we went when there was hardly anyone around—really early or really near the end of the day, when they were about to close. At those times the Cloisters were better than any gallery or that movie theater in the Village that shows all those old movies. Even better than the Horn & Hardart cafeteria, where you can put money in a machine and get a real plate of hot food like on *The Jetsons*.

The Cloisters are the best because they're like a piece of another time right at the top of Manhattan. And I'm not just saying that. They're actually made of huge chunks of French medieval monasteries that were shipped to New York and stuck together. Even the view from the Cloisters is perfect, because Rockefeller bought all the land on the other side of the river in New Jersey just so nothing could be built there. Maybe even Rockefeller needed to leave his time once in a while.

I tried hard to forget everything Greta had said, but it was there anyway, polluting the whole day. I tried not to stand too close to Finn, tried not to smile too much. But it didn't work. Maybe Greta was right. Maybe I was gross.

We didn't say much that day. Finn or me. We walked through the stone passageways without really seeing anything. I thought that it would have been good to be a monk. The kind who isn't allowed to speak. I thought of sitting with Finn in a great stone room filled with other monks, all silent, all busy illuminating manuscripts with the thinnest flakes of gold leaf. Finn and I would look at each other all the way across that room without saying a single word. And we'd hear each other. That's the kind of love I imagined with Finn. That's what I told myself. The kind that's not gross, because it's in another time and I'm not really me.

But being a monk is just one more impossible thing, like traveling to the past or having Finn here forever, because to be a monk you'd have to be a man and you'd also have to believe in God, neither of which was ever going to happen. I don't think God would create a disease just to kill people like Finn, and if he did, then there's no way I'd ever even consider worshipping him.

That day at the Cloisters, Finn and I sat on a stone bench in a dark stone corner, and he asked me what I thought happened to people after they died. I shook my head and pretended I hadn't heard him. I did that with Finn sometimes. Pretended my hearing was fuzzy so he would move closer to me. And he did. That day he slid right up next to me on that bench and put his arm around my shoulder and asked me again.

"What happens to all this?" he said, looking right into my eyes.

I shrugged and said I thought nothing happened. I said I thought everything just ended and went black.

Finn nodded and said, "Me too."

If I knew he was talking about himself, I would have made something up. I would have dreamed up a perfect Finn heaven right there on the spot.

I took Toby's note to the woods that Saturday morning. Old snow clung to every tree branch, making the whole woods seem precarious, like things might topple any second. I followed the thin icy line of the brook, listening for the wolves. I cupped my hand around my ear and closed my eyes, listening and listening, but there was nothing. Nothing at all.

I read the note again and again. It was becoming impossible to slip away from the present. Even with Finn's boots on my feet. Even with the thought of falcons. It felt like the very idea of Toby had the power to keep my thoughts in the here and now.

I'd been sure I wasn't going to meet him, absolutely sure, but I was starting to reconsider. What if he knew things? What if I'd been a secret too? What if I could turn up at the train station and be anyone I wanted?

Sixteen

Section D, Page 26!

That's what Mrs. Jansky wrote on the envelope she stuck in our mailbox that Sunday morning. Inside was *The New York Times* from the day before. My parents don't read the *Times.* They read the *New York Post* and only on Sundays, so if it wasn't for nosy Mrs. Jansky the whole portrait article would have gone completely unnoticed by the Elbus family. The painting would have stayed above our fireplace, where it belonged.

It was Greta who found the envelope and Greta who read the article out to the whole family. She called us all into the living room. I was upstairs getting dressed, because Beans and a whole bunch of her friends were going to the mall and she'd called to see if I wanted to go with them. I was pretty sure my mother had talked to her mother about me. Of course I didn't want to go, but my mom kept bringing it up, saying it'd be good for me and that you can't keep friends if you always say no to things. So I called back and said I'd do it, thinking otherwise she'd nag me about it for weeks. And there was something else. The movie theater there had an Oscar season special on Sundays. They did special showings of movies that had won over the past few years. That week they were showing *Amadeus,* which I'd already seen twice with Finn. That was the reason I said yes.

Greta had been keeping to herself even more than usual since the night at rehearsal. I wanted to ask her what Mr. Nebowitz had said to her in his office, but I knew there was no point. If she wanted to talk about it she'd do it when she was ready, which would probably be never. Not to me anyway.

That Saturday morning, Greta stood in front of the portrait, facing us on the couch. It turned out she was right. The portrait did creep out the whole living room. For the most part we all kept out of there as much as possible. Nobody wanted to sit with that portrait. We sat at the kitchen table, or Greta and I went to our rooms. My dad mostly sat in the little home office off the kitchen. As for my mother, she wasn't much of a sitter, before or after the portrait.

But on that morning, Greta called us all in there and we sat facing it. Greta stood with her weight shifted all the way to the left and one hand on her hip. In the other hand she held the paper.

"Okay, Greta, we're all here. Get on with it. I've got paperwork piling up like crazy," my dad said.

"Okay. Settle down," Greta said in an exasperated voice. "It's no big deal. We're just . . . famous."

"Come on, Greta, show us what you have there." My mom sat with her legs crossed and tapped one foot impatiently.

"Okay." Greta turned the page around so we could all see. There it was. Finn's portrait. Our portrait. Us. It was in color and took up half the page. Then Greta read.

"*When you haven't shown a painting in ten years and your name is Finn Weiss, the public is bound to get a little bit curious to catch a glimpse of your latest work. Weiss, who died earlier this month (unconfirmed reports cite the cause of death as AIDS-related)*"—Greta's voice snagged on the word *AIDS*, but then she read on—"*had apparently developed a taste for portraiture, if this recent find is anything to go by. The painting, titled 'Tell the Wolves I'm Home,' shows two teenage girls, one light, one dark, with expressions of such startling intimacy it feels as though they can see right into the viewer's own heart. As though they know the viewer's own darkest secrets.*

"*According to Harriet Barr, editor of* Art *magazine, Weiss was known for the diversity of his work. 'Finn Weiss was remarkable in his ability to adapt to any medium. He truly was a renaissance artist in the sense that he produced brilliantly original work in not only oil and acrylic but also in stone, wood, and through more conceptual installation pieces.'*

"What's baffled critics and fellow artists alike is why, almost ten years ago, Weiss went underground, becoming so reclusive that only his closest friends and family knew where he lived. Some applauded his move out of the limelight, calling it bold. The more cynical opinion is that Weiss's adoption of the hermit lifestyle was nothing more than an attempt to inflate the value of his own work. Lending credence to this theory is the fact that several older works from the artist's own collection have fetched high prices when they've occasionally appeared at auction."

"Okay, Greta, enough now." My mother reached for the paper. Greta quickly whipped it behind her back.

I was perched as close to the edge of the couch as I could be, waiting to hear the rest of the story.

"Let her read it," I said. "I want to hear."

"Go on, Danielle, it's okay." My father put a hand on my mother's knee.

"It's not okay," she said, twisting her leg away. She stood up and walked out of the room. When she was gone, my father nodded at Greta, letting her know it was all right to go on. Greta cleared her throat and tapped her chest. Then she read again.

"Despite the disagreement about his motives, all can agree that the emergence of this recent portrait offers a glimpse of the kind of work Weiss could have been producing over those 'missing' years. Indeed, Barr sees this work as perhaps the greatest piece of his career.

"A work like this shows an artist fully intellectually and, perhaps more importantly, fully emotionally engaged with his subject. Looking at this painting, there's a sense that touching the surface could burn your fingertips. That those girls are alive. That they might just bite your hand off if you come too close."

The door slammed in the kitchen and I knew my mother had gone out. Greta glanced up, losing her place in the article. She moved her finger around on the page until she found it again.

"At the moment, the location of the painting is unknown. The slide was

submitted anonymously to the Times, *and no information other than the art-ist's name and the title of the painting was included. . . ."*

Greta's arm dropped and the paper hung at her side.

"I don't like this," she said.

"What?" I said.

"This whole thing. Us, me, in an article about somebody dying of AIDS."

"Somebody? It's Uncle Finn, Greta," I said.

"I don't care who it is. I don't want a big picture of me hovering over the word *AIDS,* okay? Is that okay with you?" She chucked the paper onto the coffee table. "I never even wanted anything to do with that portrait, but everyone was all 'your uncle Finn this, your uncle Finn that.' Ugh. I could kill him if he weren't already dead. And he's famous? Like big-time famous? He never bothered to mention that to us."

"Settle down. It's just an article." My father picked the paper up and folded it smaller and smaller. "Not even a real article. It's way in the back of the Arts section of *The New York Times.* Who reads that, huh? People don't remember stuff like this."

"It's only the biggest newspaper in the country."

"It's not like it says *you* have AIDS," I said.

"Okay. Enough's enough." My father tossed the paper into the fire-place and pulled out a lighter. "This thing's upsetting everyone in the house, and so"—he bent down, flicked the lighter on, and touched the flame to the edge of the paper—"away it goes."

Above the tiny fire hung the real portrait. The painted Greta and me watching the real Greta and me watching another copy of our-selves burn away.

There was nothing I could do. I wasn't done looking at that article. I hadn't even read the whole thing yet. I wanted to read more about Finn. About how good he was. About why he stopped doing art. I knew Finn was kind of famous. The way people looked at us when we went into a gallery. The way they'd smile at him, reach out to shake his hand. I understood it, but it wasn't important to me. He didn't act fa-mous around me, and I guess I never really thought about how famous he might be.

Beans and her mom picked me up for the mall right after lunch. I told Beans I didn't mind sitting up front with her mom. I didn't want to end up squashed in the backseat between a bunch of girls I hardly knew. When we got to the mall, I told Beans I'd meet her back at the food court later. I lied and said I had to pick something up from Sears for my dad. What I really did was go straight down to the basement level to the movie theater, so I could go see the movie *Amadeus* by myself. I go to the movies whenever I get the chance, because the movie theater is like the woods. It's another place that's like a time machine. Beans didn't seem to care.

"Do whatever you want," she said. "I know you only came because your mom made you."

"No . . . I . . ."

"It's okay. I get it. Just meet us at the food court at three."

Amadeus is one of the best movies ever. Finn liked it as much as I did, but he said that they messed up the whole *Requiem* story. Nobody thinks Salieri commissioned the *Requiem* and poisoned Mozart. Still, if Finn was around, we probably would have gone to see it together again that afternoon. Just for the music and to drop into another time and because we were both suckers for movies with tragic endings.

My mother came home right after I got back from the mall. Just in time to cook dinner. Spaghetti and meatballs and garlic bread. The main topic of dinner conversation was who might have submitted the portrait to the *Times*. Every time Toby's name came up, I leaned in closer, eager for any new information. In the end we all pretty much agreed that it must have been Toby. My mother didn't say anything. She still didn't want to talk about the article, or Toby, but she seemed to have given up on stopping us from talking about it.

"It could have been Mr. Trusky," I said. "He had it overnight."

"No way," Greta said. "Why would Mr. Trusky bother with something like that?"

"Maybe he just likes art. Maybe he wants to make sure everyone has a chance to see Finn's work."

"Yeah, right."

I shrugged, but I knew Greta was probably right. Toby was the only one it could have been. Because of the title. None of us had any idea the painting was called "Tell the Wolves I'm Home." Only Toby might have known something like that.

"What does that even mean? 'Tell the Wolves I'm Home'?" Greta asked.

No one said anything, because none of us had any idea. It was just one more mystery Finn had left us with. One more thing I couldn't call and ask.

Seventeen

I went to the library after school the next day, which turned out not to be the best idea. I thought I would find the article and make a photocopy of it for myself. Then I would go to the woods to read it, maybe twice, maybe a hundred times, maybe more. What I didn't know was that the copier on the library floor was broken and I'd have to ask someone behind the desk to copy it. If I'd taken it to the upstairs librarian, who didn't know me, it probably would have been fine, but I was stupid enough to go downstairs to the children's section. I still loved the children's section, with all its bright colors and books that are real stories. But it was stupid because the children's librarian is Mrs. Lester, who's known me since I was about five, and as soon as she saw the article her face lit up.

"Oooh, Junie. This is a lovely painting of the two of you."

I nodded.

"You both look so . . . grown up. So wise."

I nodded again.

"And beautiful. Pretty as, well, as a picture." Mrs. Lester giggled. "We've got the big copier down here now. I can get most of this page all on one sheet of paper."

"Great," I said. I must have looked anxious, because Mrs. Lester scuttled off behind the counter double quick. When she came back out, she was holding two copies of the article.

"Oh, I only need one."

"I know, hon', but we need one for the board."

"The board?"

"The display board. You and Greta are famous. You're a work of art. It's nice to have a little bit of local celebrity around here. If you've got it—"

"No. Really, no. We—neither of us likes a lot of attention."

"I insist. June, you've been discovered. Don't hide your light and all that."

I knew that the only way to prevent Mrs. Lester from hanging up the article would be to tell her that the painting was by my uncle Finn who had just died of AIDS and that my whole family was a little bit touchy about the subject. Hearing the word *AIDS* would probably be enough for Mrs. Lester, but I couldn't do it. I couldn't stand there and pretend to be embarrassed about Finn.

I took my copy, folding it so the picture was on the inside, and went back upstairs, into the browns and grays of the main library. I walked to the display board to see if there might be a way to pull the article down once she'd put it up. When nobody was looking. But it was impossible. All the notices were behind a locked glass sliding door.

I took the copy of the article into the woods. I folded it small so it fit in my coat pocket, and I walked until I could hear the wolves. There wasn't much more about Finn, just this:

"This Old Man," the last painting sold by Weiss and possibly his most well known, is a self-portrait of the artist wearing a baggy woolen jacket over a bare torso. He is holding out an oversized human heart to a pool of crocodiles. Across the artist's chest is a jaggedly healed scar that reads EMPTY. It's the sincerity of the gesture that moves the viewer. There is no irony, only the feeling that you are witnessing the very moment before he will release the wet beating thing in his hand and the sense that you have truly received everything this artist has to give. The painting sold for more than $200,000 at auction in 1979. According to Sotheby's, "Tell the Wolves I'm Home" could fetch upwards of $700,000.

I guess that should have been a big deal to me, that the painting was worth a fortune, but it wasn't. We'd never sell it, so it didn't really matter. What did catch my eye was that there were no buttons. In the paper my T-shirt was plain, just a plain black T-shirt with no buttons at all.

When I got home, the portrait wasn't hanging over the mantel anymore. My parents had put the painting back in a black garbage bag and driven it down to the Bank of New York and got them to put it in a vault somewhere in the basement of the bank. I thought of our faces, mine and Greta's, staring out into that dark vault. And I thought that at least I wasn't alone in there. Even being with Greta was better than being alone in such a dark dark place.

Eighteen

My parents specialize in doing the books for restaurants. That's why the Elbus family gets free meals in places all over Westchester. We get a table even when there's a line to get in. I guess that should make me feel like someone famous, but actually it has the opposite effect. It's obvious that we're regular people, so it just looks like we're jerks who are cutting in front of everyone else. Even Greta thinks it's embarrassing. And my father. It's only my mother who likes that little bit of celebrity once in a while.

Between the funeral and tax season and Greta's rehearsals, we'd missed my father's birthday dinner completely. Almost a month had gone by since his birthday. My mother finally put her foot down and said she didn't care that it was a Tuesday in the middle of tax season. We'd put his birthday dinner off long enough and that was that.

He chose Gasho of Japan, which was perfect because my parents don't do its books and also because, if you're in the right mood, Gasho is a very cool restaurant. The person who started it took apart a whole sixteenth-century farmhouse in Japan, brought all the pieces to America, and rebuilt them and turned the place into a restaurant. The chefs cook on hot grills that are right in the middle of the tables, and in the back there's a Japanese garden with a stream and arched bridges and benches that nestle in peaceful little corners.

If you're in the right mood, it's a good place to go. But nobody was really in the right mood.

The thing was, Finn always came out to dinner with us on our birthdays. Always. Sometimes we would go into the city and Finn would arrange it. Other times he would come up here. This was the first birthday he wouldn't be there. My mother tried to suggest that we ask the Ingrams instead, but nobody thought that was a good idea. Not even Greta.

"Lookin' good, girls," my dad said as we climbed into the van. Greta and I glanced at each other for a second, then we both rolled our eyes.

Greta sat in the row of seats in front of me, in a pair of pinstripe jeans with holes in the knees. I wore a black skirt and a giant sweater. I didn't wear my boots from Finn. I couldn't bear to wear those boots that night.

The drive to Gasho was quiet except for the sound of my father's *Simon and Garfunkel's Greatest Hits* cassette. All my parents' music came from greatest hits albums. It was like the thought of getting even one bum track was too much for them to handle. As we drove down the highway, I thought of all the other birthdays we'd celebrated. My dad's thirty-fifth, in that dark Moroccan place Finn knew in the Village. Greta's tenth where we got Il Vecchio to write *Happy Birthday, Greta* in peppers on top of all the pizzas. My twelfth, when Finn reserved a dining room in an old hotel and made us all play these Victorian parlor games he'd read about. He showed up in a top hat and tails and spoke in an English accent the whole time. By the end of the night we were all talking like that. Even Greta. It was all "pardon" and "would you mind terribly much" and "swimmingly" and finding excuses to call each other cads and bounders.

Then there was my mother's fortieth, with me sitting next to Finn at this fancy restaurant that had a jazz piano player in one corner and candles in these thick square glass candleholders on the tables. I was ten and Greta was twelve, and I watched the candlelight flickering against my mother's cheek as she peeled back the wrapping paper from Finn's present. That was something about a present from Finn. You always kept the wrapping paper because it was always more beautiful than any you'd ever seen. That particular wrapping paper was a deep dark red that looked like it was made of real velvet. My mother opened it slowly, careful not to tear the paper, and then, when she had one side open, she gently slid out a black sketchbook.

That sketchbook ended up on a bookshelf in Greta's room. Inside, Finn had written a little note that said, *You know you want to . . .* next to a tiny pen sketch of my mother with a pencil in her hand. What was amazing was that even though the sketch was only half an inch high, you could tell instantly that it was my mother. That's how good Finn was.

That night everyone else was talking. My dad was having a quiet argument with Greta because she didn't want to put her napkin on her lap. The whole time, Finn sat next to me, folding and twisting his napkin until all at once he lifted it out from under the table and we saw that he'd folded it into a butterfly. We watched as he flew it over to Greta and said, "Here, I have somebody who needs a lap to rest on." Greta giggled and took the butterfly from Finn's hand and put it straight on her lap, and my dad looked over at Finn and gave him a smile. I remember thinking that I wanted a butterfly napkin too. I wanted Finn to fold something for me. I was about to ask him, but when I turned I saw that he was staring across the table at my mother. She had the sketchbook open to the inside cover and she was gazing down at that little drawing of herself. After a while she looked up at Finn. She lifted her head slowly, and she didn't smile or say thank you like you normally would if somebody gave you a present. No. She just sat there, giving him a kind of sad, hard look then shook her head at him, her lips pressed together tight. Then she slid the book back into the wrapping paper and shoved it under the table. That's one of those snapshot moments. I don't know why some memories are like that, where everything is perfectly preserved. Frozen. But that memory—Finn's eyes locked on my mother's, my mother slowly shaking her head—is exactly like that.

When we got to Gasho, we followed the hostess to one of the high tables and climbed onto our stools. Each table seated maybe twelve people around a big grill, and the chef was at the other end hacking up some meat with a little hatchet. My dad ordered two glasses of Japanese beer. Then he looked at us and asked if we wanted Shirley Temples.

"I'm not, like, three years old, you know," Greta said. "I'll have a Diet Coke."

"I guess I'll have a Coke too," I said, even though really I would have liked a Shirley Temple.

And that's about the most conversation we had all night. I don't think anybody in that restaurant would have been able to guess that we were out having a birthday celebration. My dad asked Greta how the play was going, and all she could say was "Fine." My mother remarked on a change in the menu, but that's as good as it got. None of us were Finn sort of people. I tried to remember one of the Victorian games, but nothing came to me. Maybe more was said, maybe some words disappeared into the sizzling peppers and onions, but that's how I remember it. I sat there watching the Japanese chef with his high white hat frying our dinner and wondered what would happen to me without Finn. Would I stay stupid for the rest of my life? Who would tell me the truth, the real story that was under what everybody else could see? How do you become someone who knows those things? How do you become someone with X-ray vision? How do you become Finn?

On the way home, I thought about the note from Toby again. I thought about how March 6 was only three days away and how stupid it would be for me to go meet him. Again I thought that I should go to my parents and tell them all about it. Tell them that this guy came right up to our door. That he'd asked me to meet him. That he'd asked me to keep it a secret. It wasn't too late to tell them everything.

My parents trusted me. I knew they did. And they were right to. I was a girl who always did the right thing. But this was different. I knew Toby had stories. He had little pieces of Finn I'd never seen. And the apartment. Maybe there would be a chance to see the apartment again. My mother would call it scraping the bottom of the barrel. Looking for the very last crumbs. My mother would call it being greedy, but I didn't care. If you think a story can be like a kind of cement, the sloppy kind that you put between bricks, the kind that looks like cake frosting before it dries hard, then maybe I thought it would be possible to use what Toby had to hold Finn together, to keep him here with me a little bit longer.

Nineteen

"Party. Tomorrow night. One hundred percent. No cancellations."

Greta had come into the bathroom while I was in the shower and whispered through the coral pink shower curtain.

"What?"

Greta said it again, slower, as loud as she could without our parents hearing. I still couldn't hear her right, so I turned the shower off and rubbed the water out of my ears with my palm. I stuck my head out from behind the curtain.

"What?"

She let out a frustrated breath, then said it one more time. That time I heard her.

"Mom and Dad will be at work until seven and then we can just tell them you're helping with the play again. Okay?"

I nodded, but my thoughts were racing. The party was the same day as the meeting with Toby.

"Okay?" Greta said.

"Yeah . . . I guess. Okay."

"It's in the woods behind the school."

My woods. The party was going to be in my woods. I smiled to myself. For once I'd know more than Greta. I'd be the only one there who knew anything about the place.

Greta stood there with her hands on her hips, looking at me like she was waiting for me to say something. "You know those woods, right?"

"I . . . yeah. The ones you can see behind the cafeteria."

She waited another few seconds, then nodded.

I turned the shower on to full again, letting it pound against my neck.

I could see the shape of Greta's forehead through the shower curtain, and I gave her a poke. She poked back, trying to nab my shoulder. We both laughed, poking blindly at each other through the pink plastic.

"Stop," Greta said, but she was still poking.

I reached a wet arm out from the side of the curtain and tickled Greta right under her armpit. We both couldn't stop laughing.

"Girls?" My dad's voice boomed from downstairs.

I pulled my arm back.

"It's okay," Greta hollered.

Every once in a while it was like that with me and Greta. Just for a minute or two. Just a glimpse of what we used to be like.

She stuck her head around the curtain, angling her face so she wouldn't see me naked.

"So you're still coming?"

"Yeah. Just go ahead. I'll meet you in the woods."

Twenty

I wrote down some ways to hate Toby. I wanted to be prepared. I didn't want to show up all weepy and dumb. I wanted to be hard. I wanted to be able to tell him what was what.

1) *Remember that he is the one who made Finn die. Maybe on purpose.*
2) *Remember that he is the one who sent the portrait, <u>OUR</u> portrait, to the paper without asking, even though it's ours and it's none of his business.*
3) *Remember that only someone very creepy would send a fourteen-year-old girl letters and tell her not to tell her parents.*

I looked at the list, but I couldn't make it work. I couldn't seem to hate the guy. Finn didn't hate Toby. Finn might have even loved Toby. And Toby was probably the very last person in the world who'd talked to Finn, who'd seen him alive. So I added this:

4) *Toby was the last one to talk to Finn. Toby was the last one to hold Finn's hand. The last one to hug him. Not me. It was Toby.*

That's when the list started working. *I* wanted to be the last one. Not some gangly English guy with a watery voice.

Twenty-One

If you stand on Sumac Avenue where it bridges over the train tracks and look out over the railing, you can see the whole train station platform. I turned up late, and I was freezing cold because I'd stuffed my stupid light blue puffy coat in my backpack. I'd taken the long way, up past the bike shop and the Mobil station and then across the weedy fields near the Lutheran church. As I got closer, I started to think that maybe Toby himself wouldn't show up. Maybe he would hide somewhere and watch and wait to see if I would come, just like I'd decided I was going to do to him.

I peered over the edge of the railing, trying not to get too close. I wasn't sure I would even recognize him, but I did. I saw him right away. He was sitting on a bench at the far end of the platform, his knees pulled up to his chest, his fingers fidgeting with his shoelaces. I could see that he was skinny, but not exactly in an AIDS way. He didn't look the way Finn did at the end. He looked like he'd always been like that.

I stood for a while, watching him. Every now and then he snapped his head up and looked around. Almost like he was spooked. Like he could tell I was there somewhere. Each time he did that, I jumped back out of his line of sight.

Toby looked younger than Finn. Younger than my mother or father. If I had to guess, I would have said he was around thirty, but I'm not good at that kind of thing. From where I was I could see his skinny neck and his oversize Adam's apple poking out; his hair looked soft, like baby bird feathers dusted over his head. Toby stood up and paced down the platform. He wore a small blue backpack and he had on jeans and sneakers and a thick gray sweater with a red woolen scarf, but no coat. He didn't seem like anything special, and I wondered why someone like Finn would go out with him. He stared down the track, then glanced at his watch. I heard the noise of the train edging in.

Toby peeked down at his watch again, and then, before I had time to think, he looked right up to the spot where I was standing. I jumped back before he saw me, and right then I decided I wouldn't go down there. I wouldn't meet Toby after all. I couldn't bring myself to do it. What would I say? No. I wouldn't go down. I'd watch from above. I'd wait for the train to take him away. He'd get the message.

I inched back to my place and peered down. What I saw was Toby, looking straight back up at me, staring right at my spot. One hand was shading his eyes, and when he saw me he spread the fingers of his other hand and raised them in the smallest of waves. Before I could decide not to, I did the same. I edged a hand barely above the top of the railing and spread my fingers.

Then I smiled. It was only the barest of smiles, and it came out without me wanting it to. I don't know how I could have smiled at the man who killed Finn, but I did, and that seemed to seal something. It felt like that smile had locked me in, like it was some kind of promise that made it so I had no choice but to walk down that flight of steps to the platform.

Toby kept staring up at me with a sort of worried look. The way the light was pouring down on his face, the way his hand stayed raised, made it look like he was in a medieval painting, shielding his eyes from something bigger than himself. He pointed to the platform and nodded his head downward. And before I could stop myself, I was nodding back and walking to the covered stairway. It felt like I was moving in slow motion. Like the stairs might keep going down and down forever.

But when I walked onto the platform, it was light and warm and the train had just pulled in. Toby was walking toward me, with a smile that wasn't one of those adult smiles that's too big with no thinking behind it. It was a real smile. Like he was so glad to see me he almost couldn't believe his luck.

"Come on," he said, like we already knew each other.

It was a strange time of day. Most people weren't done with work yet, and if they were they were mostly headed north, coming home from the city. I walked onto the southbound train, trying not to think too hard about what I was doing.

The carriage we picked was almost empty. Toby pointed to a set of four seats, two facing two. "Here?"

I nodded and sat down. Toby sat in the aisle seat, diagonal from me. His knees poked out across the space between us, forcing me to lean in toward the window to avoid touching him.

"Thanks for coming," he said. I could see him trying to make eye contact with me, but I didn't want that. I kept my head turned away, staring out the window at an Absolut vodka billboard on the platform. On the bottom someone had written *Def Leppard Rokz,* but someone else had crossed out *Rokz* and written *Sukz* in its place.

"It's okay," I said, still staring out the window.

"You're not scared or anything, are you? Because I know what I must have seemed like on the phone and I know what your family thinks of me, and I was trying so hard to find some kind of way to talk to you."

The train pulled out of the station, slowly rocking side to side.

"No. You're not scaring me."

"Good. That's good." He stared over at the empty seat across the aisle, then slowly turned back to me. "Did you tell your parents you were coming?"

At first I didn't answer. Then I turned and looked right at him and said, "That's kind of a creepy thing to ask, isn't it?"

Toby seemed worried for a second. He gave a tiny wince, like he knew he'd made a mistake. But then he laughed. "You're right. It is creepy. Very creepy. That's not how I meant it." He rolled his eyes. They were dark brown and soft in a way that reminded me of an animal's eyes. Like the big brown eyes of a horse. "Finn used to say . . ."

I sat up straighter when he said Finn's name. My whole body went tense, and Toby must have seen that, because he frowned and gave me a kind of pleading look. "Oh, it's nothing," he said, waving his long hand in the air. He tilted his head, trying to catch my eye again. Trying to see if I was trusting him.

"Anyway, the answer's no. I didn't tell anyone about it." I had a Swiss Army knife in my coat pocket with the corkscrew already out. Just in case.

Toby reached into his backpack and pulled out a crumpled Dunkin' Donuts bag with a cruller in it. He twisted off a chunk and gave it to me. The sticky glaze had melted a little, making the whole thing a mess. I didn't want to take it from him, but I'd come straight from school and I was starving.

"Thanks," I said.

I sat there untwisting the two strands of donut, and when I looked up I saw that Toby was doing the same thing. We both smiled, nervous, not knowing what to say. Then I was sorry that I'd smiled, because I didn't want him to get the idea that we were friends or anything.

The train slowed. The doors slid open and a blast of cold air drifted through. Toby didn't even seem to notice that we'd stopped. I thought it must have been almost four o'clock by that time, but I didn't want to say anything. I'd already said I wasn't scared, and I wasn't. The doors closed again and the train pulled out.

"It's like DNA, isn't it?" Toby held the half-separated donut up to the window. "You know, double helix."

It was the kind of thing Finn might have said to me, and I couldn't help smiling. There was something that felt familiar about Toby, and I couldn't help carrying it on. "Dunkin' DNA, Dunkin' blood cells, a twleve-pack of Dunkin' eyeballs—"

Toby threw his hand over his mouth to keep from spitting out his donut. His lips were coated in sticky glaze. "And Dunkin' bacteria and Dunkin' viruses . . ."

I could tell he hadn't meant to say that word. *Viruses.* I looked away. Toby looked down, and when he looked back up his face was serious.

"Hey," he said. "I miss him, you know."

I ate the last bite of my donut and stared out at the fenced-off backyards of the houses that bordered the tracks. Through some of the windows you could see people in their kitchens, cooking dinner. I rubbed my sticky fingers against the cloth of the seat.

"Me too," I said after a while.

"He talked about you all the time," Toby said. "You know that, don't you?"

I could feel myself starting to smile and blush, and I turned away fast. Then I understood what it meant. I hadn't been a secret. Toby knew about me.

"Yeah, right," I said, shrugging like I didn't care.

"It's true."

We sat there in silence. I saw Toby fidgeting with his train ticket. Folding and unfolding it again and again.

"So . . . are you some kind of artist too?" I said.

"Oh, no. No, I'm crap. Complete and utter rubbish." Toby laughed. "Once Finn tried to show me some sculpture stuff, but . . ." He looked over at me. I must have been frowning, because he changed his tone. "I don't know. It just didn't work out, really."

"Me neither."

"Why do you say that?"

"Because I'm not a good artist. I'm not even one of the best in my class." I didn't mean to say anything about myself, but it came out before I could stop it.

"Well, Finn thought you were good. Really good." Toby uncrossed his legs and leaned in. "Finn said art isn't about drawing or painting a perfect bowl of fruit. It's about ideas. And you, he said, have enough good ideas to last a lifetime."

"He said that?"

"Uh-huh."

Again I blushed and turned away from Toby, looking out the window. For a second it felt like Finn was on that train with us. Like Toby had a little ghost Finn on his shoulder telling him exactly what to say.

I didn't want to let myself get suckered in by all this nice talk, but it was hard not to. It was hard not to want to listen forever to every beautiful thing Finn ever said about me. I glanced over at Toby. He was probably making it all up. He was the special one, after all. I was just the dumb niece, and suddenly it felt all wrong that this guy, this stranger, had talked about me with Finn. That he knew all kinds of things about me and I knew nothing.

"So you've taken over Finn's apartment?" I said. I heard the mean edge in my voice, I heard myself sounding more like Greta than myself, but I didn't care.

Toby bowed his head. "I . . ."

"Whatever. I don't want to know."

Quiet again.

"You know, you can come down whenever you want," he said. "Whenever. I mean it. Night or day."

I shrugged. Then, before I knew it, I felt my eyes start to sting. I felt tears pressing up, and the more I tried to stop them, the more they wanted out. I turned, but I felt Toby lay a hand on my back. I leaned away. I breathed in and out as slow as I could until I felt myself coming back to normal.

"Hey, it'll be all right," he said. Then he moved his sweater off the seat next to him and laid it on his lap. Just that. Just saying I could sit there if I wanted to. I looked at the empty seat so he could see that I knew what he'd done, what he was saying, but that I wasn't going to move. I didn't need his help.

But he didn't put the sweater back down. He clutched it to his lap and left that empty seat between us. The train stopped at four more stations, and I sat there, letting it drag me farther and farther away from home. Out of the woods. Out of the suburbs and into the cold stone air of the city.

When the train pulled into Grand Central, we both got off.

He thanked me for coming about twenty more times and told me that he hoped it wouldn't be the last time we saw each other. He opened his backpack and handed me a brown paper bag. "From Finn," he said, leaning in close, then quickly pulling back.

"And there's more."

I took the bag without looking at it, as if it wasn't important.

"Well, why didn't you just bring it, then? If there's more."

Toby looked embarrassed. He twisted his hands behind his back and looked down at the dirty train station floor.

"Because I didn't think you'd come again once you had it all. And I need—I *want* you to come again. Very much."

Then he reached into his pocket and pulled out a whole bunch of money and handed it to me. It wasn't stacked neatly or anything; it was like he'd just shoved the notes into his pocket from some big pile somewhere.

"Here. You know, in case you need anything."

I didn't look at it closely, but I could tell it was a lot. Our neighbor Mrs. Kepfler used to try to give Greta and me a dollar each sometimes. Just because we looked like nice girls, she would say. But my mother would never let us take it. "You don't take money unless it's family." That's what she always said before making us return it.

"I can't," I said to Toby, handing it back.

"No, no, no. You can. It's Finn's. It's not like you're taking it from me or anything. There's still loads left. Don't worry."

"The kinds of things I want don't cost money," I said, pushing the notes back into his hands. I didn't know if he understood what I meant. That what I wanted was for time to roll back and for Finn never to have met Toby and never to have been given AIDS and to still be here, just me and him. Like I always thought it was.

"Oh," Toby said, seeming like he felt foolish suddenly. I wondered what the two of us looked like, standing in the middle of the crowded Grand Central concourse, Toby holding out this fistful of money, just waiting for someone to come up and grab it out of his hand. He tried to shove the money back into his pockets, but it wouldn't fit, and right then, just for a second, I kind of felt sorry for him.

"Okay, okay," I said. I held my backpack out. "But hurry up."

He smiled and shoved the money in. "It's what Finn would have wanted, all right?"

I was about to say that nobody knew what Finn would have wanted, but I had the awful thought that maybe Toby did know. Maybe it was only me who had no idea.

"We could . . . I don't know, maybe get some coffee? Ice cream? A drink?" Toby nudged his head toward the bar in the station.

I looked at the big clock: four-fifty. Even if I'd wanted to go somewhere with Toby, it would have been too late. I had to get back for the party.

I shook my head. "I've got somewhere to be."

"Of course. Some other time, right? I'll see you again?"

I looked Toby up and down. He stood there, shoulders stooped. His fingers playing with a loose thread on the edge of his sweater, his big brown eyes staring right into me like he really cared about my answer.

"I . . . I guess I might call you. Sometime. If I don't have anything better to do."

Toby's face lit up. He nodded and thrust his hand out to me, like he wanted to shake on it, but I didn't take it.

"Brilliant. Whenever you want, all right? Whenever. I'm always around. And if you ever need anything . . . anything at all. I mean it."

That's how we left it. Toby asked me five or six times if I would be all right getting home, and when he finally believed that I would, we said goodbye. He headed through the archway toward the exit, then he stopped and turned and looked back again. He smiled and waved and made like he was dialing an invisible telephone. Then he pointed at me. I nodded so he would go, then I bought a ticket home. I used the money I'd brought with me. My own, not what Toby had just given me. I didn't look in Toby's direction again. I stood there on the platform, staring down at the grimy tracks, waiting for my train, thinking that I would probably never see him again.

Twenty-Two

Almost the whole cast of *South Pacific* was out in the woods behind the school. Ryan Cooke, Julie Contolli, Megan Donegan. And some of the crew. Lighting and set builders. The people who wore all black and snuck around between scenes. If I was in the play, I'd be crew. I felt like stage crew right then, hiding behind a tree, watching everyone hunched around a fire. I heard Greta before I saw her. Her voice warbled through the trees. Snatches of "Bali Ha'i," Bloody Mary's big song. *Island . . . sea . . . me . . .* Then it went quiet and I spotted her. I saw Greta tipping a bottle to her mouth. A brown drink, whiskey or brandy. I didn't even know Greta drank alcohol. I didn't want to know.

I'd run from the train station right across town, and it had felt like maybe I was running for my last chance at being normal. Charging through the cold air, over the crusty little patches of snow, away from the weirdness of the whole afternoon with Toby. I didn't feel like me. It was like I was in a show about someone almost exactly like myself but not quite.

I waited for the moment when it might be right to step out from behind the tree and become part of the party, but it didn't seem to come. I stood there getting colder and colder, until finally I got my coat out of my backpack and put it on. I didn't care how I looked anymore. I took a step backward and stumbled, and a few kids saw me. One of them was Greta, who smiled for a second, then turned to say something to the boy next to her. Another was Ben Dellahunt. He glanced down at my feet and then walked over.

"So, we meet again. You're the younger Elbus."

I blushed. "Yeah. June."

"I've noticed those boots of yours."

I put one foot behind the other, trying to make the boots smaller than they were. I didn't want Ben Dellahunt looking at my boots. It had been a long day, and I didn't think I had the strength to defend my best present from Finn.

"You said that last time. What about them?" It came out harsher than I meant it to.

"Whoa there." Ben put his hands up like he was trying to protect himself. "Nothing. Just . . . they're cool. That's all. I wouldn't mind some like that."

"Well, they're not for sale."

"I know," he said, laughing. "Don't worry."

I wondered if Greta had asked Ben to look out for me. If this was why she'd asked me to go to the party. If maybe she'd seen us talking in the auditorium that night.

Ben walked over to a cooler and grabbed a bottle. He handed it to me. "Beer?"

He'd already opened it, so there wasn't much else I could do except take it from him. I thought I'd have a sip and then pour the rest out somewhere.

"Thanks," I said.

Ben eyed me up. "You're, like, way taller than your sister."

"Yeah. I know."

We stood there awkwardly for a while.

"You want to go for a walk or something?" Ben asked.

I thought about it for a few seconds. Maybe a few seconds too long, because Ben said "It's just a walk, you know. Nothing life or death about it."

So I said yes. Not because I wanted to go for a walk with Ben Dellahunt, but because at least it meant leaving the party. I didn't want to stay around that fire. Near Greta drinking, with all those people I didn't know. If we went into the woods, it would barely be like a party at all. And if anything went really wrong, I still had the corkscrew in my pocket. I'd folded it down halfway through the train ride with Toby, but I still had it, ready and waiting. And I had a flashlight, which I was pretty sure I wouldn't need but Greta had insisted I bring along.

As we walked farther into the woods, I heard one of the boys yell, "Go, Benno!"

"Ignore him," Ben said, and edged closer to me.

We were heading toward the brook when he stopped.

"Do you hear that?" he said. "That sounds like, I don't know . . . dogs or something."

"They might be wolves," I said, and then regretted it right away.

He laughed. "Yeah, right. All the wolves were killed off here, like, a hundred years ago. You have to go way the hell up north to find wolves."

"We don't know everything. Maybe wolves from the north could just walk right down here to Westchester. How would we ever know?" I took another sip of the beer, suddenly feeling bold.

"Shhh," he said. "Let's listen." He put two fingers up. "Anyway," he whispered, "not all wolves are bad."

I looked down. "No. Not all. Not bad. Just . . . just selfish. That's what they are. Hungry and selfish."

He didn't know what to say to that. "Yeah, well, anyway, it's probably just coyotes or dogs. Probably mongrel dogs." He looked around, then back at me, and picked up my hand. "If you want, we could try to find them."

Behind us, the fire was still burning strong. People were huddled close to it, tipping beer bottles to their lips. Farther out in the woods were little specks of light, candles and flashlights of other people who'd left the fire.

"I don't think I want to know." I didn't want to tell him that I liked believing in the wolves.

"Why wouldn't you want to know?" He reached into his coat pocket, then held out his palm to me. "You ever play D&D?"

I shook my head.

"Ah, well . . ." Ben kind of puffed himself up and started to explain about percentages and character alignment and experience points. Then he handed me a weird-shaped die and told me to roll it.

"Go on," he said. "Right here." He laid out both his flattened palms. He had hands the size of my father's and a voice that was low and even. He had a small patch of stubble on his chin. We were alone together, and somehow the two years between Ben Dellahunt and me seemed wider and darker than the fifteen or twenty between me and Toby only a few hours before. I didn't really understand what I was trying to do, but I let the die fall from my fingers into his hands.

"Awesome," he said.

"What?"

"I convinced you to go find the wolves."

"You did?"

"Of course I did. You have, like, no experience points."

I stood there for a few seconds, wondering whether I should turn back. What I really wanted to do was leave. But I couldn't see Greta near the fire anymore, and if I left, if I went home alone, Greta would be in for it. I wouldn't do that to her.

"Okay, then," I said. "Let's go." I pointed in the wrong direction, away from where I knew the wolves were, and we walked. Ben talked on and on about D&D and quests and his favorite parts of *The Hitch-hiker's Guide to the Galaxy*. Once in a while we'd stop and Ben would pull out another can of beer from his coat pocket and we'd sit. I wouldn't say that I was exactly enjoying myself, but it was nice. Easy. It made the party seem okay.

I led Ben in a big circle, so eventually we ended up back on the hill above the fire.

"So, no wolves," he said. He put his hand on my back.

He was the second person in one day who was not from my family to touch me on purpose, and it felt strange. Like he was made of different stuff than I was.

"Guess not." I took a step forward so his hand fell away. Then I smiled and said, "Doesn't mean they don't exist, right?"

He started to argue, but I was already jogging down the hill to the fire. It was still glowing when I got back down, smoking from the leaves people were piling on it. There was a kind of yeasty smell from the half-full beer cans, and even though it seemed pretty early, kids were starting to leave. Nobody wanted to push their luck at home. I scanned the faces. I didn't know how much time had gone by, but it was long enough that I expected to see Greta back there. But she wasn't. I saw her friends, but she was nowhere.

I stood there with no idea what to do. The weight of my backpack strained against my shoulders, and all I could think of was how much I just wanted to go home. I wanted to count out the money from Toby. I wanted to spread out everything from that crumpled brown paper bag on my bedroom floor. I wanted to sleep. All I needed was Greta.

I asked around if anyone had seen her, but nobody had. One girl said she thought she'd gone off with Rob Jordan, but she wasn't sure.

I didn't think Greta would leave me. Not this time. This time she'd be in big trouble if she came home without me.

A bunch of kids made their way toward the school. Ben was with them, and he shouted over, "You okay?"

I nodded and waved. "Fine."

He waved back, then disappeared into the trees.

Only a few kids still sat around the fire. My eyes were burning from the smoke, and I was thirsty and hungry. I took a few steps back into the dark and, without even trying, I felt like a poor peasant girl from the Middle Ages. A girl out in the woods, desperate to find her only sister.

"Greta," I whispered under the dark branches. "Come on, Greta, just tell me where you are."

I walked down the hill, away from the school and the fire, until I was next to the brook. I kept calling Greta's name. Soft and then louder, listening for any kind of response, but the only sounds I heard were above me. An owl in the branches or twigs falling. I followed the brook deeper into the woods, the same way I did when I came by myself. There was only the thinnest scrap of moon that night, but I wasn't scared. I kept telling myself that I wasn't scared at all.

I remembered the flashlight and flicked it on, shouting out Greta's name.

"Come out. It's not funny."

At first I worried about finding her with some boy. Doing things I supposedly couldn't even imagine. I thought how embarrassing that would be for both of us—all three of us even—but I didn't care anymore. My toes were going numb from cold and I needed to go home.

I kept following the brook, because I didn't know what else to do. I almost turned back, but I kept telling myself, *Just another few steps,* thinking maybe that was all it would take. I scanned the ground with my light as I walked. I picked up the shine of a beer can and once a set of keys, which I put in my pocket. And I kept calling out Greta's name, louder each time. Maybe she was gone. Maybe she'd forgotten about me altogether.

That's when the flashlight glinted off something at the base of a big tree. I looked around. This was *my* tree. The maple. And there was the old stone wall. I was in my place. For a second it was a comfort to be there, but then it quickly faded, because at night there was nothing special about it. Nothing medieval. It was nothing but cold and dark.

I angled the light at the glinting spot on the ground and walked toward it, thinking it was probably a broken beer bottle, but when I got up close I could see that the light was reflecting off a pair of glasses. The glasses were on a face. Greta's muddy face. Just her face on the forest floor, her shiny black hair pulled back tight and those round silver-framed glasses. Her eyes were closed, and for that first second my body went rigid, because I really thought it was only her head laid down on the bed of leaves.

"Greta."

I reached out for her, and right away I could feel her body, buried under a thick pile of cold damp leaves. It looked like the earth was her bed and she'd pulled up the forest floor all around her like a comforter. She looked peaceful, like she belonged in that place. If I wasn't her sister and if it wasn't so cold, I might have left her there, thinking she knew exactly what she was doing. I gave her a shake and she curled into herself.

"Greta, come on. Get up." I sat her up and leaned her against my arm. I pushed the soggy leaves off her chest and tried to shake her awake.

She let out a groan and tried to lie back down, but I held her tight. I looked behind me and couldn't see even the faintest glow from the fire anymore. Someone must have put it out. Everyone must have left. There was only Greta and me.

I shoved Greta's dirty glasses and the flashlight into my pocket and one more time I tried to wake her. I shook her by the shoulders and shouted, "Greta. Michelle. Elbus. Wake. Up."

Her eyes fluttered and she twitched her shoulders to push my hands away.

Usually I would give anything to shrink, to be small and graceful like Greta, but on that night, under that nearly moonless sky, I was glad to have strength and size. I dragged her to the tree trunk and propped her up in a sit against it. I slung my backpack onto one shoulder. Then I crouched down in front of her, my back to her belly, and stretched her arms around my neck.

"One . . . two . . . three," I said, then leaned forward and teetered to standing. Her fingers were weak, drunk person's fingers, so I stayed stooped over to stop her from falling off. I thought of all the times when it was the other way around, Greta piggybacking me around the backyard when we were little.

I didn't know what I would do when we got home, I just knew that I had to get us there. I chewed a piece of gum until it was soft and then put it in Greta's mouth, which I know is gross, but it was the only way I could think to hide her breath. Then we left, just me running with my sister, the wolves at our backs. It was like we were a story, us two. A real story, not just one I made up.

I walked, stopping to set Greta down a few times when I started to get tired. I stayed in the woods for as long as I could before coming out onto Evergreen Circle, where I knew I could cut between the Morellis' house and the Kleins' and onto Young Street, which connected to our own. Right there, in that stretch of weedy grass between those two houses, Greta whispered into the back of my neck.

"Remember invisible mermaids?" she said. Her voice was hoarse and tired. It sounded like someone else was talking, not Greta. I was breathing hard. I stopped to catch my breath.

I nodded. I did remember. There was this tropical fish place in Queens. Neptune's Grotto. A huge dim room, like a warehouse. Fish tanks stacked at least six high, almost right up to the ceiling, towering over the heads of Greta and me. Yellow tangs, lyretail mollies, emerald rainbowfish, kissing gouramis.

Greta would grab my hand and we'd run between the aisles. The story we had was that all the fish had been trapped and we were free because we were invisible mermaids. We would hide, even though nobody was looking for us. The owner of the place was a friend of my grandfather's, so even though we didn't live anywhere near Queens anymore, my dad was still the accountant for that place.

"Remember the blue place? That little blue room," Greta mumbled.

I nodded. That was the fish nursery where they kept the newly hatched stuff.

My back ached and I wanted so badly to put Greta down again. She was awake. She could stand. I could set her down on the curb and we could talk about invisible mermaids. But I knew if I did that, the moment would be over. As soon as she saw my face, she'd remember to be mean. She'd remember who she was.

"What about it?" I said.

"I don't know, just sometimes . . . sometimes I think about things like that. What it used to be like."

I almost told her that it could be like that again. That if she stopped being so mean we could go back to being like we used to be. But I didn't say it. I wasn't sure it was true.

So instead I said, "Maybe we could try to go there sometime."

"Yeah. We could, couldn't we?" And right in my belly I felt how much I'd been missing her. The real Greta. The old Greta.

"Greta?" I felt her nod. "What did Mr. Nebowitz want the other night?"

I knew asking her was risky. She struggled free of my back and stumbled onto the street. She pulled her coat tight around herself and looked down at the ground.

"Nothing," she mumbled. "He didn't want anything."

"Did he, like . . . ?" I gave her a look that implied whatever she needed it to imply. That whole idea seemed to wake her up, to turn her back into herself.

"Ugh, June. Don't be so gross." She waved the back of her hand at me in a kind of drunken flap.

"Well, what, then?"

She eyed me up, then suddenly her frown turned into a big leery smile. "Opportunities, June. Opportunities galore." Then she twirled around and headed down the street toward home. A few seconds later she stopped and turned to face me. She must have spun too fast, because she lost her balance and ended up grabbing on to somebody's mailbox to stay upright. When she'd steadied herself, she focused on me.

"You know what Megan said when I told her my uncle died of AIDS? Guess. Take a guess."

"Come on, Greta. We have to go."

"No. This is the best, June. You'll love this. Megan looked at me all serious and said, 'Wow, that would be a great college essay. You'd be a shoo-in with something like that.'" Greta laughed and laughed. She sat down on the road, shaking with laughter until she started coughing and coughing.

"Come on," I said.

"But it's funny, right? Right?"

"Yeah, really funny, Greta. Hilarious." I reached for her hand to pull her up, but she snatched it away. She stopped laughing and her face went suddenly hard.

"You think I didn't want to keep going to Finn's because I didn't care? You really think this person who I've known forever is dying and I don't care?"

Before I could say anything, she pushed herself up from the street. She flailed her arm at me dismissively and then she ran. I watched her lurching ahead, body on the edge of tipping over, stumbling down the road toward home.

The night air revived Greta enough so she could walk upstairs without falling, change into pajamas, and get into bed.

I changed out of my smoky clothes, then went down to tell my parents that everything was okay.

"You know, June," my mother said, "I can't tell you how glad I am that you and Greta are starting to do things together again."

It felt like even nodding would be a kind of lie.

Twenty-Three

This is what was in that brown paper bag from Toby:

4 cassette tapes of Mozart's *Requiem*
1 note

I scooted onto my bed and pressed my ear against the wall. When Greta and I are in our beds, our heads are right next to each other. If the wall wasn't there, we'd be lying side by side. I listened for a minute to make sure she was asleep, and when I heard nothing I unzipped my backpack and spilled the tapes out onto my bed. I recognized them right away.

They were from this one Sunday when Finn took me to Tower Records' Classical Annex on 4th Street; he bought four different versions of Mozart's *Requiem* so we could decide which one was the best. I didn't even know that it came in other versions until Finn showed me.

He said it'd be like the Pepsi challenge, where we chose without knowing which version was which. I had this bad feeling that they'd all sound the same to me and I'd have to look stupid in front of Finn, but that's not what happened.

"You'll be surprised how different they all are," he said. He had a little half smile, and I could tell that he'd seen what I was thinking.

We took a taxi back to Finn's apartment, and when we got there he made a pot of tea in the Russian teapot and put out a great big bowl of red-shelled pistachios. Then he pushed the coffee table out of the way so we could lie flat on our backs on his beautiful Turkish rug. And then we listened.

Two of the versions were so different it made me angry. They actually had different endings, which Finn told me later was because Mozart never really finished the whole *Requiem* before he died and even now people argue about which part he didn't write and how those parts should go. But I didn't care. It just sounded wrong to me. Even the other two weren't as good as our old version, the one we listened to most of the time, and I said that to Finn.

He looked kind of sad after that. He patted me on the shoulder and told me that he knew what I meant. That usually the first version you hear is the one you'll love for the rest of your life.

The other thing in the bag was a note. This is what it said:

Dear June,

If you're reading this, then it means you met me at the train station, and I want to thank you for coming. So . . . thank you!

I will admit that I had a peek in the bag and I saw those tapes, and it made me think that there are probably so many things you know about Finn that I don't and so many things I know that you don't. There are loads of stories we could tell each other. But then I thought that probably it's not going to happen.

Everything is the same, though, if you're interested. Same address, same phone number. Same as Finn's. I don't go out much. I'm usually here.

With Affection,
Toby

After I read the note, I spilled out all the money Toby gave me. There were all kinds of bills—ones and fives and twenties and even fifties. It came out to $763, which was more than I'd ever had in my life. I felt like a thief with all that money. Like a thief once removed, because it felt to me like Toby was the real thief.

I put everything in the back of my closet with the teapot and the

first note from Toby, and then I fell asleep. The bed was warm and ordinary and perfect, and it had been such a long, long day. Probably the
longest day of my life. I felt like I had proof that not all days are the
same length, not all time has the same weight. Proof that there are
worlds and worlds and worlds on top of worlds, if you want them to
be there.

Twenty-Four

"Get a look at this." My father handed a folded-over page of the Sunday *New York Post* to my mother. She was at the kitchen counter, chopping mushrooms for omelets.

"What is it?"

"Just have a look."

She wiped her hands on a towel and leaned over my father's shoulder. He raised the article up. As she read, lines formed on her forehead. She turned away.

"No, thank you," she said.

"It's something to think about though," my father said.

Greta was still asleep so it was just me and my dad at the table, waiting for our omelets. We both liked mushroom and Swiss. I sipped my orange juice from an old scratched-up Welch's jelly-jar glass that had bits and pieces of Fred Flintstone's orange caveman suit on it.

"What is it?" I asked.

"Nothing," my mother said. "Put it away."

My dad gave me a helpless look, like if it was up to him I could have seen the paper. He held on to it for a second.

"She's fourteen, Danni."

"I don't care." My mother snatched the page out of his hand. "And that's that."

I took the last sip of my juice.

"I'm not a baby," I said, to back my father up.

My mother sighed and put down her knife. She looked me up and down and sighed again. "I know, Junie. I know." She glanced at the paper, then back at me. "Here," she said, and put it in my hand.

I was expecting another article about the portrait. What I wasn't expecting was a big headline about some soldier who'd done it with both a man and a woman even though he knew he had AIDS. Now all three of them had AIDS, and the soldier was probably going to jail for it.

"So?" my father said.

"I don't know."

"That man—that Toby. It makes you think." My father didn't look me in the eye.

"You think he should go to jail?" I thought of the train. I thought how he'd brought those tapes to me all the way from the city. I thought how he didn't seem so bad.

"Yeah, of course he should. He *is* a murderer." The voice came from the doorway. Greta stood there, leaning against the wall. There'd been a rehearsal the night before and she had gray smudges of makeup all around her eyes, which made her look like some kind of ghoul. She stared right at me. "Isn't he?"

"I guess."

"You guess?"

I didn't know what to say. Greta hadn't said a thing to me since the party two days ago. Now she stood with a cup of coffee in her hand, thinking she was cool. She'd started drinking coffee only a couple of weeks ago, but she acted like she'd been drinking it her whole life.

"Why does everything need to turn into an argument with you two?" my mother asked.

Greta only smirked.

Later that same Sunday, Greta and I were sitting at the kitchen table, finishing off homework. It was snowing, just lightly, and my mother had made us both mugs of hot chocolate. She was hanging around the kitchen looking like she was waiting for something to happen. She'd been like that a lot since Finn died. Once, when she didn't know I was watching her, I saw her pick up the phone receiver, hold it up to her ear, and stand there like that, waiting. She never dialed. Now she stood there, staring at the toaster.

"Girls," she said after a while. We looked up. "These are for the two of you." She held out two little brown envelopes, one with my name on it and the other with Greta's.

"So what's in them?" Greta asked.

"Keys." My mother pressed an envelope into each of our hands. "If you go to the Bank of New York on North Street, you can look at the portrait anytime you want. Either of you."

I peeled my envelope open and let the key slide out onto my palm.

"Box number 2963. That's all you have to tell them. Then they'll take it out and put it in a private room and you can take as much time as you want."

"Like I'm ever going to do that," Greta said.

"Nobody's saying you have to go, Greta, but it's your painting. Yours and June's, and you should be able to see it whenever you want. That's all."

I dropped the key back into the envelope. I thought I would put it in the back of my closet with the notes from Toby and the teapot and those tapes of the *Requiem*. I thought I might never go to look at the portrait, but I wasn't sure.

Greta slugged down the last sip of her hot chocolate, said, "Whatever," picked up her key, and walked right out of the kitchen without looking at me once.

After dinner, after everybody had forgotten all about the newspaper, I pulled out the page about that soldier. I read it again and I hated him. How could someone be so selfish? I would never get on a train with someone like that. I would never take a donut from him.

I folded the article up, put it in an envelope, and wrote Toby's name and Finn's address on it. I got a stamp from the desk drawer in the living room, licked it, and stuck it on. I looked at it. I could send it just like that, but I didn't. I wrote my name and address in the top left corner. I wanted Toby to know it was from me.

A few days later I got a letter back. I was usually the first one home to get the mail, but Toby didn't know that, so he'd gone through a lot of trouble disguising it. The envelope was big and brown and had a return address from the League of Young Falconers typed out on the front, which made me smile, but only for a second, because almost right away it bugged me that Finn had told him about the falconing thing. At first I almost thought it was junk mail, except that my name and address were handwritten. Inside were a few folded sheets of blank paper, to bulk the letter up and make it look real, and one sheet with writing on it.

> *Dear June,*
>   *That's not how it happened. I promise you.*
>   *With hopes that this will make a difference,*
>   *Toby*

Twenty-Five

There's this statue at the Cloisters that Finn showed me the first time he took me there. It's a Virgin Mary with a very plain face made of birchwood. She's sitting down, and the look on her face isn't exactly sad, but she's not smiling either. She's sturdy and strong, and sitting on her lap is what looks like a small doll of herself. But it's not. It's Jesus as a kid, and Mary's holding him with two hands, like you'd hold a book. The main thing you notice about that statue is that Jesus is missing his head. Instead of a head, he has a thin splintery stick of wood poking out of his neck. He's holding a book, and Mary is looking out at you like she hasn't even noticed her baby's head is gone. Or maybe it's that she knows all about it, but she's daring anyone to mention it. Or maybe it's neither of those things. Maybe that solid look on her face is there because somehow she already knows everything that's going to happen to her only little boy.

Finn and I stood together looking at that statue for probably the ninety-seventh time, listening to the rain kissing down on the old stone courtyard.

"I'd like to paint a portrait," he said. "Of you. You and Greta together."

"Why?"

"Just because. Because you're at the right age for a portrait and I haven't painted one in a very long time." Finn tilted his head and squinted one eye at the statue.

"Thirteen is the right age for a portrait?"

"Of course it is," he said, turning his squinted eye on me. "It's the moment right before you slip away into the rest of your life."

"Then what about Greta?"

Finn laughed. "Well, I'll have to try to catch her before she slips away completely."

I didn't really want to be in a portrait. Even one of Finn's, which I knew would be great. But I nodded anyway.

"How long would it take?" I asked.

"Oh, that all depends," he said.

"On what?"

Finn looked at the Mary statue again. Then he pointed at it. "How long do you think it took to make her?"

I didn't know. It wasn't a very delicate carving. Not many lines. It wasn't complicated, but it had a certain feeling. Like you wanted to keep staring at Mary's face. It could have taken a day or a year to do something like that.

I shrugged my shoulders.

"Exactly," Finn said. "You can't tell until you get started."

"Yeah, well, I still don't know about it though."

"Come on now, Crocodile. Let me do this for you. For you and Greta." Finn gave me this sad look he could turn on whenever he wanted. And he called me Crocodile, which made me smile inside. "Let's go sit in the courtyard," he said. "I brought two cans of iced tea. You can have a think on it."

Finn seemed to be in such a good mood that day. It reminded me of the way you feel right after you finish one of those huge jigsaw puzzles, the kind that has thousands of tiny pieces that all look almost the same. That's the kind of happy he seemed that day.

"Okay," I said. "I'll meet you out there in a sec."

I stayed with the statue for another minute, looking mostly at the headless Jesus and wondering if there was somebody in the world who had his head. Wondering if Jesus and Mary even wanted to be art. I'll bet they didn't. Being art seemed like it might be like having a disease. Suddenly you became some kind of specimen to be discussed, analyzed, speculated on. I didn't need people staring at me, trying to figure out what I was thinking. *Look at the bigger girl, the one with the braids. Look how obvious it is that she's in love with the artist. How sad. How pathetic.* I didn't need that at all.

Twenty-Six

The next time I saw Toby, he was waiting for me right outside my school. He was sitting on the hood of the same small blue car I'd seen him get into at the funeral, which I suddenly understood was the same car I used to see parked outside Finn's building. I always thought it was Finn's car, because sometimes he'd go down and get things out of the trunk like canvases or, once, a green raincoat.

When Toby spotted me, he stood up next to the car and started waving his long arms like crazy. Like he was shipwrecked or something. A rush of pins and needles shimmied up my back because, even though I knew how wrong it was, I was kind of thrilled to see that Toby had come looking for me.

It was a bright, crisp day. The bell had just rung and kids were streaming out the doors. For a second I thought about walking the other way, but I knew I had to get Toby to stop signaling to me. I didn't even want to think about what would happen if Greta saw him there waving at me like we were best friends or something. I quickly looked down at what I was wearing—my boots from Finn (good), a long black corduroy skirt (iffy), and a maroon sweater that my mother said was three times too big on me (good). I glanced around again and then I jogged over to the car, head down, trying to look as casual as I could.

When I got to the car, Toby grabbed both my hands in his like we were long lost cousins.

"June, fantastic. I didn't realize it might be hard to find you," he said. "Come on, get in."

I stood next to the car for a few seconds, looking it up and down. My head was thinking that I shouldn't get in a car with this guy who was almost a complete stranger, but my heart was thinking, *What if there's a dropped pencil in there or a stray box of Good & Plentys or a single strand of dirty blond hair or the imprint of the place Finn used to sit? What if there's a single atom of the air Finn used to breathe in there?*

I was still eyeing the car when Toby climbed in. He reached across the passenger seat, plucked the lock open, and pushed the door open for me. I looked over my shoulder. Kids were coming from every direction, but I couldn't see anyone who might care what I was doing. And so I threw my backpack onto the floor of the car and climbed in.

The car smelled of cigarette smoke and berries. Fake strawberries. I saw that it was because Toby was chewing a huge wad of bubble gum. He was wearing a too-small tweed jacket, and underneath it he had on a green T-shirt with big saguaro cactuses printed all over it. I could tell that Finn had made that shirt, and I must have stared at it a little too long, because Toby tugged the jacket close around his body.

He gave me a sly smile and nodded. "I knew you wouldn't ring."

"Well—"

"No, no, don't worry. I understand. I'm just some stranger to you. It's my fault."

I gave Toby the barest narrowing of my eyes. "Well . . . I'm just some stranger to you too, right? So whatever."

"Of course you are," he said. He stared at me for a few seconds, like he was considering telling me more. Then he smiled and twirled his hand in the air. "You're right. Like you said, 'Whatever.'"

Toby reached into his jacket pocket and pulled out a chunky piece of gum and offered it to me.

"Thanks," I said.

He looked out the window.

"I suppose it was a bad idea. Me coming here."

I shrugged. "You're an adult. You can go wherever you want."

I regretted it right away. It was such a little kid thing to say. I waited for Toby to call me on it, but instead he smiled. Then he turned to look at me.

"And what about you, then?"

"What *about* me?"

"Well, can *you* go wherever you want?"

I looked down at my backpack. My heart raced. This whole thing was so far beyond my normal life. Here I was in Finn's old car with this boyfriend of Finn's, who everyone in my family seemed to hate. Here I was doing something really, really wrong. But when I looked up, there was Toby's warm smile, and his brown eyes, and a look that was somehow saying that if I said yes, everything would be okay. But how could that be right? I glanced around the car, and at first I couldn't see any signs of Finn. I looked across the dashboard and at the steering wheel and on the floor. Then my eye caught the gear shifter, and a smile welled up in my chest. Glued right there, right on top of that gear stick, was a tiny blue hand. The tiny hand of a Smurf. I reached out and laid a finger on top of it. There was a brand-new piece of Finn I'd never seen before. I peeked over at Toby and thought that this must be just the beginning. There must be hundreds of little things like this—thousands, maybe—and Toby was my way in to see them. And so, with the barest tilt of my head, I nodded.

"Of course I can," I said. "Why wouldn't I be able to go wherever I want?"

Right away, Toby's smile went up to full beam, and he tapped his hands against the steering wheel like this was the best news he'd had in years. And that felt good, making someone happy. There aren't many people who get a buzz out of a simple nod of my head.

Out the window I saw Diane Berger, who I have math with, heading across the parking lot in our direction. I slunk down low in the seat.

"Look," I said, "can we go somewhere else?"

"Oh, yeah. Sure." Toby revved the car up. The tires squealed as he pulled away from the curb, and I slunk down even lower. He laughed. "Oops."

We drove right through the middle of town. Past the Lutheran church and 7-Eleven, then out onto Youngstown Road. Toby turned onto the Taconic Parkway heading south.

"So . . . well . . . I was thinking . . . how about Playland?"

"Playland? With the rides?" I said.

"Yeah. But not the rides. There's something else there."

"Like what?"

"You'll see."

The Taconic is a narrow highway and Toby wasn't a very good driver. He sped the whole way down, driving so close to the guardrail that sometimes I had to close my eyes. I clutched tight to the seat. I had no watch and I had no money. All I had was my backpack, with my geometry book in it and a very short book report on *To Kill a Mockingbird,* which I got a B+ on.

A list of questions I wanted to ask Toby started piling up in my head, but when I looked over at him, ready to ask, it struck me how stupid I would sound. I should already know the answers. If I mattered at all, somebody would have told me those things. Then I remembered the article I'd sent to Toby, and sitting there in the tight little car with him, I felt embarrassed that I would have done something like that.

"I'm sorry about that article. It was mean."

Toby's long fingers tightened around the steering wheel. "It wasn't like that," he said. "I just want you to know."

I thought about asking what it was like. Exactly. But I didn't think I wanted to hear the answer. So instead I changed the subject.

"Was this Finn's car?"

I thought this was a pretty easy question, but Toby didn't answer right away.

"Well, I suppose Finn did buy it," he said after a while. "But it was mostly mine. Finn couldn't drive. Did you not know that?"

I tried to ignore the *did you not know that,* even though it felt like a sharp little needle.

"So you'd drive," I said. "If the two of you went somewhere together?"

Toby nodded. "Yeah. Well . . . all right, I don't technically have an

American driving license, but I can drive. You don't have to worry or anything."

"I'm not worried. I'm just asking."

I ran my hand over the seat under my legs. Finn had sat right here in this spot. Finn's fingers might have held on tight to the seat in the exact same place where I was touching. I wanted to open the glove compartment and look inside, but it didn't seem like the right thing to do, so instead I rolled down my window. The sky was so so bright and here I was, driving down the highway with Toby, nobody in the world knowing where I was. I wanted to touch the wind.

"You're English, right?" I said.

I saw Toby answer, but with all the wind I couldn't hear, so I rolled up my window.

"What?"

"Half."

"What's the other half?"

"My mother, she was Spanish."

"That makes sense," I said.

"Does it?"

"Your eyes. They're so dark."

"Mongrel eyes."

"No," I said. I looked out the window for a few seconds, then without turning back I said, "I like them."

I didn't know why I said that. I never said things like that. I tugged my sweater over my knees. I glanced over at Toby and caught him smiling, even though I could see he was trying to hide it.

We switched onto 287, which was wide and not nearly as scary as the Taconic. I loosened my grip on the seat edge. Toby sped up and, without indicating, pulled into the left lane to pass a big supermarket truck.

"Hey, I brought something for you. Have a look in the back."

I twisted around. There, on the seat, was a black folder.

"This?"

"Yeah," he said, glancing away from the road.

"What is it?"

"Just look."

I opened the folder slowly, cautiously peeling back the cover and readying myself for what might be inside. I saw right away they were sketches. Finn's sketches. I glanced over at Toby. He smiled and nudged his head toward the folder.

"Go on," he said.

The first page was filled with small pencil drawings of knees. Knees with just a bit of leg above and below them, each one angled in a slightly different direction. There were only a few lines in each of the sketches, but still they were better than anything I could ever do. The next sheet was covered with elbows. Some straight, some bent. Then a mouth. *My* mouth. That's what I realized after a couple of seconds. I flipped back to the knees and elbows, and on second viewing it was obvious that these were mine too. Mine and Greta's. I flipped through the pages faster. There was the hem of Greta's skirt, a thin edge of my ear poking out from my hair, one of Greta's dark eyes, the curve of her eyebrow above it. It was all us. Every piece of paper had a little detail from Finn's portrait. Me and Greta chopped up and shoved into a folder.

I kept flipping through the pile. I came to a sketch where the space between my arm and Greta's arm, the shape of the place between us, had been darkened in. The negative space. That's what Finn called it. He was always trying to get me to understand negative space. And I did. I could understand what he was saying, but it didn't come naturally to me. I had to be reminded to look for it. To see the stuff that's there but not there. In this sketch, Finn had colored in the negative space, and I saw that it made a shape that looked like a dog's head. Or, no—of course, it was a wolf's head, tilted up, mouth open and howling. It wasn't obvious or anything. Negative space was kind of like constellations. The kind of thing that had to be brought to your attention. But the way Finn did it was so skillful. It was all in the way Greta's sleeve draped and the way my shoulder angled in. So perfect. It was almost painful to look at that negative space, because it was so smart. So exactly the kind of thing Finn would think of. I touched my finger to the rough pencil lines, and I wished I could let Finn know that I saw what he'd done. That I knew he'd put that secret animal right between Greta and me.

I looked over at Toby. He'd popped a Johnny Cash tape in the cassette player and was singing both parts of "Jackson." For a second, I thought of showing that wolf to him, but then I caught myself. Finn had probably already shown him. It would just be another piece of old news.

We didn't say much for the rest of the drive. The car sped past exits for White Plains and Harrison, and even though I'd been past those places hundreds of times, they looked strange and unfamiliar that afternoon. One minute it was a regular school day and I was about to get on the bus home, and the next there I was in the Playland parking lot with a guy in a tweed jacket, chewing strawberry gum.

Only a few cars were there, and we got a spot right near the entrance. Toby's jacket was rumpled from the drive, and he smoothed it with both hands. Looking at him out in the open, I thought he looked mostly same as last time except for maybe his eyes. Maybe his eyes looked a little bit bigger.

Toby paid for us both, which was good because I didn't have any money on me. Next to the ticket booth there was a big, noisy fountain. Toby looked at it, then stepped in closer to me, leaning down. "This thing I want to show you, it's right at the back. Promise me you'll like it, all right?"

"I can't promise that."

He smiled. "Of course not. Good answer."

We walked down the main path, the one called Knickerbocker Avenue. We went past all the rides I'd been on before with Greta. The swings, that rickety old Dragon Coaster, the Scrambler, the Spider. Greta was always the one who wanted to go on the scariest, fastest stuff they had. I was always the one who got dragged into going on with her, even though it made me sick as anything.

We kept walking, and even though there was almost nobody at Playland that day, the whole place smelled of popcorn and hot sugar. Like someone was cooking that stuff just for the smell of it. Just so people knew they were supposed to have fun there. We passed a line of skeeball machines and the shooting gallery where there were creepy-looking hillbilly figures that popped up out of barrels. Toby pointed over to a narrower path on the right.

"Here," he said. "Finn said you like history, the past and all that, so . . ."

Again I had the weird realization that Toby knew all kinds of things about me, while I knew next to nothing about him. It didn't seem fair. Not at all. Every time I thought about it, about Toby and Finn talking behind my back, I felt a hot surge of anger in my chest.

Toby stopped in front of a booth with the name *Images of Yesteryear* painted on a sign above. Display boards with sepia-toned photos of people in old-fashioned clothes were spread out on the sidewalk in front of the booth. There were pictures of whole families or sometimes just kids or once in a while there was one with a single man or woman. Some were wearing Wild West stuff. One guy had on a Civil War uniform and sat scowling with a rifle and a Confederate flag across his lap. A woman stood behind her daughter, both of them squeezed into snug Victorian dresses. Some of the pictures really worked, because you couldn't see that the people weren't from the past. With others it was obvious. Not the haircuts or anything, sometimes it was just a little smirky look that gave it away.

"So? What do you say?" Toby sounded nervous. Like he'd suddenly realized that this was a weird place to bring me.

I'd seen photo places like this before, lots of times, but nobody in my family was ever interested in doing it.

"I don't come out good in pictures," I said.

"Sure you do. I've seen that portrait."

"That's different," I said. And it was. A portrait is a picture where somebody gets to choose what you look like. How they want to see you. A camera catches whichever you happens to be there when it clicks.

"It won't be," he said. He walked around to the other side of the picture board so I couldn't see him. "If you want," he said, "we could go together."

I shook my head. But then I thought about it. It would definitely make it less embarrassing if it wasn't just me sitting there like a weirdo by myself. I didn't even know what time it was, and I had no idea if anyone at home had noticed I was gone, but I suddenly felt like I really wanted to do this thing.

"Oh, okay. I guess. If you want to."

"Pardon?"

"Okay. Both of us."

Toby's head appeared from over the top of the board.

"Brilliant," he said, grinning.

A woman who was probably in her fifties, with eyeshadow in three different shades of blue, sat on a stool behind the booth. She was reading a copy of *People* magazine with a picture of Paul Hogan from *"Crocodile" Dundee* on the cover. When she heard Toby she put down her magazine, creasing it to save her page.

"Two, please," Toby said.

"Two?"

"Yes, there are two of us who'd like to have our photos done." Toby gave her the same smile he'd just given me. A kid smile. That's what I'd call it. The woman looked at Toby, then me. Then she looked harder at Toby, like she was sizing him up, trying to figure something out about him. After a few seconds she seemed to come to a decision. She reached into a drawer and pulled out a price list.

"Okay, well, what I suggest is that you have a look through some of our costumes. Feel free to try a few on and then let me know what you want. Okay? There's lots of his 'n' her stuff back there."

We both nodded. The woman unlatched a swinging door that opened up into the rear of the booth.

"Did you see that?" Toby whispered.

"See what?"

"I think that woman thought we were a couple."

"Gross," I said.

I don't know how long we spent browsing through the costumes. I tried on a Victorian dress and a medieval one. They looked okay, but in the end I settled on a ruby-red and gold Elizabethan dress. It was low cut, but since I didn't have any boobs it wasn't too embarrassing. Toby decided on a Revolutionary War soldier's uniform. It was blue, and when I told Toby blue was the American color, he said he didn't care. Plus, he said, the photo would be black and white, so nobody would ever know. I thought he really looked like a soldier in that uniform. Like someone who'd seen all kinds of terrible things. He stood against the wall, with his fake rifle on his shoulder.

We waited for the woman to get her equipment ready. She set up a tripod, then took a closer look at us.

"I don't think you understand," she said.

"Pardon?"

"Well, you have to stick with one era. You can't go combining different times. See?"

"It's okay," Toby said. His voice was calm, convincing. "We know what we're doing."

"Sir, you don't seem to understand," the woman repeated, folding her arms across her chest. "We just don't allow it. You can't mix time periods, and that's that. Like I said, there's plenty of his 'n' hers."

I looked down at my feet. The Elizabethan shoes they had were too small, so I'd left my heels hanging out. I felt Toby's hand land on my shoulder and it made me feel like we were in something together. I wasn't sure I wanted to feel that with him, but right then, with that lady acting so stupid, I did.

"I'm sorry," he said. "I mean, excuse me, but if we're paying for the photo, why should it make a difference what costumes we choose?"

"I don't want to get too technical on you, but there's the backdrops for one thing...."

"We don't care if the backdrop doesn't match. Choose something halfway between the two of us. We're really not bothered about the background." Toby's voice had lost its soft tone. I could see that the woman wasn't going to budge.

"Look, sir, take a look at every single picture we've got out front, okay? Tell me if there's a single one that mixes eras. Okay? Now, I can hear you're foreign, and I don't know how they do things where you're from..."

Toby didn't know what to say to that. There was a silence. All of us waiting for someone to shift.

"I'll change," I said in a voice that was almost a whisper.

"What's that, hon'?" the woman said.

"I said I'll do it. I'll get something colonial."

"No, June. This is for you. We'll find someplace else. There's got to be a place where we can do whatever we want."

But there was no place else. I looked at Toby and had the panicky thought that maybe I would never meet anyone again who would do this stupid thing with me. Never. And then what? And then where would I be?

"No," I said. "I want to." We looked at each other for a second, and then Toby bowed his head.

"Why do things always have to be like this?" he said. "I'll do it, then. Give me a minute to change."

I nodded and Toby disappeared. The Elizabethan costume didn't fit him right. It was too short, and the tights made it so I could see how thin his legs were. Too thin. That's what I thought at first, but then I looked again. It wasn't as if I'd seen a lot of guys in tights. Especially not skinny guys like Toby. Maybe that's what their legs looked like. Maybe the stories weren't true. Maybe he was just an ordinary friend of Finn's. Not special. Just ordinary, like me.

The woman apologized for all the fuss, then told us to experiment with different poses while she snapped the pictures. I didn't know how most of them would turn out. In one, Toby put his bony arm around my shoulder and whispered, "Don't be afraid, June," in my ear. Occasionally, Toby would give me a look out of the corner of his eye and it was like he'd known me forever, which was creepy but at the same time kind of hard not to like, and suddenly the whole thing seemed so ridiculous it took everything I had not to burst out laughing.

"That's a wrap," the woman said.

She told us she'd get the picture to us as soon as she could.

"After all that, we can't have it now?" Toby said.

"Of course not. It has to be processed."

Toby looked like a kid who'd just been told he can't wear his new shoes out of the shoe store.

"All right, but we need two copies."

The woman wrote on a pad. "That won't be a problem. By the way," she said, "where *are* you from?"

Toby didn't say anything at first. He looked over at me. Then he squinted and looked the woman straight in the eye. "Someplace very foreign," he said in a mysterious voice. "Both of us. We're from far, far away."

On the way home, we agreed we'd tell each other one Finn story each. Toby told me about this time Finn talked him into driving to a beach on Cape Cod that he and my mother used to go to on vacation when they were kids. Toby was an awful storyteller. He rambled on, going back to fill in stuff and stumbling over his words and taking big breaks while he figured out exactly how things went. Still, it was okay, because it was stuff about Finn I'd never heard before. The story didn't really have any point, but it ended with Finn and Toby both being freezing cold because Finn had convinced Toby to sleep out on the beach for the night. By the end I was kind of sorry I'd heard it, because it just made me wish that I had been there too.

The story took up most of the car ride home, so there was no time for my story, which I was glad about. I'd gotten a brand-new Finn story and I didn't have to give a thing away.

I didn't know what time it was, but I asked Toby to drop me off at the library. I could walk home from there. We sat for a few seconds, not saying anything. There were no clocks or watches in that car, and I thought I might have found my bubble. A small blue bubble where there was no time and Finn might be hiding in the glove compartment. It felt like opening the door would burst everything.

"Do you want another piece?" Toby held out a chunk of his strawberry gum and I took it.

"It's probably way late. I'll probably be in big trouble."

"Here, then." Toby rolled down his window. He reached into his jacket pocket and pulled out a penny. He pinched it between his thumb and forefinger. Then he popped it into his fist and hurled it out across the parking lot. "For luck," he said. "Go see if it's heads."

I didn't want to tell him that it didn't work that way. That lucky pennies could happen only by accident. I put the folder of sketches in my backpack, then opened the door.

"Well, bye, and thanks—I guess it was kind of fun."

"Come see me, all right? At Finn's. And if you need anything. Any-thing at all . . ."

"You said that last time."

"Because I mean it. I do."

I closed the door and walked toward the place where the penny had landed. I knew you couldn't make luck that way, but still I kind of hoped it was heads. I started to run to the spot, but even from a few feet away I could already see it was tails. I bent and picked up the penny anyway. Then I turned to Toby and gave him a smile and the thumbs-up. He didn't need to know.

Twenty-Seven

Greta was the only one home when I got there. Tax season was starting to get into the heavy stage. "Crunch time," my parents called it, which meant they barely made it home by eight o'clock most nights. Greta was lying on the couch, watching an episode of *Fame* she had on a videotape. Leroy was standing with his hands on his hips, mouthing off at the ballet teacher as usual.

Almost a week had gone by since the party, and what happened in the woods had still never come up between us. I still wondered how Greta could have found her way to my exact spot, but there was no way to ask her. Not without giving away everything I did in the woods. I watched her sometimes, when we were waiting for the bus or eating dinner, trying to see if she remembered any of what she'd said, but there was no sign that she did. When she heard me come in that night, she smiled.

"Big. Trouble."

"What?"

"Well, where have you been?"

"Why do you care?"

Something about being out with Toby, about traveling so far from home with nobody knowing, made me feel powerful. I stood there looming over Greta, and suddenly she seemed small and sad. Then she clicked off the TV and sat up straight, and like always she was the one in control again.

"So?"

"Library, okay? With Beans. Is that interesting enough for you?"

A huge smile spread across Greta's face, and she kept staring at me like she was waiting for me to understand something.

"What?" I said.

"So they were having a child prostitute look-alike day down at the library?"

"What are you talking about?"

She clicked the TV back on and turned away. Then she said, "Nice makeup," and my heart felt like it was falling right through my stomach. I was still wearing tons of photography makeup. Neither of us had wanted to put it on, but the Playland woman had insisted. Toby wiped his off as soon as it was over, but I didn't. It wasn't exactly that I liked the way it looked. It was more that it felt good to look different than I usually did. And, okay, maybe prettier.

It turned out my parents were having dinner with a client that night, so I ladled a bowl of chicken and rice soup from the crockpot and sat at the kitchen table. It was hard not to march back into the living room and tell Greta all about Toby; I knew it would make her jaw drop to the floor. I would have loved to tell her how he'd asked for me. How he came looking for me. I wanted to open up that folder of sketches and shove them right in Greta's face and say, "Look. See? I know all kinds of things you don't." But of course I couldn't do that.

The soup was hot and salty, and I ate it as fast as I could. Then I went straight up to my room and turned on all my candles. I had this set of six flickering electric candles that Woolworth's was selling out cheap after Christmas last year. The flame was way too orange, but they were the best I could do. My room has two windows, and I put one candle in each. I clustered the rest of them on my desk. When I have my own house I'll have real candles everywhere. Candelabras on mantelpieces and big candle chandeliers hanging from the ceiling. Even if I end up in some poky apartment somewhere, I'll make it like a whole other time. People will ring my bell and, when I open the door, they won't be able to believe their eyes.

I told that to Finn once. We were at an exhibit of sixteenth-century Turkish ceramics at the Met. We were standing in front of these intricately painted blue and white candleholders, and I was telling him exactly how my house would be one day. Finn turned to me, smiling, his eyes bluer than ever, and he said, "You're a romantic, June."

I was standing close to Finn, right up next to him so I wouldn't miss a word of what he knew about the exhibit. At once I stepped away and blushed so hard I could barely breathe. It felt like all the blood in my body had swum up to my face, leaving the skin around my heart completely transparent.

"Am not," I said as fast as I could. I kept my face turned away, scared Finn would see how embarrassed I was. Terrified he'd be able to read every weird thought I'd ever had.

When I finally glanced back, I saw him giving me a funny look. Just for a second. A little flash of worry shot across his face. Then he smiled, like he was trying to cover it up.

"*A* romantic, you barnacle, not lovey-dovey romantic." He leaned over like he was about to nudge my shoulder with his, but then he pulled away.

"What's the difference?" I asked cautiously.

"Being *a* romantic means you always see what's beautiful. What's good. You don't want to see the gritty truth of things. You believe everything will turn out right."

I breathed out. That wasn't so bad. I felt the blood ease away from my face.

"Well, what about you?" I dared to ask Finn. "Are you a romantic?"

Finn thought about it. He looked right at me, squinting, like he was trying to see into my future. That's what it felt like. Then he said, "Sometimes. Sometimes I am and sometimes I'm not."

I pulled out the folder of sketches and flipped straight to the one with the wolf. The dim light in my room seemed to bring it out even more. Or maybe it was just that I'd seen it before, and my eyes knew to go to the negative space. I traced around the outline with my finger, getting drowsier by the second.

That night I fell asleep with the folder of sketches under my pillow and my electric candles on, flickering right through the night. I dreamed about the wolves in the woods. I dreamed about them climbing out of the space between me and Greta. I saw them grace-fully stepping right out of the portrait and into the real world. One after the other, they shook off their painted selves and turned real, until there was a whole pack. A whole hungry pack running across the crust of snow in the woods. I dreamed I was there. That I could understand their language.

"You take her heart," one of them whispered. "I'll take the eyes."

And in the dream I didn't even run. I stayed exactly where I was, waiting for the wolves to tear me apart.

Twenty-Eight

There are two main stories in *South Pacific*. One has a happy ending and one doesn't. The one that Bloody Mary is part of is the sad one. In that one, Bloody Mary sets up her daughter Liat with Lieutenant Cable, who's in the South Pacific on a big secret mission. The daughter is young and beautiful and the two of them fall in love, but Lieutenant Cable won't marry her, because she's Polynesian and deep down he's kind of a racist.

In the other main story there's Nellie, this annoyingly chirpy American nurse from Arkansas who falls in love with this older suave French plantation owner named Emile. Emile seems pretty okay, and every time I see that play I can't even begin to imagine why he would want to marry Nellie, but I guess you're supposed to believe that love is like that. It turns out Emile is a murderer, but that doesn't seem to be a problem for Nellie. What she has a problem with is that he was married to a Polynesian woman who died and now he has two kids who are half Polynesian. And, like Lieutenant Cable, she's pretty much of a racist.

The real question for me is why Lieutenant Cable and Nellie didn't just get together. Because they would have been a perfect match. I guess the idea is that opposites attract, but I don't think that's what it's like in real life. I think in real life you'd want someone who was as close to you as possible. Someone who could understand exactly the way you thought.

According to Greta, Bloody Mary is the only one in the whole play who has any sense. She knows everything that happens on those islands.

"But she's mean," I said.

We were waiting for the bus in the morning, and it was nice because all the spring mud had dried up on that little patch of grass near the mailbox. The sun was bright, and I had to squint and shade my eyes to look at Greta.

"No, she's not," Greta said.

"Kind of. Well, she twists people into stuff anyway."

"No, she doesn't. She's just smart. That's all."

"Whatever," I said, but I was pretty sure most people did think Bloody Mary was mean.

"Anyway," Greta said, "that's not what I want to talk about. I want to hear where you were yesterday."

"I told you already. Library and Beans's, and mind your own beeswax anyway."

Greta smiled. "Okay, then. I'll ask Beans."

I didn't think she would do that, but I couldn't be sure.

"Why do you even care?" I said. And I really wanted to know. I really wanted to understand why someone who seemed to hate me so much cared about where I went after school.

Greta's smile slipped for a second, then she turned away. The bus rounded the corner and we both looked over to see it swing its great yellow body onto our street. Greta turned back to me and stuck her chin up.

"I don't," she said.

That day I carried the bank key in one of the little front pockets of my skirt. I wanted to see the portrait after school. I wanted to see how I looked before Finn died. Plus, a vault is like a crypt, and a crypt is like a dungeon, and I wanted to see what something like that looked like.

The day my mother gave us the keys, she also made me and Greta sign a form so that the bank knew our signatures. To get in we had to show our key and sign something so they would know it was really us. I was worried that my signature wouldn't look the same. I wasn't sure when that thing would happen that made it so you always signed your name exactly the same, but it hadn't happened to me yet. So far I'd only had to sign something three times. Once for a code of conduct for the eighth grade field trip to Philadelphia, once for a pact I made with Beans and Frances Wykoski in fifth grade that we'd never have boyfriends until high school. (Of the three of us, I'm the only one who kept that pact.) And then the bank form. I don't know what my signature looked like the first two times, but I was pretty sure it didn't look anything like the one I did for the bank.

It turned out that I didn't need to worry, because the man who deals with the bank vault was Dennis Zimmer's dad, who's known me since kindergarten.

"Little Junie Elbus . . ." Mr. Zimmer smiled at me. He had one of those faces that look like a turtle. Something about his upper lip. I couldn't tell whether he was making fun of me by calling me little, because in fact I was a good two inches taller than he was. Mr. Zimmer was older than most parents, and I thought he was probably just trying to be jokey to pretend like he was younger. He held the door to the stairs open for me.

"Thanks," I said.

I liked the smell of the bank—like clean dust—and I took a deep breath. Mr. Zimmer stepped ahead and led me down the long stairway. Halfway down, he stopped and turned to me, a serious look on his face. Now he was even shorter than before, because he was standing a couple of steps lower than me.

"I saw you and Greta at the library," he said.

"Oh?"

"The paper—the article about the portrait."

"Oh. That."

Mr. Zimmer's brow tensed up.

"Your uncle . . . He had AIDS?"

I looked down and nodded without looking at Mr. Zimmer.

"I . . . It's just I . . . I found out a college friend has it." He tapped his forefinger up and down against the banister.

"Sorry," I said, still not looking him in the eye.

"Was it awful? Was it . . ." There was a strange desperation in his voice.

I didn't want to be standing on the basement stairs of the Bank of New York talking to Dennis Zimmer's dad about AIDS. I didn't have any answers for him.

"Pretty much," I said. But, really, I didn't know. It wasn't me who was there at the end. It wasn't me who was allowed to be there.

"I'm sorry," he said. "Sorry to bother you like that, sorry about your uncle. It's a good painting."

At the bottom of the stairs he pointed down a hallway, and I saw the thick door of the open vault. It wasn't very dungeonlike. Not as mysterious as I'd hoped. If anything it was more James Bondish.

"Well, here we go. I'll need your key."

I showed Mr. Zimmer my key and he pulled his key out from his pocket, and the two keys together opened a door to a tall, thin safety-deposit box.

"Your mother was lucky to get such a big box on such short notice," he said.

I nodded. "Yeah. Lucky," I said.

"I'll give you room three, how about that?"

"That's fine," I said.

Mr. Zimmer flipped on the light.

"Take your time," he said, and closed the door behind him.

The room had a rich look about it, with dark red wallpaper that went only halfway up the wall and curvy moldings around the ceiling that looked old fashioned. It was like the bank wanted your valuable stuff to feel at home in its new little room, far away from its real home.

I sat for at least a minute without opening the box. It felt good to be in this small private place under the ground. I closed my eyes and imagined I was a prisoner. A rebel kept locked up by a king. I wondered if the room was soundproof. If anyone would be able to hear me if I sang the *Requiem* here.

When I took the portrait out and laid it on the desk, the first thing that caught my eye were those five black buttons. They were still sitting there like someone's lost licorice candy.

Then I looked for the wolf. It wasn't as easy to see it in the real portrait. I had to prop up the painting and walk to the other end of the tiny room to make it out, and even then I had to squint to see it. In the real portrait there's stuff in the background. A window. A curtain fluttering. Some stuff on the windowsill and pictures hanging on the wall behind us. The negative space was all chopped up, and it was almost impossible to hold the wolf there without letting it slip away. I did it for a second. I thought I had it, but then it went.

My face looked mostly the same, but I could already see that I looked a little younger than I do now. Already I could tell that the portrait would always be a kind of trick mirror that would find a way to show me what I used to be like. The other thing that felt different was that now I wanted to know what the secret was that Finn had painted into my head. I wish I'd asked.

I took a good close look at Greta. At first I thought she looked exactly the same, but she didn't. On the back of her hand was the outline of a black skull. It was maybe the size of a bottlecap and it must have been painted with the thinnest brush you could get, the kind I'd seen at Finn's where there was only a single bristle coming out of the handle. I couldn't stop looking at the skull because it seemed impossible that I wouldn't have seen it there before, that my mother wouldn't have seen it, but also it seemed impossible that someone could have painted it on after. Who would do that?

I bent my head right in close, my nose almost touching the canvas. I thought if I looked close enough I'd see where the magic came from. How it was that a delicate skull could suddenly be sitting pretty on the back of my sister's left hand. But no. Nothing.

I packed the portrait back up. When I opened the door, Mr. Zimmer was out there waiting.

"Everything okay?" he asked.

"I was wondering," I said. "I was just wondering if anyone else has been down here to see this box."

"Oh, well, I can't really say. Privacy and all that." He strummed his fingers against the metal box. "But from my understanding, it's only you and your sister who have keys at the moment. That's what your mother told us. That's what she said she wanted."

That's what I thought. But then, Greta must have been here. Greta must have come down here before me and painted that skull right on her own hand.

Twenty-Nine

Everything looked like it was starting to thaw for real. It was Saturday, and Greta had dragged a sun lounger out from the garage into the backyard. My father told her not to, but she put on her little pouty face and told him she was going to read a book for homework out there and he let her do it. So there she was, in an oversize sweatshirt and shorts, eyes closed, *The Odyssey* facedown on her chest.

My mother had gone to Grand Union to do some early-morning shopping, and when she came back she was holding a pile of mail.

"There's something here for you, Junie."

"Me?"

She held up a big brown envelope. "Young Cheesemakers of America?"

Toby. I knew it was Toby. I tried not to panic.

"Oh, yeah . . . I . . . it's a home-ec thing."

"Well, here you go." She smiled. "I'll take a nice ripe camembert. If you're making."

"Okay . . . yeah. Camembert." I tossed the envelope on the table like it was no big deal, but as soon as I got the chance I took it and scuttled up to my room.

Toby had sent the old-fashioned picture of the two of us from Playland. It made me smile because this secret thing had passed right through my mother's hands without her knowing it.

The picture was done in sepia, and if I believed in fairy-tale things I would say Toby looked almost like an angel. His hands were clasped behind his back and his head was tilted down, but his eyes were looking up like he'd just heard someone ringing a bell over his head. He was on the left side, and I was in a chair right in the middle of the picture. I wasn't smiling, which helped with the authenticity of the thing, since nobody ever smiled in pictures in those days. My hands were folded in my lap and I was looking straight at the camera. We were both wearing these great puffy ruffs, which sort of made it look like our heads were on platters. It was an okay picture, but there was something really weird about the whole thing.

After studying the picture for a few minutes, I realized what was wrong: It was a photograph, which obviously wouldn't have been around in Elizabethan times, so even though we both looked pretty good in our costumes, there was still something stupid about it. Something off. If I'd been with Finn, he would have realized right away that we should choose something from the times when cameras were invented. He would have convinced me in a second to be Annie Oakley or someone like that.

I flipped the picture over and saw that Toby had taped a note on there. *You can cut me out if you want to!* That's all it said. At first I didn't understand what he was trying to say, but then I realized that he meant that I could cut the picture in half. That if I wanted to, I could throw his part away.

The next morning, Sunday, I was sitting in the kitchen with my parents, reading the funny pages. It was an ordinary morning until Greta came down. She walked across the kitchen in her pajamas and reached for the coffeepot.

"Here she is. Our budding starlet," my dad said.

Both of them sat there beaming at her. Like they were actually starstruck by Greta.

I looked at them like they'd lost their minds. Then I looked at Greta to see if there was a hint of what this was about. Her eyes were slits.

"What's going on?" I asked.

"So it looks like Greta hasn't shared the news with you either."

I shook my head.

"Go on, honey," my dad said, "tell your sister."

"There's nothing to tell," Greta said. "I don't even know if I want to do it."

"Of course you want to," my mother said. "Opportunities don't come swimming—"

"Yeah, Mom. We all know."

I looked around at everyone. "So, what? What's this big news?"

"We had a call from Mr. Nebowitz last night, and . . ."

"And," my mother continued, "he has a friend involved with the Broadway production of *Annie,* and this friend asked if Mr. Nebowitz had any students who might be right as a summer fill-in for the role of Pepper, and, well, he said the only one he would even consider recommending was your sister. Can you believe it?"

Greta's teeth were gritted and her left foot was tapping the kitchen floor. "Mom, I'm probably not doing it, okay? Maybe next year or something."

My mother's smile disappeared and her hands were suddenly on her hips. "There's no next year. Do you think they'll wait around until next year? Even if they did, which they wouldn't, you'd be too old by then. That's not how opportunities work."

"Maybe I don't care," Greta said.

My mother's eyes widened. "Well, I do. I do care. This is the kind of thing people dream of. If you let this pass, you'll go through your life and you'll get to my age and you'll sit in your kitchen thinking what a fool you were." Her face had started to go red. "You think there are second chances? Do you? Well, there aren't. They dart right by, and before you know it . . . before you even know what's happened they're just a blur in the distance. And then what? Then what are you supposed to do? Then you'll be calling me up saying you should have listened. You should have taken your chance when it came. You . . ."

We all stood there, stunned.

"Mom, are you crying?" I asked.

She shook her head, but anyone could see there were tears in her eyes.

In the end, Greta agreed that she'd do *Annie*. The people from the city would still have to come see Greta for themselves before it was definite, but we all knew she'd get the part. She would go onstage and play a real orphan. Greta said yes, and then my mother spent a whole long time asking whether she was sure and letting her know that there was no pressure. No pressure at all.

Thirty

We were all watching *Family Ties*. Our whole family together, even Greta, who'd been more sullen than usual since the *Annie* episode. It felt really good and only seemed to happen on nights when *Family Ties* and *The Cosby Show* were on. I was pretty sure Greta only watched because she thought Alex Keaton, played by Michael J. Fox, was cute. I heard her saying it on the phone once.

"Popcorn?" my mother said after the show.

"Yeah," I said.

"Me too."

My dad had bought the air popper for Christmas and we all loved it. Watching the popped corns build up until there were enough of them to force their way over into the bowl was a show in itself.

The news came on, and the warm smell of melting butter mingled with facts about Klaus Barbie's war crimes and the Iran-Contra affair.

"So how's good old *South Pacific* going?" my dad said.

Greta shrugged. "Okay, I guess. Whatever."

My dad looked like he was waiting for more, but Greta quickly picked up the *TV Guide* and started flipping through it.

My mom walked in, holding a great big metal bowl heaped up with popcorn.

"Two batches," she said. "And more butter than I'm willing to tell you about." She smiled and set the bowl down. We reached in, grabbing popcorn by the fistful.

The local news started with a story about a fire in Mount Kisco that destroyed an apartment building. After that came a story about a judge in Yonkers who moved his whole courtroom out into the parking lot because the guy he was sentencing had AIDS. "Fresh air and sunshine," the judge said, talking about how he thought it was safer for the court staff not to be in a tight little courtroom with germs like that. They interviewed people on the street to see if they thought the judge was being reasonable. One woman said she wasn't sure, but she thought it was better to be safe than sorry. Then they had a guy who said that it wasn't the judge who was crazy, it was AIDS that was crazy.

They segued into a more general piece about AIDS. As usual, they started out with footage of some kind of sweaty nightclub in the city with a bunch of gay men dancing around in stupid leather outfits. I couldn't even begin to imagine Finn dancing the night away like some kind of half-dressed cowboy. It would have been nice if for once they showed some guys sitting in their living rooms drinking tea and talking about art or movies or something. If they showed that, then maybe people would say, "Oh, okay, that's not so strange."

I was about to go up to my room when the newscaster came on with a story about AZT, which was apparently a drug that helped people survive with AIDS. I sat back down, waiting to hear what he had to say, and when I did I couldn't get up again. The FDA had just approved it, he said. The drug would be available to the public within six months.

None of us said anything. The unfairness of what we'd heard had turned us all mute. My fists closed on the couch fabric. Finn had just missed it. Another few months and . . .

My mother stood and walked out of the room without looking back, but I was frozen to the couch. A science reporter came on, giving more details about exactly how AZT worked, but I couldn't seem to hear any of it. My dad, usually the quiet one, shouted, "Enough," at the screen. Then he stamped across the room, slapped the *off* button with his palm, and walked out.

Thirty-One

It was March 17, forty-one days since Finn died. In Earth Science, Mr. Zerbiak was talking about black holes. Black holes aren't an Earth Science topic, but Mr. Zerbiak is like that. One minute Adam Bell was asking a question about a meteoroid he found in his backyard, and the next Mr. Zerbiak was saying that he was "going a little off topic here, but . . ." and of course everyone was suddenly all interested. If teachers pretended that everything they said was "off topic," we'd have a whole school full of straight-A students. That's what I'd do if I ever became a teacher, which I'd seriously consider if the falconry didn't work out. You could see a certain look in Mr. Zerbiak's eyes when he veered off topic, like maybe he'd always dreamed of being an astronomer instead of a high school science teacher. His hands waved everywhere and he went on and on about gravity and escape velocities.

People took turns raising their hands, trying to keep Mr. Zerbiak from getting back to real work for as long as possible. I raised my hand and asked whether it was true that black holes might be secret passages to other times. I'd read that once, that there might be holes in space that would be like time machines. He said he didn't think so. "That's taking us into the realm of science fiction, Miss Elbus," he said, before deciding that we'd now gone way too far off on a tangent and had to return to course material. The whole class groaned. I saw Jenny Halpern narrow her eyes at me. It didn't really matter, though, because I wouldn't have to see Jenny Halpern or any of them for a couple of days. The next day was a teacher curriculum day. No school.

I'd called Toby a few days before to tell him I was coming to visit. On the phone he seemed like he couldn't believe I'd actually called him, and I was thinking, *Don't get too excited, buddy,* because to me the whole thing was just a mission. A mission to get whatever stuff he had from Finn.

Greta was going on the train to the Galleria in White Plains with Julie and Megan. I told my mother that I might go to the library or I might not, which somehow didn't seem like too much of a lie. She asked if I was meeting up with Beans, and I said I might, which was a complete lie, but it made my mother smile. What all this meant was that I'd have the whole day in the city without having to worry about being missed.

I took the next train after the one Greta took, and the whole way down I felt like everyone could see that I wasn't supposed to be there. I'd worn my medieval boots, and right before I left, I'd snuck into Greta's room and stolen a squirt of her Jean Naté perfume. It felt like putting on a disguise, hiding under the scent of Greta. I rode that train into the city feeling like a whole different person, someone who smelled of lemons and baby powder instead of myself.

Toby told me to take a taxi from Grand Central to the apartment. I stared out the window the whole way, because it was raining, which is how I like the city best. It looks like it's been polished up. All the streets shine and the lights from everywhere reflect off the black. It's like the whole place has been dipped in sugar syrup. Like the city is some kind of big candy apple.

Toby said he'd wait outside to pay for the taxi when I got there. Finn's apartment building isn't the kind with a doorman. It's the kind you have to buzz to get into, and as we pulled up I could see Toby standing in the little space that was between the outside door and another door that went into the building. He stepped out and smiled, and I saw that he was wearing one of Finn's cardigans. On Finn it was big and floppy, but on Toby it was too short, and he was stretching it down over his body. It looked wrong on him. Embarrassing. I must have been frowning, because when Toby ran out into the rain to open my door, the first thing he said to me was, "Is everything all right?" I told him it was. I was trying hard not to let my eyes go to Finn's soft brown sweater, but I couldn't help it. Toby saw me and didn't seem to know what to say.

"Yeah, well," he said, stooping a little, bowing his head. Then he paid the taxi driver and waved him off without even waiting for change.

"Lead the way," he said. He'd propped the door open with a fat Manhattan phone book, and he picked it up as we went in. His long arm reached over my shoulder to push the button for the elevator. The door was shiny steel, and I saw Toby looking at me in its reflection.

"Thanks," he said. "You know, thanks for coming."

"It's no big deal," I said, even though in the scheme of my life it was a huge deal to be going down to the city without anybody in my family knowing about it.

The elevator in Finn's building was slow and old, and it had always seemed like a long time before it got to the twelfth floor.

"It's open," Toby said when we got to the door. I put one hand on the doorknob, then stopped and turned to Toby.

"Is it different in there?" I didn't mean to sound scared, but that's how it came out.

Toby didn't answer; he just reached over my head and pushed the door open, and there it was. Finn's place. Just like always. The Turkish rug. The papier-mâché elephant on top of this old carved trunk he had. Those black-and-white pictures he'd taken of my grandfather's hands, which were so close up they looked like the landscape of some other planet. There was a framed picture of each hand, left and right, on each side of the huge window that looked down onto 83rd Street. The only different thing about the apartment was that it didn't smell like lavender and orange anymore. Now the place smelled mostly of stale cigarette smoke.

Toby scooped up a bunch of papers and books and clothes from the couch and piled them on one of the dining table chairs.

"There, that's better," he said. "Come in. Sit down." He seemed nervous, smiling too much and fussing over little things. Smoothing out a crumpled cushion, straightening a crooked picture on the wall. He'd taken Finn's cardigan off as we walked in and underneath he was wearing a shabby black Museum of Natural History T-shirt with glow-in-the-dark dinosaur bones all over it. After a while he sat on the couch opposite me.

"So, what did you think of the photo?"

"It's good."

"Brilliant." He sounded surprised. "I thought there was something a bit, I don't know, odd about it. But I'm glad you like it."

"Well . . . it is a *little* weird."

"Oh."

"But in a good way. Like art."

Toby's smile had faded but now was back full beam. "Yeah. Like art. Just like art." He looked at me like he thought I was the smartest person he'd ever met. "Like I said, you can cut me out if you want. There's a big space between us. I don't mind."

"It's okay," I said. "I wouldn't do something like that."

"Well, it's your copy, so if you change your mind . . ."

"I really wouldn't."

We sat there after that, not knowing what to say to each other. After a few minutes Toby stood up.

"Tea?"

While he was in the kitchen, I had a chance to look around the apartment without anyone watching me. Finn's old blue velvet chair was still there. The seat was all worn, but the back was bright because Finn was always leaning forward when he sat there, in toward the easel in front of him.

On a table in the corner was a lamp Finn had made by burying a lightbulb in the middle of a goldfish bowl full of green sea glass. There were pieces of smooth glass in every shade of green you could think of, and when you turned on the light it looked like something from the future. Next to it was this chess set that Finn had made in art school. He said he kept it to remind him never, ever to be a pretentious idiot. All the squares on the board were black, so it was hard to know whether you were in the right place. The pieces were these tiny rat skulls that he'd varnished. Each one had a small mark to tell you what piece it was. The bishops had a little cross on the top, and the knights had small horse heads. But other than that they were all the same. Practically identical unless you looked up close, and then you'd start to see the differences. Like one might have a chipped-off tooth or something. I couldn't see what was so pretentious about it. It was kind of gross, but I liked it.

I had one of the skulls in my hand when Toby came back out with the tea.

"Care for a game?" he asked.

I shrugged. "If you want." I didn't really know how to play chess, but I didn't want to admit it to Toby. I brought the board over and set it on the coffee table between us.

He'd made the tea in a plain white teapot that dribbled when it poured and was nowhere near as good as the Russian teapot. I could tell we both knew that, but neither of us said anything.

"Sugar?" Toby said, raising a spoon over a half-full sugar bag. Finn used to put sugar cubes on a little plate with tiny tongs that were shaped like the claws of a small animal. Toby must not have known about that, because he just brought out the wrinkled sugar bag.

"Two," I said.

"Excellent. I like a woman who's bold with her sugar." I turned away and smiled, mostly because he'd called me a woman. Toby stirred two spoonfuls into my cup and then what looked like about four into his own.

He pulled a pack of cigarettes from his pocket and slid one out. Then he looked over at me like he wasn't sure what to do.

"Do you . . ." He tilted the pack toward me and raised his eyebrows. That was the first time anyone had offered me a cigarette, and I wondered then if Toby knew how old I was.

I slid one out of the pack and said thanks, like it was something I did all the time. Like Greta would, not showing anything. Toby took his, then lit them both with a neon orange lighter.

"Ahhh, that's more civilized," he said, inhaling deep, suddenly seeming to relax a bit. I took the smallest puff and coughed, then put the cigarette down in the ashtray. I was waiting for Toby to laugh at me, but he didn't.

"You or me?" he asked, nudging his head toward the chessboard.

"You can go first. I don't care."

Toby lined up all the pieces, then moved one of his.

I watched what he did, then moved something on my side that was almost the same.

"Where's all *your* stuff?" I asked, scanning the apartment.

He hesitated, crossing his gangly legs. He stared at the chessboard, then moved one of his pawns.

"Well," he said, "you know, some of this is my stuff."

I looked around the apartment. I could only see Finn's things. The same things that had been in this place forever. I moved one of my pawns, barely looking at the board.

"What do you mean?"

Toby didn't look me in the eye. He had a finger on one of his knights, but he took it back off and had a drink of his tea. Then he took a long pull on his cigarette before resting it on the edge of the ashtray. He still wouldn't look at me, and suddenly I started to realize what he meant. I looked around again, this time eyeing everything with suspicion.

"Well . . ." he said, sliding the knight halfway across the board.

"So, which things are yours?" I waved the back of my hand at the room.

"I've lived here for almost nine years, June. It's hard to say *exactly* what's mine."

Nine years. Nine *years*? I was five nine years ago. He had to be lying.

"Well, I want to know. I want to see what's yours."

Toby looked at me like he was really starting to feel sorry for me. He glanced around the room, then pointed to the big wooden shelf near the door.

"That jar. Those guitar picks. They're mine, for instance."

Finn's guitar pickles. Those picks—"plectrums," Finn told me to call them if I wanted to sound like I knew what I was talking about. I used to play with those for hours and hours when I was a little kid.

Dumping them onto the carpet, the colors like candy. Hours and hours of sorting them and piling them up and setting them out into long lines like roads stretching the length of Finn's living room. I used to have contests with Greta to see who could find the prettiest one out of all the swirled marbled patterns in that jar. How could those not be Finn's?

"Are you sure?"

"June, Finn couldn't play guitar. You know that, don't you? He was a misery at musical instruments."

I didn't know that. Of course I didn't, because I didn't know anything.

"Yeah. Of course I know that. You don't have to tell me about Finn. He was *my* uncle."

I picked up my king and plonked it right down in the middle of the board. Toby slid a pawn diagonally three spaces.

"I didn't mean—"

"Well, why didn't Finn ever tell me about you?" I was trying hard to keep the anger out of my voice.

Toby shrugged and glanced down.

"I don't know. I guess I'm nothing to brag about really. Look at me. I'm a mess, I'm—"

"That's no excuse. I'm nothing to brag about either but you knew about me, didn't you?"

"June, listen, I used to be jealous of *you,* you know."

That really ticked me off, because I'm not a jealous person. Not at all. Why should *I* be jealous? What would I have to be jealous about? I looked at Toby perched on the edge of the couch, hunched over, legs crossed, trying to fold his long body down. Toby with his stupid accent. English but not real English. Not *Room with a View* English or *Lady Jane* English but some broad slurry thing I didn't know anything about. I watched him sitting there with cards up his sleeve. Decks and decks of surprise cards he could slide out whenever he wanted to. Stories of him and Finn I'd never heard. Not like me. My deck was thin. Worn out from shuffling over and over in my head. My Finn stories were dull and plain. Small and stupid.

"I'm not jealous," I said.

"All right. Sorry. Of course you're not." Toby scratched a finger over the arm of the couch, then he looked at me. "But I was. I was jealous of you. All those Sundays . . ."

He was just saying that to make me feel better. I could tell.

"And you're not jealous anymore?"

"No, not really."

"Because Finn's dead?"

Toby fidgeted with the hem of his shirt. That was something else I noticed. He was always fidgeting. Why would Finn—who could have chosen anyone he wanted for a boyfriend, a so-called *special friend*—choose Toby?

"Yeah, probably," he said. He looked at the floor, then up at me.

The rain pounded against the window and we both sat there quiet for a long time, sipping on our cold cups of tea. Toby lit another cigarette.

I stared down at the chessboard, because I didn't want Toby to see my eyes. Then I stood up and said I had to go to the bathroom. I walked down the hallway, and right away I could see that Finn's bedroom door was open—the door that had always been closed, private. Every single time I'd been there it was closed. I went up to the bathroom door and closed it, but I didn't go in. Instead, I tiptoed back down the hallway and stood outside Finn's bedroom. The room was dim, the overcast light coming through a wispy white curtain. I stared for a while, standing on the threshold. Then I did what I knew I shouldn't do. I stepped in.

There was a big red guitar in the corner. There were two pairs of slippers, two bathrobes hung over a chair. One of them was Finn's yellow one. The other was blue. The bed was unmade, and I tried to guess which side Finn would have slept on. Then it was obvious. One side table had two empty cigarette packs, half a bottle of gin, and a York Peppermint Pattie wrapper on it. The other had an old-fashioned alarm clock and a frame with three photographs in it. I stepped over and picked up the frame. The top picture was of Finn and Toby. It was black and white and looked like it might have been taken in London, because there was one of those big black taxis in the background. They both looked young and so happy. Toby was taller than Finn, and he was leaning his cheek in to rest on the top of Finn's head. I took my thumb and covered Toby's face with it so it was just Finn. Just Finn wearing my thumb like a hat. The middle picture was Greta and me when we were much younger. We were in Finn's apartment and we were each painting at an easel. The third one was the oldest. It was Finn and my mother. A holiday snapshot. A beach somewhere.

I listened for a second to make sure Toby wasn't coming to look for me, then I climbed into the bed. I slid in on Finn's side and pulled the covers up all around me. This is where Finn and Toby had sex. This might be the scene of the crime. This might be the very place where Toby gave Finn AIDS. I slid my hands over the sheets, pressed my face into Finn's pillow. Private. This was what private meant.

"Whose turn is it?" I asked Toby when I went back to the living room. I tried hard to keep my voice solid.

"Look, I don't even really know how to play chess, June. I should have said."

I looked at those little rat skulls scattered across the smooth black surface of the board, the two of us pushing them around like it actually meant something.

"Me neither."

"Well, it doesn't matter, then. Move wherever you want."

I took my time, eyeing my pieces. I put my index finger on a knight and slowly slid it straight across the board, right up to Toby's king.

"Go ahead," he said. "Do what you have to do."

Toby pushed himself up from the couch and strode across the room. His back was facing me, and with one flick of my finger I bumped his king and knocked it off the edge of the board. Then, before he could turn around and see what I'd done, I quickly picked it up and set it back in its place.

Toby asked if I was hungry, and before I had time to answer he was already putting his coat on and moving to the door. He stopped at

Finn's desk, opened the third drawer, pulled out a bunch of money, and stuffed it into his jacket pocket.

"Ah, before I forget." He spun around and ran down the hall to the bedroom. When he came back he was holding a small blue present.

"For you," he said. I took it and turned it in my hands. "From Finn. It was one of his things. He said to give it to you if you ever came to the apartment."

I could tell it was probably a book. It was wrapped in a silky kind of Chinese wrapping paper with blue butterflies all over it. I thought that if I held it or looked at it too long, I might cry right there in front of Toby, which I didn't want to do. At all. So I just said "thanks" and walked over and slid it into my backpack. Then we left.

As soon as we were out on the street, the wind and damp went right to my bones, making my teeth chatter like crazy. With Toby holding a big black umbrella over the two of us, we turned south on Columbus Avenue, then walked for blocks and blocks. After a while Toby stopped and pointed at a Chinese restaurant called Imperial Dragon. It was the kind of place with red lacquered lanterns and long fish tanks where lionfish swam over pagodas that sat on colored gravel. Toby ordered three meals, even though there were only two of us. And spring rolls. And wonton soup. And two extra bowls of crispy noodles with duck sauce. We ate everything like starved animals, not saying a word.

We'd just about finished. I was loading some sugar into my little cup of Chinese tea.

"Hey," Toby said. "For you." From under the table he pulled a gold colored napkin folded into a butterfly.

I stared at it.

That was Finn's trick. Toby was stealing Finn's trick right in front of my eyes.

"No, thanks," I said, sliding it back across the table.

"Do you not like butterflies?" he said. He had the gold butterfly cupped in his palm. He was looking at it the way you'd look at a hurt bird.

"There's nothing wrong with butterflies," I said.

"Napkins, then? One of those rare cases of napkinophobia I've been hearing about?"

I rolled my eyes. "So where'd you learn that from? Who showed you how to do the butterfly?"

I was waiting for him to say, "Finn," and then I'd say, "I thought so."

Toby set the butterfly down gently next to his teacup.

"It's only from an origami book. When I was a kid. It's one of my fiddly-hand things. Card tricks, flea circus, guitar, origami. When—if you get to know me, I'll show you some stuff."

All at once I had a picture of Toby teaching Finn how to make butterflies out of cloth. His hand guiding Finn's. The two of them laughing when Finn got it wrong. The two of them, I thought, and a billow of sadness filled my whole chest.

"Oh," I said, not looking Toby in the eye. "I guess it's just not my kind of thing."

"Fair enough," he said, and in one motion he picked up the napkin and snapped it in the air. I watched as all the knots and folds fell from the golden cloth and the little butterfly disappeared, leaving Toby with a plain old napkin in his hand.

But the sadness stayed with me. Not only sadness because I wasn't part of Toby and Finn's world but also because there were things about Finn that weren't Finn at all. Now my memory of Finn making the butterfly at the restaurant was all wrong. What if everything I loved about Finn had really come from Toby? Maybe that's why I felt like I'd known Toby for years and years. Maybe all along Toby had been shining right through Finn.

"I'm sorry about this. All of it," Toby said after a while. "I promise that if you come again it won't be as bad. The worst is over, all right?"

I didn't believe him. The worst would never be over as far as I was concerned. But just like at the train station, Toby promised he had more stuff to give me. Stuff Finn wanted me to have.

"I'll pick you up, all right? I'll find you. You don't have to do anything."

I shrugged. "If you want to."

"I do."

"Well, whatever, but it has to be a Thursday. That's the only day I can do it."

"Thursdays, then."

"*A* Thursday, not Thursdays."

Toby smiled and put his hands up like he was surrendering. "All right. *A* Thursday. We'll start with that."

Toby popped open his umbrella and we stood outside Imperial Dragon while he hailed me a taxi. When one pulled up, Toby put his hand on my shoulder and pulled me back so I wouldn't get splashed.

"Careful," he said.

That was nice. That one little thing. But instead of saying, "Thanks," I shrugged his hand off my shoulder and said, "I know how to wait for a cab."

"I know you do," he said. Then he leaned his head in and forced me to look at him. "You know if you need anything . . . anything at all . . ." Then he opened the taxi door for me and I got in. As the cab waited to pull away, Toby knocked on my window. I rolled it down. "Anything at all," he said. "Really. I mean it—"

Then, with a hiss of tires against the rain-soaked street, the taxi drove off, leaving Toby standing there mid-sentence. It didn't matter anyway. I couldn't imagine what I would ever need Toby to do for me. I couldn't imagine that at all.

Thirty-Two

When I was twelve and a half, just before I found out that Finn was sick, I got to spend four whole days at his apartment. It was over Fourth of July weekend. Greta was away at summer camp in Rhode Island, and my parents had made plans to go on a getaway to Maine with the Ingrams and one other couple. They'd tried to find somewhere else for me, but nobody was around, so I lucked out. I had to go to Finn's.

Every night Finn would pull down *Joy of Cooking* from the bookshelf in the kitchen. He'd hold it up and say, "So what shall we feed the crocodile tonight?" He'd tap his finger against the book like he was about to look for a recipe. But I knew his trick. Finn had hollowed out that book and turned it into a secret box, and inside was where he kept menus from all the best places in the city. Every night it was like that. We'd sift through until we found exactly what we were in the mood for. A different country every night. That's how it was at Finn's. It wasn't like Finn couldn't cook. What he said was that he didn't want to step on people's toes. "People should do what they do best," he said. "We're only helping them, right, Crocodile?"

On the Fourth of July I asked if we could go see fireworks somewhere. Finn shrugged.

"I'll be honest, June. I'm not a big fan. I can't see the point of it."

"Well, it's Independence Day."

"Independence from what, exactly?"

"You know. The English."

"Well, tell me what's so wrong with the English?"

"I don't know. They were taxing us and stuff, right? They were bringing all their tea over here and then making us pay all kinds of taxes on it."

"Taxes aren't the end of the world."

"Tell that to Mom and Dad."

We both laughed. Finn's hair had been getting long and he'd pushed it behind his ear, but every time he laughed a few strands fell down. I wanted to reach over and tuck them back in, but I knew it would be weird.

"I have lots of English friends, June." He paused. "You know, one of my best friends is English." He looked at me, like he was hoping I was going to ask him about this friend. And I almost did. That's the one moment I can think of when I could have found out about Toby. In all of the eight years, that's the only moment like that. I would have asked and maybe Finn would have spilled everything. But that day was like every other. I didn't want to think about Finn having other best friends. I wanted to imagine that he was like me. That all we had was each other. So I didn't ask. I let the moment go. Instead, I rolled my eyes.

"The English aren't evil *anymore*. Of course they're nice and harmless now."

Finn reached over and patted my back. "You're right. Go get your coat. I know a rooftop where we can see the fireworks."

That night Finn held my hand and we walked through the balmy city together. I knew my palm was sweating, but Finn didn't say anything about it. If there was something or someone we wanted the other to see, we'd give a squeeze. Not too hard, just enough so we knew to look. We'd been doing that as long as I could remember. Usually it was Finn squeezing my hand, because he always saw things first, and then I'd have to quickly scan around until I spotted what he meant. But that night there were so many crazy people around that we kept squeezing at the same time, our hands clenched together, palms pressed tight. Sometimes I would squeeze even when there was nothing there, just because I couldn't help it. I'd watch Finn look up and around until finally he'd give up and look at me all puzzled. Then I'd laugh and he'd bump his shoulder against mine. I loved that.

I was on the 3:37 train home. It had that commuter smell—perfume and sweat and newsprint—and it was almost full. I lucked out and found two empty seats at the end of a car. I knew I shouldn't, but I put my backpack on the other seat so nobody would sit there.

In my lap was the small gift, wrapped in blue butterfly paper. I didn't open it right away, because it was frightening to open something from a dead person. Especially a dead person you loved. Opening a present from a live person was scary enough. There was always the chance that the gift might be so wrong, so completely not the kind of thing you liked, that you'd realize they didn't really know you at all. I knew it wouldn't be like that with this present from Finn. What was scary about this was that I knew it would be perfect—completely, totally perfect. What if nobody ever knew me like that again? What if I went through my whole life getting mediocre gifts—bath sets and boxes of chocolate and bed socks—and never ever found someone who knew me the way Finn did?

I ran my fingers over the silky paper with my eyes closed, then I peeled the tape back as carefully as I could. It was fancy wrapping paper, sturdy, so it wasn't hard to get the tape off clean. The paper would go in the back of my closet with everything else that was secret and precious.

I slid the book out onto my lap.

The Medieval Woman, An Illuminated Book of Days

The cover was maroon and had a painting of medieval men and women picking apples and pears. Right in the middle of it all was a woman with a basket of apples balanced on her head. She had one hand on her stomach, like maybe she'd eaten too much fruit.

I pressed the book against my lap, scared to open it, because Finn was the kind of person who always wrote something inside books and I didn't want to find myself crying on the train. So instead of opening the inside cover, I flipped through some of the pages in the middle.

It was a nice book. There were paintings on one side and then a weekly calendar on the facing page. In July there were woman sculptors, a woman baker, and a pair of women beekeepers. In August there was a woman selling leeks, three women masons building a city wall, and a woman surgeon performing a cesarean section. In that picture, the baby is halfway out and looks like a confused eight-year-old girl instead of a newborn, which gives the whole thing a very creepy look.

I kept flipping through because it was a good book. I thought it was maybe the best book I'd ever owned. Then I landed on the week of September 13 through 18, and it was like catching a spider crawling up my sleeve. There was Finn's handwriting, his thin lines crawling over the page. I slapped a hand over his words and slammed the book shut.

A woman across the aisle peered over at me.

"You okay?"

I nodded, and she turned back to her magazine.

I eased the book open. The handwriting was a mess. Scrawly and uneven.

Dearest June,

I need to tell you.

Everything so wrong. Toby has nobody.

Please Crocodile believe me. He is good and kind.

Look after him. For me.

Need new hands. These are all used up! Can you read this?

Will haunt the Cloisters for you if I can.

With so much love,

Finn

On the opposite page was a detail of a French painting from the fifteenth century. It was called "Nurse Feeding Sick Man." The man was in a bed, all tucked under a sea-blue blanket in a room full of beds. The man looked pretty bad—gray and bald, his hand on his chest like he was trying to catch the very moment his own heart stopped beating—but the nurse, she looked even worse. She was spooning something into his mouth, and her face was all panicky and even grayer than the man's.

I shut the book and shoved it in my backpack. Then I slid the pack under the seat in front of me. I stared out the window for the rest of the journey. Building, tree, car, car, van, wall, vacant lot, van. I stared hard, trying to find a pattern. Thinking if I kept looking hard enough, maybe the pieces of the world would fit back together into something I could understand.

Thirty-Three

Sometimes I play this game where I pretend I've been knocked out of time. Like I'm really a girl from the Middle Ages walking around in 1987. It works anywhere. School. The mall. The more modern, the better. It's a way to see everything for what it is. The last time I did it was in Grand Union, getting some groceries for my mother. It was the day after I'd been down to see Toby, and I was trying anything I could to get the note from Finn out of my head.

As soon as I got home from the city, I'd shoved the *Book of Days* as far back in my closet as I could. Then I slammed the closet door. My plan was to ignore it. If I pretended not to have ever read it, then it wouldn't matter. Who would ever know?

But of course it didn't work. Once you know a thing you can't ever unknow it, and the book sat there like a fire in my closet. Like something I had to put out. Maybe it wouldn't have been so bad if my memories of Finn hadn't just been ripped to pieces. Or if he was asking me to look after somebody, anybody, other than the guy who'd pulverized everything.

I left school with my mother's shopping list in my pocket. In Grand Union I stared up at the ceiling and thought how the panel lights looked like heaps of stars that had been rolled out like pastry dough. How the shopping carts would be good for hauling wood if they had bigger wheels. How bananas and mangoes and kiwifruit looked like nothing I'd ever seen before. I was holding a banana in front of my face, staring at its waxy skin, mumbling to myself, when all of a sudden Ben Dellahunt was standing next to me, staring at me like I was the biggest weirdo in the world. My face went hot and I could tell I was blushing like crazy.

"What is this thing you earthlings call *banana*?" he said in a Mr. Spock voice.

A million different explanations fired through my head. I was ready to give Ben any one of those lies, but then I decided not to. Why should I? I had more important things to worry about. Let Ben think what he wanted to think.

I turned and looked him straight in the eye and said, "I'm weird." I could tell it wasn't what he was expecting me to say, because a huge smirk spread across his face. "Sometimes I go around pretending I'm a medieval kid dropped into our time so that everything around me looks strange and fresh and ridiculous. Okay? Now that you know just how weird I am, you're free to laugh or tell all your friends or whatever. Go for it. No questions asked."

Ben stood there stunned, the smirk still pasted on his face. He nodded slowly like he was trying to come to a decision.

"I like it," he said after a while.

Ben's response caught me off guard, and my moment of bravery disappeared. I found myself blushing again, trying to avoid eye contact.

"Well," I said, "you're not supposed to."

"Ah, *supposed to*—my least favorite words." Ben was so nerdy that it actually made me feel cool for a few seconds. I tried to subtly slip the banana back into the pile, but of course I knocked two more down in the process. Ben bent to pick them up. Then he said, "I wouldn't tell anyone. I'm not like that."

"Thanks."

"June?"

"Yeah?" ·

"Your uncle . . . I saw that article in the library." Ben looked away for a second. "He really had AIDS?"

I nodded. A few people had come up to me in school after they'd seen the article. I guess we were the first people to have any connection to this huge thing that was always on the news. The first ones anybody knew about, anyway, and it seemed to fascinate people. When they asked me about it, there was always a slight tone of awe in their voices. Like Finn having AIDS had somehow made me cooler in their eyes. I never tried to take advantage of that. When people mentioned it to me, they thought they were talking about some casual relative of mine. For most people that's what an uncle was. They had no idea how I felt about Finn. No idea that hearing them talk about AIDS, like that was the important part of the story—more important than who Finn was, or how much I loved him, or how much he was still breaking my heart every single hour of every single day—made me want to scream.

"I'm sorry," Ben said.

That's all. He didn't ask any probing questions, and I was very grateful for that.

The next day at school I wore all my old-fashioned stuff—my Gunne Sax dress with a sweater over the top, a pair of thick woolen tights, and, of course, the boots. I had my usual braids, but that day I'd tied them back with a red ribbon I'd cut out of an encyclopedia. I didn't care what anybody said. Everywhere I went, Finn's note was there, puzzling around and around in my head, and those clothes, that other me, felt like a way to hide from it.

My last class of the day was computer lab, and I plunked myself down in one of the swivelly desk chairs. There were kids in my class who were allowed to move on to programming in Fortran, but I was still stuck in Basic. Week after week, I tried to design a program that would figure out percentages if you typed in plain numbers, and still somehow my program jammed up. I didn't even bother to work on my percentage program that day, because all I could think about was *Look after him. For me.* I typed in the only program that never failed:

```
10 print "What should I do?"
20 goto 10
30 run
```

I watched, hypnotized, as the words scrolled on and on down my screen. I waited, hoping somehow the computer would be smarter than me. That somehow it would stop the stupid waterfall of words I'd forced it to spill over its screen and spit out an answer. But of course it couldn't. It just played out my dumb question over and over again, until Mr. Crowther came over and told me to do some real work.

After school, the red light on the answering machine showed two messages. I dumped my backpack on the table and listened. My mother's voice came first.

"Okay, girls, just calling in to say we'll pick up pizza on our way home. Be there about eight-ish. So don't worry about dinner. Get your homework done. Back soon. Love you."

Then Greta's voice came on.

"Hi. Mom? Well, whoever's there. I'm having dinner with Megs at the diner. Okay? Rehearsal's 'til nine . . . at least. See ya."

That night my parents brought home a mushroom pizza and a big Greek salad, all of which I usually loved, but instead of digging in I told them I thought I might be getting sick. After taking turns pressing their palms against my forehead, they let me go up to bed.

I spent the next hour turning slowly through the pages of the *Book of Days* three more times, searching for some more writing, something to tell me exactly what I was supposed to do, but there was nothing.

I heard Greta come in at about nine-thirty. With my ear against the wall, I could hear her turn on U2, "New Year's Day." I heard her singing along so I pressed my ear to the wall. I loved to hear Greta sing, especially if she didn't know I was listening.

I slipped the *Book of Days* under my pillow and picked up the two cans of Yoo-hoo I'd stopped to buy after school. Then I knocked on her door. She didn't answer, but I went in anyway.

Greta had her back to me because she was changing into her pajamas, which were flannel and plaid. Grandma Elbus always sent us matching flannel pajamas for Christmas.

"What?" Greta said.

"I don't know, I just wanted to talk."

"You have time for that in your schedule, do you?"

"Forget it."

"No," Greta said. "I'm just being a dweeb. Close the door."

I pulled the door shut and put the cans of Yoo-hoo on her desk. I moved some clothes onto her bed and sat on the desk chair.

Greta worked her bra off and pulled it out through her sleeve. When she was all safely dressed, she turned around. When she saw that I was wearing the same pajamas, she rolled her eyes.

Greta was the only one I thought I might be able to tell about the book. About what Finn had asked me to do. She was biting her nails, which I hadn't seen her do for years, and I sat there trying to make up my mind about whether to trust her.

"Supposedly the choreographer's coming tomorrow," she said, "so we'll be doing dance stuff all afternoon." She turned away again and started brushing out her hair.

"So is that good or bad?"

"It's just whatever. I don't even care anymore." She looked at me, then said, "You could come. Watch if you want."

"I don't know. It might be weird. Don't you think? Me being there all of a sudden?" The conversation felt fragile, like it always did with Greta.

"No, it won't. You can go join the geek squad and do lights. Go do whatever they do up there."

"Greta?"

"What."

"Have you ever had a kind of situation where you're not sure if you want to do something and, even if you decide you do want to do it, you're not sure how to do it anyway?"

Greta stared at me, squinting her eyes like she was trying to pry the real story right out of me. Then, slowly, a smile spread across her face. She came and sat close to me.

"I knew it," she said, slapping the bed. "There is someone. All the sneaking off. The makeup. Oh, my God, I knew you had some kind of secret boyfriend. You are so dead. If Mom finds out—"

"I don't. That's not what I'm saying—"

"June, listen to me. You should totally *not* have sex unless you are totally and completely ready. I mean it. That happened to Hallie Westerveldt, Keri's little sister, you know? And she will be, like, regretting it for the rest of her life."

"It's not sex. Really . . ." and suddenly I burst out laughing, because I was thinking about the idea of Toby being my secret boyfriend and how dumb that was.

"See. I got you. I knew it. I can see it all over your laughing face."

"No. Shut up. There's no secret boyfriend. Who would want to do it with me, anyway? Think about it."

"Good point, but somebody must. Ben? Is it Ben Dellahunt? It's Ben, isn't it? He told me he likes your boots."

"Well, he can do it with my boots, then." We both started cracking up.

"That is so gross, June. You are so gross."

The two of us in our matching pajamas, laughing our heads off in Greta's room, felt so good.

I was still laughing, but Greta had stopped, her face suddenly stern.

"June, I'm serious, okay? Just don't do anything stupid."

"Okay."

"Really. I mean it."

"Okay."

"And, no offense, but I can help you with makeup if you want. You're a little heavy-handed."

I laughed again.

"Okay," I said.

"So you're definitely going to the party next Saturday, right?" I didn't know anything about a party, and the surprise must have been all over my face.

"In the woods again. Like last time. All the cast and crew and . . . Ben."

"I don't know."

"Of course you are," she said.

And right then she reminded me again of the Greta she used to be. The nine-year-old Greta who would stand waiting for the bus with her arm around seven-year-old me. The Elbus girls. That's what people called us. Like we didn't even need separate names. Like we were one solid, unbreakable thing.

I was glad I hadn't brought the book in. It was normal things Greta wanted me to confess to. Boyfriends and sex and crushes. Things we might have in common. All I had was a strange man in the city, and secret trips to Playland, and pleas for help from the dead.

Thirty-Four

The greenroom was basically a pretty creepy place. Lonely costumes hanging on racks. Basement damp smell. Ripped old couches and chairs. Bare lightbulbs dangling from the water-stained ceiling. Creepy in all ways. But there were people down there all the time when a play was on, joking and messing around, so instead of seeming grim it actually had a great atmosphere.

I came because I wanted to see Greta dance. I wanted to be able to tell her I'd seen her. And she'd asked me, which was nice. I walked down the narrow steps off stage left that went down to the greenroom. Looking around, I couldn't see Greta, but I did see the back of Ben Dellahunt hunched over a school desk. He was wearing a long black velvet cloak that looked like part of a costume from an old play, and he had dice in his hand. He gave them a shake before letting them clack onto the table.

"Three hit points!"

Two other crew guys sat opposite him, looking glum. I was hoping to walk past without him noticing me, but he saw me.

"Hey," he said.

"Hey."

"You interested?" He pointed to a grid map on the desk. I was pretty sure it had something to do with Dungeons & Dragons.

"No, just looking for Greta. You seen her?"

Ben looked around. "Nope."

I turned to go.

"Hey, wait a sec." He nudged his head toward the game again. "Think about it. You could be anyone. Wolf Queen of the Outer Regions or—"

"No, thanks. I . . ." I heard Greta's voice echoing down the stairs. "I have to go."

I ran into Greta on the stairs. She was trailed by three or four girls I didn't know. Word had started to spread about Greta's part in *Annie,* and even though she hadn't officially been given the part, people seemed to be treating her like she was already famous. I'd see her in the cafeteria at lunchtime surrounded by a whole bunch of kids from her class, boys and girls, all gazing over at her. I couldn't tell if she liked it or not.

As I walked up past her on the stairs, I made sure she saw me. I wanted her to know I'd come to see her dance. We didn't say hi or anything, but she saw me and we scraped shoulders as I went up and she went down. Then I saw her glance over at Ben, and a little smirk flashed across her face.

I stood at the back of the auditorium and watched. Greta came on late, and when she was onstage she looked disinterested. Halfhearted. Like she was trying not to be as good as she could be. Maybe I was the only one who noticed it though, because she was still excellent. She couldn't help it.

Thirty-Five

"I don't need jeans. I hate jeans."

"Of course you do," my mother said. "Everyone needs jeans."

It was the weekend of Macy's big spring sale. It was something that my mother and Greta and I used to do together. Now Greta just got my mom to give her money and went with her friends. I didn't want to go at all. Not at all.

My mother stood in front of my closet. She tugged at a hanger that had two brown corduroy skirts hanging sloppily from it.

"Look at these." She ran her hand over both of the skirts. "It looks like you've been crawling around in mud. What do you do to get them into this state?"

I was still in my pajamas, snuggling down under my covers to hide from the sun beaming in my window.

"They're okay," I said. "They're fine."

My mother rooted deeper into my closet, and I remembered the teapot and the tapes and the notes and everything else that was back there. In a panic, I pulled up to a sit.

"All right," I said.

"What's that?"

"I'll go."

I sat on a bench and my mother stood in front of me, looking down the track. Her hair was cut short, and because it had all turned gray when she was twenty-three, she always had it dyed a deep chestnut brown. It was that color all over except for a super thin stripe at the top of her head, where the gray showed through. Sometimes I wanted to touch that place on my mother's head, that thin crack where her real self had forced its way through. Just then, in the cold March sun of the train station, it felt like if I put my finger right there, everything might go back to normal. There would be no more secret meetings with Toby. No ghosts telling me who to look after, telling me to do things I couldn't even imagine how to do. No more strange changing portraits in underground vaults. No more sisters who disappeared on you in the dark night woods. I could forget everything and go back to being a regular girl who went to Macy's with her mother and dreamed of living in the past.

I stood and took a few steps toward my mother.

She smiled at me, taking my ungloved hands between her two gloved ones, giving them a rub for warmth.

"This will be like old times, Junie," she said.

There were only a handful of people waiting for the train that morning. A few families. A group of older kids from my school. A man in a suit. My mother and I sat in seats opposite each other. She had on lipstick, which she almost never wore. My mother didn't even wear makeup to work. Only for going out at night or for going into the city. She stared at me like she was building up to something. Then, finally, she came out with it.

"How about Horn and Hardart for lunch?"

I shook my head.

"June." She let out a long sigh.

"I just don't want to."

"Honey, I know you don't want to. And I know why you don't want to." She reached over and put a hand on my knee. The train felt like it was squashing in on me, and I knew I was trapped. My mother had lured me here to talk about getting over Finn, and I was stuck.

"If you know why, then why would you want to make me do it?"

"Because one way to stop things from feeling so raw is to blanket over the memories. If we go to Horn and Hardart, then it'll be like throwing a thin blanket over the other times you were there with Finn.

Each time you go, a fresh memory will lay on top, until your times there with Finn will be muffled under it all. Do you see?"

"Some other day."

"And the Cloisters. The same thing with the Cloisters . . ."

It was like she couldn't hear me. The Cloisters? The idea of going to the Cloisters with my mother was so completely wrong. That birch-wood Mary eyeing me up, all those tight stone corners that could hold a word for centuries. All the thickest, woolliest blankets in the world couldn't cover the ghosts of Finn and me in that place.

"Can we just not talk about it?" I asked.

"June, it's been over a month now."

I leaned back in my seat. I closed my eyes, crossed my arms over my chest, and let my breath out slow. When I opened my eyes again, I looked at my mother.

"Tell me a story about you and Finn. When you were kids. One story, and I'll go to Horn and Hardart."

"Oh, June . . ." But I could tell she was already thinking about being a kid. I could tell that she wouldn't be able to help talking about it.

My mother ended up telling me about the beach on Cape Cod where she and Finn used to go on vacation when they were kids. I was pretty sure it was the same beach Toby told me about. The difference was that my mother could really tell a story. She told me how my grandparents would sleep late and how she and Finn would run across the street to the beach by themselves as soon as the sun came up. How the sky would glow the warm pink of fevered cheeks at sunrise, and how they'd have the whole beach to themselves. Like it was another time, she said. She said they'd turn the world upside down. Pretending sand was cloud and sea was sky. She told me about how Finn once found a horseshoe crab the size of a watermelon and how they'd dared each other to help it back into the water.

"It was prehistoric, June. It was like something right out of a movie."

I could tell she was there. She was right back there in that pink sky summer with Finn.

"And then what?"

My mother smiled. "Then Finn flipped it over on its back with his foot and lifted it up like a big cooking pot and carried it to the water."

The train trundled on through White Plains and Fordham, past the school in Harlem that had no windows and the 125th Street station that I'd never gotten off at. After that, it slipped into the dark mazy tunnels that wind their way under Manhattan into Grand Central.

"Why did Finn stop painting?" I said, without looking at her.

All the windows had turned into mirrors in those dark tunnels, and when I looked up I saw my mother's reflection watching me. Her face had hardened, and the way the light hit the windows made it look like she was a painting. In the window she was just bright lips and eyes, with no texture to her skin at all.

"Toby," she said.

"Toby?"

"I hold that man personally responsible for destroying Finn's life."

"He can't be that bad. Finn wasn't stupid. He wouldn't let someone force him to stop painting."

My mother crossed her arms over her chest. It seemed like a long time that she sat there, saying nothing.

"He has a past, June. Do you understand? This Toby, he's not all innocence and light. One day you'll understand this better than you do now. Love conquers all, right? Family, art, you name it. Finn was in love with Toby, and that meant nothing else mattered to him anymore."

Nothing else mattered. I didn't matter.

"Well, how come I never knew about him?"

"Because I didn't want you or Greta to have anything to do with that man. Finn knew that was the deal. If he wanted a relationship with his nieces, he would have to keep Toby out of it. You can't just take up with a derelict and expect everyone around you to be fine and dandy with it. You can't have everything. That's something Finn never understood."

I didn't understand either. Why couldn't you have everything?

"You made him choose?" I asked. She turned away. She wasn't going to answer. "You . . ." I couldn't believe she would do something like that. It didn't seem like anything I'd ever seen her do. It made me actually feel sorry for Toby.

"Enough. I've had enough of this talk."

"But—"

"Really, June," she said, "I'm the one who should be sad. He was my little brother. I was the one who took care of him when we were kids. Do you know what it's like to have a father in the military? Do you? Moving base to base. I was in charge of making sure Finn was okay. I was expected to look after him. Me, June. I simply will not allow you to continue moping around the way you've been. It's out of all proportion. This feeling-sorry-for-yourself business. I'm the one who should be a mess, June. I'm the one who lost a brother." She pressed her palms against her eyes. "You think I don't know what it is you're listening to up there in your room every night? You think I don't know it's the *Requiem*? Who do you think showed that music to Finn? He's not the only one who knows about beautiful things."

She angled herself toward the aisle and her face disappeared from the window. I pressed mine closer so I could see outside. The walls of the tunnels were covered with so much dirt, it was almost like fur. I thought those tunnels were the kind of places wolves might live. I thought they were like the vessels of the human heart.

In the end we didn't go to Horn & Hardart for lunch. We got what we needed at Macy's, then had a slice of pizza at the train station before heading back home.

When we got home, we found out that even though Greta spent all of the seventy-five dollars my mother gave her, all she came home with was one pair of Guess jeans, which weren't even on sale, and about twenty of those black rubber bracelets from a vendor on 34th Street.

My mother looked wrung out.

"It's not like they're all for me," Greta said. "Some of these are for June." Greta pulled a few of the bracelets off her arm and thrust them out to me.

"They are?" I said.

My mother looked back and forth between Greta and me. She breathed out a long slow sigh. I wanted so much to say something my mother wanted to hear, because then maybe, just maybe, she would somehow turn back into the mother who would never force someone to choose between his boyfriend and his sister.

Before I even fully thought it through, I chirped out, "I'm helping with the play tomorrow." Greta and my mother both turned to look at me. "Greta said they could use a hand with some of the backstage stuff."

"That's great, June." My mother nodded at me. I glanced over at Greta and saw that she was smiling. A real, honest smile.

"And Friendly's after. Okay?" Greta said it in this chirpy voice that sounded fake to me but seemed to please my mother.

"That's great, girls." My mother looked at both of us and cracked a smile. Then she looked just at me. "That's the way, Junie."

I nodded, and maybe I stared a little too long. Maybe I needed to get a good look at this version of my mother.

"Okay, now how about you both head upstairs for a while? I'll get dinner going."

In my room, I slid the stretchy bracelets over my hands. On Greta they hung loose and dangly. On me they sat snug, like the orthopedic wrist brace my grandfather had when he fell off the ride-on mower. One by one, I worked them back off my wrist and laid them on my desk. Then I put them in the back of my closet with the teapot. Those bracelets were the first thing Greta had given me in three years, and even though I was pretty sure she gave them to me only to get in less trouble, I still wanted to keep them safe.

Thirty-Six

I don't break promises. If I say I'll do something, I mean it. I'd told Toby I would see him again, so that's what I did. I didn't need him to come get me. I decided to go on Monday, because I had gym last period on Mondays. Even though I'd never cut a class before, never even thought about cutting a class before, I went right up to Mr. Bingman, laid my hand on my belly, and started to tell him I was having girl trouble. Everyone knew that trick with Mr. Bingman, and before I'd even finished my spiel, he had his pen out, scribbling a pass.

As I walked out of the gym, I counted the thwacks of basketballs as they hit the smooth floor, I took deep breaths of the sweaty air, and I kept a straight face. Even if I walked slow as anything, I'd still have plenty of time to get the 2:43 into the city.

"June. Brilliant," Toby said when I buzzed up, and it sounded like he really meant it. I decided to walk up instead of taking the elevator. I wanted time to prepare before I saw the apartment again. *Toby has nobody. Toby has nobody.* That's what I kept telling myself.

As soon as I walked in, I saw that the apartment had started to look different. Finnless. There were three or four dirty plates stacked up on the coffee table. The ashtray, which was a molded bowl Finn had made out of blacktop (*tarmac*, Toby had called it last time, rolling his eyes and smiling), was full, and the shades were pulled down over the big windows.

Toby stood there in this rumpled maroon corduroy jacket with that same dinosaur-bones T-shirt under it. He saw me glancing at the windows, and he strode over and snapped open the shades.

"There," he said. "That's better, right? Sit down."

Toby sat on the blue couch and I sat opposite him on the brown one. He'd made a pot of tea and we each had a cigarette, which I managed to smoke without coughing once. Toby had a small bottle of brandy and he poured a glug of it into his cup. He held it out to me, but I shook my head. I tried not to look around the apartment too much. I didn't want Toby to think I was trying to guess whose stuff was whose, but I couldn't help it. For the last few days I'd been steeling myself. I wanted to be able to look around and feel like it didn't matter that half the stuff there wasn't Finn's. *Toby has nobody,* I told myself again.

"Those are nice boots." Toby nudged his head toward my feet.

"They're from Finn," I said, a little too quickly. Then I angled myself so my skirt covered my feet.

There were a few seconds of awkward silence, then out of nowhere Toby started talking in a fake reporter's voice. Using a weird accent and pretending to hold a microphone out to me.

"So tell me, Miss Elbus, what fascinates you about the Middle Ages?"

I crossed my arms over my chest and gave him a look.

"No. Really," he said in his normal voice. "I want to know."

It was the kind of question that made me go completely dumb. I almost thought about pretending I hadn't heard it, but I knew he'd try again. My brain flicked past all the possible answers. Castles; knights; dark, candlelit nights; Gregorian chants; and dresses that came right down to your feet. Books that had to be copied out by hand and decorated by monks in the most beautiful colors. Books that were illuminated so they glowed.

"Maybe . . . I don't know . . . Maybe it's just that people didn't know everything then. There were things people had never seen before. Places nobody had ever been. You could make up a story and people would believe it. You could believe in dragons and saints. You could look around at plants and think that maybe they could save your life."

I'd been staring at the rug the whole time, because I had a feeling

I wasn't making any sense and Toby might be laughing at me. But when I glanced up, I saw that he wasn't. He was nodding.

"I like that," he said.

"Really?" I watched Toby to see if he really meant it and, when I was convinced that he did, I went on. "And, well, also maybe it seems like it would be okay not to be perfect. Nobody was perfect back then. Just about everyone was defective, and most people had no choice except to stay that way."

Toby sat there nodding. He had his hand resting on his knee and I saw how callused his fingers were. "But it was also filthy and dark and there were rats and plague . . ."

"I guess." I looked down, thinking. Then I looked up at Toby and smiled. "So not so different from New York, then."

Toby laughed. "Good point." He nodded to himself again, like he was mulling something over. "Except . . . well, except that we have AIDS instead of the plague."

It was the first time I'd heard Toby say that word. *AIDS.* He glanced away from me when he said it.

"They're not the same."

"Well, not exactly, but—"

"Not at all. You couldn't help it if the plague got you. It was no-body's fault. It just happened. Nobody was to blame." The words shot from my mouth before I had a chance to stop them.

Toby started twisting a loose thread at the edge of his jacket pocket. I thought about apologizing, but I didn't.

"June, nobody knew anything about AIDS. Do you understand? There wasn't even a word for it when Finn and I met."

"Then why does my whole family think you gave it to him? Why would they say that?"

Toby tipped his head forward and closed his eyes. He took a deep breath before opening them. "Because that's what we decided to tell them."

"Who?"

"Finn and me. Mostly me. Your mother assumed that's the way it was, and we decided to let her believe it. I told Finn I didn't mind. That if it made her feel better, we should let her believe it."

"But—"

"Let it go, June. It doesn't matter anymore."

But it did matter. The truth mattered. It wasn't right for Toby to take all the blame when it could have been either of them. When it was nobody's fault.

"Why would Finn—"

"Shhh," Toby said, and he put two dry fingertips up to my lips. I froze and he slowly moved his fingers away.

"But—"

"I'm telling you all this because I need you to understand how much I loved your uncle. Then maybe, maybe if you understand that, you'll . . . not hate me quite so much. Finn was like you, he wanted to tell the truth, he wanted everyone to know it wasn't anyone's fault. It was me who pushed it. I loved him, June. And if taking the blame made things easier for Finn, then that's what I wanted to do. Now let it go, all right? We're miles past any of that mattering anymore. All right?"

I didn't say anything.

"Please? It's what Finn would have wanted. It really is."

How do you know what Finn would have wanted? I thought. But I shrugged and said, "I guess."

"Good." He looked away, out the window.

I sat there feeling like I was about to cry. I didn't know why. It wasn't because Toby had been noble and good. It wasn't because probably nobody in the world would ever know the truth except me. It wasn't because I finally had news to tell Greta but it turned out it was news I couldn't tell anyone. I stood there letting that animal sadness drape over my shoulders, waiting for it to tell me why it was there. And then it did. It crawled in close and whispered in my ear.

He loved Finn more than you did.

That's what it told me. And I knew it was true.

I could feel a hard cold knot forming in the center of my chest. *I'm not a jealous person. I'm not a jealous person. I'm not a jealous person.* I thought that to myself over and over again, slowing my breathing down. I looked up at Toby.

"Well . . . did Finn ever paint a portrait of *you*?"

As soon as I said it, I realized how pathetic I sounded. How sad and mean. But it was like Toby didn't even hear the meanness. He held up his index finger, telling me to hold on a second. Then he jumped up from the couch and rummaged around in the secret drawer in the desk until he found a key. He held it up and smiled.

"You haven't been to the basement, have you?"

Toby was right. I hadn't been down to the basement of Finn's apartment building. But my mother had. Sometimes on Sundays, while Finn was painting us, she'd do a load of laundry for him. She'd come back up shaking her head, saying never again. "That basement is like something out of a horror movie," she said once.

Toby stuffed the key into his pocket.

"What about the basement?" I said.

"Come with me." He was beckoning me with two hands like a lanky Svengali.

"I don't know. What if I don't want to?"

"You will. I promise. There's a lockup. Each apartment has one. Like a big storage cage. Come with me."

An image of me being locked in a cage in some kind of creepy cellar came into my head. I didn't even know Toby. Not really. And he said himself he was jealous of me. Maybe he would lock me in this basement and nobody in the world would ever guess where I was.

Toby's shoulders drooped, and he cocked his head to one side and said, "Please," in the most pathetic voice ever. Then he perked back up. "Look, truly, June. You won't be sorry."

I thought about it for a few seconds and came to the conclusion that a real psycho wouldn't have mentioned the cage. A real psycho would have lured me down there by telling me there was a puppy or something.

"Okay," I said, "but you go first, and I want my coat." I wanted my coat because my quill pen was in there and if worse came to worst I could always stab Toby with it.

He threw up his hands. "Absolutely fine."

Toby pushed the *B* button and down we went. In the small space of the elevator I could smell stale cigarettes but also, underneath that, there was the nice freshness of soap.

"You won't be sorry," Toby said again as the elevator clunked to a stop and the door slid open. He stepped out and I followed. As soon as I had a chance to look around, I could see that my mother was right. The cellar did look like something out of a horror movie. The hallway in front of the elevator was narrow and lit with bare bulbs hanging from the ceiling. The whole place smelled like overheated dust, and the walls were yellowed and crumbling. As we walked, I saw that there were little dead-end hallways and rooms leading off from the main hallway. Some of them had grubby mattresses in them, like there might be people who lived down there. Over my shoulder I watched as the elevator door banged itself shut. It creaked and churned as it lifted its way up out of the basement.

I looked at Toby's shoulders in front of me and I started to feel glad that he was with me. Not that it seemed like Toby would be much help if a real psychopath was waiting in the basement, but, still, it felt better knowing I'd be hacked to death with somebody else instead of all by myself.

We passed through the laundry room. A dryer was tumbling some clothes around, but nobody was in there.

"Just here," Toby said.

We turned a corner and came into a long room lined on one side with padlocked floor-to-ceiling chain-link cages. Each one was about ten feet across and pretty deep, and each had a bare bulb hanging from the ceiling. I followed Toby along the row of cages, peering in at the stuff people kept. Most of the cages were stacked high with things like bikes and boxes and chairs. One had a stuffed fox that stared right at me as I walked by. Another had about twenty different birdcages in it. Another had three ceiling-high stacks of unopened boxes of Campbell's tomato soup.

Toby stopped at the cage that said 12H. I stood next to him, squinting at the sight of the thing. A burgundy velvet cloth, like a full-length curtain, hung from the inside on all sides so it was impossible to see what was in there. Toby pulled the key out of his pocket.

"It can be a bit . . . troublesome," he said as he worked the key into the lock.

"What's all this" I asked, pointing up at the curtain.

"Ah, there we go." Toby wriggled the lock open and off the cage door. He glanced up to where I was pointing. "Just privacy," he said. "Now, I need you to give me a minute."

He stepped in first and I waited outside. I heard a match being struck inside the cage, and then I could smell that it had been blown out. I stepped closer to the door. I stood for a few more seconds and was starting to get edgy when a metallic sound, like a big door being slid open, echoed through the basement. Then a whoosh and a loud thud.

I must have let out a little gasp, because Toby poked his head out. "Incinerator for the rubbish. That's all. It's all the way at the other end of the building. Don't be frightened."

"I'm not," I said, even though I was. I stepped toward the cage door and pulled the curtain back. "Can I?"

He offered me his hand, which I didn't take, and I stepped in.

"Oh, wow."

I wasn't planning on being impressed, but it was impossible not to be. Inside, the cage didn't look like any of the other ones we'd passed. It didn't look like a storage cage at all. It was like stepping into a Victorian parlor. Instead of a bare bulb, there was a small crystal chandelier hung from the ceiling. There was a worn Oriental carpet in blues and greens on the floor, and on top of that were two old upholstered chairs and a green velvet chaise longue. A short dark-wood bookshelf filled with little red leather-bound books nestled against one side of the room, and a fat candle burning a low flame sat on top of it. There were two side tables with lion's-claw feet. One had a deep blue glass bowl filled with miniature chocolate bars on it, and the other had one of those crystal liquor bottle sets that rich people sometimes have. Each bottle had only an inch or two of drink left on the bottom, and Toby poured some into a crystal glass.

"Take a seat," Toby said, smiling.

I wondered if this had been here all along. All the times I'd visited Finn. Another secret he hadn't bothered to let me in on. I had a sudden hope that maybe Toby had set this all up after Finn died.

"What is this place?" I asked.

"Finn made it. The annex, he called it."

I didn't want Toby to see the expression on my face, so I walked to the bookshelf. I squatted down and saw that each of the red books was a field guide to something. Sea life, wildflowers, trees, gemstones. They were beautiful. I pulled out the one about mammals and flipped through the stiff gold-edged pages without really looking. I held the book in my palm, my back to Toby, and felt my thumbnail scratching into the leather spine. Back and forth I scratched, until I was sure the mark couldn't be rubbed away.

I heard Toby stand and I could feel that he was right behind me.

"This is where I used to come when you were visiting," he said. "Not always, of course, but sometimes if I came back from somewhere and I wasn't sure you'd left yet. That's why he made this place."

Finn hid his secret boyfriend in the basement? I might have felt sorry for Toby if the place wasn't so beautiful. If it wasn't so completely obvious that a person would only make someplace like this for someone they really loved. I thought of all the times I'd been upstairs in the apartment, and now those memories were getting mixed up with the picture of Toby skulking around down here. Right underneath me all the time. I thought about the painting sessions, those afternoons after the Cloisters, that whole Fourth of July long weekend. He couldn't have stayed down here all that time. Could he?

Then I realized that this was my mother's fault. There wouldn't be any underground annex if it wasn't for her. I would have known Finn and Toby together all along. And then what? I guess I never would have been so close to Finn. I never would have thought that I might be the most important person he had. I never would have let him hook into my heart the way he did. I never would have become the pathetic girl standing here, wishing he'd made this secret room for me.

"Anyway," Toby said, "the question was, Did Finn paint any portraits of me? That's why we're down here, right? So take a look back there. Behind the chaise whatsit."

I squeezed behind there without looking at Toby. There was a wooden pallet on the floor with a white sheet draped over the top. I could see what they were without even lifting the sheet. It was a big stack of Finn's canvases. I stood there without moving.

"Go ahead," Toby said.

I bent down to lift the sheet, but then I couldn't do it. I couldn't face more parts of Finn I'd never seen before.

I shook my head. "Maybe another time."

Toby nodded like he understood. "All right," he said, landing a tentative hand on my shoulder. "Whenever you're ready."

As we turned to go, I saw what looked like a miniature stage with a blue velvet curtain. It had legs so it stood about chest level, and it looked like an antique.

"What's that?"

"Oh, that's just an old flea circus. A job's a job sometimes."

For the first time that afternoon I laughed, because that seemed like the kind of thing people usually said about waitressing or working as a garbageman. It didn't seem to fit with the idea of running a flea circus.

"It's yours?"

"Yeah, I used to set it up in parks. Or sometimes fairs."

"And the fleas?"

Toby smiled. "Of course, the fleas. My little mates."

"So . . . where are they now?"

"Who?"

"The fleas."

Toby gave me a funny look. Like he was trying to figure something out.

"Sit down," he said.

Great. This was going to be some kind of fantastically dorky performance that I'd have to try to smile my way through. I wondered if Toby came down here to feed the fleas. If they had a special flea-size cage and some kind of tiny water bowl.

"Don't hurt any fleas on my behalf," I said, trying to angle my head to get a peek at what Toby was setting up.

"What do you take me for?"

That was the thing. I didn't know what to take Toby for. I still had no idea.

He turned the whole platform around to face me. It was like a shrunk-down three-ring circus. There were tiny ladders and a tiny wire bicycle. There was a trapeze wire that stretched across two stands and a rickety miniature trapeze that hung from it. I couldn't help smiling as Toby went into full showman mode. The trapeze swung and the bicycle moved slowly around the edge of the stage. All the while, Toby gave gentle orders to the fleas, and when they did what he asked he told them how wonderful they were, praising them over and over again. "Bellissimo!" he said. "Bravo!" After a while, he told them they could have a rest and asked me to give them a big round of applause.

I gave a few light claps, then crossed my arms over my chest.

"There are no fleas, are there?"

Toby gave me a mischievous grin. "No, June. No fleas. It's a trick. Sleight of hand."

"So you're like the man with the golden hands."

I wasn't sure if I meant it to come out as mocking as it did, but once again Toby didn't seem to notice my tone. Or, if he did, he decided not to let it bother him.

"No, not really," he said. "Well, maybe for stupid fiddly things. I can't write or paint or draw. Nothing useful. And it's just my hands, really. Look at the rest of me. Clumsiest man on earth."

"So, like a superhero with one power."

"I wouldn't go *that* far. Anyway, what's yours, then? What's the one superpower of June Elbus?"

I thought about myself from head to toe. It was like being forced to read the most boring part of the Sears catalog. Like leafing through the bathroom accessories pages. Boring brain. Boring face. No sex appeal. Clumsy hands.

"Heart. Hard heart," I said, not sure where it came from. "The hardest heart in the world."

"Hmmm," Toby said, tapping a finger in the air. "That's a useful one, you know. Very handy. The question is . . ." Toby paused like he was considering this all very seriously.

"What's the question?"

"The question is, stone or ice? Crack or melt?"

Toby took his time, neatly folding away all the little parts of the flea circus. He might have kept the apartment a mess, but he seemed to take extra care to make sure the flea circus was packed away neat and tidy. I wondered how many times he'd been down here, talking to his invisible fleas, while I was upstairs with Finn. I wondered if Finn had bought him that flea circus. I wondered if Toby hated me. If maybe he hated my whole family. I couldn't have blamed him if he did. He closed the top of the box and hooked a rusted latch into a catch.

"How did you meet Finn?" I asked.

Toby frowned. He took a sip of whiskey, then tapped the edge of his crystal glass. "Oh, nothing interesting. An art class." He stood up and walked to the bookshelf, turning his back to me. He ran his hand along the spines of those red field guides. "Finn said you two used to go to the Cloisters a lot."

I could tell he was trying to change the subject, and I didn't want to let him.

"I thought you didn't do art," I said.

"No, I'm not good. It was just a class. That's all. So, tell me, what do they have at the Cloisters, then?"

"You've never been?"

He shook his head.

I turned away quickly, because I didn't want him to see my smile. I didn't want him to catch how happy it made me to know that Finn had saved that special place for me.

"Go on," Toby said. "Tell me what it's like. I want to know."

"Really?"

Toby nodded, and I started to picture the Cloisters in my head.

"Well, it doesn't look like much from the outside. That's the first thing. But once you get in it's like you're not even in New York anymore. Not even in America."

I told him how the very second you got in the doors it was like you'd been lifted right out of the city and into the Middle Ages. I told him about the wide, curving stone steps that took you up to the main cloisters and how the walls were made of big blocks of stone, just like in a castle. Toby sat himself down cross-legged on the rug to listen, and I told him about the herb gardens in the courtyards. Lungwort and bryony and comfrey and yarrow.

In my mind, I was there walking with Finn. Him rubbing a leaf between his fingers for the scent. Telling me about the doctrine of signatures, which meant that God had signed every medicinal plant so you could tell what it would cure. Red ones for blood disorders. Yellow for jaundice. Other plants I didn't even remember the names of, with roots shaped like hemorrhoids or kidneys or the heart. Finn said it was all nonsense but that it was a nice idea. Nice to imagine someone signing their name to the world. I didn't tell Toby about that. About Finn and me there. I stuck to the hard, graceful curve of the stone over the archways and the cobblestoned paths and the impossibly detailed tapestries. I never mentioned a word about Finn, but still, when I looked down, I saw that Toby's eyes were wet with tears.

"What is it?"

He wiped his eyes and tried to put on a smile. "I don't know," he said, laughing a little bit. "Everything, I suppose."

And right then I felt my heart soften to Toby, because I knew exactly what he meant. I understood how just about anything in the world could remind you of Finn. Trains, or New York City, or plants, or books, or soft sweet black-and-white cookies, or some guy in Central Park playing a polka on the harmonica and the violin at the same time. Things you'd never even seen with Finn could remind you of him, because he was the one person you'd want to show. "Look at that," you'd want to say, because you knew he would find a way to think it was wonderful. To make you feel like the most observant person in the world for spotting it.

I sat down next to Toby on the floor, close enough so our arms almost touched. We sat there for what seemed like a long time, neither of us saying anything, until finally Toby broke the silence.

"You do know that if you ever need anything, you can ring me, right? Anything at all."

I nodded. "You always say that."

"But I want you to know that I mean it. I'm not only saying it to be nice. You can ring me the same way you would have rung Finn. Just to talk or anything. Anything at all."

I told him I knew that he meant it, but I could tell the tone of my voice was saying that I'd never actually call. That he wasn't Finn. And even though he sounded like he meant it, deep down I had a feeling he *was* just saying it to be nice.

"I should probably get going," I said.

Toby offered to walk me to Grand Central. The weather had changed while we were buried in the basement. When I left school there were only a few clouds, but by the time we left Finn's building the whole sky was dark. We'd only walked a few blocks when the first fat raindrops splashed down.

"Shit," Toby said. "No umbrella."

We ducked into a deli, hoping maybe we could wait it out, but after we'd made three rounds of the aisles, the guy behind the counter stepped out and asked if we needed any help. Toby told him we were just looking for some mints, and the guy pressed his lips together hard and pointed to the candy rack in front of the register.

We walked downtown in the rain, both of us sucking on those hot, spicy mints we hadn't meant to buy. When the spiciness started to kick in, I almost spat mine out, but then I didn't. I thought it was good to test yourself sometimes. It was good to see how much you could take.

Toby asked me for one of my Finn stories. I hesitated for a few seconds, deciding, then finally I told him about how once on Thanksgiving, when everyone else was watching the football game, Finn and I snuck out of the house and walked into the woods until we were lost. "Just the two of us," I said, "because we hated football." I told Toby how good the woods smelled and that Finn made us a little campfire using only sticks and then we sat huddled in close and Finn taught me what all the Latin words in the *Lacrimosa* part of Mozart's *Requiem* meant, and we sang it over and over again in our wobbly singing voices until I knew all of it by heart. I said that Finn told me he wanted to stay there forever, that he never wanted to go back to the city again, but he knew he couldn't. Then, I said, we followed our tracks home and saw that we weren't even very lost at all. When we got back, my mother had two pieces of pumpkin pie with Cool Whip saved for us, and we ate them without telling anybody where we'd been.

"Hmmm. That's quite something, June."

"Yup."

Toby started telling me about this time Finn tried to disguise himself so he could go to an exhibit of his own work and hear what people were saying about it. Toby rambled on with his story, but I was drifting away until all of a sudden the shiny roundness of a rain-slicked manhole caught my eye and I stopped in the middle of the sidewalk.

Toby kept walking.

"Hey," I shouted to him. "What do you know about those buttons? Those black buttons on the portrait?"

Toby was a few steps ahead, but he heard me and stopped. He didn't turn right away. For a few seconds he just stood there. When he finally did turn around, he had a pleading expression on his face. He looked guilty and embarrassed, and I could see that he knew exactly what I was talking about.

He pulled me over to the side, so I was standing under the little awning of a building while he stood right out in the rain. Then he started apologizing again and again before he told me what happened.

"All right," he said, like he'd reached some kind of decision. He breathed out long and slow. "This is really hard." He paced across the sidewalk before spinning around and coming back.

"You don't have to tell me," I said, though I didn't mean it.

He seemed to think about that for a moment before shaking his head. He paced away from me then back again before saying anything. "Okay, well . . . The portrait looks good, right?"

I nodded.

"But Finn didn't think so. 'It has to be perfect. More detail. It needs more detail.' That's what he kept saying. He'd get me to bring it to him. Next to the bed. He could hardly see, hardly lift his head. If you'd seen him . . . It was all he could talk about, June. Do you see? And so I promised. I said I'd do what I could. I'd make it perfect." Toby hung his head. "There. All right? Now you know."

I pictured those clumsy buttons, and even I couldn't believe that Toby would think they made the painting better. He must have seen the look on my face, because right away he said, "Yeah. I know. I completely bollocksed it. But you don't know what it was like. It was just the two of us that afternoon, and then . . . and then it was just me." I watched his face, and I could see he was going back to that day. "It was so, so quiet, and I thought if I could only make something right. One thing . . . and I couldn't even do that. Not even black buttons."

My heart was pounding because I couldn't help picturing the apartment on that day. Finn suddenly still and gone. Toby desperate and fumbling. I bit my lip because I could feel the twitchiness at the corner of my mouth that meant I was going to cry, and I didn't want to cry in front of Toby. Rain dripped from my soaked hair down across my face, and Toby's dark eyes were staring into mine, waiting for my response. I wasn't going to cry. I wasn't, but then all at once the tears were there, unstoppable.

I started to walk away, but then I turned back. I decided to stop even trying to hold back the tears. I decided to stand there under an awning on Madison Avenue and let Toby see me. Let him understand that I missed Finn just as much as he did. And once I started, there was no way of stopping. Everything that had been squashed down and pressed into a hard tight ball in the center of my heart came undone. I stood there, shaking and heaving on Madison Avenue in front of Toby, waiting for him to run away or shove me into a taxi, but he didn't. He stepped in, put his long arms around me, and leaned his head on my shoulder. We stood there under that awning until I could feel that he was crying too. The click of Toby's mint against his teeth, and the high squeal of car brakes, and the rain plinking on the canvas over our heads all joined with our low deep sobs to make a kind of music that afternoon. It turned the whole city into a chorus of our sadness, and after a while it almost stopped feeling bad and turned into something else. It started to feel like relief.

When we pulled apart, I couldn't look Toby in the eye.

I heard him whisper, "Sorry." I heard him say, "I'm not an artist, June. I'm so sorry . . . for everything. All of it."

I gave the tiniest of shrugs, then I spat my mint into my hand and tossed it onto the sidewalk.

"These are gross," I said.

Toby smiled.

"Yeah," he said. But he didn't spit his out. He kept it in his mouth, where it must have burned at his tongue until it was all gone.

Thirty-Seven

It was late at night. That same day. Way after everybody was fast asleep. I was sitting in the kitchen, on the floor, with the *Book of Days* open on my lap. I cupped my hand around the phone receiver and whispered.

"I'm calling to tell you that I made it all up."

"Oh . . . right. You what?" Toby's voice sounded dopey, like I'd woken him from some thick kind of dream.

"The story. My Finn story. It wasn't true."

"Oh. It's you, June. Hi. What time is it?"

"Late. Sorry for waking you up."

"I wasn't sleeping. Just resting with some brandy."

I laughed with my mouth closed, trying not to make any noise. I reached over to the cabinet next to the dishwasher. The thin one that was my parents' liquor cabinet. I looked around until I saw the brandy. I set it on the floor next to me and tapped my finger against the top of the bottle.

"Anyway, so I still owe you a story."

"Are you sure yours wasn't true? I, for one, believed every word."

I smiled, even though I thought Toby might be making fun of me. "Come on."

"No, really. Very good use of detail. Top marks." Toby was whispering, even though he was all alone on his end.

We were both quiet for a few seconds, then Toby said, "You know, it's all right, June. You don't have to give me one of your stories if you don't want to." I heard him take a sip of his brandy.

I unscrewed the bottle in my hands, dipped a finger in, then touched it to my tongue.

"No. I want to. Next time."

I could almost hear Toby smiling on the other end.

"Come whenever. Whenever you can. You know that, right? If you need anything . . ."

I thought that if I was drowning in the ocean, Finn would be like a strong, polished wooden ship with sails that always caught the wind. And Toby? Well, Toby was more like a big yellow rubber raft that might pop at any moment. But maybe he'd still be there. That's what I was starting to think.

I nodded and tipped the bottle to my lips. The brandy shot through my body with so much heat that for a second I felt like my insides might have turned to lava.

"I know," I whispered.

Again, quiet.

"Well . . . Good night, then," I said.

"Good dreams, June."

I stretched out flat on my back on the cold linoleum floor and held the receiver against my chest. The only sound in the kitchen was the ticking of the yellow clock high up on the wall over the sink. It must have been a minute or two like that, and then in that quiet dark kitchen I heard my name.

"June."

I put the receiver to my ear.

"Yeah."

"Go to bed."

"Okay," I whispered. "You too."

Then I hung up, leaving Toby all by himself in Finn's apartment.

I didn't know how to seal a promise with a dead person. With someone who isn't dead, you can get a pair of scissors and snip a tiny little cut into your clothes. The clothes can't be scrappy clothes. They have to be newish ones that you wear all the time and that you'd be in huge trouble for cutting. The cut can be anywhere. Just on the inside hem or in the armpit, and it can be as small as you can possibly make it. That was one of the tricks. Learning to make really small cuts. Those are the rules Greta and I used for sealing promises when we were little. When we were too scared to use blood.

I stood and pulled a postcard of Miami Beach off the bulletin board and tossed it onto the counter. I held the thumbtack in my hand and poked it into my index finger, squeezing until a drop of blood sat there like a tiny jewel. I read Finn's note one more time, then pressed my finger down hard right in the middle of it.

Finn was right. I could tell. Toby had nobody. But it was okay. It was all sealed. He had me now.

Thirty-Eight

March was going out like a lamb. Just like in the saying. The trees were still bare, but other than that and the scrappy remnants of snow in the corners of big parking lots, winter seemed to be gone.

Posters for *South Pacific* had started to go up all over town. They put them up early so that if enough performances sold out, there would be time to schedule a couple of extra nights. It was Beans who won the contest to design the posters. She'd made the *S* of South and the *P* of Pacific look like palm trees, and the whole poster was shaped like a tiki hut. It was pretty good, and I thought I'd make sure to tell her that next time I saw her.

Everything was starting to feel springy except my parents, who were entering the haggard phase of tax season. The gray stripe in my mother's hair was getting wider, and I hadn't seen my father clean-shaven for days and days. Greta and I were on the verge of stew poisoning, which, we used to say, is when your blood actually turns into gravy.

I left school and walked straight downtown to the bank.

Gold leaf—real gold leaf—is expensive, but gold paint can sometimes look just as good and it's the same price as any other color. I bought a tiny bottle of gold paint and a thin paintbrush from Kmart. I'd been keeping them in the side pocket of my backpack, right next to the key to the safety-deposit box.

This time, Mr. Zimmer didn't say anything about AIDS. He acted normal and took me right down to the basement.

"We'll be closing up in about half an hour," he said, looking at his watch. "I'll give a knock so you have some time to pack up, okay?"

"Thanks. That's great," I said.

I laid the painting flat on the desk and touched a finger to each black button. One at a time. They didn't look so ugly now. Now that I knew their story, they were almost kind of beautiful. Shiny black pearls. Then I traced the skull on Greta's hand with my finger.

I propped the painting up against the wall and smiled at it. Finn would like—no, he would *love* this thing I was going to do. I pulled out the jar of paint and the brush from my backpack and set them on the desk. It took some effort to unscrew the lid, but I got it after a few seconds. A light whiff of paint fumes filled the room and I breathed in deep, because that smell reminded me so much of Finn. Then I dipped the brush into the jar and scraped it against the edge. I stopped, my hand hovering over the surface of the painting, suddenly scared to touch the bristles to the canvas. But I knew Finn. I wasn't like the people who tried to finish the *Requiem* for Mozart. I knew what Finn would say.

So I started, lightly at first, dragging the brush down a strand of my hair in the portrait. Then I did one of Greta's. I stepped back and looked, like artists do. Tilting my head like I'd always watched Finn doing when he was trying to size something up. I didn't want to do too much. I knew how easy it could be to get carried away. I dipped the brush again, and in that little underground room I tried to imagine Finn's hand guiding mine, barely touching, his soft palm against the back of my hand. I imagined that and let the brush slowly stroke down the length of my painted hair, the hair Finn had made. His work. How close did Finn have to look to make this other me? What did he see? Could he tell that I always wore Bonne Bell bubblegum lip gloss when I went to see him? Did he see me studying his bare feet while he was working on the canvas? Could he read my heart? I'd like to think he couldn't. I'd like to think I had enough skill to keep that much hidden.

I did a few more strands of my hair, then a few more of Greta's. I stepped back again. What I was going for was something like the wings of the angels in one of the illuminated manuscripts downstairs at the Cloisters. Something a little bit like that but not exactly, because we didn't have wings, only boring straight hair. But illuminated. I wanted that painting to beam with gold. I wanted it to sing out about Finn and how much I loved him. The way Toby's buttons did, if you knew the story.

I screwed the cap back on the paint, wrapped the brush in a piece of loose-leaf paper, and slipped them both into my backpack. We were all on that portrait now. The three of us. Greta, Toby, and me.

And the wolf. As I slid the painting back into its metal box I caught a glimpse of him. Still there, still hiding in the shadow of the negative space.

Thirty-Nine

"What are you wearing?"

I looked down at myself.

"My maroon skirt and a gray sweater."

"No, brainless. To the party. On Saturday."

"I don't know. Why?"

"Ben asked if you were going."

I rolled my eyes.

We were at the end of the driveway, waiting for the bus, which was even later than usual. Greta looked tired. She wasn't wearing makeup, and her hair was twisted into a messy bun. The strap on her usual backpack had broken on the way home from school earlier in the week, and so she had to use this old Snoopy one from years ago, where Woodstock is fluttering around Snoopy's head, just about to land.

"Why are you always trying to get me to care about Ben Dellahunt anyway? I hardly even know him."

She let out a frustrated breath. "You are so hopeless."

"No, really."

She pursed her lips, put her hands on her hips, and stared at me. "Maybe I'm trying to help you. Did you ever think of that?"

"No."

I saw a look pass over Greta's face then. Like she wanted to say something but couldn't do it. "Whatever, June. What. Ever. You . . . you . . ."

"What?"

"Nothing."

"Anyway," I said, "maybe you should think about what *you're* going to wear to the party. Maybe you're not looking so great either."

Greta spun around, hands on her hips. Her face had turned from normal to murderous in an instant.

"I know you weren't at the rehearsal on Monday. You're a big liar, June. You told Mom and me and you think nobody's gonna find out where you go? You really think you can keep your big secret forever?" She was actually shouting at me. Right out on the street. It felt like a bomb going off, and I stood there frozen. Then, just as fast, Greta turned her back to me and walked to the other side of the maple tree. She leaned up against it so her whole body disappeared. All I could see was one of her feet edging out from the trunk, tapping at the dirt. We waited another five minutes for the bus, and the whole time I watched Greta's dainty foot tapping, like she was sending some kind of Morse code message into the ground.

That night my parents came home in time for dinner. Greta had mentioned that there was no rehearsal, so they decided it would be nice to have a real family dinner together. I was glad I was there, that I hadn't made plans to go to the city. Sometimes I didn't even remember that I kind of missed my parents during tax season. It was only when they were finally around that I'd remember how nice it was to have them there. When I got my own dinner I just ladled some stew into a bowl, but when my mother did it she'd make garlic bread and a salad and she'd put a dollop of sour cream on everybody's stew. It felt like a real meal instead of just something you were supposed to do.

Greta and I were doing homework at opposite ends of the kitchen table when they got home that night. Greta had made a wall out of her biology and calculus textbooks so she wouldn't have to look at me. She laid them down when my father came in the door.

"Guess what I have," my father said, raising a Caldor bag over his head. He had a huge grin on his face.

"What is it?" I said.

"Guess."

Greta eyed the bag. "Trivial Pursuit," she said.

"Oh," he said, looking disappointed. "Well, okay. I guess you got it."

The disappointment hung on his face for a few seconds, but as soon as he had the box open, he started to get excited all over again. I figured we were probably the only family in the nation not to own Trivial Pursuit. My father always held out on buying the latest thing. He always said the smart people waited awhile, until the price came down.

"So who's up for a game?" he said, shaking the little pie pieces out onto the table.

Even though it was a weeknight we played until late. All four of us. My mother made popcorn and instant iced tea, which was sweet and lemony.

It was the first game in years that our parents were actually good at, and even though Greta refused to look at me for the whole game, it was fun.

"*Who played aging rodeo rider Junior Bonner?*" Greta read out, and right away my mother knew it.

"Steve McQueen," she said, without a second of hesitation.

I got a few of the science ones like, *What element's chemical symbol is Fe?* and *What is the scientific name for the Northern Lights?*, but mostly they were really hard. The funniest ones were the sports questions that were actually about drinking. Greta got *How do you make a Black Russian black?* which she had no trouble getting right. The answer was Tia Maria *or* Kahlua, and Greta knew both.

In the end, my dad won it with a history question: "*A 1962 agreement between Britain and France led to the building of what?*" Greta asked.

"Ummm . . . Concorde?" he said.

We all groaned, and he sat there in complete disbelief.

"I won it? I won a game?"

My mother went up to bed and Greta left to call a friend, but my father and I sat there, reading out questions from the box to each other and sipping iced tea, until we could barely keep our eyes open. Every once in a while a question like *What is a prestidigitator?* would come up, and I would think of Toby.

"Dad?"

"Wait a second, let me get a new one."

"No. I have a real question."

He nodded. "Okay, shoot."

"Did you know Uncle Finn's . . . special friend?" I nearly gagged on those stupid words, but I didn't want to give anything away.

He looked over his shoulder, down the hall. I guessed he was making sure my mother was long gone. Then he turned back to me.

"I met him a couple times. When they first moved here. That was maybe eight, nine years ago. What do you want to know?"

"Just . . . Mom. She seems to hate him and, I don't know, I can't imagine Finn being with someone who was that bad."

He picked up his plastic pie and tipped the little triangles out onto the table. Then one by one he loaded them back in. He sighed.

"Okay. I'm going to tell you a couple things, and I'm going to trust you not to make a big deal about them. I'm going to trust you particularly not to repeat them to your mother, okay?" I nodded, and he went on. "I don't want you thinking your mother's . . . I want you to see where she's coming from."

"Okay."

"You looked at Finn and your mother as adults, and it was like they were so different you'd hardly know they were brother and sister, right? Your mother the accountant; Finn in the city with his art and everything. But that's not how it used to be. When they were kids, right up through their teenage years, the two of them were together all the time. They'd move to some new army base and it was just the two of them. I don't know much about art—okay, I don't know anything about art—but as far as drawing's concerned, your mother had a talent. She talks about it sometimes. How she and Finn would go off somewhere and draw and draw. Has she ever said anything to you about that?"

I shook my head. "I never even knew she did drawings."

"Exactly."

I thought of that sketchbook Finn gave her years ago. The look on her face in that restaurant.

"You know, she still has the metal watercolor tin they used to take out with them. She said they used to have plans. That the two of them would move to New York and be artists there. They talked about it like it was real. Like it was really going to happen one day. You know Finn. When he said things, you couldn't help believing in them. She couldn't help thinking he'd find a way to make it happen. And then one day he was just gone. Of course he was young—only seventeen—but she was absolutely crushed. He left a note saying he'd come back, that he'd meet her in New York when he figured things out, but it wasn't enough. She couldn't get over it. He traveled all over the world. Paris, London, Berlin. He'd send her postcards of his exhibits, which she said was worse than hearing nothing at all. And then one day he came back. He was really in New York. But by then we were married. By that time we had you and Greta and she hadn't painted or drawn anything for years. We went down together to the city to see Finn, and she was giddy. I could be wrong here, but I think she might have secretly hoped she would finally get her chance to do her own art. That maybe we'd move down into the city and somehow she would work with Finn."

I wasn't sure, but I thought I saw a little bit of hurt on my father's face then. He tipped the pie pieces back out onto the table and let them sit there.

"That day in the city, we met Finn at a coffee shop, but he wasn't alone. Toby was with him. And all the enthusiasm Danni had carried with her into the city seeped away when she saw the two of them together. I didn't understand it then. I thought Toby seemed okay. Sort of a weird kind of guy, but nice enough. But your mother, she took an instant dislike to him. Later, she told me Finn had written to her about Toby. Told her about his past. I don't know the whole story, but apparently he'd been in some pretty bad trouble. That's what she always went back to. How he was unsuitable. How he was using Finn. And then years later when Finn got sick . . . Well, Toby was her answer for everything. He made Finn lazy, made him stop painting, took him away from his family, and then on top of all that he gave him AIDS. I think she imagined that somehow without Toby things might have been different between her and Finn. Danni always said Finn deserved better. But the truth is, I don't think it had anything to do with what Toby had done in his past or anything like that. He could have been the winner of the Nobel Peace Prize and Danni would have had a problem with him. I think . . ." My dad looked down and nudged the pie pieces. "I think your mother was embarrassed about the way things had turned out. Embarrassed that she'd gone and become an accountant. That she'd married a boring old numbers guy like me and was living in the dreaded suburbs. There was Finn, New York City artist, with his cool English boyfriend, and there she was, accountant, mother of two, in the 'burbs, sitting next to me, the uncoolest guy imaginable."

This time I was sure there was some hurt in his voice.

"Did you ever see any of Mom's drawings?"

"Just once. Grandma Weiss showed them to me. Your mother didn't know anything about it. Grandma Weiss said she'd always felt guilty about it. That Danni never got her chance to do what she wanted. I'd say she was as good as Finn. Maybe, I don't know . . . maybe even better."

I went to the fridge and got out the carton of milk. I poured out a glass for me and a glass for my dad.

"I don't think Mom's embarrassed about you."

He smiled. "Thanks, Junie. Maybe you're right."

I sipped my milk and my dad sipped his and we sat there in the quiet night kitchen, thinking our own thoughts.

"Dad?"

"Yeah?"

"So, how did Finn become my godfather, then? If Mom was so mad at him."

"Oh, she wasn't angry with Finn. Nobody ever stayed angry with Finn. It was all Toby. You didn't even have a godfather until you were five. Did you know that? Your mother always had Finn in mind. She kept hoping. Then Finn started writing, saying he was thinking of moving to the city. He never mentioned that Toby would be coming with him. He said he was thinking about coming back from England and getting an apartment downtown somewhere. That's when she asked him, and he seemed over the moon about the idea. I remember we laughed about it because he said he'd get here as soon as he could. Like it was some kind of emergency." My dad paused, like he was remembering it again. "I think maybe your mother thought making

Finn your godfather was one way to keep him. A tie to hold him. I think Finn saw it kind of differently. Like maybe he and Toby would be your godparents together. A way to settle down. A way to have their own strange kind of family or something. Or maybe that's nonsense. Maybe it's just getting way too late."

He yawned a big exaggerated yawn and patted his hand over his mouth. Then he picked up our glasses from the table and set them down in the sink. He looked at me thoughtfully and after a while said, "So, does that solve all the mysteries of the universe?"

I smiled. "Yeah," I said. "Maybe a few of them."

Forty

The next morning I sat by myself near the back of the bus. I found a blank page in my English notebook, which wasn't hard because I don't really take notes in English. If you read *Of Mice and Men,* why would you need to go through the trouble of writing down that George and Lennie had an extraordinary friendship or that Lennie's death was inevitable? You'd just know those things. Those things are impossible to forget.

At the top of the page I wrote this:

Looking After Toby . . .
Phase 1: Call him and visit him whenever possible.
Phase 2: Something big and spectacular (a work in progress).

I left school as soon as I could that day. I risked cutting woodshop and study hall so I could catch the 1:43 train. When I buzzed up, Toby answered the door in his pajamas and an old fuzzy blue bathrobe that reminded me of the Cookie Monster from *Sesame Street.* His eyes were huge, bigger than I'd ever seen them.

"Sorry it's so cold in here, but come in. This is lovely. It's lovely to see you."

I didn't think it was cold at all, but I didn't say anything. The thing that was worth apologizing for was what a huge mess the place was.

There were dirty plates and glasses everywhere, records lying around out of their sleeves, and at least three ashtrays overflowing with tea bags and cigarette butts. I didn't care much about that kind of thing, but Finn's apartment had never been a mess, so it seemed almost like a different place.

I picked up a couple of plates and headed toward the kitchen.

"No, no, no," Toby said. "Leave them." He took them out of my hands and set them back down on the coffee table.

"I don't mind. I can help with things."

"I know, but it's my mess." He stopped and glanced around. As he scanned the room, he seemed to understand something. He looked at me, embarrassed.

"It bothers you, doesn't it?" he said softly. "To see it like this."

I shrugged.

"You're right. It's appalling." He gave a sheepish grin. "Finn would *kill* me if he saw it."

No, he wouldn't, I thought.

"Come on, then," Toby said. "We'll clean things."

For the next hour I collected plates and cups and maybe a dozen little ruby-colored crystal glasses from all over the house. I shuttled them into the kitchen, and Toby stood at the sink, washing. When the dishes were all cleared, I sat down cross-legged in front of a big stack of loose records, trying to match sleeves and jackets.

"*This* Finn would kill you for," I said when Toby came in. He was drying his hands on a green checked dish towel.

"I know."

He sat down on the floor and started sorting through the records with me. I secretly watched him. At first it hadn't seemed right that some of the things I'd loved about Finn might have come from Toby, but I'd started to think that maybe there was something good about it. Maybe it would work the other way too. If I looked carefully enough, I might be able to catch glimpses of Finn shining right through Toby.

Toby slid a stack of records into a rack, then glanced down at me. He grinned and popped a cassette into the tape player. He sat down in Finn's blue chair, and all of a sudden the whole room filled with this super-intricate classical-guitar music. Bach, I thought it was. And familiar. I thought I'd heard that music before. Like maybe Finn had played this exact tape when I was visiting once.

"What is this?" I asked.

"Do you like it?" Toby turned away and bent to pick up another record.

"Yeah. It's"—I fished around in my mind for something smart to say—"complex."

"Is that good or bad?"

"Good. Complicated is the bad one. Complex is good, right? So what is it anyway?"

"Just something I used to do."

"You?"

He nodded.

"But it sounds like two or three guitars."

"That's the trick. That's why it's so difficult. Golden hands, remember?"

I looked at Toby. How his long body barely fit in the chair. How I knew him but didn't know him at all. I was starting to understand why Finn would choose him. I could see that Toby actually had something to offer. But what did I have? What would I ever have? I was doomed to mediocrity. Like Salieri in *Amadeus*. There's Salieri, knowing he'll never be as good as Mozart, and on top of all that he's the villain. He's the one everyone ends up hating.

I looked away. "Yeah," I said. "Golden hands."

I told Toby I had to go to the bathroom but ducked into the bedroom instead. I opened a few dresser drawers and rifled around in the closet. I slid open drawer after drawer, looking for something, but I didn't know what. Maybe it was something that didn't exist. Maybe I was hoping for some small object that would prove all the hours I'd spent with Finn meant as much to him as they meant to me. Instead, I picked up a pair of boxer shorts from the third drawer down. I unfolded them and held them up in front of me, trying to figure out whose they were.

"You can have whatever you want, you know."

I spun around. Toby was standing in the doorway, his shoulder leaned up against the frame. I stood there facing him, those blue boxer shorts stretched between my hands like a map. "I might not recommend a pair of my underpants as the prime choice, but, you know, feel free."

There were so many layers of embarrassment in that moment. I stood there blushing so hard my head felt like it might burst. I balled up the boxers and set them down on the top of the dresser.

"I'm really sorry, I'm . . ." I could feel hot tears starting to form, and I looked down at the floor.

"Hey," Toby said. "Don't worry about it."

He stepped into the room and sat on the edge of Finn's side of the bed. He patted the space next to him, and without looking him in the eye I skulked over and sat down. He put his long arm around my shoulders, and I found myself leaning my head against his chest. We sat in that dim room for a long time, neither of us saying anything. I could see the pictures on Finn's bedside table. Toby looking young and even kind of beautiful in his weird way, with his dark eyes and his scruffy hair. I snuggled in closer and I felt his arms squeeze in tighter. It felt good. Toby was warm and kind and, in a strange way, almost familiar. And sad. Just like me.

"Hey, you know, I've been thinking," Toby said. "You know that I'm dying, right?"

Toby had never said anything like that before. Nothing so big. So definite. I felt numb. Like cold, hard concrete had been poured into all the little spaces in my head where I'd been hiding maybes.

"I guess."

"Do you see what that means?"

"I think so."

"Tell me."

"It means you won't be here much longer."

Toby nodded. "Yes, there's that, but, also, do you see? It means I can do whatever I want. We can do anything we want." For a weird second, sitting on the bed like that, I thought Toby meant having sex. I gave him a grossed-out look and he pulled away from me so quickly I almost fell off the bed. He sat there with his arms crossed over his chest saying, "No, no, no. Nothing like *that*. Oh, June, God, you don't think."

"Ugh," I said. "Don't be so gross."

That was one of Greta's tricks. Make the other person think the gross thing was their idea and you're off the hook.

Toby's posture loosened. "Okay. All right. Seriously, June."

I stood and wandered around the room. I picked up a glass paperweight and let my fingers slide over the smooth cold surface. I thought about what Toby had said about being able to do anything. It didn't quite make sense.

"Well, no offense or anything, but *I'm* not dying."

"No. But what's the worst thing that could happen to you? Me, I could get sent to jail or deported, but now it wouldn't matter. I'm free. Do you see?"

"Yeah, I think so."

"So, tell me. If you could do anything, what would you want to do? Whatever you want, June."

I couldn't think of anything right away. Also, I didn't think Toby understood that even though I couldn't probably go to prison, I could get in all kinds of other trouble at home.

"Well, I don't know. It's a nice offer and all. I'll think about it, okay?"

"I didn't mean to put you on the spot. Take some time. Mull it over."

"Toby?"

"Yeah?"

"How long is not much longer?"

Usually I wouldn't ask something like that. Usually I wouldn't want to know. Greta always wanted to know everything. Every little detail. But I understood. You can ruin anything if you know too much. But things were different now. I was in charge of taking care of Toby. I needed to know things.

Toby shrugged. "I'm not really one for doctors." Then he put on a flaky, airy voice and said, "One day at a time, June. One day at a time."

Toby leaned over to his side table and pulled out two cigarettes. I smiled, because I'd been practicing in the far corner of my backyard when nobody was home. I sat down on the bed and tilted my head back to take a great deep pull off the cigarette. The smoke felt warm and good, like a blanket laid out all along the inside of my body.

"Finn didn't even seem to care that he was dying," I said. And it was true. Finn was as calm as ever right up to the very last time I saw him.

"Don't you know? That's the secret. If you always make sure you're exactly the person you hoped to be, if you always make sure you know only the very best people, then you won't care if you die tomorrow."

"That doesn't make any sense. If you were so happy, then you'd want to stay alive, wouldn't you? You'd want to be alive forever, so you could keep being happy." I reached over and tapped my ash into a pretty pottery dish that Toby was using for an ashtray.

"No, no. It's the most *un*happy people who want to stay alive, because they think they haven't done everything they want to do. They think they haven't had enough time. They feel like they've been short-changed."

Toby flattened both his hands and mimed pressing them up against a window. "Wax on, wax off," he said, moving one hand at a time in a flat arc. "You're turning me into Mr. Miyagi with all this talk. I feel like I'm in *The Karate Kid*."

I laughed so hard, because I couldn't imagine Toby ever watching that movie. What he'd said still didn't really make sense, but there was a tiny flicker of something I felt like I was almost catching. Just for a second it felt like I understood, and then it evaporated again.

"What about you?" I said.

"Me?"

I nodded. "I mean . . . have you been shortchanged?"

Toby took a long drag of his cigarette and stretched his arm across the bed.

"I suppose I'm in that very small group of people who are not waiting for their own story to unfold. If my life was a film, I'd have walked out by now."

"Well, I wouldn't," I said. "I wouldn't walk out."

"That's because you haven't seen the first half."

"Tell me, then. All of it."

Toby ran a hand through his hair, frowning for a second.

"Another time, all right? Another day. Look, it's nice out. For once you haven't brought the rain with you." He smiled to let me know he was joking. "Let's go out somewhere."

I understood right then that I would never know the real story of Toby's life. There was no other time. Everything between Toby and me was in the here and now. That's all there was. The here and now and Finn. No other history, just scraps and the next few months. And, you know, there was something perfect about that. It meant that everything could be put right. Everything could be new and exactly how it should be.

"Is that what you're wearing?" I said, pointing at the fuzzy blue robe.

"Only if you want me to," he said in a jokey voice. I got up and left the bedroom, pulling the door closed behind me so he could change.

When I was in the city, I always had the feeling that everyone could see right through me. Like all the real city people could see immediately that I was from the suburbs. No matter what I wore or how cool I tried to look, I could tell that Westchester was written all over me, head to toe. But not when I was with Finn. Finn was like a ticket into being a real city person. He had a glow that covered me in authentic city light. I thought it would be like that with Toby too. But it wasn't. With Toby, I felt like we were both strangers in this place. I didn't just feel like I was from the suburbs but like I was from someplace a world away from here. Like I didn't belong but also like I didn't want to. Like I didn't care. And in lots of ways that felt just as good as blending in. Maybe even better.

It was a beautiful afternoon. Bright blue sky and warm, and everyone we passed seemed to be in a good mood. We walked over to Riverside Park, which is long and thin and stretches along the Hudson right up to 158th Street. It was good to have someone to talk to again, and I talked way too much. I told Toby about Greta. About *South Pacific* and *Annie*. How Greta was probably about to become a Broadway star.

Toby laughed. "Broadway? Oh June, Finn would have loved to see her up there."

Then I told him how I'd found her all covered in leaves after the party. I told him how the two of us used to be best friends but how we weren't anymore. How Greta hated me.

"She doesn't really hate you," Toby said. But I told him she did. She really, really did.

"And there's another party Saturday," I said. "She roped me into another party and I don't even want to go."

"Maybe you'll have fun."

I gave him a look that said there was no chance of that happening. Toby gave me a sympathetic look back.

"That's why Finn painted the portrait, you know," he said after a while. "He had this idea that if he painted you together like that, then you'd always be connected. I don't know exactly what he was thinking. He wanted to do something because of how things ended up between him and your mother."

"What do you mean?"

Toby's forehead creased and he didn't answer me at first. Then he seemed to come to a decision.

"I shouldn't tell you any of this; it's not my place. But who cares? What does it matter now? Finn always felt sad that he and Danielle weren't close, that she'd drifted away from him. They used to be so close. Because of all the moving. They were all each other had for so many years. She was the one who made sure their father never had any idea about Finn being gay. Finn didn't care who knew, but she understood what it would mean. Especially with their father being this big military guy. She'd set up fake dates with her friends for Finn. And of course they all ended up falling in love with him, so it was kind of cruel, really."

I blushed.

"He told me he never meant to be away so long. You know about that, right? How Finn left?" I nodded like I'd known for years. Like it wasn't just another thing nobody had bothered to fill me in on. "He told me he wrote to her all the time. Right from the day he left. On the bus out of town. For years he didn't hear anything back. Not a single letter. And, you know, I can understand it. But Finn never meant his leaving to be hurtful. He didn't see it as leaving anyone behind. He always thought he'd be back in a few months. But when she didn't write and he started being out in the world . . . Well, he was seventeen. You can imagine."

I couldn't. I didn't want to.

"He said he even sent her money once. To meet him in Berlin. Maybe that was her chance to do something different. I don't know. But she didn't go, so that was that. Then finally he comes back and he's nothing like the little brother she knew. The young boy on the beach. And the next thing you know he's sick and there's Danni losing him all over again. None of it's fair. None of this. This thing about me not being part of Finn's relationship with you, the whole thing is about Danielle wanting to say to Finn that he can't have everything. That he needed to make a sacrifice, too. He always felt like he owed Danni something . . . and I suppose I ended up being that thing."

"But it's so stupid. It didn't solve anything."

"Of course it didn't."

I thought of my mother's story. The one about Finn carrying that enormous horseshoe crab for her.

"But if they loved each other so much, couldn't they talk it out?"

Toby gave an exasperated laugh. "You get into habits. Ways of being with certain people." He stared over at an empty bench. He gazed at it like he could see all the people who'd ever sat there and all the people who might ever sit there in the future. Or maybe he was just thinking about Finn. "It's hard sometimes, you know? Hard to stop. Finn didn't want that to happen to you and Greta. So he stuck you into that portrait together."

Two women in tennis skirts jogged by us, then we passed a man walking two droopy basset hounds. The dogs were panting, their tongues almost grazing the ground.

How would a portrait stop Greta from despising me? And then I had a thought. Maybe it was Finn who'd sent the portrait to the paper. Maybe, somehow, that was all part of what he was thinking. Thrusting us out into the world like that. The two of us in the limelight together for everyone to see. But how would that change anything?

Toby stopped at a Slush Puppie stand and bought an orange one for me and a blue-raspberry one for himself. We sat on the steps of the Soldiers' and Sailors' Monument, slurping through our thick straws.

"I'm sorry," I said.

"About what?"

"About you having to hide yourself away for me."

He shrugged. "It's not your fault."

I knew it wasn't, but somehow the thought of it being my mother's fault seemed worse than taking it on myself. It was such a childish demand to make—so desperate and petty—and I didn't want to think of my mother that way. It made me feel sorry for her.

"Hey," I said, trying to lighten things up. "Who asked Matilda to go a-waltzing?"

"What's that?"

"Trivial Pursuit. It's a question. I'm testing you."

"Oh, no. Tests aren't my strong point. Let me see . . ." He started humming the song at first, but then he began to sing. It was all out of tune, and I put my hand over my mouth to stop laughing. It was hard to believe someone could make such beautiful music with a guitar and be so awful at singing. "A jolly swagman. That's it, isn't it?"

I nodded, still laughing. "What is a swagman anyway?"

"I reckon it's someone like a hobo. A wanderer."

Sometimes, like right then, Toby's accent came through really strong. I loved those times. He spoke like nobody I'd ever heard before, and I would have listened to anything he wanted to say.

"Then who's Matilda?" I asked.

Toby tilted his cup and poked at the slush with his straw. "I suppose Matilda's the girl who felt like home."

That night I got out the *Book of Days* and read the note again. Sometimes when I read it I saw the words that said that Finn loved me. Sometimes I could only see that he loved Toby. That all he cared about was making sure Toby was okay.

I tucked myself in tight under the covers. Like the sick man in the painting. Just like that, I thought, and a hook of anger caught in my belly, because *I* wanted to be the one taken care of. I wanted someone to look after me, like it was supposed to be. I was the kid, wasn't I?

Toby was the fully grown adult. Being the sick person seemed better than being the nurse. Lying there, having people get every little thing you might need. Who wouldn't want that?

But then I thought better. The sick person would always be the sick person, but the nurse, she would have to be the nurse for only a little while. And that's when I understood what it meant, what Toby was trying to say earlier. Toby was definitely going to die. There was no time, but also there was no limit. If I was going to do something for him, something big, I had to do it soon.

I snuck down to the kitchen after everybody was asleep and called Toby. We talked for a little while, then I got to what I really wanted to know.

"What's the name of your town?" I asked him. "What's the name of the place you're from in England?"

Forty-One

It was Saturday, the day of the party, and I went in to the rehearsal for a while, just in case Greta was looking for me. They were running the show straight through, and Mr. Nebowitz looked exasperated. He was making kids do their lines over and over until he decided he was happy with them.

"You're supposed to be a nurse, Julie," I heard him say. "You can't stand there scowling. Come on, people. Step it up. There are folks from the city here today, if you hadn't noticed." He gestured to the two seats next to him: An older man wearing a cravat and a woman with bright red hair were sitting there watching the rehearsal. I wondered if they were from *Annie*. There to watch Greta. Mr. Nebowitz clapped his hands together before telling everyone to run the whole scene again.

I could see the back of Greta's head in the front row. All the cast who weren't onstage were sitting on the velvety red auditorium seats. Mr. Nebowitz said it was important for everyone to understand the *whole* play, not only their own part, and that meant that when you weren't onstage you should be watching the other scenes. I thought about sitting down next to Greta. Maybe Toby was right. Maybe she didn't hate me. Maybe it was something else altogether. But then the thought of being made to look stupid right there in the front row changed my mind. Instead, I sat in the back and waited for her to go on.

This time she wasn't anywhere near as good as the last time I saw her. Last time she wasn't even in costume, but it felt like she was the real Bloody Mary. Even I'd found myself forgetting I was watching Greta. This time it wasn't like that. This time I could see Greta through and through. Especially when she was singing "Happy Talk." All the notes were right, but, still, I didn't believe a word of it. She seemed relieved to be going offstage when the song was done. I left the auditorium right before Nellie, who was being played by Antonia Sidell, sings "Dites-Moi" for the last time.

I wandered down to the greenroom, which ended up being mostly empty. It smelled like stale sandwiches, and the only ones down there were two girls from costumes and a guy who painted sets. They stopped their conversation for a few seconds when they saw me, then angled away and kept talking. I turned back up the stairs, and when I got to the top I stood there, back pressed against the wall, wondering where I could go next. There was something so lonely about that moment, everyone around me completely involved in this thing I wasn't a part of, me with nowhere to go, waiting around for a party I didn't want to go to. The only thing I really wanted to do was call Toby. I didn't have anything to say to him. Nothing interesting at all. But that seemed okay. It seemed like he was the only one I knew in the world who I could call up and just say nothing to. I reached into my pocket, hoping there might be a few dimes, change from my lunch money, but there was nothing. So I did the next best thing. I went out into the woods.

It was windy and springtime-damp, and once I was out there everything sad seemed to blow right off me. It had been a while since I'd been there, and I'd almost forgotten how much I loved the woods. I wandered, aimlessly at first, but then I tried to pay attention. I wanted to get the lay of the land again. I wanted to make sure I knew exactly where everything was. My plan for the party was to keep a close eye on Greta and then get out of there as soon as possible.

I followed the river, which was running fast because of all the rain and melted snow. I didn't walk all the way to my place near the maple. I turned away from the river before that and walked to a big boulder not so far from the school. I tried to pretend I was in the Middle Ages, but it didn't work. Not the way it used to. Every time I got close, I'd think of something Toby said. Or a Trivial Pursuit question. Or a snatch of a lyric from a *South Pacific* song. It was like my brain had actually changed. Like some part of it, my favorite part, had died off.

I unzipped my backpack and took out a cigarette. I lit it and sat against that boulder until the last light faded. Until the space between the tree branches and the branches themselves became the same dark thing. I wasn't afraid. The party was nothing. I had a secret friend in the city. I smoked cigarettes and I had tasted brandy. I had someone to take care of.

After Toby told me the name of his hometown, I went to the library and looked it up in an atlas. I couldn't believe how lucky he was. His town was right on the edge of the North Yorkshire Moors. *Wuthering Heights, Jane Eyre, The Secret Garden.* I couldn't imagine why anyone would leave someplace like that. Finn said Toby had nobody, but he must have meant nobody in New York, because it seemed impossible that I could truly be the only person he had in the world. I decided I would tell him I wanted to go to England. I'd say *I* wanted to go, but really what I wanted to do was take him back home. I'd seen how happy he looked in London, in that picture in the bedroom. So free and easy. I didn't want to mess it up. There were details to figure out. Phone calls to make. A passport to find. There was a lot, but for once I was going to do it exactly right. This was the spectacular thing I would do for Toby.

I took a strong pull off my cigarette so the end glowed bright fiery orange in the fading light. I thought how there was a kind of power in being needed. In having a purpose. I could feel it hardening up my bones and thickening my blood. I felt older and smarter than anyone else I knew. I could do anything, anything at all.

After a while people started to come down the hill from the school. I saw them as blips of light, like fireflies bouncing down into the woods. There was laughter and then squeals as a few kids stumbled over roots, their lights falling to the ground. I stepped into a hollow behind a big downed tree trunk and watched.

I didn't see Greta, but I saw Julie and Megan and Ryan, arms linked across one another's backs, doing a cancan dance down the hill. I saw Ben, wearing the cloak, being followed by a bunch of younger lighting-crew boys. There were kids I didn't know. Someone had brought a guitar and someone else was blaring the worst music in the world out of a boom box wedged between the branches of a tree. Tiffany, with her girly voice singing, "I Think We're Alone Now."

The moon was huge, and the woods had a shine to them that I'd never seen before. There were more kids than last time, and the whole thing was louder and wilder. I watched and watched, but I didn't see Greta come past. I thought maybe I'd missed her, because I'd seen almost everyone else, but then I saw her. She was all by herself, walking down the hill slow and careful. She had on her long black coat and a neon-orange scarf. Her dark hair reached over her shoulders and most of the way down her back, and she wasn't smiling.

She walked up to the fire and pulled a bottle from the inside pocket of her coat. She put it to her lips and tipped it back for so long she must have downed half of it in that one swig. She didn't talk to anyone, and I thought of going over to her, but I didn't. I was staring so hard at Greta that when Ben Dellahunt's knuckles tapped the top of my head, I swung around and cried out.

"Whoa," he said, pulling his hand back.

"You scared me."

"I can see that." He pointed toward the fire and smiled. "Spying can make a girl skittish."

"I'm not spying. I told Greta I'd come to this thing and I'm just keeping to myself. That's all."

"Uh-huh," he said.

"It's true."

Ben had an irritating way of acting like he was way older than me. Like he was an adult and I was a kid.

"Well, I'll tell you what," he said. "I won't blow your cover if you tell me where that wolf place is."

I regretted beyond words ever saying anything about wolves to Ben Dellahunt.

"Why do you want to know?"

He reached into his pocket and pulled out a pair of weird dice. He tossed them into the air and caught them in one hand.

"A quest. D&D. Plus, those freshman boys will shit themselves if I tell them there's wolves here."

I didn't really have a choice. I needed to be left alone. I needed to keep watching Greta. So I told him about following the river to the big split tree and heading up and across the hill there. "You'll hear them then," I said.

"Cool." He smiled and patted me on the shoulder. "And, you know, if you ever change your mind . . ." He handed me one of the weird dice. "Think about it."

"Right," I said. "I'll be sure to let you know."

He stood there for a second grinning at me, then all of a sudden his face lurched toward mine and he kissed me right on the lips. Before I could say anything, he ran off. As he ran, he gathered up his cloak in his hands and called out for the other boys in a great commanding voice I never imagined Ben could have.

I stood there blushing in the darkness. The kiss probably didn't mean anything. Nobody had ever kissed me and meant it. But what if maybe for once it did? No. He was probably just trying to weird me out. I mean, if anyone looked like the Wolf Queen of the Outer Regions, it was Greta. Under that bright big moon, Greta looked like the sad queen of everything. That's exactly what I was thinking as I tried to get her back into my sight. I scanned the faces around the fire. Twice my eyes went around that circle, but Greta wasn't there.

I asked everyone I could find if they'd seen Greta: Nobody had. Ryan said he thought she was completely drunk, but he was leaning on my shoulder when he said it, like he could barely stand up himself. Margie Allen said she thought she might have seen her walking back up to the school but I shouldn't rely on that, because she wasn't sure at all if it was Greta. Still, I ran back up the hill. I walked behind the school to the greenroom door and tried it, but it was locked. I peered through the thin window—the room was empty.

If I was smart, I would have gone home right then. Greta didn't deserve to have me out looking for her. But still, I couldn't bring my-self to leave. I walked back into the woods, down that hill, and sat next to the fire, hoping she might turn up.

The crackling fire and laughing and dulled voices and boom box music all swelled into one fuzzy blob in my head. I pressed my hands over my ears, and everything shrank away. Only the bass pulse of the music was left, and I was almost enjoying it. I almost felt invisible there, right in the middle of everything.

Then I saw a few kids stand up. Then a few more. Soon people were running and shouting and there were police sirens. Red and blue lights from over the hill in the school parking lot slapped out into the darkness. All around me, kids were panicking. The whole thing was done stupidly this time. The fire was too close to the school, and the noise was too much.

Kids ran in every direction. Deeper into the woods or off to where they could cut across onto streets without going through the parking lot. Someone was kicking dirt onto the fire, and I was running like crazy, looking for Greta. The boom box had been left behind, so it was like there was a soundtrack to the whole thing. "Blister in the Sun" was on—a good song, finally—and it made the whole thing seem like a Saturday morning cartoon, as cops chased through the trees, pointing their flashlights and yelling for kids to stop.

I went tree to tree, hiding until it was safe to go on. I went deeper and deeper into those woods, looking for my sister. I didn't even need a flashlight, because the moon was so strong. Then, without thinking, I turned and ran to the spot I'd found Greta last time. I went to my place.

It was like she was waiting for me. Like she wanted me to find her. It couldn't be a coincidence that she knew this exact place. That she knew I'd also know it. But I didn't understand. She was buried in leaves, just like the last time. It was a warmer night. Much warmer than last time, and she'd snuggled herself right down under them like they were a damp blanket. Her moon-bleached face lay there, looking like something separate from the rest of her.

I brushed the leaves off her quickly. This time I decided she would have to walk. Run, even. I yanked her up and shook her hard enough to wake her. She opened her eyes and looked at me.

"June," she whispered. "It's you."

"Get up, Greta. Now." I stood and pulled her arms until she was almost standing.

"No, no, no. Listen. Shhhh. June, I think I'm dying." She was clutching on to a bottle of apricot schnapps. I'd seen that same bottle not so long ago, dusty and forgotten, in the back of my parents' liquor cabinet.

"You're not dying. You're just drunk. Now, get up."

She laughed and her eyes closed again. Then for a second they fluttered back open. She raised her finger to her lips. "We're friends, right?"

"If you walk," I said. "We're friends if you walk."

And she did. Greta put her arm around my shoulders and stumbled along next to me through the woods. It was hard work, a slow slog alongside the river. We couldn't go back up to the parking lot, because of the police, so we had to go through the woods and then cut over like we did last time. Greta hung off my shoulder like a heavy bag.

"Come on," I said, but she'd stopped and wouldn't go on.

"Remember beauty parlor?"

Here we go again, I thought. *Me dragging Greta home while she stumbles down memory lane.* At first I was angry. At the whole thing. But then Greta lifted my hand into hers and ran a finger over each of my fingernails.

"Remember those geranium petals?" she said, and the anger faded because I did remember.

Beauty parlor was a game we used to play when we were little, when we were still best friends. If it was Greta's turn, I would have to sit down on the grass. Then she would disappear all around the yard, looking for stuff. She collected things like geranium petals and milkweed fluff and those little purple violets that grow wild on the lawn. She would tell me to lie down flat on my back with my hands spread out. Then she went to work. She'd lay violets on my eyelids and sprinkle the milkweed fluff in my hair and one by one she'd lay those bright red geranium petals on my finger and toenails, finding ones that were just the right size for each and every nail. Then she'd shout out, "Snapshot," and she'd make a clicking sound and pretend she had a camera in her hand and was going to preserve the moment forever.

When she was done I would try to get up as slowly as I could, so all her work didn't tumble off me. Usually I was able to keep only the toenails and the fluff from falling. That was enough. Especially the toenails, because those petals really looked like nail polish.

What's embarrassing is that the last time I remember playing that game was when I was eleven and Greta was thirteen. We both knew we were too old for it—Greta had real makeup by then—but we also knew we liked that game, and when it's only you and your sister, you can do any embarrassing thing you want.

"Lie down," Greta said.

At first I didn't understand, but then I did. Greta wanted to do beauty parlor right there in the woods. I kept walking, tugging her along.

"No way," I said.

"Awww, Junie, come on. Like we used to."

"Like we used to? What are you talking about? You're the mean one. You're the one who wrecked how we used to be."

She didn't say anything. Her arm dropped off my back.

"Did you ever think I might have problems?" I said. "That I might be dealing with . . . situations?"

Greta stumbled along ahead of me. She turned back and laughed. "Poor old Mrs. Lucky. Poor troubled Mrs. Special," she said. "Maybe I should go out and get myself AIDS. Then everyone can come fawning around me and—"

"Shut up, Greta. Just shut up."

"Would I be special enough for you then, June? Tragic enough?" She flashed me a look, then bolted ahead, like her body had somehow sobered up instantly.

"Wait," I shouted. But she didn't. I had to run as fast as I could to stay with her. The moon lit that whole forest in the most thin and silvery light. I kept thinking Greta might get lost, but she didn't. She turned away from the river at just the right place, then cut onto Evergreen Circle, where I finally caught her.

We walked in silence the rest of the way, cutting between backyards and down the streets of our town. I stared at Greta's back. At her matted hair, decorated with brown torn leaves and dirt. What was happening to my sister? What if I'd never come? How long would she have stayed hidden in those cool, damp leaves? How long before she woke up alone and scared, with nothing but the howling of wolves to keep her company?

"Greta, you have to tell me what's going on. You are seriously scaring me now. I'll tell. I'll tell Mom and Dad if I have to."

She looked at me and smiled. "No, you won't. You're here, aren't you? And other places, right? Should I tell them about all the sneaking around? Should I tell them you're smoking now?"

"God, Greta. I'm not saying it to be mean. I'll help you with whatever it is. Really."

Greta sat on the curb between the Aults' house and the DeRonzis'. I sat next to her. A streetlight shone down from right above us, so it was like we were in a little bright circle separate from everything else. She looked at me with her tired drunk eyes.

"Are you really scared, June? For real?"

"Yeah. Of course I am."

Greta looked like she was about to cry. "That's nice," she said. Then she hugged me—a real hug, hard and fierce. She smelled of liquor and the mustiness of the forest floor, but under it all was the baby-sweet scent of Jean Naté. Then she leaned in closer and whispered, "I am too, Junie. I'm scared too."

"Of what?"

She stroked my cheek with the back of her fingers and pressed her lips to my ear. "Of everything."

Forty-Two

The next morning we both slept late. As late as my mother let us, anyway, which was ten-thirty. We were going to the Ingrams' for a barbecue that afternoon. They threw one for my parents every year, right near the end of tax season. To help them get through the final stretch, they said.

I didn't mind going to the Ingrams' too much, but Greta tried everything she could to get out of it. What's funny is that in the end she was forced to go because it would be impolite to Mikey if she didn't, but when we got there it turned out that Mikey himself had gone out with his friends. We were also told he didn't want to be called Mikey anymore, just Mike. So there we were in the Ingrams' backyard, hungover Greta and me, hanging around their rusty old swing set. Greta sat on a swing, digging the tip of her boot into the bare patch of dirt. I swung as high as I could, forcing one leg of the swing set to pull up and out of the ground again and again, making it feel like the whole thing was about to fly us both away.

"Could you stop that?" Greta said.

"Nope," I said, and kept swinging.

She stood up and looked toward the picnic table, where all the adults were sitting with glasses of beer and wine. My dad had brought Trivial Pursuit over, and even though the Ingrams had owned a copy for a couple of years, he got them to play. I heard my mother laugh, and I wanted to cover my ears because I couldn't stop thinking about what I knew about her. How could someone act so strong and normal and under it all be so desperate and sad? And mean. That was the hardest part. It was only in the past few years that I'd even thought of Finn and my mother as brother and sister. That I really believed that who they were to me—mother, uncle—wasn't all that they were. Maybe Finn and my mother sat on a swing set at a backyard barbecue, bored out of their minds, just like me and Greta. They must have held each other's secrets. Just like us.

Greta put her hand up over her mouth, made a nauseated sound, and let out a sigh before sitting back down on the swing. I was trying to think of a way to bring up everything that had happened the night before. Something that made it so Greta wouldn't turn on me right away. I had my arms linked around the chains of the swing and my hands in my coat pockets because it was cold. Too cold for a barbecue, even though everyone was pretending it wasn't. My fingers had been playing with something in my left pocket, and I realized it was that weird die that Ben gave me. I took my hands out of my pockets and waited until the swing was at its highest point, then I leapt off onto the grass.

"Hey," I said. "Look at this." I held my palm out to Greta. It was the first time I'd seen the die in daylight, and I saw that it was kind of pretty. Translucent blue with ten sides, so that it was like two five-sided pyramids stuck together at their bases. It looked like a big jewel with numbers carved into it.

She glanced at it. "Yeah, so, what is it?"

"A Dungeons & Dragons die. From Ben."

Greta perked right up. "Oooooh," she said. "Nerd courtship rituals."

I could tell I was blushing, but as painful as it was to pretend to have some kind of dishy news about me and Ben, I could see it was a way to open Greta up. I could see her loosening. And I guess there was the kiss.

"Did you see him last night? In that cloak?"

She shook her head. "Apparently *you* did, though." She raised her eyebrows and gave a crooked smile.

I nodded so the whole thing would stay kind of murky and keep

Greta thinking. She eyed me up, then gave me a look that said she understood every single thing in the world.

"You know, June, I'm just playing along here. You can drop the act."

"What act?"

"The Ben thing. There's no Ben thing."

What's funny is that for once there was something. Ben *had* kissed me. It was clumsy and quick and maybe it meant nothing at all, but it was real.

"You know what, Greta? You don't know everything. You think you do, but you are so far from knowing everything—"

"I know that I saw Ben go off with Tina Yarwood last night."

I looked away quick. What she said stung more than I would have expected. "Oh," I said after a while.

It wasn't like I'd been sitting around fantasizing about Ben Dellahunt. It wasn't that I even liked him particularly. He was smug and nerdy and he had nothing on Finn or Toby. But still, when Greta said that, about Tina Yarwood. When I thought of that kiss. How I'd blushed after, like it meant something. When I thought of all that, it hit me right in the throat. Nothing had changed. I was the stupid one again. I was the girl who never understood who she was to people.

Greta held my gaze for a second, smirking. She could see that she'd hurt me. I could tell. And even though I knew it was the worst thing I could do, that Greta was the worst person in the world to say anything to, I looked back at her hungover face and said, "Ben's nothing, Greta. I have a boyfriend in the city. He's older than me. Older than you, even. I go to the city by myself all the time, and we smoke and drink and do whatever we want." I almost kept going. I almost mentioned my plan about England, but I didn't.

"Liar," she said. She said it with so much viciousness that I knew she thought it might be true.

I shrugged. "Believe what you want."

"Don't worry. I will."

It had taken every last bit of concentration to sound so confident, and I sat on the swing, shaking for a few minutes, thinking about the stupidity of what I'd just done. About all the trouble it might lead to.

Not only for me but for Toby. I got up and started to walk away, but then I thought of something.

"How do you know about that place in the woods, anyway?"

She smiled. "I've seen you, June. The hills have eyes. . . ."

"What do you mean?"

She looked so full of power right then that I started to worry about what she would say. But I had to know.

"Tell me," I said.

"I followed you. I saw you heading down to the woods after school one day, at the beginning of the school year, and I followed you. I stayed there all afternoon, watching you play your weird stuff. Talking to yourself. Wearing that dumb old dress. Those *special* boots of yours."

"You spied on me?"

"Lots of times."

I stood there staring at Greta. I should have been embarrassed, but all I felt was rage. I turned and walked away without saying another word. I was still shaking, and I clenched my fists to stop it. I squeezed the blue die tight in my hand and thought about Ben again. Then I hurled the die across the Ingrams' lawn. In a few months it would end up shredded by their lawn mower. Good. I walked over to the picnic table and sat down with the adults. I pretended I wanted to play Trivial Pursuit until it was time to go home.

Forty-Three

The next Wednesday was April Fools' Day. President Reagan was on TV, giving a big speech about AIDS for the very first time. Apparently he'd known all about it for a while but he'd decided to keep quiet on the subject. What he said was that everyone—especially teenagers—should stop having sex. He didn't say it exactly in those words, but that was his main point. It didn't seem like too bad an idea to me. I mean, why did sex have to be so important? Why couldn't people live to-gether, spend their whole lives together, just because they liked each other's company? Just because they liked each other more than they liked anyone else in the whole world?

If you found a person like that you wouldn't have to have sex. You could just hold them, couldn't you? You could sit close to them, nestle into them so you could hear the machine of them churning away. You could press your ear against that person's back, listening to the rhythm of them, knowing that you were both made of the same exact stuff. You could do things like that.

Sometimes, if you're standing close enough to another person, you can't even tell whose stomach is growling. You look at each other and then you both apologize and say, "That was me," and then you laugh. You don't need sex for that kind of thing to happen. For your body to forget how to tell if it's hungry or not. For you to mistake someone else's hunger for your own.

Once, right after I'd turned thirteen, that happened at Finn's apartment. Finn and I were leaning out one of his big windows, watching for my mother to come back. She was out shopping at Bloomingdale's that day, some kind of wedding present for someone my parents knew through work, and we expected to see her all bundled up, scuttling across the street in her long puffy coat, with a big Bloomingdale's shopping bag. We both liked that. Seeing someone from up above without them knowing you could see them. We both understood that you could sometimes get a glimpse of who a person really was when you saw them like that. So even though it was cold, we leaned out the window, our shoulders almost touching, Finn giving my back a warm-up rub every once in a while. He had on a blue wool cap almost the exact same color as his eyes, and he'd wrapped his knitted red scarf around my neck.

"Hey, Crocodile," he said.

"What?"

"Your mom, she said she talked to you. About me. About what's happening with me."

A couple of months had passed since that day at the Mount Kisco Diner, but I never said a word about it to Finn. I never acted like I knew anything at all. I couldn't. I was sure it would ruin all the time we had left. I took the scarf and looped it around my neck one more time.

"Can we not talk about that?"

I felt Finn's hand land on my back. He nodded. "Just, you know, if you want to ask me anything—"

"Okay," I said quickly, cutting him off. I could tell he was about to go on too long. That if I let him he'd start stumbling around, telling me everything about being sick, and I didn't want to hear it. I pointed out the window. "Isn't that Barbara Walters?"

Finn leaned out even farther and angled his head. Then he smiled and bumped his shoulder against mine.

"Dolly Parton's grandmother, more like."

I laughed. Mostly because I was glad I'd found a way to change the subject. That's when it happened—one of our stomachs gave out a great bubbling grumble. I looked at Finn, all embarrassed because I was sure it was me. But then he said he was sure it was him, because all he'd had for lunch was a cup of coffee. After going back and forth about it, Finn pulled me into the kitchen and said it didn't matter.

"My stomach's your stomach, Crocodile," he said. He opened a cabinet and pulled out a box of Wheat Thins, then got this fancy cheese with a thick layer of maroon wax around it from the fridge, and we leaned up against the counter eating until my mother buzzed up from the lobby.

I had to be careful on April Fools' Day because Greta usually had some kind of trick waiting for me. It wasn't always like that. Up until a few years ago it was Greta and me doing tricks on our parents. They weren't usually the best tricks—salt in the sugar container, ketchup as fake blood on a finger, that kind of thing—but we were in it together. Then, a few years ago, it changed to Greta against me. Sometimes it would be the kind of trick where she'd say something really good was going to happen, like we were getting the day off school to go to Great Adventure or something, and then as soon as I started to get excited about it she'd laugh and say April Fools. Other years she'd do the opposite. She'd pretend something really bad had happened—like that the hamster I used to have had run away—and she'd let me get all the way to crying about it before she'd show me that she had the hamster hidden in a shoe box under her bed.

Last year she came into my room first thing in the morning with the saddest look on her face and told me that Finn was dead. She waited for me to wake up completely. She waited until her news sank right into the marrow of my bones. She seemed to be waiting for my reaction, waiting for me to break down or run over to her for support. But I was numb. I sat on my bed, frozen. She stood there awhile longer and then finally gave up. "April Fools," she said, sounding disappointed.

Usually I had no idea it was April 1, but this year I remembered, so I was waiting for Greta to pounce.

But she didn't. Breakfast was normal. It was just the two of us because our parents had left for work early. I stared at Greta's back as she leaned over the counter spreading grape jelly on her toast. When she turned around, she saw me staring at her and gave me a "what's your problem?" look before picking up her cup of coffee. I looked away and ate a spoonful of Cookie Crisp. The little disks that were supposed to taste like chocolate chip cookies had turned slimy in the milk, but I didn't mind.

"You want this other piece?" Greta said, holding out her second piece of toast and jelly.

"Okay."

She threw it on the table next to my bowl, then left to get ready for school. I had a good close look at it, then sniffed it, thinking this must be her trick this year. There must be white pepper or chili flakes or something on there. I felt relieved to get it over with. To have spotted her trick so easily. I lifted the toast to my mouth and let my tongue touch the surface, waiting for the heat to start. But there was nothing. I took a whole bite and waited again. But, no. No trick.

I decided to walk to school that morning, because I didn't want Greta to get a second chance while we waited for the bus. It was early, and it was a bright warm morning, so I walked through the woods.

The thawed leaves made the whole place smell sweet and syrupy. We had only a handful of spring days in Westchester. Usually things went from winter right to hot humid summer like a flipped switch. It could still snow in April, but then May hit and everything went hot. And that was the end of my season in the woods. You can't pretend to be in the Middle Ages when it's ninety degrees outside. In my version of the Middle Ages, it's always fall or winter. Things are always cold and damp. Coats need to be worn. And boots. Always boots.

But for now it was okay. I took my time walking to school that morning. I knew I had the woods to myself. I hummed the *Requiem* and pretended to be a girl branded across the chest for begging.

At school, I opened my locker slowly, thinking maybe the trick would be in there, but nothing. I looked out for Greta all day. Every corner I turned in the hallways. On the line in the cafeteria. In the bathroom stalls. But, again, no sign of anything.

April Fools' Day 1987 passed with not a single mean trick from Greta. When I got home there was a small padded envelope in the mailbox, addressed to me from the Consortium for the Preservation of Unsleeved Records. For just a second I thought maybe that was a Greta trick, but of course it was from Toby. He'd sent the tape of his guitar music. *I'll teach you this* was scribbled on the insert.

At dinnertime Greta and I ate the beef and vegetable stew my mother had left for us, and then I watched *Room with a View* before going up to bed.

I lay in my bed that night, trying to understand why Greta would take a whole year off. I thought maybe it wasn't too late, maybe she would try something a few minutes before midnight, but I peeked into her room at a little bit after eleven and she was fast asleep. Not me. I lay in bed, awake, thinking, and the more I thought about it, the more I realized that maybe Greta hadn't taken a year off after all. Maybe she understood that the work had been done all those other April Fools' Days. She didn't have to do a single thing anymore. I'd ruin my own day *looking* for the trick. All Greta had to do was sit back and watch.

Or maybe she just didn't care anymore. Maybe I wasn't worth the trouble. I went to sleep with that sad thought in my head, and when I woke up in the morning it was still there, like a cool black hole right in the middle of everything.

Forty-Four

I like the word *clandestine*. It feels medieval. Sometimes I think of words as being alive. If *clandestine* were alive, it would be a pale little girl with hair the color of fall leaves and a dress as white as the moon. Clandestine is the kind of relationship me and Toby had.

The next time I saw Toby, which was two days later after school, I brought him a bonsai. Only it wasn't a real bonsai, just a twig from the Japanese maple tree in our backyard that I'd stuck in some dirt.

"For you, Toby-san," I said, bowing. I was afraid he wouldn't remember the joke. I always remember jokes, but some people forget right away and then I end up looking like a weirdo for still remembering something so small.

"It is a wise student who learns from her master," Toby said, with a bow and without any hesitation at all. Then he launched into a goofy impression of the crane technique, which, with his long gangly shape, made him look not like a crane exactly but like some strange species of bird that had yet to be discovered.

I laughed and gave him a shove, but he was stronger than he looked and he didn't budge.

I'd taken the train down, as usual, and Toby made tea, like he always did. It looked like he'd been trying to keep the apartment cleaned up, but there was still a shabbiness about it. I didn't say anything, because I could see he'd been making an effort. Toby brought out a box of Oreos and I took one. I pulled it apart and scraped the white cream out with my teeth. Then I dipped the two cookie halves into my tea. Toby didn't eat anything.

"I've been thinking," I said. "About what you were saying. About how we could do anything."

"Yes?"

"Well, I'm still working on it. I haven't figured it all out yet."

"The suspense, June. The suspense." Toby widened his eyes and smiled. "I'd like to say take your time, but . . ."

"Ha-ha," I said, even though I knew it wasn't really that much of a joke. "And—"

"Yes?"

"Well, I was also thinking that maybe, if you want, we could look at those paintings. The ones in the basement."

"Are you sure? You think you're ready?"

The truth was, I didn't know if I would ever be ready, but I nodded anyway.

I led the way this time, straight to the cage, without any hesitation at all. I waited while Toby opened the sticky padlock, and then I stepped in first.

There were two piles of painted canvases on top of the wooden pallet. Maybe thirty or forty paintings in all. I turned to look at Toby.

"These are all Finn's?"

He nodded.

"But that article. Did you see that article in the *Times*?"

Toby shook his head. "I don't buy newspapers."

"There was an article and it had a picture of our portrait in it. . . ." I stopped, waiting to see if he would confess to sending it in.

"Yes?" he said, with no hint at all that he knew anything about it. I tried to catch if he was hiding something, but he only looked slightly confused.

"Well, it said Finn stopped painting. Like ten years ago or something."

Toby shook his head. "No, no. He just stopped showing his work, that's all. Could you imagine Finn not making some kind of art?"

Again, I felt stupid. Like I didn't know Finn anywhere near as well as Toby did.

"No, I guess not," I said. "But why would he stop showing it?"

"He said the whole circus of it bored him. So he sold a painting here and there when he needed money, but that was it. 'I don't have to prove anything anymore.' That's what he said."

That all made sense to me, but I knew my mother would think it was ridiculous. That Finn was a fool to let all that opportunity swim away from him.

Toby pointed to the paintings. "I can leave you if you want. Give you some time with these by yourself. Lock up and come back up when you're done." He held the key out to me.

I didn't say anything and Toby turned to go. Behind my back I heard him closing the cage door. I wanted to look at the paintings all on my own. I didn't want to be afraid, but my mother was right. The place was like something out of a horror movie.

"Toby?"

"Yeah?"

"You could stay . . . you know, if you want."

He smiled, and before I knew it he was back in the cage, stretched out on the chaise longue, pouring a drink from one of those fancy crystal bottles.

"I won't watch you," he said. "Pretend I'm not even here."

I sat myself down cross-legged on the floor and looked at the paintings one by one. Most of the canvases were small as far as art goes. Maybe the size of a microwave door. The first few were of abstract stuff. Shapes and colors. I didn't want to find them boring, but I did. I knew that if I were smarter, those would probably look like the best paintings in the world, but I am who I am and I want to tell the truth, and the truth is that I thought they were pretty boring. Still, I took my time looking at each one, in case Toby was watching me. I didn't want it to look like I didn't like Finn's work. But once I got past those abstract ones, it wasn't a problem. After about ten of those abstract paintings there was a piece of white paper with Finn's old handwriting on it. Not the scrawly handwriting he had when he was sick but the neat firm writing he used to have. *WISHING YOU HERE (23)*. That's what it said.

After that I was 100 percent hooked.

The Wishing You Here paintings looked like oversize old-fashioned postcards of places all around America. They each had intricate painted stamps and postmarks and pictures in colors that weren't quite real. The water was more turquoise, the skies so blue they were almost hard to look at. Taos, Fairbanks, Hollywood. But the weirdest thing about those paintings was that in each and every one there was some kind of picture of Toby. Not like the real Toby exactly, but like he was transformed into something else. There's one of Mount Rushmore, where Toby's face is carved into the mountain alongside the presidents. One in Alaska, where there's a grizzly bear with Toby's face. Another in the Everglades, where it took me ages to even find him, because Finn had painted him as a gnarled old swamp tree.

I glanced over at Toby. He'd fallen asleep on the chaise longue, a field guide to seashells open on his chest. I picked up the white sheet that had been covering the stack of paintings and got up and laid it over him, tucking it in at his chin. I stood there for a minute, watching the sheet move slowly up and down with his breathing. I smiled, because it was the first thing I'd done so far that could maybe count as looking after him, and it felt good to do it. Like maybe I was on the right track.

After a while I went back to the paintings. Some were so ridiculous I couldn't help laughing out loud. I think my favorite one was from Arizona, where Toby is this huge saguaro cactus with an owl living right in the middle of him. I started laughing because the whole thing was so, well, silly. That was the only word for it. I must have woken Toby, because the next second he was there, kneeling down on the floor behind me, looking over my shoulder, saying, "I don't see what's so humorous," before bursting out laughing himself.

"I can't believe I've let you see these, June Elbus."

"I can't either," I said.

And then a door slammed somewhere in the basement and we both froze.

"Shhhh," Toby said.

I could hear somebody getting their laundry. A dryer door opening and Toby saying, "Shhh," again. I flipped to the next painting. There was Toby's face on a stylized Inuit salmon jumping upstream. *British Columbia,* it said, and the Toby fish was leaping through the *C* of *Columbia.* I let out a wail of laughter and Toby looked down, seeing the exact same thing, and then he started too. We both tried as hard as we could not to laugh, but we couldn't. I couldn't.

"Hey, who's down here?" an old man's voice called out from the laundry area.

Toby pulled me in to him, saying, "Shhh, shhh," again and again. He wrapped his arms around me and put his broad palm over my mouth, trying to get me to stop laughing. His arms felt stronger than I would have thought. A lot stronger. I stayed there quiet and thought, *This is what it felt like to be Finn. This is what it feels like to be held by someone you love.* I flipped to the next painting, expecting another postcard, but instead it was Finn. A self-portrait, staring right out at us. There was nothing fancy about it. It was Finn in his blue hat, his blue eyes looking like they were trying to say something without words. The old man kept hollering and Toby's hand was still over my mouth. I could feel his fingers against my lips, and we weren't laughing anymore. We were both staring at Finn. "Come on out, goddammit." And the earthy damp of the basement and Toby's fingers that felt like lips against mine. And Finn's eyes, saying, *I love you, June.* And without thinking, my mouth parted and I felt myself kiss Toby's fingers. Gentle and soft, eyes closed, imagining everything and nothing, and I could feel Toby's arms stronger and stronger, his breath in my hair. And then I felt a kiss. A single soft kiss on the back of my neck.

Over the next few days I went down to see Toby whenever I could. Sometimes I would take the train right after school. Other times I would leave early. I'd cut gym or home ec or sometimes even Spanish if I was feeling bold.

I think New York was the perfect place for Toby to live because it was maybe the only place he would never run out of new restaurants. With Finn you had places. Horn & Hardart. The Cloisters. Places we went back to so many times that they started to feel like home. Toby was loose. Attached to nothing. Except maybe to Finn. That's what I started to figure out. Without Finn, Toby was like a kite with nobody holding the string.

One afternoon Toby tried to teach me how to do the bicycle in the flea circus. After fifteen minutes of trying to make it look like a flea was riding that bicycle, I understood how good Toby was. Sometimes, even close up, it looked to me like there really was something riding that bike. Even standing right next to Toby, I'd get that sensation. My hands moved like they were made of thick clay. And I knew my face gave away everything. Anyone could see I was moving one hand under the stage.

But Toby wouldn't give up. He made me try again and again, until by the time I had to go home I was able to make the bike inch around the ring. I knew it looked painful and slow and awful, but Toby was patient and didn't seem to mind. What I was starting to like about him was that he never lied to me. He never tried to butter me up by pretending I was some kind of budding flea-circus genius. He never said, "Good job," or "Brilliant," or any lame, meaningless comments like that. It was never like he was talking to a kid. When he said something I could believe him.

At the end of that day he said, "Keep trying. I promise you'll get better." That's all he said, but it made me happy because I knew it was exactly what he meant.

Another time we walked through Central Park and then downtown all the way to Chinatown. Toby talked about playing the guitar, his impossibly long fingers stroking at the air. I told him about the woods and the wolves and jumping rope backward and he didn't laugh at me at all. We ended up at a place called Cheng Fat Lucky Fortune, where we ordered moo shu vegetables with extra pancakes. Toby ordered a Volcano Bowl, which turned out to be a giant crazy drink that was on fire.

It came in a huge ceramic bowl with pictures of hula dancers and palm trees on the outside, and there were paper umbrellas and pieces of pineapple and maraschino cherries and big long straws. It was sweet, like coconut and Hawaiian Punch mixed together, and it hardly even tasted like alcohol. We drank and talked and ate, although I noticed it was mostly me eating. Toby only pushed the food around on his plate. That day was the first time I was ever drunk; it made me happy to know that it was a Volcano Bowl that did it. And I suddenly understood that getting drunk was just one more way to leave this place, this time. We stumbled out of Cheng Fat Lucky Fortune, and as my head spun I wondered where Greta went. Deep in the woods, buried in leaves, drunk as can be—how far away did she go?

Toby put his arm around me to steady me on the sidewalk outside the restaurant. I looked at him through hazy eyes.

"It's just us now, isn't it?" I said. But even as the words were coming out, I knew it wasn't really true. Finn was always there. Finn would always be there.

And then I thought something terrible. I thought that if Finn were still alive, Toby and I wouldn't be friends at all. If Finn hadn't caught AIDS, I would never even have met Toby. That strange and awful thought swirled around in my buzzy head. Then something else occurred to me. What if it was AIDS that made Finn settle down? What if even before he knew he had it, AIDS was making him slower, pulling him back to his family, making him choose to be my godfather. It was possible that without AIDS I would never have gotten to know Finn or Toby. There would be a big hole filled with nothing in place of all those hours and days I'd spent with them. If I could time-travel, could I be selfless enough to stop Finn from getting AIDS? Even if it meant I would never have him as my friend? I didn't know. I had no idea how greedy my heart really was.

I stood there staring at the sky over Canal Street as it faded from orange to a dusty pink. An old lady dragged a shopping cart filled with bags down the street, *click click click*ing over the sidewalk. The sun kept on with its slipping away, and I thought how many small good things in the world might be resting on the shoulders of something terrible.

I looked over at Toby. His eyes were closed and he was smiling like he was remembering the best moment in his life, and all at once I understood that this wouldn't go on forever. It couldn't. It wasn't only that I knew sooner or later I'd get caught for cutting classes. It wasn't even that tax season was almost over, so I'd have my parents watching everything I did. And it wasn't that I knew Toby would die. I don't know how to say it other than to say that the whole thing felt fragile. Like it was made of spun sugar.

But I didn't want to think about that. I'd found a friend. And I started to believe that Toby wanted to see me because of me. Not just because of what I knew about Finn. I knew I'd made that mistake before, not understanding who I was with people. With Beans. With Ben. With Finn. Maybe even with Greta. But Toby had nobody. There didn't seem any way I could be falling into that same trap again.

Forty-Five

My mother rooted around in her purse. It was Thursday morning, before school. It was gray outside, and the top branches of the maple were swaying around in the wind. My father had gone on ahead to the office, but my mother's first appointment was later so she decided to meet him down there. She was already in her work clothes—one of her navy suits with massive shoulder pads. She moved around the kitchen like it was an alien planet when she was in her work clothes, always standing back from the counter, careful not to brush against anything greasy or wet.

"You're buying lunch today, right, June?"

I usually bought lunch. Pizza. Tater Tots. Soda. All of which were much better than a soggy bologna sandwich in a soggy brown bag. I started to say yes, but then I stopped myself.

"I don't know. I was thinking maybe I could have a bagged lunch today. A PBJ or something?"

It was the thought of my mother's manicured hand holding the bread, spreading the peanut butter thin and even, spooning on just the right amount of jam. The thought of her cutting my sandwich on the diagonal, then wrapping it neatly in waxed paper. It was the thought of her doing that for me, taking care of me like that, that made me ask.

My mother clicked her purse shut and looked up at me.

"Are you sure?"

I nodded hard. "Yeah."

She put her purse on the counter and started to roll up the sleeves of her jacket. She reached into the cabinet and pulled down the jars. Then she stopped and turned to me.

"You know, Junie, you're fourteen now. I think you can certainly manage to put together a sandwich. Here." She pushed the jar of peanut butter across the counter and rolled her sleeves back down. Even though there wasn't a crumb on her, she brushed the front of her jacket hard with both hands. I stared at the jar for a few seconds.

The thing is, if my mother had any idea what I had in my backpack, she would have made me that sandwich. If she knew that I'd searched and searched the house until I finally found the little key to the fireproof box buried in the bottom of her underwear drawer, if she knew that I'd unlocked the box and taken my passport out, that I had it with me right that very second in a Ziploc bag in the bottom of my backpack, if she knew why I had it there, if she knew even a bit of all that, she might have made me that PBJ. She wouldn't have said, "You're fourteen now," like she thought I was some kind of responsible adult. No. If she knew about my plan, she would have said, "you're *only* fourteen." She would have told me that I was crazy to think about going to England when I was *only* fourteen. Crazy to even consider it. And that would be before she knew I'd be going with Toby.

But she didn't know any of that. And right then she didn't want to get her work suit messed up with sticky grape jelly. So instead of making me a sandwich, she made out like fourteen was some kind of turning point in my great journey to becoming a fully grown woman.

"It's okay," I said after a few seconds. "Whatever. I'll just take the money."

My mother gave me a disappointed look. Then I gave her one back. Mine was for everything, not just the sandwich.

Forty-Six

"Toby?"

"June?"

"Well, um . . . I was just wondering if maybe you'd want to go see *The Name of the Rose* with me. Sometime. Whenever. You know, if you want."

It was the first time I was the one asking Toby to do something. Up until then he was always the one. I'd dropped my backpack on the kitchen floor and called him as soon as I got home. I usually had at least an hour in the empty house, and I dragged the phone into the thin pantry at the side of the kitchen, where there was a stool to sit on.

I chose *The Name of the Rose* because it's about medieval monks in a remote monastery in Italy. It's a murder mystery and it was supposed to be really good, so I thought Toby would say yes right away, but he didn't. He didn't say anything for such a long time that I thought something had happened to him.

"Toby?"

"I'm not Finn, you know."

It was my turn to go quiet. After a while I said, "Yeah, so?" in a sort of *duh* tone, because I didn't get his point.

"Well, I don't know, I might not like it."

I thought about it for a second. "Well," I said patiently, "I'm not Finn either."

"Just, you know, there'll be no value added. It'll be like going to a film with any old idiot."

"I already knew *that*," I said.

He laughed, but only a little.

"So, come on. Say yes."

He laughed again, but this time it was bigger. More real.

"Yes. Yes, all right. I'm being stupid."

I told him I would make sure not to have any really smart thoughts while we were watching the movie, and then he joked some more about being stupid, and before I knew it we were both cracking up on the phone.

I said I'd call him soon, when I found out where it was playing. That's how we left it. I stepped out of the pantry and into the kitchen, holding the phone, my face all hot from laughing, thinking about what a good job I was doing looking after Toby.

It's almost slow motion the way I remember it. My arm stretching to hang up the phone. The sound of someone clearing their throat behind me, and me twisting around to look. I can see it frame by frame. My smile disappearing as I saw her, as I took in the whole scene. Greta. Sitting at the kitchen table in her silky Victoria's Secret pajamas. In front of her, every single thing from the back of my closet. The blue butterfly wrapping paper. The paper bag holding the *Requiem* tapes. The tapes themselves spilled out over the table. The Elizabethan photo of Toby and me, staring up in those big dumb ruffs. The teapot with the string of a tea bag hanging out. And, worst of all, the notes from Toby, unfolded and obviously read by Greta.

Greta sat there with no expression on her face.

"You're home," I said, trying for some crazy reason to sound innocent and casual. I realized she must have waited until she heard me come in. She must have been lurking somewhere, waiting for the moment I got home.

"Sick," she said. "Stomach flu." She shook her head back and forth, dragging the whole thing out as painfully as she could.

"Do you even know how much trouble you're in?"

I didn't move.

"Do you have any idea how much trouble Toby will be in when Mom and Dad find out that he's been luring you out to see him?"

"It's my business, Greta," I said, but she just went on.

"Nobody will care that he's gay. He's an adult. That's all. He's an adult and you're a kid, and that's all anyone will see. He'll be arrested for being a pervert, and then they'll find out he gave AIDS to Finn and he'll go to jail. He. Gave. AIDS. To. Uncle. Finn. Don't you even care about that? What is wrong with you?"

What is wrong with me. What is wrong with me?

"He wasn't luring me . . ."

"So it was all your idea, then? This is your *boyfriend*?" Greta laughed.

"No. That's not what I mean. I mean—"

"I knew you were lying. I knew it," Greta said, smiling. "As if you actually had a boyfriend. What was I thinking? You are the biggest loser, June." Her voice was shrill and scary.

"I . . . He . . ."

"He what? He's your new best friend? I heard you on the phone. Laughing your head off. Fawning all over him. *As if*, June. As if he wants to spend his time on the phone with you."

"You don't know anything about it. You're so stupid. You're such a complete idiot." I wanted to blurt out everything I knew. I wanted to tell her about Finn's note and how neither of them knew anything about AIDS. How it wasn't Toby's fault. But I knew Toby wouldn't want me to do that. And maybe I was afraid Greta would tell me things I didn't want to hear. That she would turn the story around until I didn't know what was true anymore.

Greta didn't say anything for a few seconds. She stared me down, that smile still fixed on her lips. "It's obvious, June."

And before I could stop myself, I played right into her trap. "What's obvious? What?"

"You're just a way to make him feel less guilty. He told you he didn't, right? That's what he said? But he knows he gave Finn AIDS, and now he wants a ticket out of the guilt. Why else would he waste his last days on the planet with *you*?"

Sometimes what Greta said was so sharp I could actually feel her words cutting up my insides, slicing their way through my stomach and my heart. I knew she'd be looking at me, reading my face, so I tried to harden up as quick as I could. But, still, she'd already seen my reaction.

"You know it's true," she said.

"You don't know a thing about us," I said, but my voice was shaky, unsure.

She cocked her head and looked at me. "So it's 'us,' now, huh?"

I knew that when Greta got like this, she would be able to instantly transform whatever I said. It was like she was a master sculptor and my words were the ball of clay in her warm palm. A million possibilities waiting to be formed. I could say anything and Greta would turn it stupid and naïve. But maybe she was right. Maybe it wasn't that she could change my words; maybe it was that she was able to strip away all the layers until only the truth was left. Ugly and skinless and raw.

My shoulders slumped, and I thought I might cry in front of Greta for the first time in years. There were all my secrets, spread out on the table. Like someone had taken my insides and scooped them out for everyone to see. Look, here are her stupid hopes! Look, here's her dumb soft heart!

But then I watched Greta pick up the teapot and pour tea into her mug. It poured out smooth and neat, and not a single drop spilled. She set the teapot back down on the table, running a finger around the lid before picking up her mug.

Her hands were on *my* teapot, my teapot from Finn, and in that moment everything else disappeared. I stared at her finger resting on the spout, and the anger swelled so big in my chest I really thought I could kill Greta right then and there. She blew across the top of her mug, then took a little ladylike sip, and I thought I could punch her again and again. I stepped toward her, then stopped in the middle of the kitchen. Then I screamed as loud as I could. Every mean thing Greta had ever done was wrapped up in that scream. Every snotty remark. Every sneer. Every threat made it louder and louder, until I could see I'd finally scared her.

"Get your hands off my stuff," I yelled, in a voice that came from someplace I didn't know I had. Greta slowly put the mug down on the table and stared at me, stunned, but only for a second. She ran a hand over her hair, then reached back to tighten her ponytail.

"Big, big trouble," she said, shaking her head.

"I hate you," I shouted. Then I lunged at her. I didn't care about anything anymore. I grabbed her hair and she kicked hard at my knees. I jumped back, still holding her hair with one fist. She squealed, then grabbed hold of her own hair and yanked it from my grip.

"Stop," Greta said, putting a hand in the air. "Shh. Mom." We both froze.

I heard the car door slam, and I realized that Greta had won again. She would love every minute of my mother walking in on all this stuff. She'd enjoy every second of watching me try to explain. I didn't know what to do. I turned, expecting to see Greta perfecting her innocent face for my mother, but instead I saw that she was as panicked as I was.

"Quick," she said.

She ran to the cabinet under the sink and pulled out a black garbage bag. She shook it open, and in one sweep of her arm she had most of the stuff off the table. I grabbed the teapot, splashing tea out of the spout as I went. I ducked into the downstairs bathroom and closed the door behind me. I slammed down the toilet lid and sat there, hunched over the teapot.

I could hear the muffled words of my mom and Greta in the kitchen. Then I put my ear against the door, and I could hear everything clearly. This was the spying bathroom, and for once I was going to be the spy.

" . . . really feeling much better . . . giving my room a big cleanup," I heard Greta say. I pictured her holding up the garbage bag.

"Ooh," my mother said. "Wonderful. I need to have a look at that."

"When it's done," Greta said without even a second's hesitation.

Then I heard the door open and close.

I dumped the tea down the sink and looked around that tiny bathroom for someplace to hide the teapot. There was nowhere. I opened the door just a crack and peeked. Clear.

I bolted up the stairs to my bedroom with the pot under my arm, closed the door behind me, careful not to slam it, and slid the teapot under my bed. I took a few long slow breaths, calming myself.

At least the *Book of Days* was in my backpack, but as soon as I had that thought I realized that I'd left my backpack right in the middle of the kitchen floor. I ran down the stairs three at a time.

My mother had piled her briefcase and coat on the table and was staring at the trail of tea that went out the kitchen and into the hallway. My backpack was where I'd left it, and I quickly scooped it up.

"Oh, Junie, I didn't know you were home already. I managed to get away early to check in on Greta. She was a real mess this morning. Do you know anything . . ." She pointed at the mess of tea.

"Oh, yeah," I said. "That's mine." I ripped a handful of paper towels off the roll and started to wipe it up, following the trail all the way to the bathroom.

At the bathroom door I turned around. My mother was watching me. She shook her head and walked back into the kitchen.

Greta made me clean her whole room so she wouldn't be caught lying. I sorted through all the clothes piled on her floor and draped over the desk chair while she shifted papers around on her desk. I would have loved to ask her why she saved me, why she'd gone through all the trouble of showing me what she knew, just to get me off the hook in the end, but I didn't bother. I knew she wouldn't tell me a thing. Plus, she had her Walkman on. I could hear the tinny echo of Bon Jovi shrieking out "Livin' on a Prayer" at the top of their stupid lungs.

Later, while my parents were watching the news, Greta tapped on my door, then pushed it open before I answered. She slipped in and stood with her back pressed against the door. She stared at me, then let her eyes flit from thing to thing in my room.

"What?" I said.

"I just wanted to let you know that you're hanging out with a jail-bird."

I was lying in bed and I reached behind my pillow for Celia, my old stuffed seal. She was the one stuffed animal I still kept in my bed. I put my fingers on the place in her neck where all the stuffing had worn thin, making her head loll to one side.

"What are you talking about?"

I caught the tiniest glimmer of a smile on Greta's lips. She'd gambled and she'd won. She took her time, gazing around my room, letting her eyes catch for a moment on my closet door.

"Toby. Your *special friend*. He's been to prison. He's an ex-con." Her face looked almost like the way it did in Finn's portrait. Full of the pleasure of letting a secret out.

"I . . ." My face was hot. I rubbed my thumb back and forth against the seal's fur. My dad said Toby had been in trouble, but I didn't think it was *that* kind of trouble.

"There's nothing to say, June. It's the truth. He met Finn in prison."

"Finn has not been in jail. There's no way—"

"No duh. Finn was giving an art workshop. Toby was in it. That's how they met." Greta pulled a book from my shelf and leafed through it, like she was planning on standing there all night, like she'd just popped in to do a little light reading.

"How do you know?"

She didn't answer. She lowered the book, laid it on my desk, and raised her eyebrows. She stood there shaking her head and tut-tutting at me. "I know friends are hard to come by, June, but an ex-con riddled with AIDS is sinking pretty low. Especially one that murdered your own uncle."

"You're such a liar," I said, but I knew she wasn't lying. Greta was tiny, but she seemed huge when she had information. She seemed huge then. One and a half times life size, at least. Even the way she was standing—straight, back pressed against the door again, arms crossed over her chest—was filled with truth.

"Whatever," she said.

I thought she would leave then, but she didn't. She stared down at my carpet like she was thinking something over. Then, in a voice that sounded less sure, she said, "You know . . . you know, June, why don't you just promise not to see him anymore and then I'll leave you alone."

I pulled Celia under the covers. I heard the TV go off downstairs, then the sound of my parents talking and dishes clattering in the sink.

Greta stood there, and for a second I thought she might cry. Her eyes were bulging, but she didn't look away. She kept staring right at me, like she wanted me to see that she was on the edge of tears. Like she was waiting for my answer. I didn't say anything. I didn't make her any promises about not seeing Toby, because I knew they would be promises I couldn't keep. After a while Greta's whole body seemed to sink a little, like all of it, this whole mean plan, had somehow backfired. Like she had no cards left to play. Then she pulled herself back up. She lifted her head and stared at me.

"You know . . . I thought once Finn was gone . . . I thought you and me . . ."

"You thought what? That you could torment me full-time?"

"No, I . . ." Then she did start crying, and in a voice filled up with shaky wet disappointment she said, "Jail, June. Prison," and she made her way to the door.

"I don't care," I said to Greta's back as she slipped out of my room.

Late that night I snuck out to the garbage cans. I was hoping Greta had laid the bag of my stuff on top, but she hadn't. She'd opened it up and pulled each thing out. It looked like she must have reached way down and stuck it all under the slop of a week's worth of dinners. She must have gotten filthy doing it. She'd done a good job too. The only thing I could rescue was the Playland picture. And even that was ruined. Spaghetti sauce was smeared all over Toby's side of the picture. There I was, sitting all prim and old-fashioned next to a gruesome smudge of red. Even though I said I would never do something like that, in the end I did have to cut Toby right out of the picture.

I went upstairs and checked the back of my closet. Everything was gone. Every single special thing. I moved some stuff around to see if she'd accidentally left anything behind. But, no, nothing.

Except the black bracelets. The ones she'd brought back from the city that Sunday. The ones she said she got for me. Those she'd hung neatly on one of the metal hooks on the back wall.

All that was left was the *Book of Days* in my backpack and the teapot. And the money Toby gave me, which was in my underwear drawer wrapped in a babyish white vest I never wore. I pulled the teapot out from under my bed and cupped my palms around it. At least I still had that. I still had the best teapot in the world. I traced the dancing bears with my finger. Each one teetering on only two legs, paws flailing out, clutching at the air. I stared at them and suddenly I could see that they weren't really dancing at all, just stumbling around. Like great clumsy creatures about to lose their balance.

Forty-Seven

"I can't come today."

"Why?"

"Journal. A term and a half's worth of journal entries due in English."

"You turn in your journal to be read by the teacher?"

"Yeah, and I haven't written a single entry yet."

"That's ridiculous. The whole point of a journal is—"

"Yeah. I know. It's just how it is. It's not like anyone writes down their deepest secrets. It's not like I'd write anything about you."

I sat on the floor in the pantry, leaning up against the wall, but I angled myself so I could see if anyone came into the kitchen.

"So do it after," Toby said. I thought his voice sounded hoarser than usual, ragged.

"There's four months of entries. That's, like . . . I don't know, fifty. Maybe more. I guess I'll see you next week or something."

I didn't want to say the rest. I couldn't bring myself to tell him about everything that had happened with Greta. And it was true. I did have to write the journal. It was 25 percent of our grade in English, and I couldn't afford to mess it up.

Toby was quiet. After a while he said, "I could help you. If you think that would work. Keep you company."

"I don't know."

"Oh, go on. I promise it'll be better than sitting home on your own."

I hadn't expected Toby to offer to help.

"You don't have to do that. It's okay."

He sighed. "I want you to come."

I paused. Why was I letting Greta get into my head? I could hear the way I was talking to Toby, and I didn't mean to be that way. It felt like I was testing him. Seeing how easy it would be to get him to give up.

"Well . . . help as in making cups of tea and finding some good tapes to play, or help as in luring me out to drink Volcano Bowls?"

"The former, of course, June. What do you take me for?"

I paused. I thought about telling him that I knew he'd been in prison, but I couldn't do it.

"Okay. But you have to absolutely promise you won't be a distraction, okay?"

"Okeydokey," he said, in some kind of a bizarre attempt at an American accent.

When I got to the apartment, Toby had on some mellow jazz and he was sitting in a chair, pretending to read a book. It was easy to tell when someone was pretending to read, because their eyes moved too much. Up and down and all over the page. Somehow the fact that he was pretending to read did not seem like a good sign. I was glad that I'd gotten a head start on the train.

"I brought something for you," I said.

"Really?"

I handed him a small box, clumsily wrapped in pink "new baby" wrapping paper, which was the only kind I could find in the house. He put his book down, which I saw was an old battered copy of *The Canterbury Tales,* and took the box.

"It's dumb," I said.

"That's all right. I love dumb things." Toby shook the box lightly near his ear.

"Open it later, okay?"

He nodded and put the box on the mantel.

I pushed the coffee table to the side, threw my journal down on the floor, and sprawled across the carpet on my belly.

"Go on, then," Toby said.

"What?"

"Give us a read. Let's hear what you have so far."

"No. No way."

"I thought you wanted my help. I can't help if I don't know what you've got so far."

I thought about the notes Toby had written to me. Writing did not seem to be one of his big skills.

"I don't need that kind of help. Just, I don't know, maybe some snacks or something."

"Please?"

"No. It's private."

He gave me an "as if" look.

After a while I couldn't bear to listen to Toby's pleading anymore, and I gave in. I read him one of my entries, which he accused of being painfully boring, and then he came up with something ridiculous that I should substitute. We kept going like that, haggling back and forth until finally we got into a good rhythm and settled into taking turns coming up with ideas. I made up entries about belly dancing, choosing my own falcon, and being selected as young harpsichordist of the year. Toby's ideas were darker. He had something about temporary blindness and something else about a ghost that haunted the washing machine, but only when it was run on the "delicate" cycle. We always made sure that the crazy stuff was tucked in a normal-sounding entry. We sat there smoking cigarettes and laughing and drinking tea with brandy, and I was glad I'd decided to come. I was slightly worried about what would happen if Mrs. Link actually did read the journal, but I didn't really care. That's what Toby made you feel like. I decided Greta was all wrong about everything.

Then we got to February 5. The day Finn died.

Neither of us said anything at first. Then Toby slid the notebook over toward me. It sat there on the rug, halfway between us. So far we'd found ways of avoiding putting Finn in the journal. Not exactly on purpose. It was more like we both knew not to bring him up. But it was impossible not to think of him now. That pale, empty page begging for some words.

I could have skipped over February 5. Either I could have left the page blank, or I could have written something boring in there. But it seemed wrong. Maybe it was dumb, but it felt disrespectful to Finn to do that.

I slid the notebook over to Toby.

"You first," I said.

"June, look, I can't. I really, really can't. You weren't there. You don't know . . ."

It wasn't the first time he'd said something like that, and the words hung there.

You weren't there.
You don't know.

I didn't say anything at first. I let those words worm their way through my head. I let them slither right down into my heart. I nodded slowly, then flipped the notebook closed with one finger. I stood up and pretended to look at my watch.

"Oh, June. Don't go. I . . . You don't know what it was like. You don't—"

"God," I shouted. "Just shut up. Shut. Up. Stop saying that." I felt filled with a kind of rage I didn't know I had. Like I wanted to charge at Toby and pummel his skinny arms with my fists. I'm not a violent person. I didn't think I was a violent person, but right then something dangerous seemed to be waking up. Some hard dark sleeping thing from deep in my belly had opened one eye.

And then it went. Just like that. It felt like a balloon had popped inside my chest, letting all the anger seep away. I stood there, drained. I looked at the notebook clenched in my hand, my fingernails digging into the sky-blue cardboard.

Toby's mouth was open, like he was searching for something to say.

"Sorry," I said.

"It's all right. It's my fault." He slid over on the couch and I sat down next to him. I leaned my head on the same skinny arm that only a minute before I'd wanted to punch, and Toby twisted his long fingers into my hair. I felt him undoing one of my braids and then braiding it again. Again and again he did that, all the while saying, "It's all right. It's my fault," until it felt like he wasn't even talking to me anymore.

That night I slept in fitful little naps. I dreamed of origami wolves unfolding themselves from the pages of the *Book of Days*. I saw them shaking off the creases until they were whole and muscly. Furred and running. Leaping right off my desk, in midair, hovering over my bed. Teeth sloppy with drool. I dreamed of trying again and again to fold them back down, but I couldn't do it. They knew where I lived.

"It's just a fiddly-hand thing," a green-eyed wolf said.

"Just the kind of thing a person could love," another answered, and when I woke it was like I hadn't slept at all.

Forty-Eight

There were two things in the box I gave Toby. One was the lid to Finn's Russian teapot. I thought it would be kind of like one of those broken heart necklaces that people have sometimes. When Greta was twelve she had one with Katie Tucker that said BEST FRIENDS. Each one of them wore half the jagged broken heart on a fake gold chain, until the time when Katie lied to Greta about a sleepover she was having and they weren't best friends anymore. Greta had the second half, which said *ST* and under it ENDS, like the abbreviation for Saint Ends.

I didn't know if Toby would see the lid the way I meant it. I wanted him to understand that I thought he was one of the best people. That *I* thought that. Finn or no Finn.

The other thing in that box was my passport, with a tiny note that said, *We could go to England,* taped over the top of my dorky picture.

I tried to come up with a way to go without getting caught, without anyone ever finding out, but I realized it was impossible. So my plan was to do the next best thing—I'd leave a note and call when I got there. Everyone would know I was fine, that I was coming back. Of course I'd be in the biggest trouble of my life at the end of it all, but I didn't care about things like that anymore.

We'd probably go for only a few days, but in my mind it would be just like *A Room with a View* and *Lady Jane*. I'd be taking care of Toby. It would be romantic. Not lovey-dovey romantic, the other kind. It would be the best I could possibly do. I am average at English and I am average at math, but I was not going to be average at looking after Toby. This time I was going to get it exactly right.

Forty-Nine

I was on the floor in the living room, doing a 750-piece jigsaw puzzle of one of the stained-glass windows in Chartres Cathedral, which Finn brought back for me when he went to France one time. It was only five o'clock, way too early on a weekday for anyone to be home, but then in walked my dad, looking like he was halfway to being dead.

"Stomach bug," he said, sinking into the couch. He closed his eyes and laid a hand across his belly. He sniffed the air and seemed to turn a shade greener. "Ugh, that darned crockpot."

"I could get you some ginger ale and . . . I don't know . . . a hot water bottle or something. If you want."

His eyes were still closed and a little smile spread across his face.

"What is it?" I asked.

"Oh, nothing."

"What?" I said. "Come on."

"Nothing. It's just nice, that's all. You offering to take care of your old, sick dad."

The timer bell on the crockpot dinged as I walked into the kitchen. I took the lid off and gave it a stir. I poured us both glasses of ginger ale and brought them into the living room. When I got in there, my dad was stretched out on his side on the floor, sifting through puzzle pieces.

"All right if I help?" he said.

"Sure."

It was a hard puzzle. The colors were mostly deep primaries, rich reds and blues, and even after separating them out into piles, it took a lot of time. I took the red pile and started trying to piece some sections together. My dad worked on the blues.

"It'll all be over soon, eh, Junie?"

"What will?" I flipped a piece right side up.

"Tax season. Done for another year. Thank God."

"It's not so bad, is it?"

My dad gave me an "are you kidding?" look.

"Well, why do you do it, then?"

I meant it seriously. I really wondered why people were always doing what they didn't like doing. It seemed like life was a sort of narrowing tunnel. Right when you were born, the tunnel was huge. You could be anything. Then, like, the absolute second after you were born, the tunnel narrowed down to about half that size. You were a boy, and already it was certain you wouldn't be a mother and it was likely you wouldn't become a manicurist or a kindergarten teacher. Then you started to grow up and everything you did closed the tunnel in some more. You broke your arm climbing a tree and you ruled out being a baseball pitcher. You failed every math test you ever took and you canceled any hope of being a scientist. Like that. On and on through the years until you were stuck. You'd become a baker or a librarian or a bartender. Or an accountant. And there you were. I figured that on the day you died, the tunnel would be so narrow, you'd have squeezed yourself in with so many choices, that you just got squashed.

"Why do I do it?" my dad said. "That's a no-brainer. For you. For you and Greta and your mother."

"Oh," I said, suddenly feeling immensely sad that somebody would throw their whole life away just to make sure other people were happy. "Well, thanks."

My dad smiled really big so I could see the little gap between his front teeth. "Anytime." Then all of a sudden he threw his hand over his mouth. "Oh, no . . ." he said, lurching up and running for the bathroom.

I sat there looking at my pieces. At all the different shades of red. I thought about Finn. How he did whatever he wanted. Just like my mother said. He never let the tunnel squash him. But still, there he was. In the end he was still crushed to death by his own choices. Maybe what Toby said was right. Maybe you had to be dying to finally get to do what you wanted.

I fidgeted around with the puzzle pieces for a while longer, but I wasn't lucky. Nothing seemed to fit without a whole lot of work.

Then I had this thought: What if it was enough to realize that you would die someday, that none of this would go on forever? Would that be enough?

Then I thought of something else. Something my dad had said. *It'll all be over soon.* I walked over to the calendar in the kitchen. It was the one my parents got made up to give to all their clients. *Elbus and Elbus Accountants,* it said, and it had only one picture, a cheesy scene of a bright blue lake in front of some snowcapped mountains. April 13. Two more days until the end of tax season. If I added in the week it took my parents to file extensions and get things back in order, that gave me almost a week and a half of orphanhood. This was the first year ever that I wished tax season would go on longer. The first year that I needed to be an orphan.

Fifty

I hadn't seen Greta look at me once since the day she raided my closet. If I was in the kitchen, she skipped her coffee and went straight outside to wait for the bus. If I was doing homework at the table, she went up to her room. At school she turned the other way if she saw me coming down the hall. It was like she wanted me not to exist.

And I didn't care anymore. That's what I told myself. I didn't care that her eyes were always tired and red. I didn't care that I never saw her with friends anymore. That she didn't even sit with her groupies at lunch. That she always seemed to be alone. I didn't care that at the end of this school year, Greta might be moving out. They had a supervised dorm where the kids in *Annie* stayed, and if she got the part, that's where she'd go. Then after that she'd be off to Dartmouth. And that would be the end. No more sister. Some days that sounded like a dream come true. That's what I told myself.

But still, now and then I popped into rehearsals. I thought if Greta saw me there she might think I wasn't seeing Toby anymore. It was a lame effort, and I didn't really think she cared, but I did it anyway.

I'd stand near the front of the auditorium against the wall, right next to the door, so I could leave when it got too tedious. One afternoon I was standing there, bored as could be, watching Mr. Nebowitz organize the chorus and the walk-on people, when I saw Ben Della-hunt leaning over the edge of the balcony, waving at me. He kept waving until I understood that he was trying to get me to go up to the lighting booth. I cocked my head and looked around. He nodded and beckoned me again. I didn't want to go up. Looking at Ben reminded me that I was an idiot.

"Come on, Elbus," he called down. And then I had no way not to go up.

Ben smiled, holding the door of the little booth open as I walked across the balcony. Pete Loring and John Untemeyer were in there too, and I sat down on a folding chair behind the three of them.

"Can't stay away, huh?" Ben said.

"Something like that."

"No, I mean it, you look totally bored. Why do you keep coming to rehearsals?"

For a second I thought about telling him. For a weird second I thought about spilling every single secret I had to Ben Dellahunt right there in that dark booth. Then he'd know who I really was. Then he'd know that Tina Yarwood had nothing on me. But of course I didn't.

"I told Greta I'd help," I said instead.

"Why would she care if you helped? Anyway, it's not like you're actually helping."

I crossed my arms over my chest. "Look, you're the one who asked me to come up here. I wasn't bugging you. I can go."

"No. Sorry. I'll shut up."

The other two boys didn't say anything. They concentrated on sliding switches and turning knobs on the board. John Untemeyer glanced over at me, but Pete kept his head down like he was embarrassed to have a girl, even a girl like me, in the booth. Antonia came on to sing the reprise of "Dites-Moi."

"Hey, you take French, right?" I said to Ben.

"Yeah."

"So what does *dites-moi* mean anyway?"

Ben thought for a few seconds. He tapped his index finger in the air like he was tracing out the lyrics of the song for himself.

"*Tell me why.* That's what it means. Tell me why. Then something like life is so beautiful. Tell me why life is so beautiful. Tell me why life is so . . . gay." He looked sheepish, then quickly added, "You know, like the happy gay."

"Yeah. The happy gay. I know."

Greta came on to do the scene where Lieutentant Cable says he can't marry Bloody Mary's daughter because she's not white. Bloody Mary is supposed to be furious in that scene and Greta played it almost psychotic. She poked Craig Horvell, who was playing Lieutenant Cable, over and over again in his chest. She was poking him so hard that it looked like she'd poked him right out of character. He looked scared, and a couple of times I saw him glance down at Mr. Nebowitz like he was hoping for a rescue. It was the angriest I'd ever seen Greta, stomping around onstage like she had a score to settle. Like Craig Horvell had ruined her life and she was about to make him pay. But the longer I watched, the more it looked not so much like anger but sadness. Desperation. She was flapping around up there, and what it looked like was that she was desperate for someone to notice she'd gone right around the bend. But nobody did seem to notice. Only me. Me, sitting in the balcony, watching my sister self-destruct.

When she left the stage, Ben turned to me and said, "She's really good, you know."

I nodded. "Of course I know."

We sat there quiet for a while.

"You know, the other night, in the woods, I—"

"Don't worry. I don't even remember anything."

"Well, I kissed you, remember?"

I couldn't help laughing. Most people would have just gone along with the memory loss thing, but not Ben.

"Don't worry," I said. "I won't tell Tina." Then I got up and left.

After the rehearsal, I waited for Greta outside the school. I didn't know what I wanted to say to her, but seeing her on that stage, so small and wrecked, made me want to do something. Maybe I'd tell her that I forgave her for putting all my best stuff in the garbage (even though I didn't). Or maybe I'd ask for her help with makeup so she'd tell me what was happening to her. The whole undrunk truth. The sun had turned the sky a pretty orangey pink. Like the inside of a seashell. I stared out across the school track, where a few boys were running laps. I watched them go around three times, and when Greta still hadn't come out, I turned to leave. I didn't bother with the woods. I walked on the sidewalk, right up through town, because it was longer. Sometimes it feels good to take the long way home.

Fifty-One

I stood in Finn's kitchen, leaning up against the counter. The whole place smelled charred, because Toby was making toast, which he kept burning even though he was standing right there. This was almost a week after the journal thing. He called and said he felt bad about how things had gone last time. He said he wanted to make amends. I caught the train straight after school and then I took the subway up to the apartment. It didn't bother me to take the subway by myself anymore, and it was a whole lot cheaper than taking a taxi.

"Well . . . what do you think?" I was sure Toby was going to love the England plan. He would love it because it was perfect.

"What do I think about what?"

"You know—the passport. The trip?"

So there I was, beaming like a moron, and right away I could see that Toby didn't actually look pleased at all.

"Ah. That."

"You said we could do anything, and so I was thinking England. You could show me everything there. Castles and . . . I don't know—everything. Your town—I looked it up. You could show me the moors. You know, *Wuthering Heights*? We could go in the summer. I'm still working on the details, but maybe I'd get my mother to send me to sleepaway camp and then—"

The toaster popped. Toby took out the toast, examined it, then scraped at it until it barely held itself together anymore. Then he tossed it on a plate.

"June, I'm sorry. I really am, but that's impossible." He opened a drawer in the kitchen, pulled out my passport, and handed it to me. I took it, and we walked through to the living room. Toby pulled a pack of cigarettes out of his back pocket and slid one out without even offering one to me.

I threw my passport on the coffee table between us. I was starting to feel a little bit sick, because I'd spent a lot of time thinking about this plan. I'd searched all over the house to find the place where our passports were kept, and it had taken me forever to find the key.

"Nothing's impossible. You said—"

"Castles, June? *Wuthering Heights*? Christ. I'm from the outskirts of Leeds."

"Well, okay, I don't know, whatever. Whatever you want to show me. Your England."

"That'd be a laugh a minute."

"I don't care."

"June, I can't just take you out of the country. Finn would never . . . You're only, what? Fourteen? Fifteen?" Toby thought I might be fifteen. I almost smiled, but I held it back. "Plus . . ."

"Plus what?"

"Plus they wouldn't let me back here if I left. All right? I can't go." He looked down, like he was disappointed in himself, then he said, "I'm sorry, June. I know I promised anything, but . . ."

"So? Would it be so bad to stay there?"

Toby shook his head slowly, thinking. "For me? Yes. It would. It would be awful. And the summer . . . Well, it's a long way off."

It was already halfway through April. Summer was only a couple of months away, and I was about to argue with Toby, but then I looked at him. His eyes ringed with gray circles. His cheeks collapsing as he inhaled his cigarette. I suddenly understood what he was trying to say.

"But Finn wanted—"

"You don't know what Finn wanted," he said. And for a moment it was like Greta was right there, talking out of Toby's mouth. I hoisted my backpack onto my shoulders and started to walk out. Then I turned back.

"I do. I know. He wanted me to take care of you."

Toby stubbed out his cigarette and, for the first time that day, he smiled. First a little bit, then more, until he was laughing. At me. He was laughing at me. Then he collapsed into Finn's blue chair, because something was so funny that he couldn't even manage to stand up anymore. I blushed and turned to go. Before I got to the door, I zipped open my backpack and reached down for the *Book of Days*. I opened the book, flipping through to find the page.

"You can laugh all you want, but he wrote it. In here. Plain as anything. He said, *Look after Toby*. Is that enough proof for you?"

"June, I'm not laughing at you."

And suddenly I got a burst of meanness that shot straight from my heart to my lips. "He said you have nobody. Nobody at all."

Toby didn't look away. His laugh turned into a soft, knowing smile.

"That's right," he said. Then he stood and walked over to the windowsill. He reached his hand into a big electric-blue vase and pulled out a folded piece of paper. He slowly unfolded it and passed it over to me.

It was all wrinkled and thin, like it had been read a hundred times.

My Dearest Love,

I've said everything I need to say except this. This one last thing. Please look after June for me. Please promise to take the very best care of my only girl.

With so much love my heart might split in two . . .
Finn

I read it twice, staring at each and every word, imagining Finn's shaky hand forming each sloppy letter. I looked around the apartment. There were those two pictures I used to think were my grandfather's hands, until I found out they were the hands of Toby's grandfather. There was the old carved trunk that Finn kept blankets in. There was the door to Finn's bedroom, which was closed again. Private. I reread the note, feeling stupid and confused.

"Come here," Toby said.

I shook my head hard. There it was. All along I'd been looking for Finn shining through Toby, and there he was the whole time. Every little thing Toby had done for me had come from Finn. I felt a warmth spread through my body from my toes all the way up to my scalp. I thought back to that very first day I'd seen him at the funeral. Toby trying to catch my eye, trying in his clumsy way to do right by Finn. Just like I was trying to do.

"It's all right. Everything will be all right."

I knew it wouldn't. That was obvious. But Toby stretched his arms out and I stepped into them. I walked right in, like Toby was a huge wardrobe that could take me anywhere I wanted to go.

"Shhhh," he said. "Shhhhh. It's okay," and we rocked. I cried right into Toby's chest. Right into Toby's heart. "Shhhh," he said over and over, until it felt like we weren't even two separate people anymore.

"See?" he said. "See how much he loved you?"

I clung to Toby, his ribs pressing against me like train tracks heading far, far away. I clung to him like I had the power to keep him here. I held him the way I thought Finn might have held him. With everything I had. With all the love I've got.

Then my crying turned into laughing, and I pulled back and looked at Toby.

"What is it?" he asked.

"Look at us. We must be the worst caretakers in the whole world."

Then Toby laughed too. "I don't know," he said. "I thought I was doing all right."

I raised my eyebrows. "We got drunk on Volcano Bowls last week. I'm not sure that's what Finn had in mind."

Toby gave a sheepish smile. Then he put on a fake serious face and cleared his throat. "As you head into adulthood, June, you may occasionally encounter oversize exotic beverages of an alcoholic nature. I felt it was my duty to acquaint you with these potentially hazardous drinks."

I laughed and gave him a shove in the arm.

His serious face fell apart. "Plus," he said, "it was fun, wasn't it?"

I nodded.

And I thought that maybe Toby had figured it out. Maybe that was all Finn wanted us to do. To make each other laugh. Maybe Finn just wanted to think that his two favorite people might sing and smile and stumble around the city like they were having the time of their lives.

I managed to keep the warm feeling with me for most of the train ride home, but by the time we got to Hawthorne something else started to creep in. The note meant two things. The first, the good one, was that Finn cared. That he loved me enough to make sure Toby looked out for me. But the second thing it meant was that the only reason Toby had spent all that time with me was because of Finn. Because Finn asked him to. It had nothing to do with me. Greta was right. As usual, she had it all figured out.

Fifty-Two

AMERICA'S MOST WANTED

That's what it said on the cover. The words were in bold black type, spread right across the page. Under them were Greta and me. The portrait. The two of us right in the middle of the cover of *Newsweek* magazine.

The article was about art that's missing or is maybe in people's private collections without anyone knowing about it. Hidden stuff. Apparently we were only number six. More important were an Andy Warhol painting, a painting from the 1700s showing an important battle in the Revolutionary War, two sculptures, and an American flag that had just twelve stars and was supposed to have been made even before the Betsy Ross one. Then came us.

I thought it was probably the same picture that they used in *The New York Times,* because the buttons weren't there. My T-shirt was plain black.

There was a picture of each of the top ten missing things and then there were another fifty listed below. A man from the Whitney said he was trying to put together an exhibition called "Lost and Found," and if he managed to get hold of enough of the stuff on the list, it would be able to go ahead.

In the article he said, *We know about these works only because somebody has written about them or they've appeared in a photo or a film at some point.*

We call them ghost works, because we have only a trace of them, not the real physical object.

The part about our portrait said mostly the same stuff that was in the *Times*. The only difference was that they'd interviewed the owner of the gallery where Finn used to show his work. He said that he could not think of a greater tragedy than Finn Weiss ceasing to produce art. I thought that seemed like an exaggeration, but still, I felt proud that someone would say that about Finn.

It was Beans who brought the magazine in to school and showed it to me. At first I thought of hiding it or throwing it away, but it was *Newsweek*. There were thousands and thousands of copies all over the country. It was probably already up on the library bulletin board. Someone had probably called the Whitney guy to tell him where we were.

The article ended with the guy from the Whitney saying he was like a detective. Always on the hunt for missing art. I flipped back to the cover and stared at Greta and me. I thought of that guy searching for us. Trailing us. I realized we wouldn't be very hard to find, and somehow that scared me. The idea of him knocking on our door made me shudder.

My mother brought that *Newsweek* home from work. Two separate people had given her a copy. We all sat around the dinner table. My mother and father and Greta and me. The magazine sat in the middle. There was no crockpot delight that night. Instead, my mother had cooked two boxes of Kraft macaroni and cheese. The bright-orange pasta sat on our plates, untouched.

"I've decided to call him," my mother said.

My fork fell right out of my hand. For a second it was like the portrait was right there in front of me. The gold painted hair. The little black skull.

I started to argue, but Greta kicked me hard under the table. She got me right on the anklebone and I had to try hard not to punch her back. I glanced at her, and, even though she still wouldn't look me in the eye, I could tell she had a plan.

"The longer we wait," she said, "the longer we keep it hidden, the more valuable it'll get. Right? Think about it. Even if he figures out that we have the painting, we don't have to show it to him. Do we?"

My parents looked at each other. I saw that they were reading each other, trying to work out the right thing to do.

"Well," my father said, "you do have a point, but maybe it'd be good to get it out there. Maybe it's what Finn would have wanted."

"No," I said. Greta kicked me again, but this time I ignored her. "He wouldn't have wanted that. He painted it for us."

"Honey, an artist's work belongs to everyone. In a sense."

"But it's my face. Mine and Greta's. We don't belong to everybody. Finn made it for us, and I say no."

"Just calm down, Junie." My father was always like that, trying to keep everything peaceful without taking any kind of position.

I glanced at Greta, who was leaning back in her chair and had her arms crossed over her chest.

"He'll probably just want to have a look at it and then we can take it from there," my mother said. "Nobody's talking about selling it or even showing it. Let's take it one step at a time."

I looked at Greta again. Right in the eyes. We both knew what we'd done to the portrait. I couldn't imagine how my mother would react. Or maybe I could. Maybe that was the problem. Across the table, my mother and father were also looking at each other. My mother turned and reached her hand out toward us.

"Okay. Both of you. Just . . . just quiet. The truth is, I've already called him. I spoke with him this afternoon."

"What do you mean?" I said.

"He's coming up next week to have a look."

"But it's ours. We don't want . . ." I looked at Greta.

She smiled. Slow and long. For a few seconds she stayed like that, not saying a word. Then she tossed her head back and looked across the table.

"Whatever," she said. "Maybe it's good. Like you said. Let's just see what happens next."

I didn't have any words. My mouth was probably hanging open.

The next day I went straight to the bank after school. Since the day Greta got hold of all the stuff in my closet, I'd made sure to keep my half of the Elizabethan picture and the *Book of Days* in my backpack. They were in there when I went to see the portrait. It was already getting warm, and I tied my sweater around my waist as I walked slowly through town. Along the way, I stopped at Benedetti's Deli and got a can of Yoo-hoo and a bag of Doritos.

Mr. Zimmer wasn't working at the bank that day, so I had to sign my name for the woman behind the counter to let me go down to the vault. I did my best and I could tell I was getting better, but still the woman, who was young and pretty and tidy in a way I knew I never would be, stared back and forth between the form and the signature. Then she eyed me up and asked me for my address and phone number, until I finally convinced her that I was actually June Elbus.

It was almost painful to take the portrait out of the box this time. My hope was that the gold in our hair and the skull on Greta's hand would blend right in. After all, nobody ever seemed to notice Toby's buttons. That's what I hoped, but really I knew that wasn't how it was going to be. You can't put shiny gold paint on a picture and expect nobody to notice it. I slid the portrait out slowly, with my eyes closed. When I finally looked, I saw that it was even worse than I'd imagined. The gold paint gathered every bit of light in that room and sent it right back to my eyes.

And there was something new. Greta's lips, which were a natural color before, were painted bright red. The red was the color of the Campbell's tomato soup that my mother used to make us for lunch when we were little. Instead of looking triple-pleased with herself, like she did before, now Greta looked like she was frowning. More than frowning, even. With the gold in her hair and the lips, I'd say Greta looked fearsome.

I leaned in to the painting. I wanted to see Greta's brushstrokes. I wanted to see them up close. I knew she must have seen what I'd done to our hair. That's what hit me then. In real life, Greta had been avoiding me as much as she could. She'd barely said a word to me since that day she found my stuff. But here it was almost like we were talking. Like a secret language. This portrait of us holding all the words we never said anymore.

I took out the half of the Playland picture and propped it up next to the portrait. I looked at the girl in the portrait, that girl who still had Finn, the stupid girl who used to think she was the only one who had him, and I hardly recognized her anymore. I couldn't begin to imagine her taking care of anyone. Then I looked at the girl in that big Elizabethan getup and I thought the same. I thought they both looked stupid. The kind of girls who couldn't do anything for anyone. I was glad I didn't have a mirror with me just then, because I knew I'd see the same thing there. Of course Toby wouldn't want to go to England with me. Why would he?

I pressed my back against the wall and slid down to the floor.

Why would Toby pretend to like me? Why would someone do that?

Guilt, that's why.

No. Nobody knew anything about AIDS when they first got it. That was true. Why would Toby feel guilty?

And why didn't he ever mention prison?

I don't know. I don't know. I don't know.

Of course he wouldn't go to England with you. You never get it, do you? You never get who people are to you. Ben, Beans, Finn, Greta. Why would Toby want to spend that kind of time with you? And then there's that stupid teapot lid. . . .

I closed my eyes and whispered the *Dies Irae* from the *Requiem*. Over and over I said the Latin words—*Dies irae, dies illa, solvet saeclum in favilla*—until, after a while, a little bit of the dread fell away.

I stood in that room and looked at the portrait again. At Greta and me. I dug down deep into the bottom of my backpack and found that jar of gold paint. I imagined Greta in here, coloring her lips, knowing I would see what she'd done, and suddenly I needed her to hear me. I needed her to know I was answering her call. And so instead of trying to cover anything up, I took out my little jar of gold paint, dipped the brush in, and, as careful as I could, I painted each of Greta's tiny fingernails gold.

Fifty-Three

I stood next to Toby on the platform, waiting for the monorail. We were in Wild Asia, at the Bronx Zoo, about to board the Bengali Express, which—next to the Cloisters—is the best way to leave New York without leaving New York.

The Bronx Zoo is not a sad zoo. It's huge and filled with trees and open meadows and makes you feel like you aren't in a city at all. They have it divided up into continents—Africa, Asia, North America—and each part has a feeling like the place it's supposed to be. The Africa part is all dusty, with hardly any trees, and the ice cream shacks are made to look like little huts. Asia is more lush. There's bamboo and statues of Indian goddesses and Chinese-looking archways.

I'd told Toby to pick me up at my house at ten in the morning. It was a school day, but my plan was to get up early and tell my mother I thought I was coming down with the same stomach bug my dad and Greta had. My mother pressed her soft palm against my forehead for just a second before agreeing that I did feel clammy. I crawled back into bed and waited until everyone left, then I got dressed and sat by the window in the living room, watching.

As usual, it didn't even occur to Toby that it was strange for me to be getting picked up by him at ten o'clock on a weekday. He stood outside the back door in a bulky gray wool coat, looking really happy to see me.

"It's spring," I said, eyeing the coat.

Toby seemed embarrassed that I'd brought up the coat and gazed out across the backyard.

"I've been here before, you know," he said.

"Really?"

"The teapot. That postman. It was me. Special delivery."

I thought back to that day, and it felt so long ago. It felt impossible that it had been only two months ago.

"Oh, yeah," I said. "I knew that was you."

Toby seemed to be miles away, but he came back to himself then. He smiled. "I thought you did."

I'd told him it was my turn to take him somewhere. At first I thought of the Cloisters, but I wasn't ready to give that away yet. So it was the zoo. Toby said I could drive if I wanted to. He held out the keys.

"I don't exactly know how. I don't have my permit or anything."

"I'll teach you." Toby lit a cigarette, but he only managed one breath of it before he started coughing. The keys fell from his hand and I picked them up. Before I could hand them back, Toby had slipped into the passenger's seat. This wasn't what I had in mind, but I didn't want to act scared about it, so I opened the driver's door and sat down. Then I saw the Smurf hand, that little Smurf hand Finn had glued on the gearshift, and I saw my way out.

"It's stick shift. There's no way . . ." I laid the keys on the dashboard.

Toby was still coughing, but he nodded. He picked up the keys and walked around to the driver's side.

We parked in the Bronx River parking lot, which meant that we came in through the North America section. North America was the most convincing. The big trees and grassy fields with deer and bison and wolves looked good. Like some kind of super condensed version of all the American wildlife there'd ever been. Like every kind of thing we'd killed off had been ushered back into the world.

"Okay," I said. "It's like Playland. There's something I want to show you. Not just the animals. Come on." I turned back. Toby looked old. Older than last time I'd seen him, and I saw that he was trying hard not to walk slow. "Come on," I said again, pretending not to notice.

Then, in a big burst of energy, Toby threw his arms out and bolted toward me, laughing. He looked like some kind of crazy animal like that, in that big gray coat. I laughed too and ran ahead. We raced through North America, past the meadows of deer and wolves, past the World of Birds and the World of Darkness, until after a while the woods and meadows gave way to the more exotic shrubbery of the Asia section.

"Here," I said, pointing down a flight of stairs lined with bright red and yellow Indian flags.

Toby leaned up against the railing. He couldn't seem to stop coughing. His back was bent over like an old man's. A little dart of panic hit my stomach, because I didn't know what to do. I had no idea how to help someone who might be really sick. I gave him a lame pat on the back. All the while Toby kept trying to smile between coughs, pretending like he was okay. When he finally caught his breath, I asked if he wanted a drink.

"No. Let's go," he said. "I'm fine."

We walked down the stairs. At the bottom we walked past a pen where they had camel rides. The camels were all decked out with lush carpets the colors of cinnamon and paprika and mustard under their saddles. A couple of them were toting around toddlers, but the rest stood there looking bored.

I pointed to a booth farther down the path. "This way," I said. "Promise me you'll like it."

He didn't answer for a second, and I was waiting for him to do what I'd done that day at Playland. To say he couldn't promise something like that. But he didn't.

"I promise," he said. "Even if I hate it, I promise I'll like it."

I paid for the monorail tickets, and we stood waiting under the thatched grass roof of the platform. At the other end, a bunch of little kids on a school trip were hanging off the low wood guardrail. When the train pulled up, we waited for them to pile in before choosing a quieter car at the other end.

The seats in the monorail were set up almost like a small theater: two rows tiered, and instead of facing front and back, they all faced the side of the train, which was entirely open. The ride goes for only twenty minutes or so, but the voice on the intercom makes out like you're going all around Asia, and if you don't let yourself look out too far, if you focus on the trees and water just below the train, you can believe it. You can believe those black musk deer are really in the south China hills and the elephants are really roaming over the plains of India.   ·

The train moved out. Right away we were crossing the muddy Bronx River, and a woman's voice came over the speakers saying we were in India, crossing the Ganges. I looked over at Toby and saw he was grinning, and I gave him a nod.

"Don't look out too far," I said. "It wrecks it." Greta always looked out too far. She was always the one who would point out the places where you could see the real Bronx through a gap in the trees.

On the way back across the Bronx River, the woman would say it was the Yangtze and we would be in China. Now she told us about antelope and tigers and three kinds of deer.

"Hey," Toby said.

"Yeah?"

"Come here." Toby patted the spot next to him on the bench, and I scooted over. He put his arm around my shoulder and pulled me in so my face was pressed up against his big coat.

"Breathe in."

I didn't know what Toby was trying to do at first, but I took a long slow breath of his coat and there, like magic, was Finn. The exact smell of Finn. Not only lavender and orange but other things too. The mild citrus smell of his aftershave. And coffee beans and paint and things I didn't know the names of but were just part of Finn. I didn't want to move. I sat nestled against Toby, my head buried tight in his coat. Toby held me and pulled me closer and closer, and I felt in the soft tremble of his shoulders that he was crying. I closed my eyes and it was like I was flying over the Ganges, clinging to Finn. This Finn's arms gripped me tighter than Finn's ever had. I thought of all the different kinds of love in the world. I could think of ten without even trying. The way parents love their kid, the way you love a puppy or chocolate ice cream or home or your favorite book or your sister. Or your uncle. There's those kinds of loves and then there's the other kind. The falling kind.

Husband-and-wife love, girlfriend-and-boyfriend love, the way you love an actor in a movie.

But what if you ended up in the wrong kind of love? What if you accidentally ended up in the falling kind with someone it would be so gross to fall in love with that you could never tell anyone in the world about it? The kind you'd have to crush down so deep inside yourself that it almost turned your heart into a black hole? The kind you squashed deeper and deeper down, but no matter how far you pushed it, no matter how much you hoped it would suffocate, it never did? Instead, it seemed to inflate, to grow gigantic as time went by, filling every little spare space you had until it was you. You were it. Until everything you ever saw or thought led you back to one person. The person you weren't supposed to love that way. What if that person was your uncle, and every day you carried that gross thing around with you, thinking that at least nobody knew and, as long as nobody knew, everything would be okay?

I took another deep breath of the coat as the monorail leaned smoothly into a curve, out of India, into Nepal, and I dreamed it was all true. That I was clinging tight to Finn. That the ache had been lifted right out of my belly and been made into something real. That I could open my eyes and see Finn smiling right at me.

Toby had leaned his cheek against the top of my head, and a stream of his tears ran down my forehead and onto my face, trickling over my eyes so it must have looked like I was crying. They fell down my cheek and over my lips. I didn't know if you could catch AIDS from tears, but I didn't care. I wasn't afraid of things like that anymore.

We stayed like that for the rest of the ride, and I wondered if Toby's dreams were the same as mine. I wondered if he'd been turning me into his one true love.

The monorail pulled back into the station, and neither of us moved. I turned my head to look down the car, wiping my cheek against the rough wool of Toby's coat. The mother of a family of four was staring at me. I looked straight into her eyes and I saw what we must look like, Toby and me. I saw how wrong we must look, but I didn't care. I tugged at Toby's sleeve and we both stood, our arms still tight around each other. Nobody knew our story, I thought. Nobody knew how sad our story was.

We walked out of Asia, back through North America. Back past the wolf exhibit. You could never see any wolves in there. They hid, probably trying to pretend they weren't in a cage. Probably knowing that they looked just like plain old dogs when they were behind bars. We stood for a while, leaning up against the fence, staring out over that little version of the Great Plains. Opposite the wolf field was a fake totem pole, just about the size of a man. Blue and red paint was chipping off the heads of the eagle, bear, and wolf. I stopped.

"What is it?" Toby said.

"Give me the coat."

"No. Why?"

"Just please, okay?"

Toby frowned. He had a pleading look on his face, but I stood with my hands on my hips, and after a moment he slowly unbuttoned the coat. When it was all open, he hung his head. I tugged the coat off his shoulders and draped it over my arm. Then I walked over to the totem pole, wrapped the coat around it, buttoned it up so that the eagle's head poked out of the top. I stood back, tilting my head and squinting.

"Perfect," I said with a huge smile, but when I looked over at Toby, I saw that he was still standing in the same spot. I saw that there was nothing left of him. He was wearing the same dinosaur-bones T-shirt he'd had on that first time at the apartment, and his arms were covered with dark scabby marks. He stood there in the warm April sunshine, looking like a skinned animal. He stood there with his head down not saying a word.

"They'll watch over it for us. Right?" I said, pointing to the wolf field.

Toby moved his big hands over his arms like he was holding the pieces of himself together.

"I just thought, maybe we're supposed to try to, you know, move on," I said.

Toby glanced up. I thought he'd looked older when I saw him earlier, but now, without the coat, he seemed younger. Shrunk down to nothing. He cocked his head and stared at me with a puzzled expression.

"But where would we move to?"

I didn't know, and right then I felt so stupid for having said it. I felt like a traitor to Finn. There was Toby, the loyal one, the one who would never move even an inch away from Finn's ghost. And there was me. The one with the threadbare love. *Move on.* What a cliché. What an embarrassment. I felt my face go hot. I stared at the coat, which a minute ago seemed like such a clever thing and now looked like something a kid would do. A stupid little kid who had no idea what real love was.

I bowed my head and silently unbuttoned the coat. I threw it over my arm and handed it back to Toby without looking at him.

He slipped the coat back on, and all of a sudden I felt the truth again. Of course Greta was right. There was no "us." Toby was doing what Finn asked him to do. No more. No less.

In the car, Toby reached across me and opened the glove compartment. He took out my passport and laid it on the dashboard.

"Don't forget to take this." He looked away from me when he said it.

The dark-blue book reflected onto the windshield so it looked like there were two passports. Two little reminders of my dumb plan. I picked it up and flicked through the pages. I saw that Toby had peeled the note off my picture, and my half-smiling eleven-year-old face squinted up at me. *Stupid stupid stupid.* I tossed the passport onto the floor next to my backpack. Then I shoved it away with the toe of my boot.

I turned to Toby. "I know you met Finn in prison."

For a second he looked confused. Like he hadn't heard me right. And the truth is, the prison thing didn't bother me at all. Greta thought it was this big trump card, but I felt just like Nellie in *South Pacific*. Nellie didn't care that Emile was a murderer. She could forgive that right away. Like it was nothing. It was the other stuff, the crimes he didn't even know he'd committed, that she couldn't get over.

Toby clasped his hands together and gently tapped them against the steering wheel. "You know that, do you?"

I nodded.

"And you're still here?"

I nodded again.

"And you want to know what I did, right?"

I shrugged.

"There's nothing to be frightened of."

"Like I'd really be scared of you," I said.

Toby gave me a look. Then he stared down the row of parked cars. When he turned back to me, his face was serious. "If I don't tell you, you'll imagine all kinds of things, and I don't want that." He looked worried. Or maybe trapped. He threw his head into his hands. "Ugh, this is so utterly stupid. This is from another lifetime."

I didn't say anything.

"All right. Here it is, then. I was a student at the Royal Academy. For music. On scholarship, of course. No money at all from my parents, who generally tried to pretend I didn't exist. So I'd busk in tube stations sometimes, and . . . and there was this one night . . ." He let his breath out slow. "This is what I'm trying to tell you. There was this one night, a Saturday, and I was down there, late. There were a bunch of drunken lads, and there I was with no place to go, playing guitar. I even remember what I was playing, because it was this Bach fugue, you know?" I nodded, even though I didn't think I knew any Bach fugues. "And I was lost in it. Sometimes that's what it's like. Sometimes I could forget where I was and just slip away into the playing, adding things to it and playing with it, and it was staving off the cold. But then, out of nowhere, there was a kick right to my ribs. Hard. And I flew backward, trying to hold tight to the guitar because that guitar was from my grandfather, my mother's father from Spain, and it was all I had then. I knew my body, it could heal up, but the guitar, that I couldn't replace. There were four of them, big lads, drunk, and one was taking his jacket off and another punched me in the head, and I could hear the train coming. There'd be a thud to my body and then the high scream of the train cutting through the blows. That's what I remember it like, like that train was calling me. One of them tried to pull the guitar from my hands and then I heard the train again, and all my strength poured into that one thing, that one moment, and I pushed him, June. I pushed that man onto the tracks. I didn't even know my ankle was broken— I didn't feel anything. I just plowed right to the edge, shoving and yelling, and he went over. Right onto the tracks, just a few seconds before the train pulled into the station."

"Did he . . . ?"

Toby shook his head. "Both legs." He looked down and away from me. "So that's it. That's why I went to prison. You can decide for yourself if you want to stop visiting me."

"But it wasn't your fault," I said. "They started it."

He shrugged. "It was a bad thing."

"But . . . but they stole all those years away from you. They—"

He paused for a long time. Then he said, "But they gave me Finn."

He said it like maybe it was worth the trade. Like it was something he would do again if he had the choice. Like he would take a man's legs and give away years of his own freedom if it was the only way. I thought how that was wrong and terrible and beautiful all at the same time.

I was ready for the story to end, but Toby started up again. It didn't even feel like he was talking to me anymore. It felt more like he was talking just to let the story of him and Finn out into the world. He told me he was twenty-three when he met Finn. That Finn was thirty, in London doing a master's degree in art, and part of the course was community work. Finn chose this art-in-prisons project, where they ran classes for inmates.

"So it's his first day and we're in a classroom. There's me and then there's this room full of real criminals. And Finn standing up front. I can see he's trying not to look lost. He's scanning the room and I can't stop watching him, his face, the way he's biting nervously at the corner of his lip, his perfect little narrow shoulders. And I'm thinking, 'Look at me. I'm the only one here who matters.' And the room is starting to get restless. There's this one wiry cockney wanker—oh, sorry, June. This one guy who shouts up to Finn, 'Art is for homos,' and the room goes quiet. Everyone's waiting to see how this art teacher will play it.

I see a smile come up on Finn's face—you know that smile—and he looks down, trying to hide it, but then he decides not to. He decides to take a risk. He looks the guy straight in the eyes and says, 'Well, you're in the right place, then,' and right away he had the whole room—well, the whole room except for that one guy. Everyone's laughing, banging on the desks, all sorts. Not me, of course. I sat there quiet, and that's when he noticed me. I looked at him, trying to tell this man, this stranger, everything with my eyes. He cocked his head just the tiniest bit, and I stared back. For a few frozen seconds we were the only ones in the room, and I took my chance. I had to. I mouthed, *Help me,* knowing that he'd probably turn his head away, embarrassed. But he didn't. He kept looking at me. That's how it started. We wrote letters, and I never missed one of his classes. He would brush by me, casually running his hand against my back. Or he would drop a pencil and touch a finger to my ankle as he stooped to pick it up." Toby closed his eyes and smiled, like he was going back there. "There was something so electric about it. So dangerous. Those little touches were everything. I lived for them. You can build a whole world around the tiniest of touches. Did you know that? Can you imagine?"

Toby's eyes had started to water. I wanted to say of course I know that. I know all about tiny things. Proportion. I know all about love that's too big to stay in a tiny bucket. Splashing out all over the place in the most embarrassing way possible. I didn't want to hear any more of the story, but I couldn't help listening. The pain of it almost felt good.

"He saved me, you know? He stayed in England far beyond his visa. He waited for me. He was already known. He was already selling his work for an absolute fortune. He could have gone anywhere, but he waited. For me. The day I got out—"

"I don't want to hear it."

Toby looked embarrassed. He put his hands up in apology. "I understand," he said.

"What do you understand?"

"Your feelings for Finn. I'm sorry. It wasn't sensitive. I'm an ass—"

"What feelings?"

"June—"

"No, tell me what you think. You think I have *feelings* because I don't want to hear about you throwing yourself at my uncle after being locked away in prison?"

"June, it's all right. We know how you felt." He looked at me intensely when he said it, tipping his head slightly to make sure I understood.

And suddenly, like a brick falling on my head, I did understand. Finn knew. Finn knew and Toby knew. They both knew. Of course Finn would know. He always knew my heart.

I lost all my hearing. My head felt filled with every buzzing creature on the planet. I wanted to turn to wax and melt away. I wanted to erase every wrong cell of my body. It felt so bad to be alive in that moment, I would have done anything to end it. If we weren't in the Bronx, I would have jumped out of the car and run all the way home.

Instead, I had to sit there right next to Toby for forty-five whole minutes. Forty-five minutes staring out the window, twisting my body as far away as possible. Forty-five minutes that felt like years. Forty-five silent minutes, except for the one moment on the north side of Yonkers when Toby reached out and put a hand on my back and said, "You think I don't know about wrong love, June? You think I don't understand embarrassing love?"

Toby parked a block from my house. He gave his usual "If you need anything . . ." spiel. I got out of the car as fast as I could, and when I glanced back in, I saw my passport laying on the floor mat, all muddy from my boots. I looked at it there, a little book made of all my stupidity, and I hoped maybe it would get lost forever.

Toby got out of the car and walked around to my side. I forced myself to act like nothing had happened. Like it was no big deal. I forced myself to look at him with a pasted-on smile. We made plans to meet the next Tuesday. He said he thought he was still okay to drive. I told him to park in the Grand Union parking lot, in the back where it slopes off, where it's overhung with trees, next to the Goodwill bins. They were just numb words spilling out of my mouth. They didn't mean anything. I said I'd be there at three-thirty. Toby nodded. That's what we arranged. That's exactly the way we left it.

Fifty-Four

There was the smell of cinnamon French toast, and there was my mother humming "Some Enchanted Evening" and the sunshine billowing into my bedroom window and the thump of Greta's stereo coming through the wall behind my head. There was my father clunking around in the closet at the bottom of the stairs, and there were two chickadees on the branch outside my window. This is how that Saturday started, and I lay in my old, warm bed, smiling because there was no Toby, there were no secrets, there was nothing but home. Nothing but normal things, and that made it feel like it might turn out to be a really good day.

That night was going to be the first performance of *South Pacific*. Opening night. We all had tickets, and Greta already told us that we were supposed to have flowers sent to her at the school. She told us that usually kids sent each other a carnation and parents sent roses or even a whole bunch of flowers. My mother nodded and told her not to worry.

"Promise you'll remember, okay?" Greta said.

"Honey, you'll get flowers. You need to calm down. Stop worrying about everything. You'll look like a wreck by the time the show starts." My mother put a hand on Greta's shoulder and gave it a rub.

I didn't say it, but the truth was that she already did look like a wreck. Her skin was dry and flaky, and her hair looked coarse instead of shiny and smooth like it usually was. She didn't even bother to do her fingernails anymore. It looked like she'd been biting them ragged.

My mother smoothed her hand over Greta's hair.

"You'll do great. I know you will. Sit down, have some breakfast. You too, Junie."

She brought over great heaping plates of French toast with maple syrup. After wiping down the counters and washing a few dishes, my mother left to go into town, and Greta and I were alone together for the first time since the day she raided my closet. Greta pushed most of the French toast over to one side of her plate, then cut up the one piece that was left. We didn't say anything to each other. I could have sat right through that whole breakfast without saying a word, but I looked over at Greta cutting her French toast into the tiniest of pieces, I looked at my small, tired sister, and I thought what a big day this was for her.

"So . . . are you, like, nervous?" I said.

At first I thought she was going to ignore me, but then her brow furrowed and she shrugged. "I don't even want to do it," she said without looking at me. "I wish I'd never auditioned. I wish I was an extra. Or nothing. I wish I was nothing."

The kitchen window was open and I could hear the echoey thump of Kenny Gordano dribbling his basketball in his driveway next door.

"You'll be great."

She pressed the back of her fork into a piece of French toast. "Maybe I don't want to be *great*. Maybe I want to be average. At everything. Maybe I want to be like you."

"Trust me. You don't."

"No, June. You trust me. You know what being great means? It means having a year stolen from your life. There's a whole extra year in there that's lost. And, you know, I want my year back. I want second grade. I'm only sixteen. And now . . . now I'm supposed to be leaving home for good? Does that seem right? You know, I used to love *South Pacific*. It was like this little place in my life where I could just hang out and sing. No pressure or anything. And then next thing you know it turns into this huge chance of a lifetime. Why is everything like that for me? All my life I've listened to Mom. Opportunities. Chances. And

I don't want to be ungrateful. I don't want to miss out, but sometimes I lie in my bed and I look around at my room and I can't believe I'm not supposed to be a kid anymore. What about that opportunity? Where's the second chance for that?" Her voice had gone shaky, like she was about to cry. She reached into her jeans pocket and pulled out one of those tiny bottles of vodka. She didn't even try to hide it from me, she just opened the top and poured half of it into her orange juice. She drank half the glass, then leaned in to me and said, "I'm not going to *Annie,* June. I don't care what I have to do. I won't go."

"I'll help you. We'll figure something out. Tell Mom you changed your mind or something."

Greta finished off her juice and laughed. "Yeah. Right. Whatever. So, are you coming?" she asked. "Tonight?"

"Of course I'm coming. I have a ticket."

"Not the play. After. The cast party." The combination of everything she'd said and the vodka and the matter-of-fact way she'd just asked me to the cast party left me stunned. I sat there staring at her.

"You've got to be kidding."

"No. No, I'm not. I'm asking you."

"You spy on me in the woods. You go into my closet. Destroy all my private stuff—irreplaceable stuff. And then you sit there like I'd actually consider going to a party with you again? I mean, I feel bad about the whole overachiever thing, but—"

"But Ben—you know, maybe . . ."

"Ben went off with Tina Yarwood. You said so yourself. Remember?"

"Oh," she said, suddenly looking sad. "Yeah."

"I'm not part of the cast or crew, and—" I cut myself off. Why should I explain?

Greta didn't say anything for a few seconds. She gently set her fork down on the edge of her plate. "You still go to see him?" she asked.

"Who?"

"You know who."

"Why should I tell you anything? You sit there . . . You sit there like we're best friends or something. Inviting me to parties, always in my business. Well, I've had enough. The. End." I twisted my chair to face away from Greta. Upstairs, my father was singing "Younger Than Springtime" in his booming voice.

"Two words, June. Ryan. White. Okay?"

"Yeah, whatever, Greta."

"Just think about it."

I turned to face Greta again. "What about Ryan White?"

All I knew was that Ryan White was some kid somewhere in the Midwest, who'd caught AIDS from a blood transfusion.

"Someone shot a bullet through his house. People canceled their newspapers because they didn't want him delivering them. Paper, June. They thought they would catch AIDS from paper."

"So what? I'm not afraid. Toby has nobody, okay? And to me—unlike to some people—that actually matters. So just stay away from me. If you hate me so much, if you hate Toby, why didn't you take the opportunity to get us in trouble when you had the chance?" I was almost shouting at Greta, but at the same time I was feeling sorry for her. Here was this person who wasn't a big sister at all anymore. Drinking vodka at breakfast?

Greta didn't say anything. She slurped the last sip of her orange juice, then stacked her glass on top of her plate and started to stand. She stayed like that for a few seconds, then she put her plate back on the table and sat down again. Her eyes were wet, and she reached out and took my hand in hers. She rubbed her index finger over each of my fingernails, then she tapped her own and smiled. "I like the gold," she whispered.

For a second I didn't understand, but then I did, and it felt strange and explosive to have her mention what we'd done to the portrait right at the kitchen table. I gave her a little smile back, and after a while I whispered, "I'm glad," and right then, right at that moment, I felt the wall between the world of secrets and the real world start to collapse. I felt the girls from the portrait becoming us and us becoming them, and I felt my eyes welling up. I nodded hard. "I'm really, really glad."

We sat there, quiet. Kenny's basketball kept thumping, and I wanted to go out there and grab that ball away from him and throw it right over the top of the Gordanos' cedar hedge.

"I shouldn't have gone in your closet."

"Why did you have to spill everything out? You could have just—"

"I know."

I looked at Greta's plate. All the French toast was still there. "You should eat something."

She shrugged. "So . . . will you come? Tonight? To the cast party? We'll talk, okay? You're the only one . . ."

We looked at each other. It was like she hadn't heard a word I'd been saying.

"Why can't you talk to me now?"

She shook her head.

"Same place," she said, and she looked at me long enough to make sure I understood that she meant the woods. "Promise me, June."

"No."

"Promise," she said again, and this time she squeezed my hand so hard it hurt. So tight it was like it was the only thing saving her from falling. "Promise?"

She didn't let go until I gave a little nod. "Okay. I promise," I whispered.

Greta stood to leave. She got as far as the doorway, then turned. She didn't look at me.

"Toby, he has nobody, right? Right, June? Well, who do you think I have?"

Then, before I could say anything, she was gone.

My father had his golf bag slung over one shoulder when he came into the kitchen. This was at about ten-thirty, an hour after breakfast. I was washing the dishes because I told my mother I would. My father grinned at me as he leaned his golf bag up against the refrigerator. "I've got it, June Bug. This year I've finally got it."

"What?" I said.

"Mother's Day's only two weeks away. We're all going to the champagne brunch at Gasho. Reservations are made."

"Good job, Dad," I said. I hadn't even remembered Mother's Day. Usually I was really good at stuff like that. Greta and I used to go out into the backyard and pick flowers and try to cook scrambled eggs.

"She's had a rough year. Let's make this a good one for her, okay?"

"Yeah, good idea." And maybe it was a good idea. Maybe if I tried to see my mother exactly the way I used to see her—hardworking, smart, kind—I could forget what I knew.

"Greta," he shouted. "Let's go." Mr. Nebowitz wanted all the cast and crew at the school by noon, and my father had said he'd drop her on his way to golf. After a couple of minutes, she came down the stairs with a big bag of stuff she needed for the show.

"See you later," she said to me as they went out the door.

After they left, the house was empty, and even though Mother's Day was two weeks away, I went up to my room and started to make my mother a card. Like I used to. With construction paper and markers and colored pencils and glitter. And right then it was almost impossible to believe that there was a whole other me, who drank Volcano Bowls and smoked cigarettes and took care of people who used to be strangers.

About a half hour later my mother knocked on my door.

"Honey?"

"Yeah?"

"Come out here a second."

I stashed my card-making stuff under a few books and stuck my head out the door.

"Yeah?"

"You can come with me into town."

"Why?"

"We need to stop at the bank. Bring your deposit box key."

The panic must have been all over my face, because my mother smiled and said, "Don't worry, we're not selling it or anything. The man from the Whitney, he's coming to see it on Thursday evening, and I won't have time to pick it up during the week."

"I'm kind of busy."

"June."

"I'm working on something. A project."

"Just get the key and get dressed, okay?"

I started to close the door, then popped my head back out. "I could get it for you. On Monday," I called after her. I didn't know what I would do on Monday, but it would give me time.

"Stop this, June. There's nothing to worry about. I expect you downstairs in fifteen minutes, and that's that."

I got dressed as slowly as I could, trying to think of some kind of plan. I thought if Greta was there she'd know what to do, but maybe not. Maybe even she couldn't get us out of this one.

In the kitchen, my mother was leafing through papers in her purse.

"The car's open. You do have the key, right? I honestly wouldn't put it past you to leave it behind."

I nodded.

"Show me, then."

"Mom—"

"I'm sorry, June, but you're making it very hard for me to trust you this morning."

"Well, maybe I'm finding it hard to trust you too," I said.

"June, I have no idea what's gotten into you, but I want to see that key."

I reached down into my pocket and pulled it out. I had actually thought of leaving it in my room, but that seemed like a dumb plan. I held it up and my mother watched me tuck it back in my pocket.

"Okay," she said. "Go on. Out the door."

"I don't think the bank is even open on Saturdays, is it?"

"Of course it is. They've been open 'til one on Saturdays for at least a year. Now, get yourself in the car. We're running late."

My mother shaded her eyes with her open hand as she backed out of the driveway. It was a warm day, probably the hottest of the year so far, and the car was stifling. I kept my eyes on the van's digital clock right in the middle of the dashboard—12:17.

It was the quickest drive into town I'd ever been on. Every light on the way was green, and there was hardly any traffic at all.

"Here, June. Run these in for me." My mother pulled into one of the drop-off spots in front of the post office and handed me a stack of envelopes. "They're all stamped, except for this heavy one." She handed me a dollar and told me to have them weigh it before dropping them all in the box.

I glanced at the clock—12:29.

"Make it quick."

"Yeah, okay," I said, and jumped out of the van. I ran into the post office like I was trying my hardest to be fast, but once I was in there I slowed right down. I slipped behind the door and stood, waiting, then snuck back out and went next door to the pharmacy.

When you have a watch, time is like a swimming pool. There are edges and sides. Without a watch, time is like the ocean. Sloppy and vast. I didn't have a watch. So I had to guess how long I'd been stand-ing there next to the display of decongestants. After what I thought was about ten minutes, I slipped into the post office and joined the end of the line. It didn't feel particularly good to do this to my mother, making her wait out there, getting angrier and angrier, but I thought it was my only chance. If I could push us past one o'clock . . .

When I finally went back out, my mother was not in the van. The doors were unlocked, so I got in and waited. The clock said 12:42. Not as late as I'd hoped, and I considered jumping back out. But then my mother came marching toward me. The van was parked so the sun shone right down on the windshield, and I had to squint to see her. Her arms were folded across her chest and her whole body was stiff as she marched diagonally across the street. When she got in she didn't say a word to me.

We parked behind the bank. The clock said 12:49.

I used to think that if I could time-travel just once, I'd go back to the Middle Ages. Then I thought I would time-travel to the day Finn met Toby, so I could save Finn's life. Now I think I would go back to 12:49 on Saturday, April 25, 1987. I would go to exactly the moment when my mother and I stood in the bank parking lot. Then, I would run or faint or snatch the key from my pocket and hurl it into the scrubby weeds. I'd do whatever I had to do to stop us from going into the bank that day. But there is no time travel, so I had no idea how the rest of the day would go, and instead of running away, I walked in si-lence to the front door of the bank and went in.

Mr. Zimmer was there, and he led us straight downstairs.

"How's Dennis doing?" my mother asked.

"Can't complain, really," he said. "Big into music these days."

"June, you could ask Dennis over for a visit sometime, couldn't you?"

"I guess," I said, only because his father was standing right there.

Mr. Zimmer opened room number two and lowered the box onto the floor.

"All righty," he said. He looked at his watch. "We close in . . . well, we're about to close now, so—"

"I guess we'll have to leave it until next week," I said, in a voice that was probably a bit too pleased.

My mother flashed me a stern look.

"We need to take it with us anyway, Dave. So I guess we'll just have to skip the viewing session."

My mother started to walk out with the whole box.

"I'm afraid we can't let the box itself go out. You'll have to take the painting."

"Oh," my mother said, and then I saw her give Mr. Zimmer the same sad look that Finn could put on. The very same sad look he'd given me when he was trying to get me to agree to the portrait in the first place. She put on a little half smile and I could see Mr. Zimmer changing his mind, right there in front of us.

"Oh, what the hey," he said. "I've known you for years."

"Thanks, Dave. It's just," she lowered her voice, "well, it's quite valuable."

"Of course," he said. "Get it back when you can."

And so we rode home with the portrait in the backseat, and the whole way I couldn't stop wishing for miracles. I imagined that somehow the painting might swallow up everything we'd added to it. I called on the ghost of Finn with my mind, staring at the sun until I couldn't get rid of the black spots on my eyes, thinking if there was a ghost Finn he could slip his vaporous self right into that box and erase everything we'd done. I looked out between the trees and across the front yards of strangers. I looked under cars and up at the bright blue sky, like the answer to everything might be there, but there was nothing. Only shadow and bright. Shadow and bright, over and over again.

I went straight to my room when we got back. I closed my door and put the *Requiem* on really loud and waited for whatever was going to happen. Ever since that day on the train when my mother said she was the one who'd shown Finn the *Requiem,* it felt weird to play it. Like it was some kind of conversation between Finn and my mother, like it was Finn trying to say that he still remembered everything that had been between the two of them. I hated playing it after that. I didn't like being used like that. But I couldn't help myself. I'd been aching to hear it again, and that afternoon I gave in. I pulled out the card I was making for my mother. I'd drawn the outlines of butterflies, colored each one in, and delicately put glitter in just the right places on their wings. I opened my case of colored pencils and took out three shades of blue. Then I started furiously coloring in the sky. So hard I thought I might go right through the construction paper. And for a moment I believed that even if time travel was impossible, doing kid stuff might have the power to slow time down. Stop it just long enough to make everything okay.

Fifty-Five

There was thunder. Way off somewhere. I'd fallen asleep, and when I woke up that's what I heard. Other than that, the house was quiet. My alarm clock said four-thirty. When I peeked out my window, I saw that the sky had turned darker and that both cars were in the driveway. I had to check, because day-sleeping is like that. When you wake up, you feel like you could be anywhere.

I moved quietly through my room, then out my door to the top of the stairs. I stood there for a while, hoping I might somehow hear whether my parents had seen the portrait yet. Would they have woken me up if they'd seen it? Dragged me right out of bed?

I tiptoed down the stairs, listening. No TV. No radio. No lawn mower or food processor. Not even the flicking of pages. When my feet hit the floor at the bottom, I stopped again, barely breathing, trying to sense where my parents were. Trying to catch a glimpse of the safety-deposit box. Nothing.

I popped my head into the kitchen, which was empty, and then into the living room.

There it was. The portrait. Out of the box, propped up on the mantel. There was still no sign of my parents, which felt strange. Just the portrait and me, alone in that room. No magic had erased what we'd done. Our hair glowed gold, making us look like girls from a story. Girls who knew everything there was to know. Greta's lips were even redder, even more pouty than I remembered them. The skull on her hand was more obvious, and her nails looked like the claws of some kind of mythical cat. Even the buttons, which used to be almost invisible, seemed intense. Bright and dazzling compared to the stuff Finn had done. It was almost like we'd made Finn invisible with all our clumsy brushstrokes.

Then there were footsteps on the stairs. Soft. Slippered. My mother's feet. I sat on the couch, facing the portrait. Waiting. I heard her go into the kitchen and open the fridge. I heard a cabinet open, the sound of a glass against the counter. A drink poured. I heard thunder again, still low and far away. Then the swish of my mother's slippered feet came toward the living room until I could see the shadow of her in the doorway. She was in her bathrobe. Clean white terry cloth.

"I know," I said before she could start.

She walked over to the sideboard and put her glass down. She didn't even bother to use a coaster. "I'm not sure you do know, June. I'm not sure you know even the most basic rights and wrongs anymore." She cinched the tie on her robe tighter and walked slowly over to the portrait. With her eyes she traced along the strands of our illuminated hair, lingering for a moment on Greta. "What upsets your father and me most—more than the fact that this painting will have lost at least half a million, *half a million,* dollars in value because of your childish acts—is that you seem to have particularly gone out of your way to deface your sister."

"How do you know it was all me? Why am I always the one to blame?"

My mother huffed and shook her head. "Greta's been so busy with that play, do you really think I'm going to believe that she would have time, would want to spend her time, going to the bank to deface a valuable piece of art? That's the difference between you and Greta. She has better things to do. She gets involved in clubs, activities. She has friends. But you? You slump around in that room of yours—"

"I thought Finn might like it."

All the anger slipped from my mother's face then. Her brow furrowed and she looked scared. Like she might cry. "What's happening to you, Junie? Huh?"

"Nothing," I said.

"Your uncle made that painting for you and your sister. The last painting he ever made. Did you even read the articles? In the *Times,* in *Newsweek?* Do you understand who Finn was? And you come along, a fourteen-year-old girl, thinking you can improve on his work?"

The kitchen door opened and slammed shut. My father came into the living room in torn sweatpants, his gardening hat, and muddy hands, which he was holding away from his body. He looked from my mother to me, then lifted his hands. "I'll just wash up, then be right down."

"Do you see? Look at your father. He works more than full-time, plays golf, and still has time for gardening on the weekend. And Greta. And me. We all find ways to stay busy. From now on your time will be booked. I'm signing you up for after-school activities every day of the week, and I'll be checking if you've been attending. We haven't kept you involved enough. Too much time on your own. Too much time filled with nonsense. I see that now."

There were many things I could have said about keeping busy. About filling your life up with stupid clubs and sports and plays where people start singing for no reason at all. But I didn't. Of course I didn't say a word.

My mother kept going. "And on top of that, you're grounded. Anything outside of supervised, structured activities is off limits to you until we can see some improvement."

The implications of this flashed through my mind. Toby came to me first. Then, after a few seconds, Greta.

"I told Greta I'd be at the cast party."

"You will not be going to any party of any kind tonight. Do you understand?" My mother threw her hands up. "It's like you really don't understand the magnitude of what you've done here."

"But I promised her . . ."

My father came back into the room. He'd changed into fresh clothes. "She'll get along just fine without you," he said.

"What you don't realize is that you've hurt yourself more than anyone else. That man, the one from the Whitney, he said if the painting all checked out he'd be willing to offer ten thousand dollars to include the painting in an exhibit. And do you know what we were planning to do with that money? Do you?"

I shook my head.

"We thought we'd take a trip. All of us. Europe, England, maybe Ireland. We knew you'd had a rough year and we thought, *You know, June would love that. June would love to visit castles and all that kind of stuff.* So there you go. Sit with that for a while."

I couldn't look at either of them anymore. I stared at the light blue rug, my eyes catching the patterns of flattened and fluffy strands of yarn.

"Now it's just going to be an embarrassment. That man's going to think we're all nuts."

My dad put his hand on my shoulder. "Look, June, if this is some kind of cry for help, we're hearing it. Okay? Loud and clear."

I sat there listening to a long list of things that were wrong with me. And I listened to several more repetitions of the half a million dollars figure, which, for something that wasn't the most important thing, seemed to be pretty close to the most important thing.

After a while my dad put his hands up and said, "Okay, enough now. Head on upstairs and start getting ready."

They'd decided that I should still go to the play. They said it wasn't fair to Greta not to have her whole family there supporting her.

I shut my door and sat on the edge of my rumpled bed, listening as hard as I could to my parents arguing downstairs. But I couldn't make out what they were saying. I could still hear the thunder, though, grumbling and grumbling from somewhere far across that dim Saturday sky.

Fifty-Six

The play was sold out, like it was every year. This year Mr. Nebowitz specifically told the cast that he'd invited a few of his actor friends from the city to watch. He wouldn't say who exactly, but he said they might be recognizable and if anyone did recognize them in town or at the performances they were specifically requested not to harass that person. Maybe these were the same people who would be watching Greta. The ones who would decide if she was good enough for Broadway.

I sat in the back on the drive to the school, and nobody talked. When we got there, I saw that someone had put colored cellophane over the lawn lights so the grass glowed red and orange and yellow. My mother gave me a warning look as we went inside, then I saw her switching herself back to normal mode. Chattering with other moms, saying how proud she was of Greta.

I tried to slip away, because I thought that at least if I found Greta, I could tell her about the portrait and let her know that I wouldn't be at the party and then maybe she wouldn't pull the whole burying act. She'd know she had to take care of herself, because nobody was going to go looking for her in the woods.

My dad and I stood against the wall near where the PTA was selling cups of bright red punch and home-baked brownies and cupcakes. I turned to walk away down the hall, but my dad held on to my shoulder.

"I don't think so. Strict orders from your mother. You're staying with me."

"What could I possibly do wrong here?"

"I don't know, but this is Greta's night, and we're not taking any risks," he said. Then he gave me the most disappointed look I think he's ever given me and he said, "You've broken our trust, June."

"I know," I told him.

I stared back and forth down the hall, hoping to see somebody I could send the message with, but there were only parents and little kids, who were no use at all. Then the lights flashed on and off a few times and we all filed into the auditorium. She'd be fine on her own. That was probably true. She'd have to be.

There was a live professional orchestra in the pit, and as the lights dimmed they started to play the overture. The overture is by far the most boring part of the show. It's the most boring part of any show, and I don't think anyone knows why it even exists. I was wedged be-tween my mother and father and I glanced around, trying to see if there really were any famous actors there. I noticed one man who I thought looked like Danny DeVito, but then I realized that it was just Kelly Hanrahan's dad.

The play was old news to me, because I'd already seen it so many times. The main fun was trying to spot any mistakes. The only one I saw was when Gary Jasper, the kid who played Luther Billis, started to laugh a little bit during one of his lines. That was no huge surprise though, because Gary Jasper was not just class clown, but the whole school clown which is why he got that part in the first place.

Greta came on, and my dad reached over and squeezed my hand as if I might not have noticed her otherwise. There she was, looking fan-tastic. All made up and in character. Both my parents were smiling. They looked so proud of her, and I realized I couldn't remember the last time they looked like that over something I'd done. She had to prance around on the stage while a bunch of the scruffy sailor guys led by Gary Jasper sang that song "Bloody Mary," where they tell her that her skin is like a baseball glove and she doesn't use toothpaste but she's the girl they love. It's not a very nice song, and on top of that, the school made Mr. Nebowitz take the "damn" out of the chorus lyrics, so now they sang *ain't that too darn bad,* which doesn't sound nearly as good.

It was only when Greta sang "Bali Ha'i" that I started to think there was something wrong. That song's got a kind of dreamy quality. Bloody Mary is trying to make Lieutenant Cable imagine this amazing island, so at first I thought Greta was swaying around because she was in character. But then I watched her and listened to her singing about a place somewhere where you'd never have to be lonely. It starts out being about a place, but by the end you start to realize that Bloody Mary is talking about herself. She's the island. She's the one floating way out in the middle of the ocean waiting to be found.

It was like she was thinking about the words she was saying. She slowed down, so the orchestra was out of synch with her singing, the instruments trying to follow her, and I thought, I don't know if this is true, but I thought, she might have been looking out into the audience for me. For a couple of seconds, when she was singing those words, I thought she could have been singing them just to me.

And I could tell that she was drunk. Right up there onstage in front of everyone.

I glanced over at my parents, but they didn't seem to notice anything. Nobody did. Bloody Mary was a weird character, and I guess people thought that's how Greta was playing her. Like an old drunk lady.

After the intermission, I watched Greta do "Happy Talk," clicking her fingers together like her hands were having a cute little chitchat, and I could feel myself getting angry. It felt like a tightening all through my body. When I looked down, I saw my own hands clenched. Greta thought she could do whatever she wanted, get drunk as anything, and I'd be there to carry her home. She thought after everything she'd done, ruining all my Finn stuff, making me look stupid again and again, that she could rely on me. Well, she couldn't. This time she'd find that out. I wouldn't be there to rescue her, and that was that.

As we were leaving, I saw Ben in the front lobby, dressed in his all-black backstage clothes and buying a cup of Hawaiian Punch at the PTA snack table.

"Hey," I said as I passed.

"Oh, hey, June." He smiled. "You going to the Reeds'?"

"The Reeds'?"

"You know, the cast party. You'll be there, right?"

My parents were behind me, talking to Mr. and Mrs. Farley, but my dad must have been ready to go, because he tapped my shoulder and nudged his head toward the door. I nodded. Then I turned back to Ben and whispered, "So the party's not in the woods?"

"The Reeds always do the cast party. Have you seen their house?"

I shook my head.

"It's this awesome modern thing with huge windows. You know, it's one of those up on Woodlawn Court." He pointed toward the window, where the wind was shaking even the sturdy school window-panes. "Look at the weather anyway. Who'd want to be out in the woods?"

"Yeah. Right. I . . ."

"So you'll be there?"

I shook my head. "I can't." I rolled my eyes and glanced at my parents.

"Ahhh, I see." Then he smiled even bigger. "So I can borrow your boots, then, right?"

I started to tell him that there wasn't a chance, but then I saw that he was joking. "Ha-ha," I said, smiling.

As I left the school, flanked by a parent on either side, all I could think about was Greta. Was she actually going to the woods by herself? Waiting for me? Or maybe that wasn't it at all. Maybe it was just an-other trick. Maybe she wanted to send me off on a stupid chase through the woods at night by myself. But, no. I didn't think she would do that. Not after everything we said that morning. I looked at the school, then at my parents, and in a flash I turned and ran.

"I'll be right back," I shouted over my shoulder.

I stumbled up the steps and through the doors and charged up to Ben, slapping my hand on his back. A splash of his bright red punch spilled over the edge of his paper cup and onto the floor.

"Hey," he said.

"Sorry, sorry. Look—I need you to go tell Greta I can't come to the party, okay? Please. It's important."

"Hey, calm down," he said, putting a hand on my shoulder. "I would if I could, but Greta left as soon as the curtain closed. She didn't even change out of costume. She went right out the greenroom door and cut through the woods."

My whole body slumped. "Oh," I said.

"If I see her . . ." Ben started to say.

As I turned to leave, my parents stared up at me from the bottom of the stone stairs outside the school. Both of them had their arms crossed tight across their chests. But all I could think about was Greta. I shouldn't have cared, it wasn't my problem, but still, I couldn't get the picture out of my head. Greta's beautiful face shining up from the ground. Waiting. Waiting for her sister to come and find her.

Fifty-Seven

As the night went on and I sat awake in my room, listening to the growl of thunder, I couldn't stop myself from worrying about Greta. What if she was already passed out, deep under the cover of leaves? What if she drank so much she couldn't wake up? I'd seen that kind of thing on the news. What if she'd taken something else? Drugs or something I couldn't even imagine? And what if there was lightning? What if lightning came and twisted its way down that tall maple tree in the woods? What if it shot right down to the ground, right to Greta's skull? My thoughts kept spinning out. She said she'd find a way not to do *Annie*. What did she mean? What if she tried to do something to herself? I didn't want to care, but somehow, like always, I did. She was wired into my heart. Twisted and kinked and threaded right through.

It was the first flicker of real lightning that made me panic. I thought of the rain that would come soon. Heavy, drenching. How the ground around Greta might dissolve into mud. How the river might rise and flood if the rain was hard and fast enough. I imagined Greta floating away. And the wolves. What if the wolves were there? What if they were real? And what if they were hungry? I thought of that look on her face when we were talking about invisible mermaids. Like a little kid. Even if the wolves were only coyotes, they could take Greta and tear her to pieces.

The eleven o'clock news was on, and then came *Saturday Night*

Live, which my parents watched because they thought it was still funny. Every few minutes my dad would call up to me, waiting to hear me call back. I knew my parents thought I might sneak out. And maybe I would have if I wasn't such a coward.

Instead, I walked down the hallway, past Greta's closed door, past the bathroom, and into my parents' bedroom. Their bed was always made and stretched tight, so I slunk down on the fuzzy beige carpet next to the night table on my father's side of the bed. I lifted the phone receiver off the cradle, and slowly, taking my time over every number, I dialed Finn's apartment. It rang twice, then three times, and for a moment I thought Toby might not be there or he might not want to pick up. I held the receiver to my ear and decided I'd give him six rings before I hung up. He picked up on the fifth.

"Toby?" I said.

"June? It's late. Are you all right?"

I didn't say anything at first. It felt awkward to talk to him after last time. Nothing had changed for him, but for me everything had. I'd become transparent, naked. The girl with the see-through heart. The stupidest girl in the world. A pulse of anger shot through my body.

"You know how we're supposed to be there for each other? If we need anything?"

"Of course. Of course I know. What is it? Are you all right, June?"

"I'm okay. It's not me. It's Greta."

"Greta? What's happened?"

"I'm scared. I don't know. I'm grounded. I can't get her home. I . . ." My voice was rising higher and higher, the words rushing out.

"June?" my father called up from the living room.

"It's okay." I yelled back down, trying to sound calm and happy. "Just singing to myself. It's okay."

"Shhh. Slowly," Toby said.

"Okay." I let out a long breath. "Okay."

I told him about the parties again, and Greta, and how I'd found her the last two times.

"She was waiting for me there. And she'll be there again tonight. I know she will. She said she wanted to talk. And she had no idea I'd be grounded or anything. There's lightning out there, and thunder. She was already drunk in the play. She was completely wasted. I could tell. There's more, but there's no time."

"Why are you grounded? It isn't me, is it?"

"No, no. Later, okay? Just this now."

"All right, all right."

"So where is she? Exactly."

"Remember where you parked when you picked me up at the school that time? That day we went to Playland? Remember how that parking lot wrapped around to the back of the school?"

He did, and from there I described exactly where to cut into the woods. How to follow the river and find the maple where Greta would be. I told him once, and then he asked me to tell it to him all over again, twice.

"You'll need a flashlight, okay?"

Toby didn't say anything for a few seconds. "June?"

"Yeah?"

"Well, I'm a bit concerned. I'm probably—I'm bound to frighten Greta, aren't I? She doesn't know me. Your family . . . well, they hate me. You know that. I don't know . . ."

"Well, if you don't want to . . . I mean, you said *anything,* and first you say we can't go to England and now . . ." It made me feel bad to play on his guilt like that. And I wish I hadn't done it, but I did. It's the truth. I made him feel as guilty as I could.

"All right. Okay, then."

"If she wakes up, tell her I sent you. Tell her this, specifically, and she'll believe you: Tell her our parents saw the portrait, okay? Tell her I was grounded because of the portrait and I called you to get her. She might not even wake up. In that case, just get her outside our door. Park down the road a little. I'll keep checking the back door. I'll bring her inside. It'll be fine."

"I'm sorry, I don't know about this, June."

"Don't worry, Toby. Don't be afraid."

He didn't say anything. Then he sighed. "Okay. All right. I'll go. For you."

"You will?" And I realized I was surprised. Maybe I'd been testing him. Maybe I expected him to fail.

"For you. Don't worry. I don't want you to worry. I'll be there soon."

I hung up, and right away I felt a shiver hit every part of my skin at once. I should have just told my parents. I should have just let Greta get in trouble. I sat there on my parents' bedroom floor, letting what I'd done sink in. Then I grabbed the receiver back up and dialed the number again. My fingers fumbled, and when I finally got the number right it didn't even matter. The phone rang and rang. Toby had already left. I can't say what I would have said if he'd been there. Would I have begged him not to go? I don't know. I don't know my heart that well. All I knew was that Toby's promises were good. He'd dropped everything, just like that, and came when I called.

Downstairs, my parents were laughing at *Saturday Night Live,* and I slipped into the living room. My mother was all cozy in pink sweatpants and a huge oversize sweatshirt. They were on the couch, and her head was leaned up against my dad's shoulder. I sat cross-legged in the recliner.

Dennis Miller was on the show, doing that comedy news thing he did. Both my parents were laughing at some stupid joke about Gary Hart. A commercial came on and I looked over at them.

"I'm sorry," I said.

My mother glanced over at my father. Then she looked at me for a long time, her lips pressed together tight. Her face hard. Finally, she seemed to lighten a little bit and she nodded her head very slightly. "It's good to hear you say that, June."

"I mean it. Really. I am sorry."

My mother patted the spot next to her on the couch, and I slid off the vinyl recliner and snuggled up next to her in a way I hadn't done for years. It felt warm and good.

When the commercials were done, *Saturday Night Live* came back on and there was a sketch with Jon Lovitz about a package-delivery service called Einstein Express, where, because of Einstein's theories about the space-time continuum, packages could actually arrive before they were sent out. It was a good idea but, like most stuff on that show, the skit wasn't all that funny.   ·

But I didn't care. This day would be over soon, and my mother's shoulder was soft and the couch was soft and Suzanne Vega had come on and she was singing "Luka," about that sad boy who lived on the second floor, and it was soft and soothing and just right.

The minutes seemed to pass in slow motion that night. My mother's body shook when she laughed, just like Finn's, and my father snored lightly. After *Saturday Night Live,* my parents went up to bed and I went into the kitchen to watch for Toby at the back door. Everything would work out fine. Of course it would. That's what I told myself. I would thank Toby for doing this for me and everything would be back to normal. The rain pounded the kitchen window and I stared into the darkness of our backyard, at the skeletal shadow of the swing set, at the rhododendron bushes whipping around in the storm. I stood there for a long time, staring out, waiting for the shadow of Toby to arrive.

Then the front doorbell rang.

Fifty-Eight

The two policemen stood in the doorway. I knew one was Officer Gellski. He'd been coming to our school once a year since I was in kindergarten, to tell us about stranger danger and the third rail and bike safety. He was older than my parents. The other one was young.

Between the two of them, looking small, was Greta. She stood stiff, staring down at the ground. She was still in her grass skirt, her Bloody Mary costume, and she was soaked. Her hair was plastered with mud and leaves, her face filthy with smeared stage makeup. The rain pounded down behind the three of them, but my father just stood there, one hand on the edge of the door, and stared.

"Greta—what on earth?" he whispered. "Is she okay?"

"May we?" Officer Gellski asked.

"Yes. Yes, of course. Come in." My father opened the door wider and the three of them stepped into the front hallway. The younger cop looked down at his muddy shoes, then over to my mother.

"Don't worry about it," she said, shaking her head. "Come into the kitchen. In here."

The police walked ahead. Greta hung back. My father put his arm around her and guided her into the kitchen. He pulled a chair out for Greta and sat her down. The two policemen made the kitchen seem tiny. Their navy uniforms and their bulky pistols made everything in our house seem flimsy.

"Take a seat," my mother said to them.

"It's okay. We're fine standing," Officer Gellski said, forcing a smile. The younger cop held out a plastic bag.

"Your daughter's coat," he said. "It was soaked."

She took the bag from him and held it out, away from her body.

"Throw it in the bathtub, please, June," she said without looking at me.

I'd been standing in the kitchen doorway, and I went over to my mother and took the bag. I walked as close to Greta as I could, nudging her arm as I went past, trying to get her eyes. But she wouldn't look at me. Not even for a second.

"June, move it," my mother said. "It's dripping all over the floor."

As I left the room, I heard both my parents frantically questioning the two cops about Greta. All I could think of was Toby. What had happened to Toby? Did this mean he hadn't made it to Greta? Was he lost in the woods? Was he too late? Would he spend all night out there searching for her, trying to keep his promise to me? I ran up the stairs two at a time, then flipped the light on and dumped the coat out of the bag and into the tub.

I barely looked at it at first, eager to get back downstairs, but as my hand reached for the light switch, I turned. The coat wasn't black. Greta's coat was black. I stared at the wet lump in the bathtub for a few seconds, not quite registering what I saw. It wasn't Greta's coat in the tub. Slumped in the bottom of the bathtub like some kind of dead animal was a big gray coat. Finn's coat. Toby's coat. The one he'd worn to the zoo.

I ran down the stairs two at a time.

"Tell us what's going on," my mother was saying.

I stood in the doorway watching. Trying to catch Greta's eye.

"Well, first of all, we think Greta's just fine," Officer Gellski said.

"Where did you find her?" she said, wringing her hands together.

"Behind the school, Mrs. Elbus. In the woods. Kids throw parties back there sometimes. We like to keep an eye on it." He stretched his arms out across the kitchen counter. "It looks like she's had a bit too much to drink. Partying a little too hard, that kind of thing, but we're not too worried about that right now."

Look at me, Greta. Look at me. I was thinking at Greta as hard as I could, but still nothing.

"You're not?" my father said.

The young cop kept shifting his weight from left foot to right. He seemed uncomfortable, like he had no real job to do now that he'd handed the coat over.

"No. That's not what's worrying us right now," Officer Gellski said.

"Well, what is it, then?"

"There was a man, Mr. Elbus."

My stomach felt like it had turned to stone. Heavy and cold and too much for my body to hold. *Look at me, Greta. Please look at me.*

My father's voice sounded alarmed now, louder, higher pitched. "A man? What kind of man?"

Then Officer Gellski described exactly what they saw. He said he and the young cop were sitting in the cruiser in the school parking lot. Some people who lived on the street had called in, complaining of noise, which, he said, was not unusual for a Saturday night. What was a little bit different was that the neighbor had reported a scream. Not only the usual party noise, but also a girl screaming. So the two of them were sitting in the cruiser with the headlights off, watching, looking for any movement in and out of the woods. Anything to indicate that there was a party.

"We got out of the car, about to walk in a ways, and it started raining. Hard. We looked at each other, thinking that it wasn't worth getting soaked over. The rain was bound to get everyone out of there anyway."

My thoughts were wild. All over the place.

"We were about to leave. I'd just turned the key in the ignition, just switched on the lights." Officer Gellski mimed starting the car up. "We were backing out. The car was facing the woods so the lights were shining right into the trees, lighting the whole place up, and that's when he came out."

"I don't understand," my father said.

The younger cop stepped forward. "The man in question was coming out of the woods, holding your daughter, Mr. Elbus." He put his arms out in front of him, like he was holding firewood, demonstrating.

"To tell you the truth, at first we thought he was holding a dog or something. A dead dog." Gellski held up a hand. "No offense."

"It was that big coat," said the young cop.

As Gellski described what had happened, I could see the whole thing in my mind. Toby, like that lanky Ichabod Crane, running through the woods, cold and wet, cradling the bundled-up Greta. Charging along, faster and faster, his good heart pounding. I could see him so clearly, trying to do right by me, by Finn, his eyes squinting as he stumbled out of the woods, shocked by the headlights aimed right at him. Clutching Greta tighter, both of them drenched.

"We put the two of them in the back of the car, cuffed the man. We haven't been able to get a word. From either of them."

"The man," my mother said, looking between the cops and Greta. "Greta, who is this man? What are they talking about? The cast party was at the Reeds', wasn't it? I don't . . ."

My father pulled a chair out and my mother sat down, looking defeated. I edged into the room, pulled a glass from the cabinet and filled it with water.

Greta didn't answer, and my mother turned back to the two cops.

I walked over to Greta and knelt, handing her the glass. From down low, I peered up into her face. As the adults kept talking, I looked right into her eyes until I forced her to look back. For those few seconds, once our eyes met, it was like we were the only two people in the room. I put a hand on her arm, and with everything in me I tried to make her understand that it was all me. That none of this was Toby's fault. My eyes were begging her to save him. I would forgive every awful thing she'd ever done to me for this. For this one thing. I kept staring, waiting for some sign from her. But I saw nothing. It was Greta who could read people, not me. After a few seconds, she took a long slow sip of the water and turned away.

"The man's name is Tobias Aldshaw. Does that mean anything to you?"

My mother and father looked at each other like they'd just been told Martians had landed in the backyard.

"Toby?" my mother said.

"So you know the man?" said Officer Gellski.

"Well . . ."

"There's something else," Gellski said.

Something else? Was Toby drunk? Had he been drinking when I made him drive out?

Gellski reached inside the chest pocket of his shirt.

"We found this in his back pocket." He tossed a small navy-blue book on the table, and everyone stared. I gasped, then put my hand over my mouth. My passport. The confusion on my parents' faces was so deep by that point, I thought it might stay there forever. My mother picked up the passport and flipped to the picture page. She stared at it for a moment, then she looked at me. I stood, but looked away.

"June? This is June's passport. This is starting to really scare me," my mother said, turning to my father. "I don't understand . . ."

I saw everything then. I saw how deep the trap was that Toby was in. If nobody said anything, if it looked like he was here on his own, like a crazy person, with my passport, with Greta, he'd get arrested. And maybe even more. Prison? Sent back to England? But if I did tell them everything—if they all knew he'd been meeting up with me, meeting alone with a fourteen-year-old girl in the city—I didn't know what would happen. To either of us.

"Greta," I said, under all the adult voices.

She turned slowly and looked at me over her shoulder. She seemed older than sixteen, in a haggard way, and so tired I couldn't imagine how she was still sitting upright.

Please, I mouthed.

The words *kidnap* and *AIDS* and *illegal immigrant* flew around the room, but I just watched Greta. She turned slowly back and for a few seconds she sat there, saying nothing. She wasn't going to help. She was going to leave me drowning in all this mess. She was going to let me watch Toby get everything she thought he deserved.

"Mom," I said. She didn't hear me, so I said it again, louder. "Mom."

"June, it'll be okay, honey. Don't worry."

I shook my head. "No. No, it's just—"

Then Greta stood up. She stretched her arms at her sides and reached through her grass skirt and into her front pocket for a hair scrunchie. She twisted her hair into a neat bun, wrapping the scrunchie around to hold it in place. Then she took a deep breath and, as slowly as she could, gently blew the air back out. She scanned the room, looking right into the eyes of each person there, and with a voice as loud and clear as the one she used in *South Pacific* she said, "It's my fault."

The room went silent.

The yellow clock ticked.

My hands trembled so much I had to stuff them in my pockets.

As Greta started talking, the only thing I could do was stand and stare in amazement at that person who was my sister. At the way she could invent a whole story on the spot. She told them that she knew Toby. That she'd seen him once when she was in the city with her friends. She'd gone to Finn's old neighborhood, right past Finn's building, and there he was, walking out the front door. She said he recognized her, from the portrait, from pictures Finn had in the apartment, and he'd called her over. She said he explained who he was, and then she remembered him from the funeral. "It was the guy you pointed out, remember, Dad?" She described the whole thing in such detail. How she and her friends had all gotten drinks at Gray's Papaya. How she got the piña colada—nonalcoholic, she said, glancing at my parents—but the other two had mango, and she was about to throw her empty cup away when she saw him. She said she wasn't going to go over to Toby at first, but then she decided she would, for only a minute. And they started talking.

"It was stupid, I know it was," she said. "But he looked so sad, and he started going on and on about how much he was missing Finn. How it was so lonely. It was just so totally weird and I didn't know what to say to him, so I ended up inviting him to the party. I said that maybe getting out would make him feel better and that there was this party." She'd crinkled her brow, looking helpless. "I . . . I didn't know what to say to him."

Nobody said anything, so she went on.

"I didn't think he'd come. I mean, I was just saying it, I didn't mean it, you'd think he'd have better things to do—"

"You would think that, wouldn't you?" my mother said, her lips pursed.

"Let her finish, Danni," my dad said.

"But in the end, it was a good thing, wasn't it? I was drunk. Way drunk. If it wasn't for Toby, I might still be out in the woods, passed out in the pouring rain."

"But the party was at the Reeds', wasn't it?"

"The *official* party's at the Reeds', but . . ."

She didn't look at me the whole time she was talking. It was like she was giving a performance. Like a perfect actress, pausing exactly long enough when she needed to make a point. Changing the expression on her face at just the right time. Choosing which person to glance at when she was saying a particularly hard thing.

"That doesn't explain anything, Greta," my mother said. "A grown man with AIDS out in the woods at a high school party? No. Nothing makes that right. Nothing makes it right for him to be carrying my daughter across a parking lot. And June's passport. There's still that. Why on earth would he have June's passport in his pocket?"

"Those passports are in a locked box in our bedroom," my father said to Officer Gellski. "It doesn't make any sense."

I wanted so badly to have the kind of brain Greta had. I would have given anything to step forward with some elegant explanation of why the man called Tobias Aldshaw had my passport in his back pocket. But all my thoughts seemed to blur and mingle. The possibility of a sensible story coming out of my mouth was zero.

"No. It's just plain ridiculous. On every level," my mother said. "Why on earth would that man have June's passport in his pocket?" she repeated.

I looked at Greta. I thought she'd been flustered by the passport thing, because she didn't say anything. I kept watching her until I saw something change. I actually saw the exact moment when she switched on a guilty face. She looked down at the floor, then back up, peeking through her bangs, as much like a little girl as she could make herself. Then, cool as anything, she told the whole room a story about making fake IDs to buy alcohol.

"I'd made one for myself a while ago. It's wrong, I know, but June wanted one too. I thought she was coming to the party. I said I'd try to make something for her, and . . ."

Both cops stood there, nodding their heads.

"We've seen this kind of thing, Mrs. Elbus," the younger one said. "I know it's difficult to believe when it's your own kid."

"Are you saying Toby was helping you make fake identification, Greta?"

"No, no." Greta shook her head hard. "The passport must have fallen out of my pocket. He must have picked it up for me."

My mother and father looked stunned. It was hard to tell if they were believing Greta's story. But then, I thought, what else was there to believe? That this dying man was trying to kidnap Greta and me? Would they want to believe that? Could they really think Finn would be with someone that crazy?

"Well, where is he now?" my father asked. "I think we need a word."

Officer Gellski didn't answer right away, like he was considering something.

"We have him in the cruiser." Everyone's eyes went in the direction of the living room window, the one that overlooked the driveway. Toby was out there. Right outside the house.

My father took a step, but Officer Gellski put out his hand.

"I don't think now's the time, Mr. Elbus. We'll get him down to the station. Let us talk to him first, then maybe in a day or two—"

"I have to go to the bathroom," I said.

"Go ahead. Quickly," my mom said. "You're in this too, June."

I left the kitchen, and what I wanted to do was run right out the door to Toby. I wanted to apologize over and over again. To say sorry until I was sure he believed me. Until I was sure he knew it was coming from the deepest part of my heart. But I couldn't do that. I had to keep my head straight.

I snuck away to the cellar as quietly as I could. I got a big white cardboard box, and on the side I wrote, DON'T TELL THEM ANY-THING!!!!!!! with a fat black marker.

You could see the driveway from the living room but also from my bedroom. I tiptoed up the stairs and cleared my windowsill of the fake candles. Then I threw the window wide open.

There was the police car, and there was Toby sitting in the back. His arms were bare, his hair still wet, and even from inside the house I could see that he was shivering. All I wanted to do was walk down the hall and get one of my father's big coats and wrap Toby up in it. I wanted to pull all the blankets off my bed and run to the car and cover him up so tight that he'd stop shivering on the spot. But I couldn't. This was all my fault. He was right there and still I couldn't take care of him. I flicked my light on and off a few times to get his attention, then I pressed the box up to the window. I held it there for a few seconds, hiding my face behind that sign. Then I lowered it.

Toby tipped his head slightly, his thin face framed in the police-car window. Then he looked away, embarrassed or angry with me for getting him into this mess.

They would not be able to charge Toby with anything. Not after everything Greta said. That's what Officer Gellski told us. He also told us that Toby's name would be passed on to immigration. He said it looked like Toby was years over his visitation limit.

My parents thanked the cops for bringing Greta home safely and then they both showed them to the door. They watched as the cops walked down the front steps and out to their car.

"I almost feel sorry for the man," my father said, staring out at the police car.

"I know, but you can't," my mother said. "He's the kind of person who's bound for problems. Look what he did to Finn. . . ." Her voice was cracking.

"It'll be okay." My father put his arm on my mother's back and they walked upstairs, looking like they'd both been through some kind of epic battle.

Greta had already gone up, leaving me alone downstairs. I wandered from room to room, turning off the lights.

In the living room, I stopped to look at the portrait. There we were. Those same two girls. Illuminated. I thought that it wasn't that bad. The stuff we'd added. There was beauty in it. There was at least some small beauty in what we'd done.

I flicked the light off and we disappeared.

Fifty-Nine

Upstairs, I brushed my teeth, then sat on the edge of the bathtub, looking at the coat. There it was, dead wolf, all the beautiful scents of Finn washed away. I touched it, lightly at first, petting it with my open hand.

"I'm sorry," I whispered, stroking the coat harder, over and over again.

Even though it was dark and way past midnight, that Saturday would not let itself end. It stayed, keeping me up, making me drag it right into Sunday. I lay in bed, over and over again running through what Greta had done for me. For Toby and me. And then over and over again I thought of Toby and hated myself for the trouble I'd dragged him into. I wondered if they had him all cold and wet, sitting in that small jail cell in the police station in town. The one they made our whole class squash into when we went there on a class trip in fourth grade. "This is where you don't want to end up, right, kids?" the policeman said. Everyone except Evan Hardy nodded. Evan stood there with his hands on his little-boy hips and said, "Yeah, yeah, I do." I remember being afraid for him. I remember thinking they might just keep him in there if he kept talking like that. And now it was Toby, and all I wanted to do was run through the streets of town, right to that cell. I wanted to bring him dry clothes, and I wanted to tell him how sorry I was.

I tried pushing it all away. I counted backward from one thousand. I listened to the rhythm of my father's snoring, trying to breathe in time to it. I opened my curtain and lay on my back. The storm had petered out, and I watched the after-storm clouds whizzing over the moon, covering it, then letting it shine. Then, through all of that, I heard the sound of crying.

I pressed my ear up against the wall next to my bed. The crying went on, then stopped for a while, then started again. Greta was awake.

The lights were off in her room except for the blue heart night-light under the desk. When I nudged her door open, she instantly slouched deeper under her covers and turned to face the far side of the room.

"Can I come in?"

Greta shrugged, and I quietly crawled into her bed, pressing my back against hers. We lay there, saying nothing, our bodies stiff and tense.

"Thanks for saying all that," I said.

I felt her wiping her eyes against the blanket.

"I shouldn't have called him. . . . I know you hate him. . . ." I heard my voice cracking.

Greta started to laugh. It wasn't a happy laugh. More sad and frustrated.

"You just don't get it, do you?" I felt her shaking her head and I turned. She was sitting up and reaching under the mattress. She pulled out a bottle of some kind of liquor. "Go get some soda from the fridge, okay?"

"What kind?"

"I don't care, but be quiet."

I slipped out and came back with a half-full bottle of cream soda and a glass. Greta poured some of the liquor in and then topped it up with the soda.

"Here," she said, passing me the glass. I took a sip. It was sickly sweet and then there was the heat from the liquor. I handed the glass back, and Greta downed the rest in one gulp. Then we both crawled back under the covers.

"What don't I get?" I lowered my eyes, in hopes that Greta might answer if I wasn't staring right at her.

"How lucky you are." She whispered it, then turned away.

"Oh, yeah, right."

"Do you know what it's like to hope for someone to die?"

"I—"

"Did you ever wonder how I knew about Finn being sick way before you did? Even though he was *your* godfather?"

I thought about it for a second. "No—I mean, you always know everything before me. That's just how it is."

Greta pushed closer to me, her small body against my bulky one.

"Do you remember that day when Finn took us out for those frozen hot chocolates at Serendipity? Do you remember that place?"

I nodded. Serendipity was this old-fashioned fancy ice cream parlor on the Upper East Side. Inside, it was dark, with lots of wood, and I remember those huge frozen hot chocolates with loads of whipped cream. Greta and I shared one with two straws.

"This was before he'd even started the portrait. I was your age, or maybe younger. Maybe I was still thirteen, I don't know. You, Mom, and I were all at Finn's apartment after Serendipity. I was in the bathroom and I'd left the door open a little, and Mom walked right in and saw me using Finn's ChapStick. I still remember the look on her face. I remember it like I'm looking at a picture. Terrified. I stood there, frozen, holding the ChapStick, all embarrassed and guilty, and then she slapped it right out of my hand. Hard. So hard it hurt. She pushed into that tight bathroom and closed the door on the two of us. I didn't know what was going on. I knew I shouldn't be using Finn's stuff, but he always had that lip stuff that smelled like coconut and pineapple. You know? It always smelled so good."

I did know. I knew exactly the smell she was talking about.

Greta scrunched herself up tighter and tighter as she spoke, until her spine was curved and pointing hard into mine.

"I didn't know what was going on. I had no idea. And Mom started shouting at me but trying to keep it quiet at the same time. Then all of a sudden she got teary and hugged me. She asked me if that was the first time I'd used Finn's ChapStick. I told her it was, and she looked relieved, and she hugged me some more. That's when she told me. About Finn being sick. About AIDS. She told me and she made me promise never to use his stuff ever again. She said I shouldn't worry

about it because it was only once. She said over and over that it would
be okay. It was okay, she kept saying, all the time wiping hard at my lips
with some toilet paper. I promised her I would never do it again. Do
you remember Finn's lips, June? Do you remember how cracked they
always were? How every winter they'd bleed?"

I nodded. I didn't know what to say.

"But you know what?"

Greta swiveled her body around so she was looking right at me, so
our faces almost touched. I shook my head.

"I wasn't even scared. When Mom closed the door and went back
to the living room, I sat down on the bathroom floor and all I felt was
happy."

"What are you talking about?"

"I thought if Finn . . . if he was dying, then maybe we would go
back to how we used to be. How evil is that? How totally evil am I?"
Greta pulled the covers over her head.

"But you hate me."

Greta huffed. "You're so, so lucky, June. Why are you so lucky?
Look at me." She peeked out from the cover, talking through tears.
"All these years I watched you and Finn. And then you and Toby. How
could you do that? How could you possibly choose Toby over me?"

"But Finn always asked if you wanted to come along. You know he
did. You always acted like it was the last thing you wanted to do."

"Finn always asked—of course he would. But I knew you hoped
I'd say no. Don't even lie. I know you hoped that. It was like a trap. If
I came along, you'd resent me. And if I didn't, well, then I wouldn't be
a part of any of it."

It was true. Of course she would have seen that.

I reached out for Greta's hand, but I couldn't find it. Instead, I gently touched her shoulder. "I didn't know."

"Don't you even remember how we used to be? I kept thinking
that you'd find me in the woods and maybe . . . maybe you'd be worried. How could I compete with Finn? How could I be better than
Toby? I'm leaving, June. A couple months and I'll be gone and then . . .
I don't know. What if we end up like Mom and Finn? What if I leave
and that's the end of us? It's like . . . It just feels like I'm being pulled

out to sea. Do you know what I mean? Those days I followed you into the woods, you there playing like a kid. Like a real kid, you know. Like we used to play. I wanted so badly to shout out, 'Hey, June. I'm here. Look. Let me play too.'"

She turned onto her back, and so did I, both of us staring at the ceiling, under Greta's white comforter with the rainbows and clouds all over it. The one she's had since she was ten. My father's snoring roared through the quiet room. A slice of moonlight shone in from the edge of Greta's curtains and lit a dusty world globe sitting on her desk.

We talked for hours in the dark. I told her everything that had happened that day. The portrait. How our parents thought it was all my fault. How I let them think that, because it was the right thing to do. The noble thing. Greta told me that she'd been trying to wreck the portrait, but it never seemed to work. The skull and the lips. They kind of made it more beautiful, she said. She said she went down to the vault sometimes and sat there, hoping I'd walk in. That I'd catch her. It was the same with Bloody Mary. She kept trying to mess up, but somehow the more she tried, the better everyone thought she was.

"I saw it," I said. "I saw you onstage and I knew you were trying to mess up. I was the only one who seemed to see it."

"I know you're the only one. That's the thing. We were orphans together. I knew you'd see me. I kept asking you to those rehearsals, thinking . . . I don't know." Her voice caught in the back of her throat. "I don't want us to be mean anymore."

"I never wanted to," I said. And I finally got that it was both of us. It had always been both of us. It was never only Greta. Everything she said was true. After all the years of being best friends, I'd abandoned her. How could I not have seen that? How could I have been so selfish?

Greta slipped out of bed and turned the radio on really low. She had a coat hanger attached to the antenna so she could get WLIR all the way from Long Island. WLIR was the cool radio station, because they played mostly English stuff. That Echo & the Bunnymen song, "The Killing Moon," was on, and we lay there listening.

"Tell me what happened in the woods," I said after a while.

"Go to sleep."

"I'm sorry if Toby scared you," I whispered. "I didn't know what else to do."

Greta turned farther away from me so we weren't touching anymore. It seemed like she wasn't going to say anything, but then, after a long wait, she cleared her throat.

"I think I scared him more than he scared me," she said.

"Were you by yourself out there?" I spoke carefully. I knew that any second Greta could disappear into herself.

"I thought it was you at first. Then there was a man's voice. Really hoarse. He was saying my name, telling me not to be frightened. He didn't say *afraid,* he said *frightened.* That's when I screamed. And I can scream when I want to. Loud. He stood up, and it looked like he was thinking about running, but then he started mumbling something about Mom and Dad knowing about the portrait. He said you'd sent him. He said he was Finn's friend. And then everything clicked into place. I tried to scramble up. I shoved the leaves off myself, but it was all mud out there. It was pouring. I slipped. I didn't want his help, but I had no choice. I could barely keep my eyes open. And then he took his coat off—I remember that. He took his coat off and laid it on the ground and lifted me onto it. And then he told me to go back to sleep. That everything would be all right."

"He's not like you think, Greta."

Then I told her everything I knew about our mother. All the jealousy and sadness. All the meanness that could come out of loving someone too much.

She laughed to herself. Just a little sad puff through her nose.

I closed my eyes and let Depeche Mode and Yaz and the Cure erase everything that had happened. I didn't want to let my mind go beyond right now, because every time I did I saw Toby's hapless face in the window of the police car and I couldn't face that. Not yet.

We lay there quiet for a long time, but I could tell neither of us could sleep. After a while Greta nudged my back.

"What?"

"Did you hear WPLJ banned that stupid George Michael song 'I Want Your Sex' because of AIDS?"

I shook my head. "As if listening to that would ever get anyone in the mood."

Then we both started cracking up. We laughed until Greta fell right out of the bed. And then she kept on laughing on the floor. I couldn't even remember the last time we laughed together like that, and I knew that it meant my sister was starting to come back. That somehow Toby had gone out into the woods and brought back Greta for me. He'd brought me back my sister.

We listened to more music and drank brandy and cream soda, and we talked and talked, and that Saturday never did end. Not for us. We stayed up until the world started to get light again. Until we saw the pink sunrise over the top of the Gordanos' freshly trimmed cedar hedge.

Sixty

I called Toby at five-thirty in the morning on Sunday. Only Greta and I were up. The phone rang and rang and I thought he was probably asleep, so I let it keep going. I let it ring twenty-three times before I finally hung up. I wasn't really worried, because I figured he was still at the police station. It didn't feel good to imagine him there, but I wasn't worried. He just hadn't gotten home yet.

After all those hours of talking and all the brandy and cream soda, Greta and I finally crashed. We found our way to our own beds and slept until lunchtime, when my mother woke us both up.

She knocked on my door, then eased her head in. The way she looked at me was different than I'd ever seen before. It was like she was looking at someone else. A stranger.

"June," she said. She said my name in a businesslike way. Calm and with purpose. "Your father and I want to move on from this."

I heard Toby's voice in my head—*But where would we move to?*—and I'm not sure if I disguised the smile that must have rushed across my face.

"June? Are you listening?"

"Yes. Of course I'm listening."

"Tax season's over, and after this week *South Pacific* is done, and we think we should start doing some more family things. Pull together for a while, until you girls seem back to normal. We haven't been there for you. We know."

I wanted to say that if she hadn't made Finn keep Toby a secret, none of this would ever have happened, but I couldn't. It was my fault. There was no point dragging my mother into it. And, anyway, I understood exactly how she felt. I knew the way lost hopes could be dangerous, how they could turn a person into someone they never thought they'd be.

All day I kept expecting Greta to ignore me or say something snotty or mean. I waited for her to do something that proved that she hadn't meant any of what she'd said the night before, but she didn't. When she saw me in the kitchen she smiled. A real, actual, non-snotty smile.

Later in the afternoon, the two of us sat on the couch, staring at the portrait.

"Don't tell Mom, but I kind of like it," Greta whispered.

I nodded. "Me too."

The gold in our hair looked so perfect right then, and I knew we both saw it. We could see the way it made us look like the closest of sisters. Girls made of exactly the same stuff.

Sixty-One

There was no answer when I called Toby that night. Or early on Monday morning. I thought maybe he'd decided to hate me because of what I'd made him do. I hoped that wasn't true. But I thought that it might be.

Life went back to being more normal than it had been in a long time. I wasn't making secret trips into the city. There were no Volcano Bowls or secret rooms in basements. There wasn't even an underground bank vault anymore. Maybe the normality of it all was the worst thing about it. I had lost Toby. He was missing, and I was the only one looking for him. He was missing, and it was my fault.

After school on Monday I went to the library. Ben was there, checking out books for a report on Hiroshima. He was just in jeans and a plain black T-shirt. No cape. He spotted me heading for the pay phone.

"Hey there," he called. "Wolf Girl."

I put my hands on my hips and turned to look at him. "What?"

"Have you seen it?"

"What? Seen what?"

"In today's *Gazette*."

"No," I said cautiously. Was there some kind of big article about Toby being in the woods?

"Your wolves. They existeth no more," he said.

"What do you mean?"

"Feral dogs. A whole pack of them. Scary stuff. You know that dirt road? Wrisley Road? Some old guy died out there, like, a year ago, and all his dogs—seven or eight of them—went feral."

I was pretty sure I knew the house he was talking about. Driving, you'd have to go up Rampatuck Road, which was dirt, to get to Wrisley Road, which was also dirt but even narrower. But if you were walking, you only had to go over that ridge past the river in the woods behind the school.

"What happened?"

"Some people complained about dogs getting into their garbage cans, and when the animal patrol came and saw what was going on out there, they shot them. All of them. You're lucky you were never attacked out there."

"But why were they shot?"

"Because they're feral dogs. Hello in there. Didn't you hear me? Dangerous things. Filthy, diseased, wild . . . What should they do, re-home them as gentle household pets?"

"How about just leaving them alone?"

"Consider yourself lucky. That's all I have to say."

"I don't. I don't consider myself lucky at all, because there was nothing to be afraid of in the first place."

Ben smiled, and I saw exactly what he must have been like as a little kid. "Can I still call you Wolf Girl?"

"No," I said, giving him the sternest look I could muster. Then, before I could help myself, I said, "Why don't you call Tina Yarwood Wolf Girl? I'm sure she'd let you."

Great. Now I looked like a complete jealous idiot. Over Ben Dellahunt, of all people. I didn't even care about Ben Dellahunt. He was okay, he had a few good points, but that was as far as it went.

He seemed confused. "Why would I call Tina anything?"

I shuffled my feet, wanting to leave. "Well, you're going out with her, right?"

"Uh, you do know she's my cousin? I know you're into the whole Middle Ages thing, but . . ."

"Oh . . . No, I didn't know that. God. Obviously that's gross. Like so gross . . . I'm sorry, I—"

"Okay, okay. You didn't know. Whatever. No need for total morti-
fication."

"Yeah, all right. I mean it, though. I didn't know. I'm not into that
kind of thing or anything, okay?"

Ben put his hands on my shoulders and looked into my face. "June,
do you think I believe you'd be *into* dating relatives? Really? You have
seriously got to find a way to lighten up. Listen, next weekend, after
the play's all over with, you can come over to my house and we'll roll
you a character. No obligations. We'll just roll, see what happens. What
do you say? I'm pegging you as maybe assassin material." He took a
step back, tilting his head and squinting at me. For a second it reminded me of the way Finn looked at a piece of art and I smiled,
which probably gave Ben the wrong idea, because he smiled back. "Elf
assassin . . . with magic. We'll hope for a good charisma roll, and I'd be
willing to fudge the constitution numbers to give you a fair chance.
What do you say?"

I realized I was twirling one of my braids in my fingers and I let it
go. I looked down, away from Ben, and mumbled, "Okay."

"Really?"

"Yeah. Okay. I'll do it."

It felt good to say yes. To agree to something so ordinary. To agree
to spend some time with a guy who didn't think it was possible I
might want to date my relatives. For a few minutes I stood there with
Ben and I forgot about everything terrible. Then he said goodbye and
turned and left, and it all came rushing back.

I walked out to the pay phone in the lobby and called Toby. Still no
answer. Then I tried again, dialing more carefully, thinking that maybe
I'd been getting the number wrong. But, no, it rang and rang until I
hung up.

I ran home from the library and went straight to the mailbox. I would
have given anything to find a letter from one of Toby's crazy places.
The League of Volcano Bowl Drinkers, The Miyagi-San Appreciation
Society, Golden Hands United. Anything. But there were just two bills
and a Grand Union flyer.

A few minutes after I got inside, my mother was on the phone, calling from work, making sure I was there.

Greta was staying late at school, because there were *South Pacific* performances at seven o'clock on Monday, Wednesday, and Friday nights that week. So I sat alone at the kitchen table and pulled out my homework. Geometry proofs. I drew a line down my paper and made two columns.

I looked at the problem sheet. Postulates. Axioms. Congruence. The words sat there. Pointless and dead. I tapped my pencil against the paper. Then, instead of working out two separate proofs of Pythagoras's theorem, I wrote: *Proof for Why It Is Impossible That I Will Never See Toby Again.* I looked at it for a few seconds. I wanted it to be an easy proof. Like the one for showing that a straight line is always a 180-degree angle. But it wasn't like that. I could only come up with arguments for the other side.

Like, what if the police had taken Toby straight from our house to the airport and shoved him on a plane back to England? Or what if he packed his stuff up and left to go someplace I'd never know? Or what if the police had beaten him up and were keeping him in a deep dark cell so nobody would find out? Or what if it was worse? What if it was something I couldn't even imagine?

"No," I said out loud, before crumpling the paper in my hand. Then I tried his number again. It just rang and rang.

Sixty-Two

I could come up with a list of reasons why I'd made that phone call to Toby on Saturday night. Convincing reasons. Reasons that would be easy to believe. I was worried about Greta. It seemed like the best option. I panicked. There are more. I could come up with more in an instant. But underneath all of them is the reason I'm afraid of. The one that still haunts me at night. The one that still wanders around dressed in wolf's clothing. Baring sharp, shiny teeth.

The one I don't want to believe is that I did it on purpose. That I called because of all those Sundays I waited for the phone to ring. All those Sundays I imagined Finn was probably having the time of his life with Toby. I called because of how embarrassing it must have been for Finn to have me fawning over him all the time. I called because sometimes I imagined I could hear them laughing. At me. At every dumb thing about me. How funny it was that I didn't know a thing about the two of them. How hilarious it was that I had *feelings* for my own uncle. I lay in bed at night and I could hear Finn's beautiful laugh in my ears. "Hm-hm-hm," his laugh went. Like he'd swallowed the sun. I called because I could hear it so clearly. And I wanted more of it and I didn't want any of it. I'm not a jealous person. That's what I used to say. That's what I used to believe.

But maybe I am. Maybe that's exactly what I am. Maybe all I wanted was for Toby to hear the wolves that lived in the dark forest of my heart. And maybe that's what it meant. Tell the Wolves I'm Home.

Maybe Finn understood everything, as usual. You may as well tell them where you live, because they'll find you anyway. They always do.

I started to think that maybe my mother and I aren't really so different. Not in our hearts. And maybe Toby was the one who got the worst of it. I say maybe, but really I know it's true. I knew he'd go when I called. I knew it was dangerous, and I knew he'd do anything to keep a promise to Finn.

I used to believe in all the good reasons I made that call on that stupid stormy Saturday night, but with each day that passed, with each Tobyless day, I lost that belief. I started to know the truth.

That night I didn't sleep. I snuck downstairs every hour and tried Toby. Each time, the phone rang and rang. In my dark night kitchen, I could imagine it ringing out into Finn's messy apartment. Trilling over the dirty plates, around the books, and over the Turkish carpet. Searching and searching for the right ears to hear.

Sixty-Three

"Have you heard anything?" Greta had come over to sit with me in the school cafeteria. It was the first time that had ever happened, and it was nice.

I shook my head.

"He'll turn up," she said. "Here." She handed me half of her sandwich.

"No, thanks."

"Come on, you have to eat."

I shook my head. "I can't."

Greta nodded. "It's not your fault, June, okay? He's an adult."

"He's sick." I was about to say that I was supposed to be taking care of him, but I knew that was something only I would ever know.

"It'll be okay," she said. She put her arm on my shoulder, like girls do sometimes. Other girls, real girls.

Wednesday. It had been four days since I'd last seen Toby. I hated myself.

I found the number for the police station in the phone book. I asked for Officer Gellski and they put me through.

I told him I was wondering, just out of curiosity, if he could tell me what happened to Tobias Aldshaw after he left our house on Saturday night.

"You a friend of Mr. Aldshaw's?" he asked.

I didn't know what I should say. I didn't want to do anything at all to make things worse for Toby, but there was a place in me, right in the center of my heart, that wanted to yell out that he was my friend. I wanted to tell that cop that he was actually my best friend. That I had no better friend in the world than Tobias Aldshaw. But then I didn't. I didn't say that.

"I'm Greta Elbus's sister. Mr. Aldshaw was a good friend of my uncle's. I knew him a little."

He didn't say anything at first. "Okay. Okay then. Well, we were going to hold him here until the morning, but . . ." He paused, and I could feel him thinking about whether to go on. "Well, your mother, she told us about the AIDS, and, to tell you the truth, everybody wanted to get him out of here as soon as possible."

"So you just let him go?"

"The guy was burning up. Fever. Like I said, if it wasn't for the AIDS, we would have kept him awhile."

He kept calling it *the* AIDS, like it was some kind of animal or household appliance.

"Are you saying you let him go?"

"Ambulance. The EMTs picked him up."

"Do you know where they took him?"

"Not sure. With the AIDS and all, they might have shipped him right to the city."

"Is there a way I could find out which hospital?"

"Yeah, hold on a sec." He had a loud voice, and I could hear him calling across the room, then the mumble of someone answering.

"Yeah, Bellevue. In the city. Like I said, probably they took him right down there because of the AIDS."

"It's AIDS," I said.

"Yeah. That's what I said."

"It's AIDS. It's not *the* AIDS."

"Okay, kid. Whatever you want."

I called the hospital. I asked for Toby by his real name, which I'd been turning around in my head since Saturday, when I first heard it. Tobias

Aldshaw. It sounded like the name of somebody famous, not the name of an invisible man who had nobody in the world except me.

The hospital told me he was unavailable. They told me his room number was 2763 and that I should call back later.

"What do you mean, 'unavailable'?" I asked.

"No idea. There's just no answer when I try putting the call through," the nurse said. "Could be tests. He could be sleeping. Try later."

"He's okay though? Right? He's still a patient."

I heard the nurse shuffling through some papers.

"His name's still on the register. Try later."

My mother had tickets to all the performances of *South Pacific*. My dad and I went to only one, but she wanted to see it as many times as she could. My mother and Greta got back at around nine-thirty and Greta showered and changed. My parents finished watching the ten o'clock news, then went up to bed. I'd been in my room all night, and when I heard my father's snoring kick in, I snuck downstairs.

I dragged the phone out the back door, so I was crouched down under Greta's bedroom window, and I called straight through to Toby's hospital room. I expected it to ring and ring, because after all these days it seemed hard to believe that Toby would really pick up. But he did.

I could hardly hear him at first. His voice was almost gone. He cleared his throat then tried again. "Hello?"

"Toby?"

"June?"

"Oh, Toby, I'm so, so glad—"

"June, I buggered it all up, didn't I? I'm so sorry."

"*You're* sorry? I dragged you out there and now . . . Are you okay? You must hate me."

"June. Of course not."

"I didn't know where you were. I had no idea what happened to you."

"I couldn't ring your house. Not after—"

"It was a bad idea. The worst idea. I'm so sorry. Are you okay? Are you sick? What did the police do to you?"

"I'm all right," he said, but the sound of his voice said something different. He sounded wheezy, like he was trying as hard as he could not to cough. "And you? You and Greta?"

"We're okay. Don't worry about us." I wrapped and unwrapped the curly phone cord around my finger.

"Good. That's good."

Then we both went quiet, and I thought that it felt hard to talk to Toby, in a way it never had before.

"When will you be back home?" I asked.

He coughed, and it sounded horrible. All chesty and deep. I listened while he struggled to get his breathing back to normal.

"June, listen, I might not be going back. . . ."

"Of course you will," I said, but I was starting to get scared. "I'm in huge trouble right now, but I'll figure something out. I'll come down as soon as I can, okay?"

"June, I'm serious. I might not—"

"Why wouldn't you? Your guitar's there, and your fleas, your little mates, and—"

"June . . ."

"No, Toby. No. Because I still need to take you to the Cloisters, and then when you're feeling better you can meet Greta properly. You have to. There's no choice."

"June . . ."

Toby's voice trailed off and he started to cough again. He kept hacking and hacking, and I heard a nurse saying something to him in the background.

I wanted to tell him all of what had happened over the last few days. I wanted to find more ways to say I was sorry. And I wanted to make us both believe that he would be going home. But I sat out there without saying anything. The moon was a sliver, and there was no breeze at all. I stared out, watching powdery gray moths fluttering up against the patio light.

I felt tears welling up. "Toby?"

But he kept coughing and coughing until I couldn't bear to listen anymore.

"Toby, look, I'm coming. As soon as I can, okay? Just hang on. Please wait."

"No, June. I'll be fine. I'm being stupid. Don't get yourself into more trouble."

"Just wait for me, okay? Please?"

When I looked up, Greta was staring down at me from her open window. We looked at each other for a few seconds. I couldn't tell what she was thinking.

"Will you come with me?" I whispered up to her.

She closed the window and breathed out onto the glass. With her finger, she wrote, *yes* into the fog. Without even thinking about it, she'd written it backward, mirror image, so it looked perfect to me.

That night, Greta drove. We waited until after midnight, after our parents would be sound asleep. I wasn't worried about getting into trouble. There was no bigger trouble left to get in. And Toby had nobody. In his world, I, June Elbus, was it, and I was going to put everything right. I was going to undo all the mess I'd gotten him into.

It was a clear, warm night. Greta rolled our dad's car out of the driveway and, like she did with everything, like she always could, she managed to drive as if she'd been doing it for years, even though she'd only just gotten her permit. We drove down the empty Saw Mill Parkway, and Greta pushed in my parents' Simon and Garfunkel cassette. I got out two cigarettes from my bag. I pushed in the car lighter and waited.

"What will you do when you get there?" Greta asked.

"I don't know."

"You'll be fine."

I tried to believe her. I tried to believe I had the power to make the story end any way I wanted it to. I pushed the tip of each cigarette against the lighter, then I breathed each one to life.

"Here," I said, passing one to Greta.

"You know, the smoking. It surprised me."

"Just something I picked up," I said, grinning, and I realized that Toby was shining through me so strongly then that for a moment I was almost completely invisible.

Sixty-Four

Up until then, all the times I'd been in the city at night was with Finn. Once he took me to see a special showing of *It's a Wonderful Life* at Radio City Music Hall. Another time we went to *La Bohème* at Lincoln Center. And another time, not too long ago, our whole family met him in the city and we went out for a huge Italian meal for my mother's birthday. The city at night was supposed to have Finn in it. So somehow I thought he might be there. Not really, but so much a part of the night city that I would feel him there. But that wasn't what it felt like. It was just Greta and me standing on the sidewalk in front of the building, me fishing in my pocket for the key on the red ribbon.

We had decided to stop at Finn's apartment first. I wanted to bring Toby a change of clothes. Plus, we realized we had no idea where Bellevue Hospital was.

I imagined the apartment would be a wreck. Worse than last time. I was getting ready to explain it to Greta somehow, to make excuses for Toby, but when I pushed open the door the place was neater than I'd ever seen it. Everything in the right spot. No clothes draped over chairs. No saucers heaped with tea bags and cigarettes. Even the stale smell was gone. The big windows were open a few inches, letting in a breeze that must have been working to freshen the air. I tried not to act too surprised.

"This is weird," Greta said. "Being here like this."

"Yeah," I said, thinking that she didn't even know how weird it was, because she hadn't seen the mess the place was just a few weeks ago.

I grabbed a plastic bag from the kitchen and walked down the hall to the bedroom to get some clothes. The door was closed, like it used to be, and I gently pushed it open and walked over to the chest of drawers. Greta followed behind me.

"So this is the private bedroom," she said.

The bed was made and the cigarette packs were gone from Toby's side table. Greta was about to open the closet, but I put my hand on hers.

"Let's not," I said. "Okay?"

Greta looked up Bellevue in the phone book. It turned out that it was pretty far downtown and all the way over near the river on the East Side.

"We should go," I said. I was standing near the door, looking across the living room. I shivered, because it was late and I was tired but also because I had a sudden feeling that it might be the last time I saw that place. But I couldn't let myself focus on that. Greta was walking around, looking at every little thing. Like a detective looking for clues. "Come on," I said.

We drove all the way down West End Avenue, right past where it turns into 11th Avenue, until we got to 23rd Street. At that time of night, West End was quiet. Almost creepy. And in my father's smooth sedan it felt like we were floating slightly above the city.

By the time we got to Bellevue it was almost two in the morning. Greta pulled up on a side street.

"Go ahead home," I said.

"You can't go all by yourself."

"You've already had a show, you must be totally exhausted. Plus you have to tell Mom and Dad where I am. They'll go crazy if we're both missing in the morning."

She seemed to think about that for a few seconds.

"I want to make sure you get up there first. Then I'll go. Okay?"

I nodded.

I was about to walk right through the big automatic sliding doors, but Greta stopped me. "Look, hospitals don't let anyone visit any time of day or night," she said. "Just wait."

Greta pulled me away from the doors, over to the side. She put her hands on both my shoulders and looked at me. And it felt so good. In the middle of that terrible night, there was nothing better than feeling Greta's hands on my shoulders. Having her teach me how to do something the right way. I felt tears pushing their way into my eyes. I felt my legs go soft and weak. Greta squeezed my shoulders.

"Stop," she said.

I nodded, wiping my face with my sleeve.

"It's all going to work out fine. They'll ask you who you are. If you're a relative." Greta kept looking at me. Then she neatened up my hair a little bit and looked at me some more. "Okay. This is what you should do. Tell them you're his sister. From England. He called you and said he thought he was in really bad shape. You're the only one he has and you're not sure how much longer he has left. Okay? Put on an accent. Not a stupid one. Try to imitate Toby or something."

I thought of how Toby talked. Not with the regular English accent, but the kind where all his *u*'s sounded like the *oo*'s in *books*.

"What about you?" I said.

"I'll keep an eye on you. Make sure they let you up. Then I'll drive back home."

"Mom and Dad will kill you. What are you going to tell them?"

"I'll sneak in, and if you're not back by the time they wake up, I'll figure something out. I'll worry about all that. You just go, okay?"

I nodded. "Okay."

"Now, remember, the trick is to walk in like you expect to be let in. Like you belong there. Got it?"

I nodded again and let those big white doors open for me.

Bellevue did not look like the kind of hospital a person would choose to go to if they had any other option. Part of the lobby was having work done on it, and there were roped-off areas with signs that said EXCUSE OUR APPEARANCE . . . But there was no excuse. Most of the chairs had rips in their orange vinyl seats, and in one corner there was a bucket under a brown water stain in the ceiling. People were slumped on chairs sleeping. A mother held a toddler bundled up tight in a blanket that looked like it used to be pink. One guy looked like he might have been shot in the arm. He sat there wincing, pressing a brightly patterned beach towel against his upper arm. A TV bolted onto a shelf near the ceiling played an episode of *Columbo,* but there was no sound.

Bellevue seemed like the kind of place where they wouldn't really care who visited when or where. It didn't look like the kind of place where the staff would notice much of anything. But it also looked big. Too big to find Toby by myself. So I walked through that lobby to the information desk.

It was just like Greta said. The receptionist tried to send me away, but then I did everything Greta told me to and it worked. I headed down the hallway to the elevator and glanced back toward the lobby. There was Greta, legs crossed, sitting next to a lady who looked about thirteen months pregnant. Greta had a magazine held up high over her face, and when I squinted I saw it was our issue of *Newsweek.* I laughed, then put my hand over my mouth to stifle it. Greta lowered the magazine, looked up at me for a second, and smiled. As the elevator door started to close, she stood and put up one hand to wave goodbye. That's one of those frozen memories for me, because there was something in Greta's solemn wave that made me understand it was about something bigger. That as the elevator door eclipsed the look between us, we were really saying goodbye to the girls we used to be. Girls who knew how to play invisible mermaids, who could run through dark aisles, pretending to save the world.

Toby was on a wing on the eighth floor. It looked like the place they were putting all the guys with AIDS. I knew it wasn't polite, but it was impossible not to stare into each room as I walked by. In almost every bed there was a man. Most of them were alone, but one or two had people sitting in the room with them. The light, sweet sound of violin music was drifting out of one of the rooms, and when I looked in I saw a man staring right back at me. When he saw me, he tried to turn his head away, then gave up and closed his eyes instead.

I peeked into Toby's room and saw him lying there. The room was dim. The only brightness came from a small fluorescent light above the sink. His face was gray, his hair more featherlike than I'd ever seen it. He was wearing an oxygen mask, which I hadn't expected.

His eyes were open, and when he saw me he pulled the mask off his face and smiled as big and genuine as ever. It was the same way he'd smiled at me that very first afternoon at the train station. Like he couldn't believe his luck. The difference was that this time it took effort. This time he managed to hold it for only a couple of seconds before it slipped away. I took a few steps into the room, never taking my eyes off Toby, and I felt myself falling apart. My eyes started watering up and my hand went over my mouth.

"Out. Try again," Toby said in the hoarsest voice ever, angling his eyes toward the door.

I nodded and dashed out of the room. In the hallway I stood against the wall, bent at the waist, heaving. I slowed down my breathing. *Okay, okay, okay,* I said to myself. I blew out a long breath, trying not to think about this being all my fault. I had to stop thinking about that or I would never be able to step back into the room. I breathed in and out nice and slow a few more times, then turned and went in.

Toby had turned his back to the door. Maybe he was trying to give me a chance to ease into the room. Or maybe it was just that he couldn't bear to look at me anymore.

I stood watching his blanket move up and down to the rhythm of his wheezy breathing. I slowly walked over to the side of the bed and bent in close, pressing my ear against his back.

"You came," he said into the silence.

"I brought you some clothes," I said, holding up the bag even though he was looking the other way. "For when it's time to go home."

Toby turned his head and smiled, but it looked painful because his lips were so dry. He started coughing and I poured him a glass of water.

"Shhh. It's okay," I said.

"Here, help me up a bit, would you?"

At first I stood there awkwardly, not knowing how to help. Then I slid my arms under his body and scooted him up on the bed. I'd expected that it would take some effort, but there was nothing at all left to Toby. The lightness of his body was so shocking that I had to try hard not to gasp out loud. It felt like I could have lifted him right up and out of that bed with barely any effort at all.

I fluffed his pillows and wedged them behind his back so he was propped up to sit.

"Is that better?" I asked.

"Perfect," he said.

I pulled the chair as close to the bed as I could get it and wrapped a spare blanket around myself. "The apartment is clean."

"Why, June, you sound surprised." He'd put on an offended-housewife voice, but it was in a hoarse whisper, so it sounded like an offended housewife who smoked five packs of cigarettes a day. I laughed.

"It looks good. Like it used to when Finn was there."

Toby smiled. Then his smile faded. He took another sip of water, but even that made him cough. After a while the cough turned into a frail kind of bark. He held his side, squinting in pain, and he looked at me, his dark eyes bigger and deeper than ever. His face was all eyes now, and he stared at me for too long. Like time had slowed right down for him. After a while he reached his hand out for mine, then he held it, rubbing his thumb over my palm.

"This isn't your fault, you know. You do know that, don't you? This would have happened anyway. Maybe in a month. Two months."

I looked down. I stared at Toby's long fingers in my hand. At the swirled linoleum squares of the floor.

"How can you say this isn't my fault?" I asked in a whisper. "How can you keep being so nice to me when I'm . . . I'm just not a good person. Can't you see that?"

"Oh, June."

"I keep trying to think of some way to make it up to you—"

"Shhh," he said, reaching for my other hand. "Shhh." He started hacking again, and I sat there, helpless. He pointed to a shelf across the room. I looked and there was a half-empty roll of butterscotch Life Savers. I nudged one out with my fingernail, then put it in Toby's mouth. My fingers brushed his lips, and they were so rough and dry it almost made me pull my hand back. After a while the coughing stopped, and he looked at me and gave a soft laugh. I sat down on the edge of the bed.

"Do you know that all this time I've been waiting for some way I could do something huge and magnificent for you? But it never happened. And then the one thing you finally asked me for I couldn't do. I never dreamed you'd ask me to take you to England."

"No, *I* was taking *you*. I wanted to take you."

"It's the same thing, isn't it?"

"No. Not at all."

"But I knew I wouldn't be able to bring you home. Even if we somehow worked out every other reason why we couldn't go, I knew I wouldn't get back into the country. I've outstayed my visa by a good number of years now. And then there's the criminal record. They're not so good with that sort of thing at immigration control. I couldn't do that, do you see? I couldn't let you find your way home all by yourself. Finn wouldn't have wanted that. I wouldn't have. If things were different . . ."

"Why didn't you just say that to me?"

"What? Say, 'I'm terribly sorry to disappoint you, but I crippled a man for life and I'm also an illegal immigrant, so leaving the country wouldn't be such a brilliant idea for me at the moment.' What would that have sounded like to you? You might have been gone."

I thought about what he was saying. "So is that what it was all about? Keeping your promise to Finn? All our time together?"

He shook his head so slowly it was barely perceptible. "Is that what you really think?"

I looked away. "Sometimes."

"Don't you see? It's like we've known each other all these years. Without even seeing each other. It's like there's been this . . . this ghost relationship between us. You laying out my plectrums on the floor, me buying black-and-white cookies every time I knew you would be coming over. You didn't know that was me, but it was."

It was true. There were always soft, sweet black-and-white cookies from a bakery over on 76th Street when we went to Finn's. In a white box tied with red-and-white cotton string.

"Do you know how Finn would fix things for you sometimes? A

windup clock once, and that music box. That little music box shaped like a cupcake that played 'Happy Birthday' when you opened the top. There were teeth missing, some of those tiny metal teeth."

"That was you?"

Toby nodded and held up his hand. "Fingers," he said.

"Why are you telling me all this now? Why are you waiting until right now to let me in on this?"

He looked away. "Because maybe I don't want to leave the planet invisible. Maybe I need at least one person to remember something about me. And . . ."

"And what?"

Toby closed his eyes and breathed in deep. I thought maybe he was about to fall asleep, but then he reached over for my hand again and looked right into my eyes. "He was both our first loves, June."

The words hung there and I felt my cheeks getting hot. I turned away so Toby couldn't see my face.

"We're bound together. Do you see?" He stopped, waiting for my reaction.

I couldn't meet his eyes. "I should go . . ."

"Don't, June. It's all right."

I turned to him then. "Finn was my uncle."

"I know," he said, looking at me like he felt completely sorry for me.

"Uncles can't be your first loves."

Toby nodded slowly, his eyes closed. "Nobody can help what they feel, June."

"I . . ."

"He was so beautiful and patient and so clever and talented. And maybe for you he was two people. Do you see? Who could resist the two of us all squashed into one beautiful person, right?" He smiled. His voice was getting hoarser and hoarser, but still he kept talking. "I told him, you know. I told him he would make you fall in love with him, and he didn't believe me. He never understood that he had that kind of power. And I was like you. Always doubting myself. Always wondering why he would be with me. June, I think if you say it, if you get it out, you might be free. He was my first love too, June."

I was going to tell him that it wasn't true. That Finn was just my uncle. That uncles can't be your first loves. But suddenly the weight of it all felt too much. Suddenly I couldn't understand why I'd been carrying it around with me for so, so long.

"Okay," I said in a rush. "Okay, I was in love with Finn. There. Okay. Okay?" I couldn't look Toby in the eye, but I felt him pull me to him. His hand on my arm.

"That's better, isn't it?"

I nodded. And somehow it was.

We stayed like that for a while. Me perched on the edge of Toby's bed, slowly rubbing his thin arm, him squeezing my hand. Like the oldest of couples. That's what it felt like. Like we were two people who'd known each other forever. People who could tell each other anything or just sit there saying nothing at all.

"Come on," I said.

"What is it?"

"Let's go. I'm taking you home. To my house. You can't stay here." I hadn't known that would be my plan until the moment I said it, but when I did, I knew it was right. I knew it was the perfect thing to do. I unwrapped myself from the blanket and walked over to push the door closed. I spilled the bag of clothes out on the chair.

"June, I can't go there. Your parents . . . your mother."

"Shhh. We can do whatever we want. That's what you said, right?" I gave Toby a huge smile. Then I offered him my arm. He winced as he swung his legs around the side of the bed.

"I'm starting to think I never should have said that. I'm starting to think it was a bit on the open-ended side."

I laughed. "Here." I handed him an orange-and-black-checked button-down shirt that I'd never seen him wear. There's something about picking out clothes for someone else that made me want to choose the things I'd never seen before. Like maybe there was a chance to catch a glimpse of a whole other version of a person buried in the bottom of a dresser drawer. Toby held the shirt away from his body and looked at me.

"What's this?" he said.

"I've never seen you in it."

Toby gave me a look that said there was a good reason for that, but then he slipped the shirt over his head without bothering to undo the buttons. I'd brought him a regular pair of jeans, which he seemed relieved to see. I turned my head away as he slid out of the hospital gown. When I turned back he was still sitting on the edge of the bed and he'd changed into the jeans, but he was hunched over, like just changing clothes had exhausted him. I sat next to him on the bed and leaned my head over so I could press my ear to his chest. There was so much rasping and wheezing it was hard to see how he was getting any air at all. Then I remembered the oxygen tank, and I reached across the bed, grabbed the mask, and passed it to Toby.

He nodded and pressed it over his nose and mouth. A look of relief spread across his face.

I followed the tube from the mask, hoping it would lead to some kind of little tank I could pick up. Instead the tube connected to a pipe that ran right along the wall and seemed to be connected to the building itself.

"We won't be able to take this," I said. "Maybe it's a dumb idea."

Toby moved the mask away from his face and shook his head. "No, it'll be all right. We'll be in the fresh air."

"Are you sure?"

He nodded, but in my heart I knew he was making a choice. I knew what it meant.

"Toby?"

"Mmmm."

"You . . . You don't mean Finn was your first love ever. You don't mean real first, right?" I turned away, embarrassed to be asking. But I needed to know.

He didn't say anything for a long time. I sat there listening to his wheezy breathing, thinking it was probably wrong to ask a question like that. That maybe sometimes what's private should stay private. I was about to tell him to forget it, but then he picked up my hand in his and spoke in a small thin voice.

"Finn never knew. It's just between you and me now, all right? It doesn't matter. It's nobody's fault."

I felt his fingers squeeze my palm, and it was like he was pressing this secret into my hand. Suddenly all the smells in that room—rubbing alcohol and pine disinfectant and raspberry Jell-O—grew harsher and brighter. Like they were trying to obliterate this revelation that changed everything and nothing at all. Toby had closed his eyes, but mine were wide open and I couldn't stop staring at him. *This is what love looks like,* I thought. Then I squeezed his hand back.

"It's safe with me," I said. "I promise."

With his eyes still closed, he smiled. "I know."

I was right about Bellevue. It was the kind of place you could walk right out of without anyone noticing at all. I took a blanket from Toby's bed and a wheelchair from near the nurse's station and wheeled Toby into the elevator. A few nurses glanced at us, but they all seemed too busy to care. I left him in the lobby, then went out to hail a taxi. It didn't take long. I told the taxi driver to wait, then I ran back in for Toby.

When we got out there, the taxi driver stared at the two of us, and I could see he was trying to figure out who we were to each other. I thought of Playland, of how the woman there thought we were some kind of weird couple. I knew there was no way anyone could come to that conclusion now. No way at all. And maybe it was some of Toby's mischievousness rubbing off on me, or maybe it was just that I wanted to test the word on my lips—I wanted to see if my lips could hold such a huge and powerful word—but I looked that driver straight in the eye and leaned in and said, "Excuse me, but would you mind helping my lover into the car?" It was the first time all night that Toby laughed. He turned his head away, trying to keep up the game. The driver's mouth actually hung open, like a dumb guy in a cartoon, but I kept my eyes on him, like I didn't understand what the problem was. I let the word *lover* hang in his mind until finally he gave a little lift of his hand, as if to say, "Whatever," or "Only in New York," or "To each his own." The kinds of things people say about things they know they'll never understand. Then he reached for Toby's arm and eased him into the backseat of the cab.

"So where to?" the driver said.

I gave him my address. Not the apartment, but my real address at home.

"But—" Toby began.

"It's okay."

"You have the money to go all the way up to Westchester?" the driver said. "I'm gonna need a deposit."

I reached into my pocket and pulled out a wad of the bills that Toby had given me all that time ago. "Here," I said handing him two fifties.

"Okay, okay. No questions asked," he said, as he pulled away from the curb. He looked over his shoulder at us. "You two mind some music?"

Toby smiled. "Music, yes, music," he mumbled. The driver fumbled around with the radio dial, and a few seconds later he caught the NYU station and someone was saying, ". . . and now for Frankie Yankovic and the 'Tick Tock Polka.'" The taxi filled with Frankie and his accordion and this silly, silly polka, and I looked at Toby and he looked at me and we laughed so hard it hurt.

And that's when I finally gave away one of my Finn stories to Toby. It was just a small story, like all my stories were. I told him about that day Greta brought the mistletoe with her to Finn's apartment. I whispered the story into his ear. I told him about the weather that day. The pellets of sleet as we drove down. The way Finn looked. What he was wearing. I wasn't even sure Toby could hear me, but I told him about the *Requiem* on the stereo. How the portrait was almost done. How scared I was. How stupid. And how, in the end, none of that mattered, because Finn saw through it all. I told Toby about Finn's soft butterfly kiss on the top of my head. How he saw exactly what I was feeling and made it all right. Like he always did.

Toby leaned on my shoulder and I felt him nodding just a little bit. He wasn't coughing much anymore, but his breathing had turned thick and gurgly. Like he was breathing water instead of air.

I would have ridden around like that for hours and hours. Maybe weeks, months. Maybe the rest of my life. The taxi took us out of the city, all the way up First Avenue and across the Willis Avenue Bridge, past Yankee Stadium, then away from the brightly lit streets and out, out onto the dark highway. Window open. Cool night air pushing in at us, and the radio buzzing out polkas about clocks, and beer, and yellow roses, and blue eyes crying. There was Toby's drowsy head on my shoulder and my open hand on his head, and the rough wool blanket that covered both of us, and the feeling of having laughed and laughed and cried until there was nothing left at all. But stillness. The best kind of stillness. That's how I remember that night. That's how I want always to remember it.

Sixty-Five

Toby was right. Finn was my first love. But Toby, he was my second. And the sadness in that stretched like a thin cold river down the length of my whole life. My signature would probably set, and tax seasons would come and go. I'd eventually tuck the medieval boots way in the back of my closet and start wearing sneakers and jeans like everyone else. Maybe I'd grow some more, or maybe I wouldn't. Maybe I'd become the Wolf Queen of the outer regions, or maybe I'd just stay June Elbus, Queen of Jealous Hearts. Maybe I'd spend my years alone, waiting for someone to come along who was even half as good as Toby or Finn. Even a quarter as good. Or maybe I wouldn't. Maybe I already knew there was no point waiting for that. Maybe I was destined to forever fall in love with people I couldn't have. Maybe there's a whole assortment of impossible people waiting for me to find them. Waiting to make me feel the same impossibility over and over again.

But then, I guess it's what I deserve. No. That would be kind. I deserve much worse.

Toby slept on the couch in our living room. The painted Greta and the painted me and the real Greta and the real me all watched over him through the night. He slept covered in all the blankets from our beds, blankets printed with rainbows and balloons and Holly Hobby in her big straw ribbon-tied bonnet. He slept with our eyes on him.

Greta had waited up for me. She didn't say anything when she saw

I had Toby; she gave me a graceful nod so I'd know she understood. Mostly we sat silent, but every once in a while Greta would sing snatches of whatever she could think of, and every time she did we saw a little smile pull at the corner of Toby's mouth. So she kept going. Songs from *South Pacific* and James Taylor and Simon and Garfunkel. We were careful to keep our voices low, and other than Greta's soft, sweet singing, we hardly said anything. I sat on a chair next to the couch and kept my hand on Toby's fevered head. Just like he probably did for Finn.

And then the world started to wake up. At the first sign of light, Greta pulled the curtains closed so tight that not a crack of brightness could leak in. But even without light, the day was starting. Car doors slammed. The grind of tires on gravel driveways. My parents' radio alarm clock, the serious voice of 1010 WINS. All news. All the time. The bathroom door closing, then opening again, and then slippered footsteps padding down the stairs.

"Let me—" Greta said.

"No." I shook my head, then scooted my chair even closer to Toby. I wanted everything to be plain and true. I wanted my mother to come down and see my hand on Toby's head.

And she did. She stood on the stairs in her bathrobe, squinting into the dim living room. "June?" she said. But that was all she got out, because as she looked from me to Toby to Greta, there was nothing else to say. The whole story was there. Her hand flew up to cover her mouth and then she turned back up the stairs to get my father.

There was a lot of talking after that. Some of it was angry, hurt. But mostly there were just questions, and by the end of it all, there was nothing left to say. Both of them understood that Toby had been my friend.

For a long time, the four of us sat in the living room in the kind of brittle silence I'd only ever felt in churches and libraries. The kind everyone is careful not to break. We watched Toby's chest rise and fall, rise and fall, the only proof that he was still with us.

It was my mother who stood first. She walked across the room, knelt on the floor next to Toby, and laid her open palm on his head. I watched as she ran her hand over his soft feathery hair, and even though her back was to me, I think I heard her say, "Sorry." I want to believe that's what I heard. I needed to know that my mother understood that her hand was in this too. That all the jealousy and envy and shame we carried was our own kind of sickness. As much a disease as Toby and Finn's AIDS.

In the end it was just the two of us in the room. My mother and me. Toby's body stilled, and she reached out and laid her hand on my shoulder. That was how one person's story ended.

Later that night, long after Toby's body had been taken away and everyone was fast asleep, I saw something I mentioned only to Greta. I couldn't sleep and so I crept downstairs. The living room was dark except for a single lamp on a table near the mantel. A dining-room chair had been dragged over next to the fireplace, and standing on it was my mother. She had a thin paintbrush in one hand and in the other was a plastic ice cream lid that she was using as a palette. I watched quietly, just out of sight, as she delicately dipped the brush into the paint. I saw her tilt her head and eye the portrait before she touched her brush to the canvas, just like Finn. I stood there in complete disbelief as I watched my mother make her own small strokes on the painting. In the morning I woke before anyone else to see what she'd done. Around my neck was an intricate, perfectly painted silver necklace. On Greta's finger was a silver ring set with her birthstone.

Sometimes I tell myself that it wasn't so bad. Being responsible for killing someone who was dying anyway. Murdering a person who was already almost dead. That's what I try to think sometimes, but it never works. Two months is sixty days, 1,440 hours, 86,400 minutes. I was a stealer of minutes. I stole them from Toby and I stole them from myself. That's what it came down to. My family would go on forever thinking Toby was a murderer, but they'd never know about me. They'd never guess that there was a real killer living right in their house. It doesn't matter that Toby forgave me. That he really truly left this world with not a single bad feeling for me. That we ended as the sweetest of friends. None of that changed anything. There are dark black buttons tattooed on my heart. I'll carry them for the rest of my days.

But there is another place in my heart that knows that I finally kept my promise. I was the one who took care of Toby right up to the very end, who stayed with him so he wouldn't be alone. Just like Finn would have wanted. And sometimes, when I don't want to be sad anymore, I think that makes it almost even.

One thing I do know is that my superpower is gone. My heart is broken and soft, and I am plain again. I have no friends in the city. Not a single one. I used to think maybe I wanted to become a falconer, and now I'm sure of it, because I need to figure out the secret. I need to work out how to keep things flying back to me instead of always flying away.

Finn set it up so when Toby died, Greta and I would get everything. Even the apartment. Sometimes I imagined our lives in the future. Both of us shooting out in different directions. College and husbands and kids. Maybe we would live thousands of miles apart. In separate countries. Separate continents, even. I imagined even further on, when we were old ladies. Stooped-over old grannies with great big handbags and glasses and hand-knitted shawls. I imagined us all those years in the future, coming back to Finn's apartment. Our secret place. The place Finn and Toby left just for us.

But that room in the basement, that small magical place, that will always be mine alone. I found Toby's copy of the silly picture of him and me at Playland and I had it framed. I used some wire to hang it on the wall of the lockup. That's the only time I've been back there. I took the elevator down and I wasn't scared at all. Not even a little bit. Toby told me once that when he and Finn first found out they had AIDS, instead of feeling damaged and like time was running out, they felt just the opposite. He and Finn felt all-powerful. Like nothing could touch them. Maybe I'd caught some of that, because walking across that basement, past all those creepy mattresses and dark dead ends, all I felt was strong and hard. Like I wanted to shout out, "Come and get me." Knowing that nothing could.

There wasn't a funeral for Toby. And he didn't want to be buried. He'd told me that once, joking around. "I don't see myself as a grave kind of bloke," he said. And I probably told him that I didn't see him as an ash kind of bloke either. Something like that. I don't remember exactly.

All along I'd wondered where Finn's ashes were, and after the hundredth time I asked, my mother finally admitted that she had them. They were in a beautiful polished wood urn that she'd put on the very top shelf of her closet. I imagined her taking that urn out late at night. I imagined her running her palm over the smooth curve of it. I imagined her saying how sorry she was for how unkind she'd been to Toby. Sorry for how everything had turned out. I imagined those things because I needed to. I needed to think everything she'd done was out of love. Because I could understand that. I could forgive it. It made me think that maybe one day I might be able to forgive myself.

Instead of having a real funeral, Toby was cremated, and finally I thought I had a plan. I wanted to give Toby back to Finn. I wanted the crematorium to open Finn's urn and put Toby's ashes in there with his. I expected my mother to argue about it, but she didn't. She said she thought I was right. That it was the least we could do. The least we both could do. And after it was done, I felt that for once I'd gotten something completely right.

When I go to the woods now, I always head out along the brook and go straight to the big maple. I run there, like Toby must have done on that stormy night, then I bend down and crawl on the earth. Because what if there's a clue? What if there's a piece of chunky strawberry bubble gum still bundled up in its waxy wrapper, or a weather-faded matchbook, or a fallen button from somebody's big gray coat? What if buried under all those leaves is me? Not this me, but the girl in a Gunne Sax dress with the back zipper open. The girl with the best boots in the world. What if she's under there? What if she's crying? Because she will be, if I find her. Her tears tell the story of what she knows. That the past, present, and future are just one thing. That there's nowhere to go from here. Home is home is home.

Sixty-Six

We were all sitting in the living room when the doorbell rang. It was a Saturday morning and we were expecting him, the man from the Whitney. My mother stood and looked at all of us.

"I don't want a scene," she said, turning to stare right at me.

"What?" I said with my best "I would never do that" look.

"No inappropriate comments and no scenes, got it? This whole thing is embarrassing enough."

I did agree with her on that. It had been embarrassing. Only my mother, Greta, and I were home when the man from the Whitney had come to see the portrait the first time. I think we were all expecting some nice laid-back art person, but he seemed more like someone from the army than someone involved with art. He had a crew cut and wore a white shirt buttoned right up to the top. He carried a black briefcase and like my mother predicted, he thought we were nuts. He told us that he was appalled by what we'd done. He said it three or four times with a deep frown on his face. I could tell that even my mother was intimidated by him, because she forgot to offer him coffee, and she never forgot to be polite. We sat there in the living room while he stared at the portrait. He pulled a clipboard with a yellow legal pad out of his briefcase, and he jotted down a few notes as he analyzed it. Every now and then he took a few steps closer, then back, then left and right, scribbling on the pad all the time.

I wasn't sure if he understood that Greta and I were the ones he was looking at, that we were right there behind him. I wasn't about to point it out to him, but the longer he stared, the more angry I started to feel about it. How dare he look at us like that? What right did he have to tear us apart with his eyes? All those hours Finn spent trying to get us just right. Because he loved us. Because he wanted to do this thing for *us*. All that love didn't mean anything to this Whitney guy. That was obvious. He looked at us like we were specimens. He stared and stared, and suddenly all I wanted to do was protect us. And Finn. I wanted to protect Finn's work.

I stood up. "Have you seen enough?" I asked. I had my hands on my hips. I expected that my mother would tell me to be polite. To be patient. I looked over at her and, instead of seeming annoyed at my rudeness, she stood up as well.

"Yes," she said, nodding. "I think that's enough."

Then Greta stood too, but she didn't say anything.

The Whitney guy looked at us slowly, one at a time, and I wondered if he went through his whole life that way, appraising everything he saw. After a while, he gave a slight nod.

"All right," he said. "Let's discuss our options." He pointed at a chair. "May I?"

"Of course," my mother said.

We all sat down and listened.

He told us again what a shame it was that so much damage had been "inflicted." He used words like *travesty* and *abomination,* and it didn't take long for all the boldness we'd felt a few minutes before to completely evaporate. After he seemed sure we understood the magnitude of what we'd done, he told us he thought a good restorer would be able to clean it all off.

"It won't be an inexpensive task," he said, "but it's necessary, and I think you should all feel relieved that it will at least be possible."

We nodded, and after some negotiation we agreed to let him take the painting with him to the museum. He told us we should have it back within the month.

Then he left, and usually this would have been the kind of moment all our stifled feelings exploded, the moment we all burst out laughing. But there was a big empty space on the wall, which somehow made it seem not very funny at all.

Now he was on the other side of our front door again, this time with the portrait in his hands.

"Okay, I promise," I told my mother. "I won't say a thing."

The man looked the same as last time. I imagined a closet full of crisp white shirts. After some pleasantries and coffee, which my mother remembered this time, he laid the portrait down on the kitchen table. It was bundled in layers and layers of bubble wrap, and I thought about how he would probably keel right over and die if he saw the way all those paintings in Finn's basement were kept. The way they were un-wrapped and all stacked on top of one another. I smiled at that thought, because he would never know. Nobody would. Ever.

My father was there too this time, and we all watched as the man peeled back the tape and unrolled the wrap.

"I think you'll find the restoration work to be top quality," he said.

And there it was. Everything we'd done—the buttons, the skull, the lips, the illuminated hair and fingernails—all of it was gone. The paint-ing was back to the way Finn left it.

Almost. I noticed that the two things my mother had added—the necklace and the ring—were still there. That's how good she was. She was so good that even an art expert couldn't tell her painting apart from Finn's. She'd be part of that portrait forever. I watched my mother as she looked at the painting, but she didn't give anything away. I thought of trying to catch her eye, so she'd know I understood what she'd done, but I decided not to. Everyone needs to think they have secrets.

My parents were nodding and Greta looked relieved. I was the only one who seemed to think there was something sad about losing all that stuff. But I didn't say it. It was the kind of thing I didn't think anybody would understand. Plus, I'd promised my mother I wouldn't make a scene.

My parents thanked the man again and again, and even though he nodded, I could tell it was killing him to have to leave the portrait with stupid people like us. But that's what he had to do.

And so the portrait was hung above our mantel. Back where it belonged. At first, anytime one of us walked by it we would look, but after a while it faded into the background of our house. Of our lives.

But the thing is, even with all the restoration, all the erasing, I could still read that painting. I'm the only one who knows about the wolf, and I'm the only one who knows that if the light hits the canvas just right, if it's deep-orange end-of-the-day light and it comes through the window from the side at just the right angle, and if you know what you're looking for, if you know exactly the right place to look, you can still see the five black buttons. Not the way they were, not clumsy and thick, but more like shadows. Like small eclipsed moons, floating over my heart.

Author's Note

It warms my heart that most of the time the facts of the world have fit my story just right. But on those occasions where they haven't, I've taken the liberty of tailoring them—as gently as possible—to suit.

Acknowledgments

I have been graced from the very start with readers skilled in combining honesty and encouragement in perfect balance. Many thanks to these readers and their words of wisdom: Sarah Crow, Sondra Friedman, Julia Wherrell, Jerry Horsman, Clive Mitchell, and Clare Blake.

Thank you to Mollie Glick for ushering *Wolves* into the wider world in the best possible way. I couldn't have asked for any better. Many thanks also to everyone else at Foundry, particularly Katie Hamblin and Stéphanie Abou, and to Caspian Dennis at Abner Stein.

My greatest appreciation to my editor Jen Smith. Thank you for your always insightful, always kind, and always thoughtful reads and for pushing me that final mile. Thank you also to everyone else at Dial Press: Susan Kamil, Hannah Elnan, Kathleen Murphy Lord, and everyone else who has worked or will work on this book.

Thanks to Jenny Geras at Pan Macmillan. How lucky am I to get two fantastic editors working on my book? Thank you also to Jeremy Trevathan, Ellen Wood, Michelle Kirk, Chloe Healy, and the whole Macmillan team, whose enthusiasm makes my heart flutter.

Thanks to everyone at New Writing Partnership, particularly Kate Pullinger and Candida Clark, for selecting me for the fantastic New Writing Ventures Award. I still think dreamily of that Ventures year. And thanks to Judith Murray, whose early feedback made me ask all the right questions about this book.

Thank you to Arts Council England for awarding me a generous grant to write the first draft of *Wolves*.

Many thanks and much love to family and friends near and far who have always been there in so many ways: Mom, Dad, Wendy and Josh, Cindi, Shirley, Kristin, Lynne, Dilys, Mike, Steven, and Irene.

A respectful nod to the ghost of Ged Stewart.

And, most of all, with love to Chris, steadfast and ever tolerant. You never doubted that this would all turn out well. I couldn't have done it without you.

ABOUT THE AUTHOR

CAROL RIFKA BRUNT's work has appeared in several literary journals, including *North American Review* and *The Sun*. In 2006, she was one of three fiction writers who received the New Writing Ventures award, sponsored by the University of East Anglia/Arts Council England, and, in 2007, she received a generous Arts Council grant to write *Tell the Wolves I'm Home,* her first novel. Originally from New York, she currently lives in England with her husband and three children.